I0700935

ALL MY LIFE

BRIANNA GUSTAFSSON

Brianna Gustafsson

Copyright © 2024 Brianna Gustafsson.

All rights reserved. No part of this publication may be reproduced, distributed, or transmitted in any form or by any means, including photocopying, recording, or other electronic or mechanical methods, without the prior written permission of the publisher, except in the case of brief quotations embodied in critical reviews and certain other noncommercial uses permitted by copyright law. For permission requests, write to the publisher, addressed "Attention: Permissions Coordinator," at the address below.

ISBN: 979-8-9904699-0-7 (ebook)
ISBN: 979-8-9904699-1-4 (Paperback) ISBN:
979-8-9904699-2-1(Hardcover)

Any references to historical events, real people, or real places are used fictitiously. Names, characters, and places are products of the author's imagination.

Front cover image by Rica Graphics. First

printing edition 2024.

G&G LLC
506 S Spring St #13308, SMB#60684
Los Angeles, CA 90013

www.penandprose.org

Brianna Gustafsson

All My Life playlist

https://open.spotify.com/playlist/0bSUeAuhUt4ur6va8MBTDv?si=428d3558ebb44ea7

Brianna Gustafsson

Brianna Gustafsson

Warning

Though this book is a work of fiction, it was created from real places, circumstances & situations. If you are at all uncomfortable reading books with themes of controlling & jealous partners, criminal behavior, drug-references, difficult co-parenting of a young child, physical/emotional/mental abuse, mentions of past child abuse/previous suicide attempt or SA—please do not read this book.

Brianna Gustafsson

To my husband.
Always, for all my life.

Brianna Gustafsson

"Tell me every terrible thing you ever did and let me love you anyway."

-Edgar Allan Poe

Brianna Gustafsson

TRISTAN

1

inety seconds, I reminded myself as I paced just behind the line of thick trees. Cigarette smoke pumped out from between my lips as I sighed heavily.

It's fucking freezing, I shuddered under my thin sweater. I glanced down at my watch, the glow-in-the-dark hands crept forward towards the mark slowly, heart pounding in my ears with anticipation. I absentmindedly patted the right pocket of my jeans where my kit was hidden. Next, my hand brushed across the 9mm wedged in my waistband.

Movement from beyond the trees snagged my attention. The lone security guard walked out of the short, square building and the door slammed closed behind him. He was hard to see in the dark, the sparse light from the streetlamps stretched lazily across the grass towards the barbed wire fence that wrapped the perimeter of the building.

I threw a quick glance at the grassy hill below the fence, Donovan's silhouette blurred into the shadows. With another long drag of my cigarette, I flicked it into the distance and readied to sprint. Every muscle in my body coiled tightly. The moment the guard disappeared around the corner; I sprinted.

Donovan was up and running before I hit the line of trees, our timing perfect. He reached the fence just before me, in time to throw the slab of carpet up and over the barbed wire just as I hit the fence with a shrieking impact. I scaled quickly, my practiced grabs finding their spot expertly before I barrel rolled over the carpet and landed squarely on my feet on the other side.

Without a word, Donovan snatched the carpet and ran in the opposite direction. My heart hammered loudly inside my ears, my lungs on fire from the cold air as I darted across the lot towards the goal: the '65 Camaro on the far left of the line of cars. *80 seconds.*

It took three seconds to slide the Slim-jim through the slit of the window down into the car door and pop it open. *77 seconds.* It was cold and quiet inside the car; my heavy breathing filled the space. I popped open the paneling under the steering wheel to expose the wires like eviscerated entrails. The blade of my knife reflected sharply as I sliced the wires I needed. Sparks sprayed from the connection, landing painfully on my exposed wrists as I brushed the metal wires against each other. Nothing.

"*Fuck,*" I spat. I tried again, the wires refusing to ignite the engine. I glanced up through the dark window, but the guard was nowhere in sight. *Sixty seconds.* If I didn't get the car started and off the lot in time, the guard would be back. He would put a bullet in my brain if he caught me attempting to lift this car.

These weren't ordinary cars, and these weren't ordinary security guards. If it just came down to throwing a few punches to render him incapacitated, that wouldn't be a big deal. I towered over most men I knew, and I was one of the best bare-knuckle boxers in the county. However, strength and size don't mean shit against a gun.

All My Life

Sweat dripped from my hairline into my eyes and I quickly brushed it away with the back of my hand holding the knife. I knew Donovan and the others were eagerly waiting for my return. It never takes this long. In another ten seconds, they would tear out of here, leaving me behind. A dark shadow moved in my peripheral vision but was quickly forgotten as the interior lights of the car turned on. I had power. *Fifty seconds.*

Glass erupted around me; pain seared across my neck as a bullet tore through the car. The guard sprinted towards me as blood seeped down the back of my neck and pooled between my shoulder blades. I barely had time to register that I had been shot. I rammed my knife into the ignition and cranked the engine over.

It roared to life; the entire shell of the Camaro vibrated around me. The guard skidded to a halt in the blinding headlights, his gun aimed directly at my face. I threw the car into drive and slammed my foot onto the gas pedal in one smooth motion. The man didn't have time to jump out of the way before the front of the heavy car collided with him.

There was a large bump as I drove over his body. I caught a glimpse of Donovan sprinting towards the trees where his own vehicle was parked. Part of my mind was coherent enough to be grateful that he'd stuck around long enough to slide the gate open, I'm sure the other guys had taken off the moment they heard the gunshot.

The car hit the threshold of the gate with a heavy bounce, the tires connected with the asphalt with a loud screech as my vision began to tunnel. Pain erupted through my head like my nerves had been set ablaze. Blood seeping into my sweater caused the fabric to stick to my sweaty skin, trickling down to the small of my back.

Headlights appeared in my rearview mirror, following too close and I knew it was Donovan. We didn't have a long drive back to the shop, but I wasn't sure if I would make it there. My vision began to swim, and the lines in the road took on strange shapes as my eyelids began to droop. *Almost there,* I thought, the words slow and hazy in my head.

The black edges around my vision pulsated. My stomach churned, a sour taste filled my mouth, and I thought I was going to be sick. The next thing I knew, my hands were in my lap, my chin to my chest as the front end of the Camaro slammed headfirst into a wall.

Ophelia

2

My phone buzzed under my notebook, interrupting my train of thought. I looked away from the molecular model my professor was holding up to check the message that came through.

JIMMY: I need you to bring more diapers next time
I frowned down at the screen.

Me: I brought you an entire box two weeks ago. You only have him twice a week, how could you be out already?
I watched as the gray dots appeared, indicating that he was texting me back. They disappeared and reappeared a minute later.

Jimmy: Just bring some dont be a bitch

Angrily, I turned my phone face-down and went back to my lecture. Since my divorce from Jimmy, I had been taking classes whenever I could to apply for nursing programs in my area. My dream had always been to be a nurse, to help others in their time of need and it had taken me a long time to get this far. It didn't hurt that the pay would catapult our lives in such a way that I couldn't fathom.

Jimmy had our son Hunter on Fridays so I could take classes at Berkeley City College. He had our son for half a day on Thursdays and overnight on Fridays between working at a hotel kitchen, getting drunk, and going to strip clubs. I had left and divorced him before Hunter's first birthday when I realized he would never change.

That he wasn't the type of man I wanted our son to grow up into.

Now, our relationship is cordial at best. I didn't have the means to hire a lawyer during our divorce which meant I wasn't able to fight for custody and the judge granted him 50/50 custody of Hunter with me. Which Jimmy never seemed able to stick to…or want to.

After class had finished, I slung my backpack over my shoulder and headed out of the building. My college classroom was a rented-out building on the edge of a busy area. To my left was a large park, to the right would take me further into downtown. I had an hour before my shift started at the senior living facility a mile down the road.

It was an easy walk once I passed the busy intersection, cutting through mostly residential areas. I worked as a certified nursing assistant part-time and picked up shifts when I could. It was hard, thankless work but I enjoyed it. I loved the residents of the facility, and it gave me an opportunity to work with nurses and pick their brains.

The part of my walk I hated the most wasn't darting through traffic but having to cross the park—a large grassy field with a small playground set off to the side towards the trees. The perimeter of the park was lined with cement benches where the homeless liked to camp.

I tightened my grip on my shoulder strap and kept my head down as I attempted to hurry to the other side where the intersection divided us. I was painfully aware that I was wearing shorts and a tank top as a group of men leered at me from where they congregated. Unsteadily, I tugged at the hem of my shorts and hurried.

Me: How's he doing?

It was time for my lunch break. I sagged heavily into the hard plastic chair in the break room as I devoured my reheated dinner leftovers.

Jimmy: Fine

I rolled my eyes, too tired to argue. I had urine on my shoes, I smelled like sweat and my face was flushed from the busy shift. I was scheduled to be off for the next two days, and I couldn't wait. I wanted a cold shower, a beer, and a nap. *Maybe I could take Hunter to the park before it got too hot, I could pack us a lunch*, I mused. My Walkie Talkie crackled in my pocket.

"Ophelia, are you on break?" Kim's voice barked. I smashed down the talk button.

"Yes, Kim."

"Next time leave your Walkie Talkie with whoever is covering you."

I rolled my eyes again.

"I forgot, will do next time." In my haste to fill my growling stomach, I had forgotten to hand it over. The Walkie remained silent, so I went back to finishing my lunch.

The heat was unbearable in this tin can. Stifling like a hand over my mouth even though it was only after sundown. My head rolled forward, snapping me awake. Frantically, I glanced around the empty BART car. I had collapsed into the first empty seat next to the window after my shift. I squinted out into the dark to the platform, frantically trying to read which stop we were at.

I scurried out of my seat when I realized I hadn't missed my stop but was dangerously close. The station was dark, near closing with me inside. I swiped my pass and lurched through the turnstile. Safely on the other side, I stretched my arms above my head until my muscles pulled in protest.

I had a twenty-minute walk back to my apartment and it was nearing midnight. I preferred to stick to the busier streets instead of cutting through alleys which would save me time. The air was cooler at this time, and it felt soothing against my sweaty skin–heat clung to my body under my filthy scrubs. I was thinking about how gross I felt as I approached a set of low buildings.

They had roll-up garage doors, signs hung loosely above them. Most of them were closed except for one, the door rolled up all the way to the top, and light poured out from inside along with the sound of music.

As I got nearer, I saw a group of men standing off to the side of the open garage with beers in their hands. One of them spotted me and jerked his head in my direction, bringing the attention of the others to me. My breath caught in my chest as I met the tense eyes of the tallest man, standing in the middle with his hands in the pockets of his dark jeans. He stood head and shoulders above the others. His brows were furrowed slightly as he watched me closely, his square jaw flexed as an unreadable expression flashed across his handsome face.

My face flushed and I glanced away, my stomach twisting. I hurried my pace. I was heading towards the busy street when my phone buzzed. The first thing I saw was that my battery was dangerously close to being dead. I cursed for forgetting my charger at home. I swiped away the alert to the message beneath it:

Jimmy: I'm bringing Hunter early i gotta work

Normally I picked Hunter up from Jimmy on Saturday mornings around 9 so I was surprised that Jimmy would offer to drive him over to me. I was musing over being annoyed that Jimmy, once again, was chomping at the bit to get rid of our son as soon as possible but also glad that I wouldn't have to drive back across town in the morning traffic.

I didn't hear the shouts.

I didn't notice the headlights that were too close and approaching much too quickly.

Something solid and huge slammed into my side, throwing me to the ground. My momentum was propelled further as I was twisted around sharply, my world a blur. I was dazed momentarily as I rolled to a stop. I expected pain but there was none.

Someone grunted from underneath me, and it took me a moment to realize that I had been gripping onto the front of someone's gray t-shirt. Large hands cradled my face, brushing my hair back to look at me. My spinning eyes settled on a pair of bright green-blue eyes searching my face frantically.

"Hey, are you okay?" he asked. I nodded jerkily like my head wasn't completely attached to my body.

"I-I think so," I breathed. Hurried footsteps and shouts reached my ears then as I realized the group of people, he had been standing with were running over to us. It took my slow, still-spinning brain to realize what had happened.

"That stupid fucking truck almost hit you," he explained as he pushed me gently off him so he could sit up. His strong hands gripped my upper arms and with just that he was able to lift the weight of my body off him and set me down gently on the cement next to him as the others approached us.

"Wow! You guys okay Tristan?" the one who reached us first asked.

"That was pretty gnarly dude," a shorter, second guy laughed once he saw we were okay.

"Tristan! Oh my god!" a girl shrieked once she caught up, as she shoved through the rest of the guys that jogged over. Her long, blood-red hair brushed the ground as she dropped to her knees beside Tristan and grabbed desperately at him. Her hands groped him frantically, searching for an injury. I glanced away awkwardly, uncomfortable at all the sudden attention. I located my phone in the grass next to where we had fallen, luckily it wasn't broken. Tristan made a face and pulled the girl's hands away from him.

"Cherry, stop I'm fine."

"Why would you do something so *stupid*?" she cried.

"She was going to get *hit!*" He gestured one large hand toward me, and I felt my face redden as they all glanced at me again as if remembering that I was there.

"Ay, you, okay?" The first guy nodded at me.

"Y-yeah, I think so."

"You're shaking."

I glanced at Tristan who was staring at me intently, his beautiful face serious. I looked down at my hands in my lap, gripping my phone like a lifeline. They were trembling.

"Oh," I frowned. Tristan snapped his fingers at the first guy.

"Donovan, get her bag, it's in the street. Cherry let go." Tristan roughly removed Cherry's claws from his shirt despite her pout and complaints. He offered me both of his hands and I took them cautiously. He pulled me to my feet in one swift motion that caused my stomach to drop.

"Oh," I breathed as I wobbled towards him. My vision blurred and my legs turned to jelly before my forehead connected with his hard chest. A concerned sound emanated from deep inside him as he steadied me, dropping his head so that his face was inches from mine.

"What's your name?"

"Ophelia," I said.

"Ophelia, I'm going to carry you." As soon as he said it, his arm swept under my legs, the other held me closely to his chest. The world pitched and my stomach dropped for a second time.

"Stop doing that," I groaned. He chuckled softly and muttered an apology. His chest was large and strong, his arms like vices around me but he cradled me gently. He walked swiftly back towards the garage, barking at someone to lower the music and to bring me water.

Tristan bent and set me gently on a leather couch, the smell of oil, weed, and alcohol permeated the bright garage around me. It was some sort of mechanic shop, cars in different stages of being worked on lined the cement floor. Tristan absently swatted away a cloud of smoke above my head and offered me a bottle of water.

The guy named Donovan placed my bag next to me on the couch and stepped back quickly to give me space. He intercepted Cherry and tugged her after him, while she stared daggers over her shoulder at me.

Tristan's finger gently tipped my chin back so he could study my face. My vision stopped swimming as his face came into view, as the last few minutes sank in, and my heart began to pound.

Tristan was absurdly beautiful. He had dark black hair, wavy on top and cut close on the sides. The front of his hair fell forward over his forehead, above his dark eyebrows. A scar cut through his left eyebrow above his ocean eyes that touched his sharp cheekbones. His perfectly straight nose, broad lips, and square jaw.

A thin gold chain peeked out from the top of his gray t-shirt that stretched over wide shoulders. The letters ML were tattooed over the front of his throat, a rose tattoo peeked out from under the stubble over his jaw. His eyebrows pinched together as he studied me with a severe expression that made my stomach twist. "I tried to make sure you didn't hit your head." He sounded irritated that he might not have succeeded. I shook my head gently, swallowing a hard knot in my throat. "I don't think I did."

He released my jaw, and I dropped my eyes. I took a sip of the water Donovan handed to me. He was tall and lanky with shaggy black hair that fell into his eyes. I thanked him and averted my gaze. It was unnerving to have so many eyes on me after almost being run over. The room slowly crept to a standstill, no longer stuck in the leftover inertia from the almost-accident.

It dawned on me that I was in some strange shop with a room full of strange men. They were no longer leering at me, instead, they all seemed to glance at Tristan as if waiting to see what he would do next.

"I need to get home," I said softly. He nodded, still frowning to himself.

"Don, get me the keys," he called over his shoulder without looking away from me.

"Which ones?" Donovan called back.

"Whatever." Tristan stood up and offered me his hand again. I glanced behind him at Cherry, her face contorted in jealousy. I stood up shakily without taking it. "I'll drive you."

I opened my mouth to protest but he turned away to snag the keys out of the air as Donovan tossed them. Wordlessly and self-conscious of the eyes on us, I hurried after Tristan's long strides out of the garage.

He walked over to a dark car parked out front and opened the door for me with a polite smile. I muttered a thanks and slid inside. He walked around quickly and got in next to me. The car was ablaze with static electricity as the darkness settled around us. His scent filled the air between us, and my heart pounded against my ribs.

"You seem nervous," he pointed out. He was looking down at me from the corner of his eye. Electricity snagged in the air; I was suddenly very conscious of being locked into a small car with this very large man.

"I just don't know you," I said. My answer made him laugh; the sound bubbled from his chest. He extended his hand to me, tattoos snaked out from under his short sleeve, across thick forearms down to his hands. A rose trapped in a spider's web covered the wide expanse of the back of his right hand. The knuckles of his hands were raw and bloody from cradling me as he tackled me out of the way of the truck earlier.

"Tristan Lawrence, nice to meet you."

I smiled back and placed my hand in his. "Nice to meet you too, I'm Ophelia Black."

"Are you a nurse?" He nodded towards my scrubs as we pulled away from the garage.

"Not yet, I'm in school right now to be a nurse. I work as an aid at Sunset Ridge."

"The old folk's home?" He looked at me quickly. "My grandma lives there, she's on the dementia wing."

"Memory care," I corrected with a laugh which made him laugh in return. "Take the next right." I directed him. "You're a mechanic?"

"Yeah." His answer was short, his body stiffened.

"Your girlfriend doesn't seem happy that you're helping me…thank you by the way."

He laughed again, his body relaxing.

"Cherry? Nah, she's not my girlfriend." He shook his head. He glanced at me again, his green-blue eyes blazed. "What about you? Is your boyfriend going to be concerned with some strange man dropping you off at 1 AM?"

I balked at the time, realizing it was so late.

"No." I shook my head and his shoulders fell incrementally. "I mean, no I don't have a boyfriend."

His eyes lightened again. I directed him a few more streets to my building. It was a tall, brown building of only a dozen units. Rickety wooden stairs led up to my apartment. My roommate Crystal was either asleep or spending the night at her boyfriend's, hopefully, she wasn't home so I wouldn't have to worry about waking her. I gathered my things and unlatched my seat belt, pausing to look back at him. *God, he is so beautiful.* He leaned forward suddenly until he was less than a foot from my face.

"It was really nice meeting you Ophelia," he breathed, and my heart leaped.

"Y-you too," I stammered. I hesitated for a moment, unsure of how to end the entire encounter with him. Awkwardly, I smiled up at him before I darted out of the car. I hurried up the stairs. I fumbled with my keys to the front door until I finally fell inside, kicking the door closed behind me.

Leaping onto the couch in front of the window, I peeked out of the thin curtain. Tristan's car was still there but he was standing outside of it. A squeak escaped me as I ducked down, hoping he didn't see me. A moment later, I steeled myself to take another look. He stood motionlessly, staring up at my apartment with a cigarette to his lips.

The cherry burned brightly in the night, smoke obscuring his face. A few minutes later, he flicked the butt and got back into his car.

Ophelia

3

The excessively loud knock on my door ripped me from my sleep, jolting me awake. I struggled all night, replaying the events of the night through my head. The way Tristan's enormous shoulders molded into my body; his steel-cage arms wrapped around me fiercely yet gently as he threw our bodies to the ground out of harm's way. He had scraped his arms up on the asphalt as we rolled but he hadn't complained once. His ocean eyes had been so intense.

I scrambled out of bed, tugging on a pair of sweats, and made my way to the door. Crystal's door was still closed, I assumed she would be home later. I opened the front door to Jimmy, an annoyed expression on his face.

"I've been standing outside for ten minutes," he complained. I ignored him as my attention focused on Hunter, my chest full at the sight of my baby coming home. His large brown eyes lit up when he saw me, chubby hands grabbed for me. I scooped him out of Jimmy's arms and held him tightly to my chest. Though he wasn't with Jimmy for very long, not often at all, I always worried about him being with his dad. Jimmy was by far the least responsible person that I knew.

Jimmy handed me back Hunter's diaper bag, it didn't look touched other than the missing diapers. Jimmy was living with some roommate in a small apartment that smelled of stale beer and unwashed clothes. I knew Jimmy still hated me for divorcing him, but it wasn't like either of us had wanted to stay in the marriage. I was home alone with Hunter so often, fending for ourselves and going to bed just the two of us that it was like we had broken up before.

Jimmy stood on my porch now in a pair of dirty jeans, his white tank top clung to his skinny sides. Jimmy had been so handsome when we met five years ago, he wasn't so sunken in and drained looking. The hollows of his cheeks were covered in patchy stubble, his dull hazel eyes looked exhausted.

Greasy brown hair peeked out from under the beanie hat he always wore. Dirt lined his nails. Part of me hurt looking at what he had become but it was quickly snuffed out, he had treated me so poorly during our relationship and chose every opportunity now to continue treating myself and our son badly. I hated him.

"Thanks," was all I said as I took the bag and closed the door. I spent the next hour bathing Hunter and feeding him. His diaper had been so full that it swayed beneath him as he staggered across the living room. Worse yet was the red, angry diaper rash. If Jimmy went through all the diapers that I had supplied him in just a day, there was no reason for Hunter's diaper to be so full or the rash.

I soothed the angry skin in a lukewarm bath, skipping the bubbles so it wouldn't dry his skin out more. Hunter whined as I poured water through his blonde hair, rinsing the time at his dad's off him. I wrapped him up in a soft towel and covered his face with kisses until he was squealing with laughter. Slopping his bottom in diaper cream, I put a new diaper on him loosely and dressed him in comfortable clothes. I was feeding him his second bowl of oatmeal when Serena walked in through my front door with her daughter Alicia.

Serena and I had been friends since high school, and each had our own issues with the fathers of our children. We were as close as sisters which is why she let herself into my apartment any time she wanted.

"Morning!" I greeted, happy to see them. I took Hunter out of his highchair so the two kids could play. Alicia was a couple of years older than Hunter, but they loved to play together. Serena and I dropped onto the couch as the two got into the plastic bins of Hunter's toys on the floor. Serena handed me a hot Starbucks coffee and I took it happily. She sagged into the back of the couch, throwing her head back. Her black hair was a curly mess, tied up haphazardly to the top of her head. She was hungover, which was usual for her.

"I met this guy last night," she began.

Sleepily, I listened to her story of going to the bars downtown last night and hooking up with some guy she met. Serena had a free lifestyle; she was a firecracker of a woman and loved the thrill of being chased by men. Her voice tinkled familiarly as I sagged deeper and deeper into my couch. Serena noticed me falling asleep and elbowed my side. "Why are you so tired? Did you work a double? I thought Hunter was at his dad's today."

I glanced at my sweet boy playing with a firetruck on the carpet. "No, Jimmy brought him by early this morning."

"Figures," she rolled her eyes.

"I...I also met a guy last night," I admitted, my cheeks burned. Serena's eyes flew open wide, and she jumped on the couch so that her legs were crossed beneath her, her body facing me.

"You bitch! You let me go on and on about some guy fingering me in my car and you met a guy?"

I laughed and looked down at my hands wrapped around my drink. I didn't know where to start—I didn't even know what to say. *Did I really* meet *a guy last night?* He did save my life, injuring himself in the process but he hasn't even asked for my phone number. I didn't know if I would ever see him again. A frown pulled my eyebrows together as I realized that I may well never see him again.

"His name is Tristan Lawrence and he's *gorgeous*," I whined the last word which made Serena beam excitedly. Her black eyes filled with lust as I told her the story. Her hand flew to her mouth as I told her about the truck that almost hit me, the gold bracelets on her wrist clanging gently against her deep, mahogany skin.

As I described Tristan–his golden skin, full lips, and impossibly large shoulders and chest–Serena moaned deeply, her eyes fluttered to the back of her head dramatically as her palm skated down her throat, over her large chest down to her pants. I laughed at her reaction, but the sound died on my tongue. "I don't know if I'll ever see him again. I didn't even give him my phone number–he didn't even *ask* for it!" I groaned.

"Who gives a fuck? Go see him! You know where his shop is." She threw her arm out in an arch like that should've been obvious to me. "Oh my god *yes* bitch, wear something super sexy and a little slutty. Go show up at his shop and demand to see him. Oh my god, I'm wet thinking about it." She grabbed the front of her crotch and laughed wildly.

I laughed, a burn seeped into my cheeks from my chest at the thought of doing something so brazen, so…Serena. I wish I had her confidence. She was beautiful and she knew it. It's not like I wasn't attractive, I'm very beautiful and I know it as well. I'm tall and shapely with long, straight brown hair and green eyes. My skin is fair no matter how often I try to tan. However, I grew up being told by my father that I was fat and ugly.

It stuck with me as an adult. I realize now that my father had his own insecurities that he projected onto me. Mostly because I looked like my mother who had left him after their short time together and broke his heart.

"I have an idea!" I grabbed my phone and immediately pulled up Instagram. My eagerness quickly died when I couldn't find him. Serena used her phone to join in my search, but her own quest came up empty-handed.

"Wait—is this him?" She sat up straight and shoved the phone into my face. It took a moment for my eyes to adjust to the sudden proximity. My heart leaped into my throat when I saw his picture staring back at me.

It was an Alameda County Jail mugshot. The police shield was embossed over the bottom right of the image. Tristan's hair was disheveled, and the collar of his white shirt was torn. His devastatingly handsome face smirked at the camera, his full lips pulled up to one side. Though his eyes burned furiously, murderously.

"That's him!" I laughed.

Serena snapped her phone back around, tearing his image away from me too quickly.

"Ugh, *girl!*" She exclaimed, drawing out the last word. She threw herself back over the arm of the couch, her large chest heaving. "He is *so sexy*, Jesus! If you don't go down to the auto shop and claim him, I will."

An irrational feeling of jealousy made me bristle. The thought of Serena slinking up to Tristan's eager eyes, and outstretched hands made me shift uncomfortably.

"What was he arrested for?" I changed the subject.

"An assault charge two years ago," she said. She stared at his image for a long, pregnant moment and sighed. "Damn bitch, good for you."

My stomach sank. I had a feeling that Tristan was a bit rough around the edges, I got that just from our brief encounter. The devilish look in his eyes, the energy at the mechanic shop, and the way his friends were looking at me.

But a part of me had been hopeful that he wasn't the *same* as the other guys I always went for. The ones who were trouble, mixed up with a bad crowd, and going nowhere in life. He'd obviously made a mistake but if that was the worst he'd ever done...was it really that bad? Could I pass judgment so quickly when I wasn't perfect either?

After Serena left, I took a short nap with Hunter. I held him close, listening to his little breath as his tiny shoulders rose and fell. His long, dark eyelashes fanned out over the curve of his cheeks peacefully. I kissed his ear softly.

"I love you," I breathed as I drifted to sleep.

Around five, Crystal came home briefly to change and head back out. We muttered polite greetings to each other before she was gone again.

I found myself checking my phone. Tristan's mugshot made my stomach twist and heat spread from my chest. I groaned and slammed my phone face down onto my couch. I hated myself for not giving him my phone number. For not being brave enough to go find him. Irritated, I pushed my laptop away and stretched my sore back.

My eyes were aching from staring at my Cultural Anthropology homework. I threw open the window behind the loveseat and gulped in fresh air. I closed my eyes, feeling the blazing sun hot on my skin. Someone in the complex was barbecuing on their back patio, the smell of cooking meat made my mouth water.

I opened my eyes to try and see who was cooking, maybe it was someone we knew and could come over. As my eyes swept over the parking lot in front of the complex, I stopped. A car I didn't recognize was parked across the street. The apartment complex was so small that I knew almost everyone who lived here and recognized their visitors by their cars, but this was one I didn't know.

Not one to know the makes and models of cars, I did know when I would see the same cars repeatedly. The energy radiating from the black car made goosebumps flitter across my bare skin. The windows were tinted dark, there was no chance to see who was inside. It idled, the rumbling sound of the engine loud enough to reach me.

As I squinted to see better, the driver's side window rolled down. My breath caught, suddenly self-conscious at being caught staring. But the window stopped just an inch or two down. My heart began to beat strongly against my chest, but I couldn't look away. A billow of smoke wafted out of the open window, drifting upwards into the blue, hot sky.

Something about the act told me they saw me staring at them and they were watching me in return. A small shiver trickled down my spine and across my shoulders. I shut the window quickly and pulled the curtains tight.

Tristan

4

She has a kid. A little boy, in fact, about two years old or so. I had gotten there just in time to see some scrawny guy pull up in some piece of shit car and stagger out. He walked around to the other side of the car and picked a small boy up from the backseat. My jaw clenched as the scrawny dude swayed suspiciously under the small boy's weight, nearly dropping him.

Was he drunk? A heat filled me as I watched him walk too comfortably up the stairs to Ophelia's apartment, but it quickly halted when I saw him stop at her door and knock loudly. *Who the fuck does he think he is, banging like that?* I was relieved to see that he clearly didn't live there. Ophelia had said she didn't have anyone, but she could've been lying. Or maybe she and her ex were on such good terms he felt like he could just walk in without knocking. I was pleased to see that neither was the case.

A smirk pulled up the corner of my mouth as I saw the guy grow visibly irritated. Despite his angry banging, Ophelia didn't feel the need to rush to answer the door, to appease his frustrations.

"Good girl," I growled softly. A few minutes later she opened the door and my heart leaped painfully. I could immediately see she had a lot of baggage in her life, but she was doing her best to improve her situation. For her and her child. She stood in the doorway with her sweats hung low on wide hips, the bottom of her tank top barely covering her stomach. My hands gripped the steering wheel until my knuckles turned white.

This is how she answers the door for her ex? With her stomach and tits practically visible?

The man left shortly after, not long enough to exchange pleasantries. *Good*, I thought. He sauntered down the stairs, eager to be away from Ophelia or their kid, I couldn't be sure. I waited until he got into his old, red Saturn and drove down the street before I followed. I'm not sure why I followed her ex, honestly. Their relationship was clearly over but I wanted to see what kind of people Ophelia had in her life.

"What a shitty car." I lit a blunt. I was behind him at a red light. It would be impossible to see through the dark tint of my car, not that I cared much if this fucker saw my face. My chest tightened as I watched the end of the blunt smolder in the flame of my lighter, catching fire.

The light turned green as I brought the blunt to my lips and sunk down low in my seat. The car I borrowed was too small for me. My knees hit painfully against the dashboard, my head brushed the roof and made my hair frizz. For the life of me, I have no idea why Donovan had chosen this car for me to take Ophelia home in, but I had chosen it to drive to her house in hopes she would see me. See me and recognize this car.

I took my phone out and typed a new message to Donovan.

Me: Look this car up for me, red 2001 Saturn SC1. #77THGLL

A cloud of weed smoke was building in the small confines. I hit a button to open the sunroof above my head. The smell of summer penetrated my car, heat bristled across the nape of my neck and over my shoulders. Summer was my favorite. I loved the sticky heat. I cranked the radio up until the car around me shook with the bass. Impulsively, I grabbed the back of my shirt and pulled it off over my head, having to put my arms through the sunroof to have enough room to do so. I tossed it onto the seat next to me and relished in the feel of the Bay Area heat across my bare chest and stomach.

As I contemplated, the weed began to seep into my bloodstream. It bled into my head, dulled the irritation that was churning there. With a sigh, I relaxed my grip on the steering wheel and sank into the leather of the seat. I let up on the accelerator until I was two car lengths behind him. My phone buzzed.

Donovan: Registered to Ophelia Black and Jimmy Heinz. Isn't that the chick from the other night?
Donovan: What're you doin man?

Jimmy. A lousy name for a lousy guy. Jimmy turned and I followed him closely. Through his window, I watched as he lit a cigarette. *Did he forget about the car seat in the back of his fucking car?* My bumper inched closer to his. I smoke weed anywhere but smoking cigarettes in a car or house is disgusting. All those thousands of poisonous chemicals. That coupled with him appearing inebriated earlier, clearly doesn't give a shit about his son.

Me: Tell me about Jimmy.

Jimmy pulled into the parking lot of a row of single-story apartments. Half-dressed; dirty kids ran around the parking lot unsupervised. Trash littered the asphalt. A few apartments had broken windows fixed with plyboards.

Donovan: Age 30. Arrested five years ago for a DUI, no active driver's license. Arrested two years ago for a bar fight, spent two nights in jail and was released on bond. No show for court. Arrested a year ago for possession of meth and active bench warrant. Court ordered drug rehab—no show.

My skin crawled. He looked like someone who would be into meth. Was he doing that shit around his kid? The joints in my hands popped loudly as I curled them into fists on my lap. No license but he's out driving around in *Ophelia's* car. Though I met her briefly, I knew better than to assume Ophelia was okay with this shit. That's probably why they aren't together anymore. Another text buzzed.

Donovan: Divorced 1.5 years ago from one Miss Ophelia Black

Divorced? My eyes widened, staring at the words on my screen. *She actually married this loser?* A heavy sigh escaped me as I rolled my head back onto the seat and looked out my side window as Jimmy began to crawl out of his Saturn. Whatever her reasonings were, she clearly wised up and left the loser. As Jimmy approached his apartment, the door opened, and another sickly- looking guy greeted him. They were exchanging pleasantries of some sort as I turned down my radio while simultaneously rolling down my window.

The movement caught the second guy's attention. With a nod of his chin, he directed Jimmy's attention to me. Slowly, Jimmy turned, squinting through the bright sun at me. I extended my long arm out of the window, curling my fingers into the shape of a gun, and pointed it directly at Jimmy. His eyes widened. Gently, I flicked my wrist as if letting off a single shot. Jimmy shoved his way past his friend, and they ducked inside, slamming the door behind them.

"It's on bitch." I watched his closed door for another minute before I turned around to head back to Ophelia's house.

Ophelia

5

There was a delay in the train schedule which meant I was rushing to clock in on time. I swiped my badge and sighed in relief when it chimed. I stuffed my things into my locker and went out to the receptionist area to get my schedule. Most times, I had the same assignment, but I liked to check for any last-minute changes.

Gloria was the off-going aid, so I found her to get report on the residents, mostly for any last-minute changes to their health status or need to know information. After report, I made my rounds greeting all my residents. These places could be so bittersweet. They were underfunded and understaffed which made the elderly residents so thankful for a sliver of kindness. This side of the large facility was for those who required minimum assistance, so it was mostly independent residents.

After throwing a few loads of laundry in the wash and tossing the garbage, I was stopped in the hall by one of the nurses.

"Hey *chika*," she smiled as she popped a pill from a package into a small serving cup. Her large medication cart took up half the width of the hall though she was hardly tall enough to see over it. "How's school going?"

"Good!" I smiled and wiped the back of my hand across my sweaty forehead. "I have one last year until I apply to the nursing program."

"That's great, sweetheart." She smiled back, the dimple in her left cheek popped. Maria was old enough to be my grandmother, she had worked here longer than I had been alive. She slipped the pill card back into the drawer and slid it closed. "You're going to make a great nurse. You're so smart and you *care*, that's not always a common combination." Her brown eyes gave me a knowing look as she typed something into the laptop on her cart.

"Thanks," I grinned, a bit embarrassed and then sighed. "I'm just tired, Maria. Jimmy is absolutely no help with Hunter, if anything he makes it harder. I'm trying to make something out of myself for *our child*, but he doesn't care."

Maria gave me a sad look and reached up to grab my shoulder.

"You'll get it done without him and then you can leave him in the dust." She nodded with finality and started pushing her cart down the hall to her next patient. My shift started at lunch, so I had a free moment to go through the rooms and straighten them up while the residents finished eating. A couple of ladies wanted to go to the in-house salon and one resident needed to be changed.

I pushed his wheelchair back to his room and helped him get into his bed. It took quite some time cleaning the dried bowel movement off, careful not to tear his fragile skin. We talked about his day, that his grandchildren were going to be visiting later that evening, so he wanted to get cleaned up before they came. I put a new brief on him and helped him back into his wheelchair. After I got his shirt changed and hair brushed, it was already time for me to go.

Because my shift was short, I didn't get a lunch break and I was starving. I brought leftovers from dinner in my bag that I planned on eating on the train. The possibilities of what I could do with my day filled my head. I was lost in my thoughts as I replaced my Walkie Talkie on the charger behind the receptionist's desk and I didn't notice who she was speaking animatedly to across the lobby.

I did notice the way she was smiling too brightly, her cheeks pink, the way she leaned on the counter as if to be closer to him though he was at least ten feet away, leaning against the wall. I felt their eyes shift to me as I returned the Walkie and turned to walk away but I ignored them, my eyes on the floor.

I reached out a hand to open the glass door to my freedom when the man leaning next to the door reached over and pushed it open for me. I stared at his thick forearm covered in tattoos, the large hand that held the door. My heart squeezed painfully; my stomach jumped into my throat.

"Let me get that for you, Ophelia." The sound of my name drawn out in his deep voice made me shiver.

"Tristan—w-what are you doing here?" I stammered, my face on fire.

"My great grandma lives here, remember?" he teased. My heart was beating so loudly, it made my breath come in staggered puffs. "Where are you going?" His eyes moved to my shoulder where my bag hung.

"I'm off early today." I tore my eyes away from his beautiful face to look out the door that he still held open for me. It was hard to think when he was looking at me.

"Okay, let's go then." He shrugged and pushed towards me, causing me to sidestep through the door quickly, otherwise be plowed down by him. The receptionist called out something to Tristan, but he ignored her, letting the door close behind him.

"What do you mean?" I asked once we were safely outside. He shrugged again; his massive shoulders were like two boulders. He was absurdly *large*. His white shirt was purposefully purchased so that it wouldn't be overly restricting across his massive chest and arms, but it did nothing to hide his sheer muscle mass.

This was my first time seeing him in daylight, it hurt my heart to realize he was even more gorgeous when I could take in every detail. He had a dusting of small freckles on his left cheekbone that crossed the bridge of his nose. What looked like a red birthmark resembling a small heart lined the column of his throat, on the other side of his tattoo.

His hair was a deeper chocolate brown in the sunlight. He wore diamond studs in both ears that glittered in the light. The stubble from his sharp jaw was gone, the tattoo of the rose that brushed the bottom border of his cheek more visible.

"What're we doing? Are you hungry?" He walked swiftly towards the parking lot, leaving me to scramble to keep up.

"I-I actually brought my lunch," I said lamely. He cocked an eyebrow at me as he approached a large, white Oldsmobile Cutlass. It was boxy and mean looking, the way it sparkled in the bright sun.

"How fun," he joked. "I'll feed you."

"No, no it's–" I began to protest, my face warming but his eyes turned intense.

"Get in the car, Ophelia," he demanded as he opened his door. Without hesitation, I got in.

The inside of his car was warm and smelt like leather. And like Tristan. The moment the door was shut, the same electricity flared between us. It was stifling.

"What happened to your other car?" I frowned down at the blue leather as I slid my bag onto the floor between my feet.

"This is my car," he corrected. He reached towards me, and my breathing hitched. He grasped the strap of my backpack between my legs, careful to not touch me, and gently tossed the bag into the back seat. "Working at the shop gives me lots of access to other cars but this one is mine."

He turned the key and the roar that answered made me jump. The car seemed to vibrate around us. He twisted the knob on the radio, turning the music down to a low whisper but it was still too loud to have a comfortable conversation.

"What kind of food do you like?" He rested his elbow on the window ledge, gripping the steering wheel with his right hand. He glanced down at me out of the corner of his eye.

"Honestly, you make me too nervous to eat," I blurted. That caught him off guard and he laughed loudly; the booming sound reverberated off the car.

"You like breakfast food?"

"It's four in the afternoon."

"Breakfast doesn't have a time," he rolled his eyes, but it was full of humor. "It's my favorite kind of food. I love this place down the street, I take my great grandma all the time. I'll take you."

The thought of this large, slightly terrifying man helping his frail, older grandmother into a restaurant, being sweet and helping her eat made my heart swell.

We drove the rest of the way in silence. He stopped the car and got out immediately, leaving me to scramble. The seatbelt was stuck. A blush filled my cheeks as I struggled with the clip, feeling stupid. My car door swung open suddenly and Tristan leaned into the car across me. My heart jumped painfully as his body crowded me into the seat, his shoulder gently pushing into mine as he reached across me. With a flick of his hand, the buckle sprang open. He tilted his face towards me, his lips just inches from mine. His eyes were on fire with something that made my stomach tighten.

"The buckle sticks," he explained, his voice rough and scratching. I absentmindedly bit my bottom lip in response. His hand that had released the belt suddenly balled up, turning white over the tendons. Then he was gone. He stepped back away from the car, giving me space to tumble out awkwardly.

Silently, we walked into the small restaurant together.

"Tristan!" A man greeted us as we entered. He was short with a large belly, sweat covered his bald head.

"Hola Luis, como estas?" The Spanish rolled off Tristan's tongue effortlessly.

"¡Bien bien! ¿Como estas mi amigo? ¿Quién es?" Luis' bushy eyebrows lifted towards me.

"Estoy bien, esta es mi amiga Ophelia." The sound of my name, nestled into the Spanish twang made goosebumps sprinkle my arms.

"Ophelia, welcome my friend. Lovely to meet you." Luis walked around the counter to take my hand in his, a large smile on his face. I smiled warmly back. "Will you two be eating here?"

"Sí, claro," Tristan nodded. He grabbed two menus from the counter and dipped his head, indicating that I was to follow.

"Nice to meet you," I smiled at Luis. He chuckled and shook my hand before releasing it.

"Mucho gusto, Ophelia. Enjoy your breakfast."

Tristan led me to a table in the back, away from everyone else. It was hard to not notice all the eyes that turned to latch onto Tristan as we made our way passed. One teenager's eyes grew wide as he leaned to whisper to his friend: "That guy is a fucking *wall*." I pursed my lips to keep from laughing and saw Tristan doing the same.

Tristan made a point to sit in the chair furthest from me, angled so that his back was flush with the wall.

"So, you speak Spanish?" I said to hide my disappointment in our distance.

"Todo mi vida," he nodded, his eyes studying my face. Then in English: "All my life, just picked it up."

I busied myself with the menu, not reading a single word. He intertwined his long fingers together over his menu and leaned over it, closing most of the distance between us. "You know, you don't hide your feelings very well."

A blush filled my cheeks and it only deepened as I saw how close he was to me but more so because of his own heat coloring his neck red. If I didn't know any better, he was feeling the same about our proximity as I was. A waitress approached our table then, but Tristan didn't break his focus on my face.

"Uhm," I swallowed hard, blinking heavily. My eyes scanned the menu until the words made sense. "Can I get the Spanish omelet please?"

"Two please," Tristan added, still staring at me intently. His pulse was beating strongly in his neck, his gold chain vibrated against it. I imagined pressing my lips to that spot and my blush deepened further. Tristan's eyes blazed as if reading my mind. He sat back and let go of a shaky breath I hadn't realized he had been holding.

"Tell me something about you," I said, forcing the silence to end.

"Like what?" He cocked his scarred eyebrow.

I shrugged. "Anything–all I know is your name and that you're a mechanic, plus your grandma is a resident where I work." *Also, your mugshot,* I thought.

Tristan shrugged, bored and leaned on his elbows.

"Not much to tell. Dropped out of school when I was sixteen, worked at the shop ever since."

I pursed my lips and nodded, not sure what else to say. Tristan dropped his head, trying to catch my gaze with his own. His eyes were earnest. "Does that bother you? That you're going to be a successful nurse and I don't even have a GED?"

His implication made me bite my bottom lip but also guilt flooded me. I shook my head.

"It doesn't mean anything," I resolved. My answer seemed to dispel whatever anxiety was behind his eyes and a smile fluttered across his face. The food came then but I was too jittery to eat. The implication in his words thrilled me, my hands trembled as I lifted my fork.

My mouth was too dry to eat but the food was without a doubt, delicious. Tristan ate his faster than I would have thought possible but judging by his sheer size, I'm sure he eats much more than that just as quickly.

"Are you done?" he asked once I set my fork down. He pulled out a wallet from his back pocket and dropped a surprisingly large amount of cash onto the table, clearly much more than what we owed. Without a word, I followed him back through the restaurant and into his car. He held my door open for me.

"Thank you for breakfast," I smiled up at him, pausing just on the other side of the door from him, standing close enough to force him to look down at me. His eyes were cautious as he realized what I was doing. A wicked expression flashed through his indigo eyes and suddenly his face was next to mine, his cheek softly brushing mine as he whispered in my ear: "Thank *you* for coming with me." His breath tickled my ear and I shivered.

I fell into his car with no semblance of grace. He laughed as he walked around the front of the car and got in. The engine roared to life, and he backed out so quickly the car spun sharply, throwing me against the door. I gasped and clutched the handle as he straightened the car expertly and took off.

"Do you like coffee?" he asked.

"*Love* it," I emphasized.

He smirked and drove to a spot down the street. Instead of going through the drive-thru, he parked. I hurriedly undid the seatbelt before he could help me and scrambled out after him.

"How much longer do you have for school?" he asked.

"Two more semesters—a year and then I apply to the nursing program."

"Is it hard to get into?"

"Extremely," I grumbled. "I'm applying to schools all over the area hoping to get in. I have the grades and work experience so…we'll see."

"You'll get in," he nodded. He sounded so sure. I wish I had his confidence. He gestured for me to stop walking. "Go behind the building, there's a picnic table there. I'll order and meet you." With a shrug, I did as I was told. I found the paved path between two yellow utility poles and made my way to the picnic table. Down the grassy hill a few yards away was a river floating by lazily.

"You're gonna love this." His voice surprised me and made me spin around. He held out a brown coffee cup to me and I thanked him. He watched me closely as I brought the cup to my lips and took a sip. The bitterness of the dark coffee was muted by something sweet and tingly—mint. He chuckled when my eyes grew wide.

"Wow that's good," I laughed and took another long sip. He nodded and began walking past me towards the water. I followed him.

"Hidden gem, that's for sure."

We followed the paved path until it became dirt and continued walking until we were under an overpass. The river rushed by quicker here, echoing off the cement around us. There was graffiti coating most of the underpass, an abandoned tent, and some other trash here. Part of me wondered if this was a safe place but glancing at Tristan, I felt safer. It wasn't lost on me that I had eagerly followed this huge, beautiful man who I barely knew to a vacant underpass. I didn't even know where I was.

There was another picnic table here, Tristan stepped up onto the bench and sat fluidly on the table. Feeling brave, I sat on the bench his feet rested on.

"Who do you live with?" he asked, taking another sip of his coffee.

"My roommate Crystal…" I trailed; my mouth clamped shut tightly. He looked down at me, sensing my hesitation. "I don't think she likes me very much. But that's fine, she pays her half of the bills and leaves me alone. I hate when her boyfriend comes over though."

"Why's that?" His voice was low.

I shrugged and took another sip of the delicious coffee.

"He's lazy, he takes up the entire couch. Eats all our food, leaves beer cans everywhere."

"Sounds like a dick," Tristan said finally. He set his coffee down next to him and reached into his pocket. I wasn't surprised when he pulled out a pipe stuffed with weed. He held it to his lips and sparked a lighter. His massive chest expanded as he pulled deep. A moment later he spoke. "You want me to say something to him?"

The image of Tristan leering over Steven, huge and oppressive, made the heat burn in my stomach. I shook my head, dropping my eyes to my lap in an attempt to break the tension.

"No, I couldn't ask that of you."

He lifted my chin softly with the tip of his finger, the way he did in the garage.

"I have a feeling there isn't much that you could ask me that I wouldn't do."

I froze under his touch, his fierce gaze. Words escaped me along with the air from my lungs. Tristan let the silence draw out painfully, refusing to release me. His gaze drifted slowly over my face, coming to a rest on my lips. He made a soft sound in his chest and released me. I practically had to brace myself against the table, feeling faint.

"Since you asked me, do *you* live with anyone?" I asked when I could speak again. I was desperate to know more about this hauntingly beautiful man. It wasn't fair the way he looked at me, the way he teased the heat out of my body. I gripped my hands around my cup tightly, not caring if I crushed my drink.

He took another long drag off his pipe before answering. "I don't." He shook his head as he spoke, the words coming out in smoke. He stuffed the pipe back into his pocket and stretched his arms above his head.

His joints popped loudly. I imagined him in his bedroom, no one there to hear him…I had to look away and take a deep breath of air to clear my head. I stood up and walked slowly down the edge of the river, leaving my drink on the table. He turned and watched me intently.

"Do you have any siblings?" I called back at him.

"No." Was his only reply.

I kicked a rock into the water and watched it sink.

"Do you?"

"I have one sister…we aren't very close." I made a face, but he couldn't see it from his angel.

"Why not?" His voice was soft. I craned my neck to look at the graffiti all around me. Some was beautifully done but most of it looked like it was done by a bunch of rebellious teens. I shrugged.

"We didn't have a very good upbringing, I guess she handled it better than me." My voice was low, but I knew he could hear me. He leaned forward, his elbows on his knees. He watched me closely, his expression unreadable.

"But you're making something of yourself," he said. "I have to," I replied simply.

He let the words hang between us. The air had shifted, a cool breeze reached us under the bridge. The sky had turned a dark blue tint and I sighed.

"You need to go," he said as if reading my mind. He hopped down from the table easily and gathered up our drinks. I could feel the finality of the day creeping up on us, ending much too soon. As we approached the car, my heart rate slowly increased step by step until it was hammering in my ears. He didn't open the door for me this time.

"I have a son," I blurted out suddenly. I knew Tristan had sensed my hesitation. I felt the need to protect my son, to put him first. But I also didn't want to hide him or lie to Tristan. Whatever this was between us, whatever was brewing, was undoubtedly intense and I wanted to put all my cards on the table.

"Do…we need to go get him or something?" His eyebrows knitted together.

"No–no, he's at daycare."

"Oh." His face smoothed but I could see the confusion still etched into his eyes. "I just wasn't sure why you said it so frantically." His response made a nervous laugh bubble from inside of me.

"I just…I just wanted to be honest. I don't know how you feel about single moms…" My face was burning. I felt humiliated. What if I was reading too much into this? Maybe he was just being nice. He surprised me by rolling his eyes.

"It's going to take a lot more than having a kid to make me leave you alone," he said. "Get in the car Ophelia."

Obediently, I scrambled in after him.

I couldn't stop smiling the entire car ride to the BART station, like a moron. Tristan had offered to drive me to where my car was parked at the other station instead of dropping me off to take the train back. It was a thirty-minute drive.

"Tell me about your son," Tristan said. His hand was on the gear shift, close to my knee, his other arm draped over the steering wheel. The position made his body turn towards me, bringing us closer.

"He's a year and a half," I began, my smile unintentional as I thought of him. "He's my everything. I didn't know I could be so happy until I had him."

Tristan studied me closely, his eyes slowly moved across my face, reading something there.

"You light up when you talk about him," he said. I caught the glimpse of something in his expression, but I couldn't figure it out before he turned to look at the traffic.

"He's such a sweet and smart little guy." I pulled out my phone to show him the screensaver of us. We had gotten ready for the day a few weeks ago when I had realized that I accidentally dressed us in matching outfits. I had sat on the closed toilet of my bathroom, pulled Hunter into my lap and taken a picture. The corners of his mouth pulled up into a smile, but it didn't touch his eyes.

"He's cute, he looks like his mama."

I smiled bashfully and put my phone away. We were approaching the station much too fast, I wanted to draw out our time together. A sadness swept over me as my car came into view. I chewed my bottom lip, not sure how to end our time together. I turned to say something, but the words caught in my throat. Tristan had leaned over close to me, his eyes sad.

"Ophelia Black, if it's okay with you, I would very much like to get to know you better," he breathed. My heart jolted and I fought hard against the smile that was pulling my face into a stupid grin.

"Can I give you my n-number?" My voice broke, embarrassingly. His relieved smile made me laugh. I don't know in what world he would have thought that I would have said no, to *him*. Wordlessly, he handed me his phone. I was surprised to see that he didn't have a lock code, it opened right up. I typed my number in and called myself so that he would have my number but also so I would have his.

Without saying anything, Tristan threw his door open and got out of the car to walk around to my side.

"I had a nice time," I smiled up at him. Tristan smiled back and suddenly bent down to wrap his arms around me. He softly placed his lips to my cheek and heat erupted from where his kiss landed.

"I'm glad I met you." His voice vibrated in my chest against his. "You'll be hearing from me." He released me and I had to try my best to not melt into a puddle. He watched me as I awkwardly got into my car, backing up so that I could get out of my space. Lamely, I waved as I drove away.

It was just turning eight o'clock as I pulled into my mother's driveway. The gravel crunched softly under my tires, her neighborhood quiet and still. I pulled up into her large, wooden awning and cut off my engine. Through the windows of the back of her house, I could see that all the lights were off save for the soft lamp in the living room.

My mother and I had an odd relationship. My mom had been a young, single mother herself and made plenty of mistakes along the way. She was a heavy drinker back then, had boyfriend after boyfriend through the house over the years. When I was eight, my mother lost custody of me to my father who I only knew from weekend visits. He and my mother's entire relationship was long enough for my mother to become pregnant and leave my dad.

He also drank and had quite the temper. I didn't blame her for leaving him, but I blamed her for having me anyways. After high school, we reconnected, and she's admittedly been a great grandmother to Hunter. Over the years, my mother had matured and grown into the type of person I wished she was when I was a child.

But now Hunter has her. She married twice after my father, the second lasting the longest but still ended in a messy divorce. Tamara owned her house in a nice neighborhood, had a good job with the county and drank only occasionally.

I was lucky to have her when my marriage to Jimmy dissolved. We stayed with her for a few difficult months. It was an arrangement born of necessity, but it strained our relationship until Serena told me someone in her complex was looking for a roommate. Tamara helped me with picking up Hunter from daycare when he wasn't with Jimmy, and I relished in knowing that Hunter was much safer with his grandmother than his father. Right now, Hunter was more than likely tucked into my mother's bed, sound asleep with a full belly and a fresh bath. I could see the TV light flickering in the living room while my mom watched her shows.

I walked through the back door with a soft knock. Tamara was sitting in her favorite pink bathrobe, perched on the edge of the couch.

"Hi baby," she greeted. "Did you have a nice afternoon?"

"Yes, thanks mom," I said. "It was nice having a few hours to myself." The last few hours replayed like a flash through my head, and I turned to look at the TV to hide my blush.

"Hunter is asleep in my room; he ate a lot of dinner tonight." My mom smelled of a fresh shower, her damp blonde hair clipped up perfectly into a bun on the top of her hair, her youthful face fresh of any makeup. We were often mistaken for sisters. Same high cheekbones and full lips, the only difference is that her hair was blonde and mine was brown like my father's. I thanked her and quietly went to retrieve Hunter. He was sprawled out on his back, his belly moving slowly with his deep breaths.

Love swelled so sharply in my body as I watched my beautiful son sleep for a moment. His rose bud lips were open as he breathed deeply, his eyelids fluttered while he dreamt. Eagerly, I scooped him into my arms, wrapping his blanket around him tightly. I slung the strap of his diaper bag over my shoulder and made my way back into the living room.

"Thanks mom, same time tomorrow?" I whispered. She nodded as she clicked the power off the TV.

"Love you baby, drive safe." She bent and kissed Hunter's head.

I buckled Hunter into his seat, he didn't even wake as the dome light came on. It wasn't a long drive out of her neighborhood to my apartment but there was a sharp contrast between the neighborhoods. Hers was safe and quiet while mine was always loud, and the sense of danger buzzed in the air like electricity. I couldn't wait to finish nursing school, get a good job and move into a neighborhood like my mother's.

I groaned as I pulled into my parking lot. Steven's car was parked across the street which meant he and Crystal were probably inside, drunk and smoking. I hated when they did that, and I had tried to ask them to stop but Crystal reminded me that this was *her* apartment.

Tonight, I cradled Hunter to me as we entered the smoky apartment. The music was on, but they had it low as they passed around a blunt, beer cans littered the table. Steven was here with his friend Marco who I couldn't stand. Marco's eyes were always glued to my ass.

I waved to them as I rushed into my bedroom and shut the door behind me. I gently lowered Hunter onto his bed, which was just a crib mattress on the floor next to my own mattress on the floor. Once he was tucked in, I grabbed the rolled-up towel I used to block the smoke from coming under the door and shoved it in place. I cranked on the box fan in the window that was facing outwards to blow out any smoke that did leak inside.

My room was a tiny box. My queen-sized bed was on the floor next to Hunter's mattress. An awkwardly big end table took up all the space between the foot of my bed to the wall which held an equally awkwardly big TV. The three things I had taken from the house I had shared with Jimmy. To the left of our beds was the closet, stuffed to the brim with all our clothes, toys and a plastic dresser.

It wasn't much but it was freedom.

I slunk out of the room, careful to not let the smoke in and went to the bathroom. I showered quickly, brushing my teeth in the shower to not waste time. The water heater supplied the entire building which meant you only got a few brief minutes of hot water before it was taken by someone else. I scrubbed the workday off my body and shaved every inch while I thought of Tristan.

Just conjuring his image to mind made my heart leap and the heat return to my core. I thought of his large hands and how they would feel on my body. The way his full lips felt on my cheek.

The sound of his laugh and the intensity of his eyes. My hand drifted down to the apex of my thighs; my breathing hitched.

I imagined him shirtless, his strong chest and broad shoulders naked above me, the gold chain swinging freely against my cheek. It didn't take long for the heat in my body to grow until I was choking on it, my hand working faster on myself. I remembered the way his breathing escalated when I stood close to him, the pounding of his heart visible in the veins of his neck. I came undone, burying my wet face into my arm as the pleasure racked through me, seizing me sharply.

When my heart settled, I got out of the cold shower feeling like my skin was on fire. The smile on my face wouldn't dissolve as I toweled dried and changed into yoga pants and a tank top. When Steven was over, I didn't like to walk across the short hall to my bedroom in a towel, *especially* not when Marco was here. I finished changing, put away my bathroom things and opened the door to leave. Marco stood just inches from the door, causing me to yelp and fall back a step.

"Oh sorry," he laughed. He was a tall, gangly guy with an awkward haircut, bad skin and a pencil mustache.

"It's okay," I grumbled. I attempted to sidestep around him, but he was too close to me.

"You just get off work?" he asked casually.

"Mm-hm," I hummed, attempting to get passed him again.

"Marco!" Steven laughed from the couch. He had Crystal's legs in his lap as she lounged backwards with the blunt to her lips. "Leave the poor girl alone. She don't want you." He laughed again and took a long swig from his beer.

"I just gotta take a piss, man!" Marco called over his shoulder, but I could tell he was embarrassed. He finally stepped aside, and I was able to slink by and lock myself into my room. I tucked the towel sharply under the door. Hunter hadn't moved while I was in the shower, my little heavy sleeper.

I collapsed onto my bed, spreading my arms and legs wide in the cool sheets. I was already half dry from the warm summer air leaking through my open window. The delicious warmth had all but dissipated in my stomach as I stretched and groaned. I glanced at Hunter and pulled his blanket down to his legs so he wouldn't get too hot in his sleep. I grabbed my phone to plug it in and saw a text message. My heart flipped violently.

Tristan: I can't stop thinking about you

My face tore into a wide grin and I rolled onto my belly so I could softly scream into my pillow. My head snapped up with a gasp when I realized his text had been delivered over an hour ago.

"Ugh!" I groaned. I had kept him *waiting*, I reprimanded myself. My thumbs poised over the keyboard, wanting to respond immediately but too bewildered and self-conscious to even think straight.

Me: You're pretty memorable yourself…I think I'm going to like getting to know you

Tristan

6

My entire body was on fire. She was *everywhere*. Her scent filled my car, clung to the leather, it was weaved into the fabric of my shirt from our brief hug. I groaned softly as I remembered the feel of her soft body against mine. She's tall but she still only comes up to my chest. The way Ophelia's body melted into mine in that fleeting embrace, the way her soft cheek felt against my lips. If we had locked eyes when I went in for a hug, it would've been a wrap. My dick hardened in my jeans. I would make her wait–make myself wait. Ophelia was far too precious for anything but patience.

Too often had I thought I saw something I enjoyed in a woman only for her to take me to her bed or into her mouth too soon. It tarnished whatever I believed that I saw in them. God knew how badly I wanted Ophelia, the feel of her cool skin beneath my blazing body, her legs wrapped around my hips, my hands in her hair…Even if she begged me to fuck her tonight, there's no way I could ever turn away from her.

"I'm so fucked," I laughed in realization, leaning my elbow onto the door of my car and running my hand through my hair. After I had dropped Ophelia off at her car, instead of going home or to the shop, I went back to her apartment. I couldn't risk her spotting me in the Cutlass, so I parked down the adjacent street a ways so that I had a full view of her complex but her view of me would be obscured.

I watched as her roommate came home, followed shortly after by her boyfriend and some other guy. It was immediately obvious who Steven was—he walked right up to the apartment without knocking. The guy behind him carried two large cases of beer and I frowned. Ophelia hated when they drank at her house, around her son. Ophelia had asked me to not confront Steven's punk ass and tell him to fuck off so I would have to respect that.

For now.

Soon, we would be face-to-face anyways. Ophelia would introduce me as her boyfriend and that's when I would set shit straight. First, I had to get myself into the house. But for now, there's other things I could do to deter Steven from coming over, so they'd stop fucking *partying* around a child.

The sun had set behind the horizon a few minutes ago.

Donovan had installed a self-made app into my phone that could track anyone's mobile device, I only needed their phone number. I loaded it quickly and typed Ophelia's number in.

"Shit," I spat. She was only a few minutes from home, not enough time for me to do anything worthwhile like cut out Steven's catalytic converter. On an impulse, I reached over the seat to the floor behind me. I slunk out of my car, careful to not make too much noise and draw the neighbor's unwanted attention. Music blared loudly from Ophelia's apartment and her shit roommate, loud enough to mask any noise I made.

I raised the crowbar back over my shoulder and swung with all my might. Vibrations shot up my arm as it connected with the driver's side window. Glass sprayed against my face and fell to the asphalt. It crunched under my feet as I made my way to the next window.

The glass fell easily. Lastly, I took the bar to the windshield, aiming for where Steven's head would be if he were driving. I wanted it to be pointed, to be obviously against Steven so I left the rest of the windows alone. The windshield splintered and spiderwebbed. It took another four hits before it cracked.

Breathing heavily, I checked my phone and saw that Ophelia was only down the street. I jogged back to my car; my long legs took me the distance quickly. My engine was roaring to life just as Ophelia's Toyota Corolla pulled into the lot. As much as I wanted to see her face, I threw my car in reverse and backed up so she couldn't see me.

I've never text someone so much in my goddamn life. I had to bring my phone charger with me everywhere so my stupid fucking phone wouldn't die. I even turned my ringer on so I would know when she text me. I would be so embarrassed by my behavior if I wasn't so completely consumed by Ophelia. I wanted to know everything. She told me about her childhood, how CPS took her from her drunk mom's house only to transplant her to her abusive dad's house.

He remarried but the wife wasn't much better than Ophelia's own mother. They fought constantly, drank just as often and poor Ophelia was dragged into the middle more often than not. When she was 10, her stepmom had another daughter, Braxton. The sisters weren't very close since Ophelia got herself legally emancipated when she was 16.

That impressed me. Ophelia had to prove to the court system that she was able to take care of herself, that she had a good reason to be out of her abusive home. She got a job as a hostess and finished high school. She lived with her friend Serena until graduation when she met her ex, Jimmy. I could tell the way her texts came in slow and choppy that she didn't like talking about Jimmy.

Eventually, I would have to do something about him. Something more than an idle threat from across the parking lot. Jimmy wasn't a fool; he obviously had some street smarts about him. He may not know who I was, yet, but he knew something was going to go down. I would make good on it.

I tried my best to be present when I talked to Ophelia but sometimes my job got in the way.

"Who're you talking to?" Cherry screeched. Her voice startled me out of my concentration on Ophelia's text. She stood in the middle of the shop, her hands on her hips. She had her excessively long and excessively red hair braided on one side, the rest flipped like a red wave over her head. She looked like a clown. Her eyes were staring daggers into me.

"Loverboy's talking to his girl," Donovan teased. He threw me a wicked smile from his bent over position into the car we were working on. I was supposed to be helping him change out an engine but was too busy staring at my phone. Cherry's face turned so red it almost matched her hair.

"Ugh," I groaned. Donovan snickered; his laugh lost in the hood of the car.

"Your *who*?" She cocked her head as she folded her arms over her chest, her low-cut shirt barely covered her tits. I'd be a liar if I didn't admit that I'd let Cherry suck my dick once or twice but that's all I ever wanted from her. It was a short-lived want, gone as quickly as it came once I did. Her eyes narrowed when realization kicked in and she laughed darkly. "That *Ophelia* bitch?"

"Oops," Donovan's eyebrows shot up. The commotion in the shop stalled. Everyone who was working or otherwise paying attention to something else, were all staring at us. My entire body burned. I shoved my phone into my back pocket and clenched my hands until the joints popped audibly.

"You need to watch your *fucking mouth* Cherry," I warned. My breath escaped me like a bull huffing. She flinched but held her ground.

"Or what, Tristan? You going to fuck my mouth? *Again?*"

In an instant, I was looming over her, my entire body shook with rage.

"Everyone knows you're trash Cherry; you don't need to remind everyone how fucking easy you are to make yourself feel like a bad bitch." My words hurt her, but it only ignited her fire. She squared her shoulders and raised her chin defiantly at me.

"Ophelia's pussy is used up from having that fucking kid—"

My hand lashed out before I could process it, palm connecting with a sharp slap across her face so hard she spun around, her hair whirling.

"Tristan, that's enough." A deep voice commanded from behind me. My entire body shook so hard I clenched my teeth to keep them from chattering. Charlie's voice stalled me. I didn't have to turn around to know that he had a shotgun pointed at my back. My jaw flexed as I considered. "Leave her alone."

Fuck it, shoot me, I thought. I bent closer to Cherry and spat a large wad of saliva at her feet.

Donovan and I rode together once the sun had set. We had the windows rolled down, the warm summer night breeze plummeting us as we drove at alarming speeds down the packed highway. I expertly maneuvered the matte black Saab 9-5 Turbo through the trickling cars. Donovan lazily blew a cloud of weed smoke out the window, comfortable with my driving abilities.

The Saab was my favorite car to take when we were on a boost—it was matte black with illegally tinted windows all the way around, fake license plates and a fake VIN number. I cranked the gear shift, releasing the clutch as I dropped it into the sixth gear. We had put so much work into this car making it a speed demon, it clung to turns effortlessly and handled well.

It had gotten us out of a few sticky situations with cops in the past. I pushed us to the front of the traffic over the Bay Bridge and shot out, throwing us into the seat as we blazed like a bullet away from the city.

Though it was still around eighty degrees outside, Donovan still wore his black hoodie—mine was thrown into the back seat. The lights of the Bay Bridge danced through the open window across my naked chest. We always wore all black when we went on a boost, the best to conceal our identities, hoods pulled over our heads. Sneaking into car lots or auto body shops wasn't exactly safe and far from legal. We stole cars straight off the lot and dismantled them for parts, piecing them out and making more money that way.

Sometimes, if we had a buyer, we would keep the car whole, change the VIN and sell it for twice what it was worth. Most times, I was the driver and Donovan oversaw getting me in and out in one piece. I've taken a bullet twice so far in my five years boosting and been bit by a dog once. I had tried to stay away from boosting, when I started at the shop as a teen, I mostly kept the shop clean. A few years later, I got into bare knuckle boxing and was damn good at it. Until it went too far and cost me everything.

"So, man…what's up with you?" Donovan asked, not looking at me. Instead, he opted to look out his window at the water.

"What do you mean?" I got off on the Walnut Creek exit, fishtailing around the curve and sliding into the traffic below on the 24 highway just in front of a new Mercedes C Class. The Mercedes slammed on their brakes and laid on their horn, but I was already gone, throwing the Saab into gear, and smashing through the traffic. He sighed heavily and I knew this conversation was going to piss me off.

"This Ophelia chick. You seem pretty…invested but I mean, c'mon man," he rolled his head dramatically, as if exhausted. "You've known her like what? A couple of weeks?"

"So?" My voice was tight.

"I mean, you were pretty rough with Cherry." He shrugged one shoulder. "Are you guys even together? I mean, I've seen you with a lot of chicks, man. But I haven't seen you *with* a chick…not since Katherine."

The sound of Katherine's name hit me like a punch in the gut, my mouth turned sour. The unexpectedness of her image tore through my brain like a bullet, rendering me silent. Donovan stared at me, knowing now was the time to strike but carefully.

"That shit royally fucked you up and it's been what—five years? When was the last time you spoke to her?"

I leaned heavily against the door as if I could get away from him. The energy in my body deflated. Everything was suddenly too much. I stabbed my finger into the radio, silencing it. With the music gone, I could hear my heart pound in my ears.

"A year," my voice broke. "She won't tell me where they are. Everything is on her terms."

"Do you think you're using Ophelia and her kid…to replace Katherine and Millie?"

A black wave brewed around me, threatening to suck me down and under it like it had so many times before. I knew he was right. At least partly. Maybe I was holding onto Ophelia like I had talons because of what happened. A memory of coming home to an empty house, Katherine's shit cleared out, a few scattered baby toys of Millie's left behind leaked into my brain before I could stop it. My jaw flexed as the darkness threatened to pull me under again.

"Fuck you," I whispered.

Donovan dropped his gaze, his shoulders slouched.

"Just be careful man," he said then clapped my shoulder. "C'mon, Charlie has a job for us."

Ophelia

7

I'm on a cloud. I floated through my day, absentmindedly and blissful. *I've met someone*, I repeated to myself over and over, my smile wider each time. My world was muted by a golden glow that tainted everything. I didn't even mind getting called into work on my day off, nothing could get me down. To top it off, Steven's car had been vandalized when he was here last, so he hasn't been back since. I haven't seen Tristan since our spontaneous lunch together, but we've talked nonstop day and night.

I stayed up well into the night, smiling like an idiot at my phone as my thumbs flew a mile a minute. He was *funny* and more often than not, my stomach was full of butterflies by his intensity. He didn't hide his feelings about me, he made it very evident he was attracted to me and my mind. He encouraged me when I had a bad day at work or if I was struggling with an assignment. Even more surprising, he was very good at math. More than once, I sent him a picture of some problem I was stuck on, and he would walk me through solving it.

"You look happy," Crystal had commented one morning. I was feeding Hunter some slices of avocado and toast before we were to go to the park on my day off. My permanent smile was starting to make my cheeks hurt. I took a deep breath, my heart squeezing tightly.

"I met someone," I told her. She raised an eyebrow at me, her curly blonde hair hung loosely from its ponytail. She filled her cup of coffee from the pot I made, yawning as she said: "Who?"

"His name is Tristan, he saved me from getting hit by a truck a month ago."

Her tired, blue eyes widened but she didn't care enough to ask about it. I don't know why I was telling her, we barely liked each other. The excitement was getting to me. She yawned again and started back to her bedroom.

"Wild," was all she said as she slipped back to her bedroom, closing the door behind her. *Bitch,* I thought to myself. Just then my phone rang. I cradled it between my shoulder and my ear as I wrestled Hunter out of his highchair.

"Hello?"

"Yeah, so I can't have Hunter tonight," Jimmy stated. I rolled my eyes, my earlier excitement immediately drying up. I carried Hunter to the sink and leaned him over so I could wash his hands.

"Jimmy," I sighed. "It's your night." Serena and I had plans to go to the city tonight for a much-needed break. We planned on getting drinks and watching a sideshow which I hadn't done in forever. It was illegal and could be dangerous–people blocked off major intersections or highways to whip donuts in their cars. The atmosphere was electric. They always attracted some of the roughest crowds and when alcohol was involved, there were usually fights. I was always scared of getting in trouble, but Serena lived for it and of course, I was easily manipulated.

"I'm aware Ophelia," he hissed. He was pissed, he hated when I fought with him. But it wasn't fair. Hunter was his son just as much as he was mine, I hated when he blew him off. "But I've gotta work–sorry." He said it with such venom and finality that it was clear that he wasn't actually sorry. He was telling me to deal with it.

"You need to be more reliable Jimmy, he's your son too. He's not going to know you if you keep this up."

"Whatever bitch," he spat, and the phone went dead.

I put a hat on Hunter to protect his sensitive skin from the bright sun and searched for my keys.

A few minutes later we were at the park. We found a spot to sit in the grass with a large blanket and dropped our stuff. I loved this park; it was all ramps and AstroTurf so I could just let Hunter wobble around and not worry about him falling or getting tan bark in his shoes. My eyes trained on my son like a hawk in case he needed me. He laughed as he made his way over the little bridge carefully.

My heart broke for him. I had wanted him to have a good life so badly, but he was dealt a mediocre card. Two poor parents, one who had a drug, and a drinking problem that repeatedly chose those addictions over his son. Jimmy claimed he needed to work and that was why he never saw his son, but I wasn't stupid. More times than I could count, I was told my mutual acquaintances that he was either at a strip club or fucked up at some bar.

Though I knew he was better off with me, my heart still broke for Hunter. He was too little to fully understand, most of his life he spent going back and forth between our houses, he didn't remember when his parents were together. The best thing I could have done for Hunter was to leave Jimmy and try to give him a better life. But I fucking hated myself for putting him in this position. My phone rang then, and I answered without looking.

"Hello?" I grumbled.

"Hey beautiful!" Tristan's bright voice greeted me. I stuttered, unsure of how to process that he was calling me. Up to this point, we had only ever text each other. Which I didn't mind, I was usually too busy and I'm far too awkward to hold a phone conversation.

"Oh! H-hi," I stammered, my entire body turned hot.

"What're you doing?" He breathed, the sound delicious.

"Hunter and I are at the park." My eyes suddenly scanned the area, panicked that he was attempting to surprise me. I wouldn't put it past him, he was very spontaneous. But I was with Hunter and regardless of how I felt about him, or was beginning to feel about him, I didn't want Hunter to meet Tristan just yet. My shoulders fell in relief when I didn't spot him.

"That sounds fun," he said. "Listen babe, I have a…work event tonight so I might be unavailable, but I'll try to text you back when I can. Okay?"

The stupid grin was back, I bit my lip to try and control it. Hunter squealed as I pushed the swing gently. The sound of him calling me "babe" turned my insides to jelly. Plus, the fact that he was calling to tell me he would be busy but didn't want me to feel like he had forgotten me. I swooned. It's the little things.

"Yeah of course. Serena and I are actually going out tonight."

"Oh, cool…" His voice sounded stiff. "Do me a favor and be careful, okay? Have fun but be careful." I didn't understand the concern in his voice, but it delighted me all the same.

"Yeah of course."

We hung up, him promising to see me soon. Hunter started whining so we took a break from the park to enjoy our little picnic. After two string cheese and a handful of goldfish, his eyes started to close.

"Ready to go baby?" I asked with a chuckle.

"Yeah mommy," Hunter nodded eagerly, his chubby hand rubbing his eyes.

I did some homework while Hunter napped. I had stripped him down to his diaper, opened the window and turned the fan on for him in our bedroom. The heat was stifling up here, sweat beaded on my skin but Hunter was nice and cool in our room. Papers covered the surface of the dining room table, flickering as the weak breeze from the back door trickled through.

My mom had called and demanded that I bring Hunter this weekend–a lucky coincidence since I was just about to tell Serena that I couldn't make it tonight. I told her of Jimmy canceling and she sighed and said: "I figured." So, her perfect timing was more than just that. Having been a single mom herself, she knew what it was like.

Serena's messy car smelled of bubble gum and body spray. I had to shove a bunch of empty water bottles, fast food wrappers and kids toys just to get inside.

"Sorry," she said as she tossed some toys onto Alicia's car seat. "Damn bitch, you look hot."

I laughed as I buckled my seat belt, and we took off. I was wearing a tight-fitting black dress that had quarter sleeves but was backless. The material was thin so hopefully it wouldn't get too hot, anytime my armpits are covered I sweat like a pig. I had lathered myself in glittery body lotion, so I shimmered in the lights. My long hair was straightened, and my lips painted red. Serena wore tight leather pants and a red bandana wrapped around her thin body like a shirt. Her black hair was piled into a sleek, messy bun on top of her head, and she wore giant silver hoops.

We laughed and sang along to the radio as we made our way through the Bay Area down to Oakland. Most sideshows happened on the spur of the moment and were rarely planned but occasionally, we would catch the whispers of one brewing. Anxiety fluttered in my stomach as I stuck my arms out of the window, singing loudly to the night sky. I closed my eyes and relished in the hot summer night wafting over my skin, caressing me softly. I thought of what Tristan might be doing. A work event?

"Maybe a swap meet or something," Serena said when I told her about his phone call earlier. "Too bad he can't see how you look tonight. Send him a picture, make him jealous." She smirked. Feeling ballsy, I did just that. I hiked my leg up so he could see the hem of my dress and the shimmer of my skin. I screamed internally as I hit *send* and the picture whisked away.

"I can't believe I just did that," I laughed. "I feel like a dumb teenager trying to make her boyfriend jealous."

"You are trying to, that's the point," she laughed in return. "Is he the jealous type?"

"I'm not really sure," I shrugged as my phone pinged.

Tristan: Yum ;)

My face ablaze, I showed her his response and she nodded knowingly.

"Yup, he's the jealous type—and he wants to fuck you."

I bit my lip. Did I really want to make him jealous? He hadn't been anything but sweet and gentle with me, but a darkness blurred around his edges. It was visible in the way he set his jaw. The way he stared at me so intently like he wanted to eat me.

Serena and I parked on Lakeshore Drive next to Lake Merritt in Oakland. The breeze coming off the water did little to cool our skin, a mixture of excitement and summer burning through us. We held hands as we hurried across the busy street to the Red Room, a bar we frequented.

As advertised, the Red Room was cast in red light, giving it a sinister feel. Serena pulled my hand through the throb of bodies to the bar, the throng laughing and cheering as the female bartenders set the bar on fire. The blaze heated the already stifling room in an inferno that was briefly lived before the it was snuffed out as the patrons took their shots.

My eyes stung from the sudden flames.

"Two Jager bombs please!" Serena leaned through two men to shout at the bartender. The men turned and looked at us curiously.

"What's your name?" the man on the left asked. He was at least ten years older than us with shaggy brown hair.

"None of your business," Serena retorted. She took our shots from the bartender and turned away from him, but he was persistent. His friend joined in. His friend was taller and thinner with glasses.

"That's not very polite," the second man said.

"Fuck politeness." Serena didn't turn to speak to him. We clinked our shots together and dropped them into the larger glasses. In unison, we chugged them deeply. Serena took my glass and set it on the bar, ordering a second round. We took our shots and ordered mixed drinks to chase them down and made our way to the back of the bar.

Pool tables and tables were already packed full of people. The music thundered in my veins; the red glow of the room made my eyes adjust painfully. But to my delight, I noticed how my body reflected the glow–sinister and sexy. The alcohol was quickly kicking in, making me feel weightless. We played a round of pool with two guys our age, one who worked with Serena at the pizza shop, his name Tanis. He was adorable. Just slightly taller than me with light brown hair that curled out around his ears.

I had met him briefly once before when I had dropped off a shirt I had borrowed from Serena at work. He always seemed shy around me but evidently, he was also intoxicated. He missed his second shot in a row and decided to give up and come stand next to me. I was atrocious at playing pool, there wasn't any connection between what my brain wanted to do and what happened with my hands. I played half-heartedly, knocking back another shot.

"How've you been?" Tanis asked as he leaned against the wall next to me.

"Good!" I said too eagerly. "Just the same old stuff–school, work and my son. How about you?"

"Good, good," he nodded. "Serena had said that our boys were close in age. This one is mine." He pulled out his phone and showed me a picture of his son. The image was doubled as my eyes swam in alcohol.

"Aww cute," I guessed because I could hardly see it. "Hunter needs friends, we should get them together for a playdate." I had meant the words platonically but even though I was drunk, I could see the light in Tanis's eyes.

"I would like that."

"Bitch it's time!" Serena cut in then and grabbed my hand. I pushed the pool cue into Tanis's hand and followed her clumsily out of the crowded bar.

As we exploded from the doors, I could hear music drifting from the street over and the sound of squealing tires. We ran hand in hand towards the sounds, laughing as we tripped over each other and bumped into people on the sidewalk.

There was a thick crowd of people blocking a busy intersection. Already, a line of cars had developed in all directions, honking angrily but no one budged. Cars circled the outside of the intersection, creating a sort of perimeter. Music pounded from large speakers hanging out of one of the cars, another one had its trunk open and was full of alcohol. Serena and I beelined for the second car.

"Tits or twenty bucks," the guy standing at the trunk barked. He was a fat guy, wearing a 49'ers jersey and a backwards hat. Serena rolled her eyes and lifted the hem of her bandana shirt to reveal her full tits. Impressed, the fat guy handed us two solo cups with unknown contents.

We chugged our drinks and elbowed our way through the throng of people to get a closer look at the cars circling each other dangerously in the intersection. Part of the appeal was for people to come from all over the Bay Area to show off their cars and the other part was trying to not get run over when the cars spun out. Serena and I cheered until our throats burned, dancing against each other, not a care in the world.

Serena disappeared and remerged moments later with two new, full solo cups and I took one happily.

"Whoa, bitch is crazy," Serena said, her eyes on the squealing cars. I sipped my drink and turned to see who had entered the circle. A boxy, white car was squealing expertly in a circle, growing larger and larger but managing to stay out of the way of hitting the second car.

Hanging from the passenger's side was a vaguely familiar woman with extremely long, vibrantly red hair. The crowd screamed wildly as she leaned backwards out of the window, holding herself with just her thighs, her long hair dangerously close to the spinning, smoking tires. Her full breasts bulged against her white top. With a sinking feeling, I recognized the white Oldsmobile Cutlass as Tristan's and the girl as Cherry.

Tristan's car spun wider and wider, the windows too tinted and blurring too fast for me to see him. His circles caused the second car to back out into the crowd, purposefully so that he was the only car in the pit. "I gotta pee! Meet me back at the car if we get separated!" Serena shouted into my ear.

I watched, frozen, as the Cutlass screeched to a stop, smoke spewing from the tires. Cherry rolled the rest of the way out of the window as the driver's side door flung open. Tristan unfolded from the car and walked with long strides towards Cherry, his face pulled into a wide grin. Cherry ran to meet him, slamming into his front, her hands in his hair as she pulled his face down towards her. My heart dropped when their lips met hungrily. Ice trickled through my chest down my arms and dripped in my stomach.

I watched as Tristan pulled out of her hands, laughing deeply, his eyes bright. He turned, scanning the crowd before his eyes locked onto mine. His face fell. We stared at each other momentarily, both shocked. He mouthed something but I couldn't hear over the music and my heart pounding in my ears. I turned and ran.

I felt so fucking stupid. Why was I even upset? We hadn't talked about dating or being exclusive with each other. *I'm just drunk*, I told myself but at that moment I felt eerily sober. Tears streamed my flushed cheeks as I pushed and shoved my way through the crowd. I wanted to go home. I needed to find Serena; she was probably in the bathroom at the Red Room.

"Ophelia! Hold up!" Tristan called after me. I ignored him as I broke free of the crowd and came out to the sidewalk. Drunk and stupid, I bolted for the street. I could hear Tristan running after me, cursing as he darted through cars trying to catch up. The security guard at the Red Room was distracted so I was able to slip passed him. The darkness of the bar only blurred my vision more. I stumbled into someone on my way to the bathroom.

"Sorry," I muttered, pulling out of their hands. They had steadied me when we collided, but I was hurrying. I was sobbing now, embarrassingly. The bathroom was dark, a single red bulb in here, walls painted black, and every inch of the room was spray painted in graffiti. The contrast disoriented me momentarily as I searched blindly with my hands for the sink. I felt the cool porcelain and cranked the water on. I splashed handfuls of cold water onto my burning face, willing myself to calm down. My phone buzzed in my bra where I had stuffed it, but I ignored it.

"Fucking *asshole*," I hissed, slapping the side of the sink. The bathroom door flew open and suddenly Tristan was standing there. He kicked the door closed behind him and spun the lock closed.

"Would you *stop running?*" he shouted; his eyes were on fire in his reflection. I refused to turn to face him, instead I glared at him through the mirror. "I know it looks bad but–"

"With *her?*" My voice cut through. God, he looked so good. He wore a black shirt, dark jeans and the same gold chain. His skin was bathed in the red light, giving him an unearthly glow. He winced.

"I know how it looks Ophelia, but I didn't know she was going to kiss me."

I ripped a paper towel down and used it to roughly blot under my eyes. Luckily my makeup was waterproof, but my eyes stung from crying.

"I didn't know you'd be here–*why are you* even here?" His voice turned disapproving. His eyes skated over me, suddenly realizing what I was wearing. His jaw flexed; his breathing hitched.

"I thought you had a 'work event'," I said sardonically.

"This is the event I was talking about." His voice was tight, his eyes locked onto my exposed back. "I didn't think you'd come to something like this."

"I usually don't. Lucky for you."

His eyes snapped up to meet mine, full of acid. I took a shuddering, calming breath. The tears had stopped for now. "Look, Tristan–it doesn't matter. It's not like we're dating."

His hands shot out like a blur, spinning me around and pinning me against the sink. The full length of his strong body was pressed against mine. His grip was like a vice on my upper arms, but it didn't hurt. His face was tight, but his eyes were wide, pleading.

"Ophelia, please." His voice ached. A whimper escaped my lips then I suddenly noticed. His left eye was badly bruised, the skin purple and angry. A jagged slice ran down his cheek through the rose tattoo, his bottom lip was sliced open, in a state of healing. "She's nothing to me, she's like a puppy dog that I can't get rid of. I want *you*."

He bent and pressed his hungry, desperate lips to mine.

I slapped him. Right on the bruised side of his face. He jerked back in shock, both of us staring at each other incredulously. Our hearts hammering against each other's, our breath shaky in the small distance between us. His face twisted into a furious mask, and I shrunk from him.

His fist flashed out just passed my head to the mirror behind me, connecting with a booming explosion. Glass shattered; splinters hit my bare skin. I gasped but didn't move. He stared down at me, breathing heavily. I watched as realization pulled his expression down, softening it into a blank mask.

Wordlessly, I pushed passed him and he let me, stopping before I left to glance back at him. He was standing with his back to me, his face in his hands. Without a word, I left.

I found Serena at her car; she was standing outside of it with her phone in her hand. Her shoulders fell when she saw me. "There you are!" she said, full of relief. Then her face pinched in alarm when she saw me. "What the fuck happened?"

I collapsed into her car and let another sob shake through me. Serena got in after me, waiting for me to speak. When I shook my head, she started her car and headed home.

I was embarrassed. Mortified by my behavior and my reaction yet I didn't regret it. I felt played and used, how many girls did Tristan have on his roster? Did he rotate them based on his moods, the weather? It was ridiculous to be so upset we had barely known each other for a few weeks and yet I was crushed. We had spent hours talking, sometimes staying up until 3AM. The thought of how my heart would lurch so painfully when his name appeared on my phone, my anxiety between messages.

But I couldn't bring myself to delete his pictures from my phone, to put an end to the lost potential. Numbly, I swiped through them: his smirk no longer reading as alluring and instead now was just taunting. I groaned as a pang sliced through me the longer, I looked at his smoldering eyes.

"Fucking asshole," I whispered at the screen. Hunter was asleep in my bed, selfishly I had slid him from his mattress onto mine. The heat from his little body was comforting while my own was breaking. As insane as it was, I felt heartbroken. Tears could no longer flow through my swollen eyes, my head throbbed painfully.

I traced my lips with my fingertips as I remembered the feel of his full lips against mine—they had been desperate, fervent. Like he could drink me down into his core, begging me. He made me feel like a fool and I made the right decision, I told myself, but it didn't make it hurt any less. It felt like my flesh had been torn from my body, leaving a raw and bleeding wound behind. In the short amount of time Tristan and I had known each other, I had fallen for him harder than I had realized until it was ripped away from me.

I rolled onto my back and stared up at the dark ceiling. Our meeting had been intense, charged with electricity. Every moment after had been just as electrifying, the fire in his eyes had consumed me, reduced me to ash. The embers in my chest smoldered, raging against another feeling. The way he had punched the mirror behind me, the anger in his eyes that peeked through the cracks of his mask showed me who he really was. He was passionate and yet he was also dangerous. Two characteristics that could cause a combustion as they fed off each other. I was afraid of him.

It had been two days since the sideshow, two days of silence. Tristan hadn't tried to reach out once since I left him standing in the bathroom of the Red Room, too ashamed to look at me. Serena had held my hand quietly as I blubbered on my couch about Tristan making out with Cherry in front of a crowd of people. She didn't judge me or say that the alcohol had tainted everything and stretched it out of proportion. She didn't tell me to call him. Serena could see how hurt I was, so she sat silently, offering a supportive and sorry presence.

I woke up the next morning and decided that was enough. I showered, letting the hot steam burn away the last of my sadness and tears over Tristan. I put on a full face of makeup, got dressed and went back to my life.

Serena: I'm glad you're feeling better.

I had told Serena of my decision to grow the fuck up and move on with my life. The summer term was coming to an end which meant I had finals to study for and Chemistry had been kicking my ass all semester. Hunter and I had a lot riding on me being successful. It was this newfound determination that made me agree to a date with Tanis.

He picked me up from my house one evening, the air had a chill in it which meant summer would be ending abruptly soon. Very typical of Bay Area seasons, they started as suddenly as they ended without any sort of warning. We would be plummeted into the rainy season. We had a nice time over dinner getting to know each other, sharing a few laughs.

He had a son Hunter's age and an older brother himself that he was close with. It was a very decent evening, so I gladly accepted a second date. It was easy falling into a slower, less dramatic pace with Tanis. He was sweet and timid; he had a shy smile that made him approachable. When he kissed me at the end of our second date, I kissed him back earnestly.

Though I was having a pleasant time getting to know Tanis better, I was painfully aware of the weeks that trickled by that I didn't hear from Tristan and the ache in my chest didn't ease up as they did.

Tristan

8

Wing 2 west side, housing unit D pod, 2 Delta in Rita Santa Jail in Dublin, California, Alameda County. It's home to nearly 4,000 inmates, most coming from Oakland.

It's the fifth largest jail in America and I've been here before.

The intake–known as ITR–was always the same. 3:30 AM start time through a metal detector, searched until my pockets were turned out and I was barefoot on the cold, filthy floor and my every crevice checked. I opened my mouth for the male officer doing my booking and he stuck a gloved finger into my mouth. He roughly swept his finger in the space between my teeth and cheeks. He ordered me to stick out my tongue and then looked under for any crack rocks or razor blades I might be hiding.

"State your name and birth month and date," he drawled.

"Tristan Lawrence," I said. "June thirtieth."

The officer waved his hand at me to move along.

Fingerprinted and given the same yellow outfit that just further classified me as a violent inmate. The officers drilled me asking about my criminal past, violent history, what points I received last time I was in jail and took pictures of all my tattoos. That part always took the longest. I had to stand with my arms stretched out as they snapped images of my torso, my back, my hands, my face, my legs, and feet.

This jail was no joke—it was hardcore. Like a training facility for a real prison. Having this many hot-headed individuals slammed into one place, their rights and daily lives stripped away was bound to make blood boil. Gangs ran amok in these walls, if you didn't belong to one then it was highly likely they were going to try to punk you. Luckily my size deterred most attempts but being big like me didn't mean shit against 5 or 10 other dudes with razor blades or knives. On the streets, I didn't care if you were black, white, brown or green but in this jail, if you didn't pick a side—a side was gonna pick you.

Hands down.

There were vultures out in the yard, watching you and waiting to pick you off. It didn't matter that I had been here before, had spent two years here one time, being back behind these walls set my nerves on high alert.

After sitting in the holding room for 12 hours with nowhere to lie down, the bright lights blazing against the white, stone walls and a dozen other dudes; they slapped a wristband on me with my inmate number and picture, gave me a pair of canvas slip-on shoes and took me to my housing unit. I was exhausted, I'd been awake for well over 24 hours, beaten, thrown to the asphalt by the police and arrested all because I lost my shit on some smart mouth at the sideshow.

The night before I had been out on a boost that went smoothly but still rendered me little sleep. Then the shit with Ophelia. A groan escaped me. I was too tired to fucking think about her. I would have to log that away for now to pull out later when I had a chance to fucking breathe. Right now, I had to focus on spending my thirty days and getting out. This was my second strike; California only had a Three Strike Law, and I was dangerously close to overstepping that line.

By the time I was assigned my cell, given my pillow and bag of toiletries–I hit the thin mat and fell asleep. It was not a restful sleep; I was a fresh face amongst suspicious men. No doubt that my arrival had already been spread amongst all the other inmates. Santa Rita had a whole underground working; the officers might think they ran this place but that was a joke.

My cellmate–my celly–was crazy, literally talking to himself all night. Any time his voice hit a certain octave, my eyes flew open, my heart hammering my chest and my muscles coiled. I wouldn't be getting a good night's sleep until the block became comfortable with me.

The next morning, I woke up with a killer headache and a gnawing feeling in my lower back from being crammed onto the small bunk. My celly had given me the top bunk which meant I was constantly being jolted awake from almost rolling off. The cell itself was like a long closet. It consisted of two bunks built directly into the wall, topped with thin, plastic mats, one low and long shelf that served as a sort of desk and a toilet. The back of the silver toilet where a tank would be, was the sink. My celly, a short white dude with long and greasy brown hair, was finally asleep. I got down off my bunk and stretched my aching body.

Out in the day room, it was loud and chaotic. Some dudes were playing dominos at one of the metal benches, another group was sipping coffee out of Styrofoam cups, other dudes were hanging out on the stairs and others were just sleeping on the floor. But the moment I stepped onto the floor; all eyes were on me.

"Ay, young blood," a familiar voice called out to me. I turned to see Nashville, aka Big Nash sitting at one of the metal benches. He had a deck of playing cards in his meaty hands, in the middle of a game of Solitaire.

"Ay, man," I chuckled and slapped his outstretched hand. "They still got you in this place huh?"

"Supposed to be transferring me out, that's what they said last year." He laughed and placed another card down, the big gap in his front teeth in full view.

Big Nash and Charlie were old friends, got into a lot of shit together that's for sure. I had grown up with Big Nash always hanging out at the house, smoking weed with Charlie and playing cards like he was now. Like his name implied, he was a big dude– all fat. A black man in his late fifties, Big Nash could always be counted on for a laugh and an ass whoopin'. He got serious suddenly, whipping his head up at me.

"And what the fuck are you doing here? When I heard you had come in last night, I about busted down your cell door and whooped your ass."

"Same old shit." I sat down at the bench across from him and grabbed a cigarette out of the pack that he offered. "I had a bench warrant for failure to appear or some shit. Got caught up at a sideshow for bustin' some dudes head in." The cigarette smoke was hot in my lungs, it burned.

"Those court ordered anger management classes didn't pan out?" He said sarcastically and went back to his card game. I blew out a cloud of smoke and noticed a tall, skinny black dude across the pod staring me down. Big Nash slapped the table suddenly, making the dude jump. "Damnit Terry if you don't stop eye fucking Lawrence, I'ma fuck your shit up."

"No harm Big Nash," Terry nodded, with his hands up. "Just checking out our new boy here."

"I ain't new," I said. "Just been on vacation."

Terry laughed and went over to the dudes hanging on the stairs, no doubt to tell them about our encounter.

I followed Big Nash to the cafeteria to get breakfast, though my stomach cramped. The food was typical jail food but what I hadn't accounted for was the razor blade in my oatmeal. It was hidden at the bottom of the grey sludge, wrapped in plastic, a razor blade melted into a toothbrush handle. I glanced up casually as if surveying the room and locked eyes with Big Nash. With a slight nod of his head, he glanced to my left to a tall white guy with mustache handles.

"Name's Tim," he said without looking at me, scraping up his watery eggs. "Figured you could use something seein' how it's been a while since you last been here."

Of course, I was getting in with the fucking skinheads. Denying the blade or their protection meant I would have a hit out on my head. When we had pod time, I was free to kick it with whoever I wanted but, on the yard, it meant I had to stick with these tweaks. If it was the difference between me getting out of here in a month without a third strike or getting my throat slit in the shower, then that was it.

After breakfast, I hit the shower to clean up. The toothpaste tasted like chalk and the water never heated up fully. Tim met me on my way out of the showers with a cup of instant coffee, his attempt at comradeship before he went in and grilled me about who I was, why I was here, where I spent time before, my previous charges and who all my previous cellies were. This was typical. I gave him all the info he needed, knowing it was going to filter around the jail all the way to the East Block.

A sort of underground background check. We made our way to the yard where segregation was heavy. Each racial group stuck to their own sides; the whites stuck to the basketball courts so that's where I followed Tim. He introduced me to the other white guys, vouching for me. My job while on the yard, mostly due to my size and my rap sheet, was to be a bodyguard.

I posted up in front of the guys while they played ball, smoked cigarettes, or just stood around. Being a guard meant I stood around looking hard and mean muggin' anyone who came too close. But if shit popped off, I was fully expected to participate. *Twenty-nine more days*, I told myself.

After lunch, I stood in line for the phones. It was a long ass line, but no one attempted to cut in line for fear of getting a knife in the kidney or jumped in their cell. My turn came up, I had ten minutes. A CO stood by the phones; his thumbs hooked into his belt, but he wasn't paying any attention.

"Hey man," Donovan answered on the fourth ring. "You find Big Nash?"

"Yeah, and the Aryan brotherhood," I rolled my eyes and he laughed.

"How much time did you get? Charlie's pissed. We have that run for some parts tonight."

"Thirty days–man fuck Charlie, his old ass can go on the run himself." The CO glanced at me, and I made a point to lower my voice. "Look bruh, I need you to do something. Ophelia's number is in my phone, but they got that shit in a bag somewhere–"

"Tristan, I don't think–" he tried to interject but I continued, raising my voice slightly.

"I need you to go to her house. She's off Holly Ave in the brown apartment building, top right unit. I need you to tell her I'm locked up but the day I get out, I'm coming to see her. Tell her I fucked up, I get it–"

"Would you fucking listen to me, man?" Donovan startled me. I've known him my entire life and he never raised his voice. "You need to let his chick go. She ain't an option for you man. I know you're bent over this girl but she's not like Cherry. She's a good girl, I think you need to let her go."

My grip on the phone caused the plastic casing to groan in protest. A sinking feeling came over me, like being sucked under a wave.

"I know." My voice was clipped. I closed my eyes and rubbed my face exhaustedly. "I know man, but I just need her to know. I need her to know that I didn't just dip, I didn't ghost her. Okay man? Can you just fucking do that for me?"

Donovan sighed, just as tired.

"Yeah man, I'll tell her."

The robotic voice came through the phone, warning that our call would end in two minutes.

"Holly Ave, brown building. Her unit is the top right one." I hung up the phone harder than I meant to.

"Back up inmate," the CO barked at me. I held up my hands in apology and dragged my exhausted, aching body back to my cell. Luckily it was empty.

It was like a hole had been ripped through my chest, the edges raw and angry. All I could do was lie there motionlessly; a tightness formed in my throat. The kiss with Cherry had been innocent–at least on my end. We were both swept up in the thrill of spinning weightlessly, the energy of the crowd pumped through our veins. If Ophelia hadn't been there, I would have just shrugged Cherry off.

Why the fuck was she even there? Sideshows didn't seem like her usual scene. If one of her friends brought her there, she had some stupid fucking friends. I knew she had seen some shit between being emancipated as a minor then her marriage to a drug addict. She had told me about being homeless with him before she got pregnant.

The way she had to beg her estranged father for money just so she could eat. The fact that she lived in a house for 6 months that didn't have walls and rats the size of cats. She still had scars on her stomach from the bugs that chewed on her skin while she slept on a futon.

Jimmy had put her in countless sketchy situations with bad people–himself included. But she had worked so hard for some stability for her and Hunter. She had tasted like alcohol; her eyes swam with it as she looked up at me with disgust…and hurt. I fucking hated alcohol but I couldn't necessarily be mad at her right now about that. When she was mine, she wouldn't need to numb her feelings. To hide from reality.

Donovan's words played through my head. He felt like I was bad for her. He had told me to leave her alone. I didn't know if I could. I hadn't felt for someone like this since Katherine–I didn't know I even could. Katherine had been my first girlfriend when we were 15 and over the years, she had sliced me down to nothing, taken everything from me–my friends and my daughter.

Her jealousy was made known by fucking a good majority of my friends. She wanted to isolate me and she sure the fuck did.

She showed me that I couldn't trust anyone, that everything I had believed about myself had been a lie. Then she came crawling back, crying, and begging me to take her back. And I did—every time. It was fucking stupid, but we were so toxic. She brought out the beast in me, the thing that made me my father. I had transformed into the shell of a man, angry and distrusting.

Katherine and Cherry used to be friends. Katherine would hang out at the shop frequently, mostly because she couldn't hold down a job and because she didn't trust me.

When she got pregnant, it was the happiest I had ever been. Running jobs and boosting now became about providing for my family. I got us a place, a trailer—hard to rent an apartment when you can't show how much you *actually* make on paper—filled it to the brim with baby gear. Millie was such a good baby, so easily pleased and slept through the night so early. But it didn't fix our fucked-up relationship.

Too many times, I came home to Katherine being drunk while Millie was unsupervised in the living room. Her diaper soiled and her stomach growling. There were things that Katherine did that I had overlooked because I loved Millie so much, I just let them slide but this was the last I could take.

That was the first time I ever hit Katherine.

Part of me said it was because I wanted to scare her, scare her sober and show her what would happen if she drank around my daughter again.

That's when I first got court appointed anger management. I didn't go—that's on me. We fought constantly, Millie a witness to all of it. The holes punched in the wall, the skin gouged out of my face and chest, the bruises on her mom's face. When Katherine finally left, slinking out in the middle of the night while I was out working, a small part of me understood.

But my entirety was broken. When it was obvious that she wasn't coming back this time, I tried to kill myself.

Donovan found me in my kitchen with my arm slit to the fucking bone from wrist to elbow. It had taken forty-six stitches to put me back together, twenty-three internal and twenty-three external. Almost a year of physical therapy and I still lose my grip or the feeling in my hand at times. A long stem rose tattoo now covered the scar.

It had been five years since I'd seen my daughter.
Katherine randomly felt sympathy and would send me pictures to the trailer. Millie was 8 now, with long chocolate colored hair and in the third grade. I framed every picture I ever received. There's not a lot that I regret in life and losing my daughter is something I will never forgive myself for. She didn't even know me and honestly, I didn't know her. Did she still hate strawberries? Did she still snore? When Katherine left, she had forgotten one of Millie's baby blankets, a fuzzy blue and white Finding Nemo blanket.

I slept with it under my pillow every night.

I hated Katherine, loathed her to her very fucking being and I would never understand why she did what she did. No matter how bad our fights were, how many times I was arrested or if she accused me of fucking some chick–I didn't deserve this. Millie deserved to know me.

A whimper escaped my lips, and I turned my face to the wall. I rarely cry but every time I thought of losing Millie, of who she might be now, it was like acid had been poured down my throat. There's no way I could fight for Millie. I didn't even know where they were. Katherine's dad was a retired sheriff for Alameda County. I was a high school dropout and criminal with a domestic violence, multiple misdemeanors, and aggravated assault charge. I didn't have a chance. They would say my trouble began when I beat the future out of Viktor Petrov, but my shit began way before that. Before I was even born. I never stood a chance.

And now I was losing the only good thing that's happened to me, the only person who ever just made me feel *good*. If I lost Ophelia too–I don't know what I would do. Whatever it was, Donovan wasn't going to save me this time.

Tristan

9

Jail is sure as hell a lot like those documentaries you see on Netflix–loud, with everyone trying to assert dominance over the pod. There's so much gang shit going on here, rivals and old beefs coming to a head on the yard. The shank given to me by Tim wasn't just a part of the jailhouse uniform, it was a necessity.
I kept it in the waistband of my underwear and another one had been stuffed into the thin rubber of my canvas shoes.

This jail in particular was fucking stressful, it was a lot like prison in some ways. Guys like Big Nash could do over a decade here before getting transferred out, the hooch was made the same way and in the same trash bags as prison and there's a stabbing more often than not. Man, I wanted to get the fuck out of here. I had twenty days left and each minute felt was as excruciating as my skin being torn from my body.

"What's got you so twitchy young blood?" Big Nash nodded at my leg as I bounced it nervously under the table. "You act like you've never been here before." He put a domino down to connect a line of 3's. We were playing Chicken Foot, and he was kicking my ass.

"It's gonna sound corny as shit," I chuckled dryly. "But I need to get back to my girl." Big Nash looked up at me, his round face full of surprise. His bushy salt-and-pepper eyebrows up high on his wide forehead.

"Oh, it's like that?" He made an impressed look and nodded at me to play my turn. I placed down my domino without much thought. He stuck out his bottom lip and nodded. "It's been a minute."

"A long fucking minute," I chuckled again. "She's not the type though–I don't know how she's gonna take me being locked up. She's going to school to be a nurse." I added on, showing off a little bit. Big Nash rolled his enormous frame back, his hand on his thigh.

"You got yourself a good girl." The surprise in his voice was fucking offensive. "How does she feel about you boosting?"

"She doesn't know," I admitted with a groan.

"She's gonna find out when you get shot again." He slapped the back of my neck with a hardy laugh. Flashes of that night came back in clips–Donovan as he dragged my limp body into the garage. Everyone freaking out–Cherry screaming as they pulled me up onto a table, shoving things off to make room. The blood that splattered on the floor at their feet.

"What if I get out?" I cocked an eyebrow at him, gauging his response. He quickly went back to the game on the table, shaking his bald head.

"Not gonna happen. Charlie would kill you first, you make him too much money." We let the words hang in the air between us, heavy and sour but way too fucking true. We played in silence for a few more minutes, each placing a domino down trying to block each other from making a foot. When Nash spoke next, his voice was softer. "You give her the black phone yet?"

My veins turned to ice. I shuddered.

"No." My voice was tight. I don't know who or how it started but each of us in the shop each had a black, disposable phone that only we had the number to. The deal was that if something happened–one of us ended up dead, then one of us would call that phone. It was supposed to always be charged and on in case we had to tell a family member that their son/boyfriend/husband/father was dead. Unfortunately, it's happened a few times when shit went south. My own phone was dead and in my locker at the shop. I didn't have anyone to give it to.

The sun outside had decided to peek out from behind thick, black clouds while we were all out at the yard. It had been cold as shit for the last few weeks, I welcomed the burst of mediocre warmth, it heated up my bones and woke up my brain. I had taken my shirt off when the sun came out and stuffed it into my back pocket.

My skin managed to produce some sweat beads as I worked out in the yard. Since the whites were isolated to the basketball court, there wasn't much to do here. I made do by wrapping a towel around the neck of the basketball hoop and used it to do pull ups.

My biceps burnt like fucking crazy; the skin of my wrist threatened to slip right off the bone from all the friction of the cheap, rough ass towel. When I thought my shit would give out, I dropped to the ground and pumped out push-ups on the cold asphalt.

"That how you get all them muscles, boy?" Tim chuckled. He was being guard today so I could take some time to stretch my aching body. It turned into a game. Tim was close to my height but also hella older than me, with long and lanky muscles. We started competing to see who could do the most pull-ups or push-ups could do– laughing when one of us got a cramp or needed to catch our breath. The commotion attracted other groups and they started filtering over to our rectangle of asphalt.

"Squat something!" Someone yelled out.

I made quick eye contact with Terry who was the closest standing person to me and moved fast. Before he could object, he was lying straight as a board across my shoulders.

"Whoa man!" Terry called as I dropped down quickly into a squat and popped back up straight. The group of men around us burst out laughing as I continued to squat with Terry across my back. Terry squirmed until I damn near dropped him on his ass, I let him go with a hearty laugh as he flipped me off.

"Damn you a big boy," one Hispanic guy laughed.

"Lawrence used to be a bare-knuckle boxer," Big Nash elbowed the guy. "So better watch your fucking mouth or Lawrence'll put yo ass on a ventilator." I winced but Big Nash either didn't notice or didn't care.

"For real?" The guy cocked an eyebrow at me.

Donovan and I would spar whenever we had a spare moment at the garage. A little too often, I would be too fast, not control my punch and clip him. I kicked off my canvas shoes, forgetting about the shank and hiked my pants up at the legs to get better leverage. The guy nodded eagerly, falling into a stance with one fist up by his face, the other straight down.

We went for a few rounds, each throwing a careful but meaningful punch. He was too slow; he gave away when he was about to strike so I was able to sidestep before he even committed to the move. I landed a couple of body shots to his sides, easing back my hits so that it smarted but didn't injure him. A much larger crowd had gathered, this time placing bets. The first guy got tired and tapped out, but another immediately replaced him. Each one became more eager, surer of themselves but each time, I landed a final blow that dropped them and made them give in.

Before the shop and boosting, I went toe to toe with a young guy named Viktor Petrov, he was a year older than me but a foot shorter than my already six-foot-five at only seventeen years old. He was undefeated up until that night. It went too far, my rage still wholly unchecked in those days. The blood had seeped from a deep laceration through my eyebrow, tainted my vision red. Viktor had kicked my ass fairly well up until something in me snapped.

I didn't stop when Viktor fell, I landed blow after blow against his skull. The referee and Charlie had jumped into the ring in an attempt to pull me off, but my fury was all consuming, turning their attempts feeble. Useless. They managed to get ahold of my arms and were attempting to pull me back when I landed one last illegal move that sealed both Viktor's and my fate. The heel of my foot connected with a sickening crunch into his face.

Blood was everywhere. It coated my face, turned my hair red, it bubbled out of Viktor's unconscious body and splattered the mat.

"What did you do?" Charlie screamed in my face; his hand gripped my hair tightly. "What did you do?"

My breath came out of me in strained puffs through my mouth guard. Charlie released me and placed his hands on his head, his face screwed up in shame. More often than not, Charlie counted on my anger, my rage to get a job done. To protect the crew. To make him money. Beating some guy into pulp wasn't enough to be Charlie's undoing, he was heartless. What I'm sure it was, was that no one would ever agree to face me in the ring after that. Which meant I messed with Charlie's money.

Bodies had swarmed Viktor, frantically trying to revive him. My breathing slowed, everything around me slowed and tunneled until all I could see was Viktor laying in a puddle of blood. He would spend the better part of a year in the hospital, poles screwed into his skull to keep his spine aligned. He would be on a ventilator, rendered a vegetable. Eventually, he would open his eyes, the ventilator removed but Viktor would never be the same again. The shame and guilt would end up driving me to quit and join the crew. I worked my way up, being a runner or tagging cars until Charlie decided one day that it was my turn. It was a wrap.

Back in the jail yard, the COs broke us up, uncomfortable with the groups congregating together even if we weren't actually brawling. Breathing heavy, I picked up my shoes as I caught Big Nash's eye. He nodded once at me as he fell into line with his guys and headed back inside. I realized then what Big Nash had done.

He had asserted me as one of the Tops in the yard, showed off my strength and ability to throw down so that no one would fuck with me. My size alone was obviously a contender but now everyone knew I wasn't one to fuck with. Sometimes dudes tried shit when you were close to your date, to get more time added on. I chuckled and went to put my shoe back on when I noticed the shank I had hidden in the sole was missing.

I made sure to fall into line at the end, suddenly very on edge. Big Nash might have done a good job setting up a presence for myself but that didn't mean there wouldn't be some dumb fuck head that wanted to try me. I ate dinner later that evening without looking at my plate, my eyes constantly revolved around the room. I showered while Tim did so that I would have back up if something went down. I knew I was being paranoid but in Rita Santa, you couldn't be too safe.

I finally relaxed slightly later that night on my bunk. My celly was strung out on some medication from the infirmary so he could finally stop the voices in his head and get some sleep. Sleep wouldn't come despite how much as I willed it. These last few weeks had dragged by painfully but luckily uneventful.

I was getting out tomorrow.

Ophelia
10

I had picked up an early shift today which meant I was off by 3:30 in the afternoon—a treat. Though it was cold outside, rain drops splattered on the plexiglass windows of the BART train, inside the train was warm and stale. I unzipped my hoodie and loosened my scarf as I sunk into the hard, filthy plastic seat. Though it was nice to be off while there was still daylight out, the day shift was the hardest of the three shifts to work. Instead of just one meal to prepare the residents for, there were two. Plus, showers, appointments, family visits, activities and so on. I was exhausted and couldn't wait to shower.

Hunter was with Jimmy this weekend; we had traded a day earlier in the week so Jimmy agreed to have Hunter for two days this weekend–we would see if that actually happened or not. The turn of events meant I was free on a weekend–a rare occasion.

Tanis had asked me on a date tonight to get a drink and dinner. I liked spending time with him, he was gentle and funny.

He had a boyish charm that reminded me of the boys I crushed on in high school, especially the way his hair curled out over the tops of his ears and his forehead. I half expected him to show up to my house on a skateboard–luckily, he didn't.

Serena had gone out with us a few times but tonight she was home with Alicia since Alicia had come home early from school with a fever. "Are you going to fuck him tonight?" Serena asked as she

sat on my toilet seat. Alicia was in their apartment taking a nap, her soft snores echoed from the baby monitor on Serena's lap. I balked at her reflection in the mirror as I applied mascara.

"What? He's super cute and he really likes you." She smiled sweetly back up at me.

"I don't know." I shook my head, a blush already warming my cheeks. "I *do* like him, and I also don't have Hunter tonight…"

"Perfect!" She threw up her hands. "Do you have condoms? I feel like it's been a while since you slept with anyone."

"I have condoms," I rolled my eyes.

"I think you should do it. Fuck his brains out and make him crazy about you. You need something nice in your life."

I shrugged and pretended to be busy looking for my lipstick.

"Mommy….mommy come here," Alicia's little voice spoke up then. Serena waved the monitor at me as she stood up.

"Okay sexy bitch, tell me how he is." She kissed my cheek and let herself out of my apartment.

I took a step back to examine myself in the mirror. It was cold out, so I wore black leggings with thigh-high black boots and a cropped, rose-gold top. My light brown hair was loosely curled and cascaded down my back. My fake eyelashes gave me a sultry, seductive look. I had spent extra time on my makeup and hair—Serena was right, I looked fucking *great*. A knock sounded on the front door then, breaking my admiration.

Tanis wore a jean jacket, black pants, and a band t-shirt. He has his hands stuffed into his front pockets, looking sheepish and adorable. I smiled widely and kissed him in greeting.

"Damn," he sighed, his eyes roving over me. "You look

great."

"Thank you," I smiled as I locked the door behind me.

"I kept the truck running so you wouldn't be cold." I climbed into the warm cab of the truck and smiled at the smell of an old, well-loved car.

We held hands on the seat between us, his thumb smoothed the skin of the back of my hand. Things were easy with Tanis. He wasn't much of a talker, but he listened closely to what I had to say. He hummed softly to the radio as we drove downtown. I wanted a more laid-back evening, so we stayed local. We ate a casual meal at a busy restaurant–as every restaurant is in the Bay Area–and talked about our boys. After, we walked across the street to a bar that also had a dance floor. We played pool, Tanis beat me easily as I was never a good pool player.

A few drinks later and I was too busy laughing to even hold the stick correctly. I dragged Tanis onto the dance floor, and he obliged sheepishly. He was close to my height, so it was easy to rest my head on his shoulder, hold him close and grind my body against his. His hands gripped my hips, pulling me closer to him as we danced.

His hand brushed my long hair to the side so that his other hand could caress the bare skin of my back and I shivered. His lips found mine in response and I kissed him earnestly. Heat began to build between our bodies wherever we touched, the music gave it a tempo. It was obvious in the way his hands held me, the hunger in his lips that he was getting turned on. I could feel it through his jeans, pressing into me. Briefly, I imagined what it would be like to sleep with him, sweet and slow, his lips never leaving mine.

"I'm thirsty!" I shouted over the music. Tanis nodded and took my hand, leading me back to the bar. I flagged down the bartender and ordered a Jack and coke with a water back.

"I'm gonna go to the bathroom," Tanis said into my ear. I nodded in response, swaying absentmindedly to the music.

I frowned. Something on the edge of my subconscious was vibrating–alerting me to its presence. It was so faint that I barely noticed it, it seemed more like a beat to the music that vibrated my insides. It stopped. I shrugged and took a long drink of my Jack, relishing in the sweet and biting taste as I finished it and reached for my water. The vibration came back. This time it was closer to my conscious and I ran through a mental list of what it could be. The music? An earthquake? *My phone!* With a small gasp I realized that my cell phone was in my back pocket.

Was it Jimmy trying to call me for Hunter? Panicking, I nearly dropped my phone as I scrambled to flip it up right. My eyes took a moment to focus, swimming in alcohol and casting double images of the screen saver and my phone.

Firstly, I noticed the time. It was already midnight?

"Fuck," I hiccupped. Concentrating, I focused intently on what was on my screen. My heart lurched as the notifications came into view.

Missed Call: Tristan Lawrence (x3)

It was like my entire body had a major shock. The floor beneath my feet disappeared and I dropped into the abyss. I hadn't heard anything from Tristan in over a month since the incident in Oakland. I thought surely that had been the end of us. It had been so painful, outrageously so for not knowing each other for very long. I hated to admit how broken I had felt. With great intent, I had turned all my focus on this new relationship with Tanis. Both to forget Tristan but also because I genuinely liked Tanis. Another text message came through then. I opened the thread to read all the missed texts from Tristan.

Tristan: Baaabbbyyy! I'm finally done, I'm out.
Tristan: Where are you? Can I come see you?
Tristan: ?

I didn't know what he meant, finally done with what? His last text was a simple question mark, I could feel the impatience behind it. Numbly, I jammed my fingers into the screen.

Me: Been a while.

Lamely, I hit send and placed my phone face down on the bar. My heart was hammering so loudly I barely heard Tanis walk up and say something into my ear.

"Huh?" I gulped at him.

"Are you ready to go?" He repeated, louder this time.

"Mm-hmm," I nodded quickly. "I'm um, actually not feeling very good. Today at work was tough." The concern in his eyes made my heart hurt.

"Oh, for sure, let's get you home."

I stiffly followed Tanis out of the bar and back to his truck. No messages from Tristan came in during the drive. I could imagine Tristan staring at his phone with a frown, unsure of what I meant by my response. Tanis attempted to check on me twice during the drive, but I just nodded and assured him I was okay, that I just needed to sleep.

"Thanks for tonight," I grinned at him, already unbuckling my seatbelt before he stopped the car.

"Let me know how you're feeling tomorrow and text me if you need anything."

"Thanks!" I called out as I slammed the door behind me and sprinted up the stairs to my apartment.

Crystal was in her room with Steven watching a movie and probably having sex–that was the only time they weren't hanging out in the living room and smoking weed. I roughly tore my boots off, struggling with the laces as they got caught around my thighs. My entire body was shaking I felt stifled. I just wanted to get out of these clothes, I suddenly felt ridiculous…and shameful.

I put on a pair of short black shorts that I usually wore to bed and a flowy red tank top. I took my phone into the bathroom, but it remained silent. Panic took over fully then and I gripped the sides of the sink, gasping for air.

What was I supposed to do? Act like this last month didn't happen? That Tristan didn't just ghost me and leave me hanging after what he did? I remembered the way he grabbed me roughly, forcing a kiss onto me and the way he punched the mirror in anger, barely missing the side of my head. The look of fury in his eyes. It was so unfair, the way I felt for him and the way I hated him.

My phone rang.

I picked it up and slid to the floor with my back against the counter. It was like a bomb, vibrating and ready to explode.

"Hello?" My voice came out a shaking whisper.

"Oh baby," Tristan's voice was full of light. "I'm so sorry I went away. I'm so sorry for the way everything went down."

"Where did you go?" I rested my elbows on my knees, the phone to my ear and the other hand gripped my hair painfully.

"What do you mean?" His voice was full of confusion. "Did…didn't Donovan tell you I was in jail?" His voice came out slow and even, but the last few words turned hard.

"In *jail*?" I snapped in disbelief. "For what?"

There was a long pause on the other end.

"I'll fucking kill him," he whispered finally. He let out a long sigh then. "After you left me at the Red Room, I got into a fight. It was stupid but I was just so *pissed* about how everything happened. I lost my shit on some guy that ran his mouth and wound up doing 30 days–but baby, baby I'm out now." He said the last words in a hurry, attempting to bury the rest of what he said. "Can I come see you–I need to see you."

I squeezed my eyes shut. "Tristan…I'm seeing someone."

Another long pause.

"What the fuck does that mean?"

Ophelia

11

I rolled my head back against the counter and stared up at the ceiling. I needed to do the right thing. Tristan obviously wasn't up to any good, he clearly has issues he needed to work on, and his lifestyle wasn't something I needed to get involved in. Tanis was sweet and gentle; he didn't deserve this.

"When I stopped hearing from you, I went on a couple of dates with someone."

"A *couple of dates*," he laughed dryly. "Whatever, I get it. But I'm out now." The hope in his voice made my eyes sting. There's what I *should* do…and what I *wanted*. Taking a deep breath, I steeled myself.

"Tristan, it really hurt me when you disappeared."

"I know, I know," he sighed heavily. "I told Don to tell you, but I guess…he never got around to it." His voice suddenly became lively, panicked. "But don't do this Ophelia, we didn't have a chance. I…I, fuck, I just gotta keep it lit. I fell hard as fuck for you.”

My chest burned painfully; my stomach twisted. “You love me?” My voice was just a whisper, the silence in the room around me vibrated.

“Yeah,” he breathed, his breath caused a burst of static through the phone. “I do.”

I pinched my eyes shut and bit my bottom lip hard, deliberating.

“I love you too,” I whispered back. I hated how much I meant it; it was as if I had been drowning. My lungs on fire and those words were me breaking through the surface of the dark water.

“Can I *please* come see you?” His voice burned. I nodded and realized he couldn’t see me.

“Yes.”

“Good, I’m outside. Come out.” The phone went silent. I scrambled up to my feet, tripping awkwardly on the floor mat and skidded to a halt in the dark living room, in front of the closed door. I could see his massive, looming silhouette through the square window in the door.

I threw the door open, and his bright, emerald eyes flashed down to mine the moment he saw me, full of intense hunger that made my stomach clench. He looked like an animal that locked on its prey. I opened my mouth to speak but he moved so fast it was a blur.

His mouth was on mine, starving, as if he could drink me down. His large hands twisted into my hair, pinning me to him. I kissed him back just as hungrily, smashing the front of my body along his entire length. He kicked the door closed behind him and pushed me forward without breaking our kiss.

His hands ran up and down my body as if he was trying to memorize the shape and feel of me, while pulling me to him as if he was trying to make us one. His palms brushed every inch of my exposed abdomen and back and I leaned into it deliciously, relishing in the trail of electricity his touch left on me. We managed to walk backwards into my bedroom without coming up for air.

He paused only briefly to shut the door behind him and when he turned back to face me, he was starving all over again.

I crawled backwards across my bed, inviting him to join me. He paused once more to grip the back of his black hoodie and pulled it up and over his head along with his shirt. My eyes widened as I took in his naked torso. It was obvious he was muscular even under his sweater but the sheer mass of him was astounding. He was also a lot more tattooed than I had thought, the markings covered most of his chest and stomach.

There wasn't much time to admire him because he was already pulling off his pants so that he was only in a pair of boxers and crawling into bed with me. His cyan eyes were excited, longing and they never left my face as he moved closer to me.

My heart hammered; my entire body was shaking. Resisting going back to kissing me, he gently grabbed the hem of my flowy shirt. He quirked his scarred eyebrow in question, and I nodded. He slipped the fabric off me, I shivered as my hair fell onto my naked back, giving me goosebumps. He leaned back on his haunches as his eyes roved over my naked breasts. I felt embarrassed suddenly, being so exposed under his excruciating gaze.

My nipples were hard from the shivering and from the heat that was brewing between my legs. A low groan escaped his chest, and I bit my lip. The moment suspended between us as he admired my body slowly, taking in every inch of me. I realized, delightfully, that he was shaking.

He was a bit rougher as he grabbed the waistband of my shorts on either side of my hips and pulled them off. Another growl escaped him, and he was on top of me, his lips hungry for mine again. I moaned into his mouth; my fingers laced into his hair as he pressed his hard length against my burning flesh. He pushed me down suddenly against the bed, his large hands pinned my shoulders beneath him, I was trapped. His lips trailed down my chin and along my jaw as he worked his hips, creating overwhelming pressure between us. I moaned and craned my head back into my pillow.

His teeth grazed my neck as his own moan answered mine.

His large hands gripped my legs, pulling me tighter against him. His bites grew gentler as he made trails down my chest to my breasts. He ran his tongue, flat and warm over my nipples and my hips arched against him with a gasp. He sucked the little buds into his warm mouth and twirled his tongue around them, taking his time on each until they were both hard.

He snaked a hand between our bodies and brushed the tips of his fingers against my clit. I bucked again with another gasp, and I felt him smile against my stomach as he bit the skin over my ribs. He pressed the pads of his fingers firmer into my clit, eliciting a pulsating throb from my body. He worked them in a circle and my eyes rolled into the back of my head. Roughly, he shoved two long fingers inside of me at the same time as he sucked my nipple back into his mouth. I clenched around him, and he groaned.

"Tristan," I whined. Both in yearning for him and for wanting him to ease up. The feeling was too strong, too delicious. He knew immediately what I meant and again he sat back on his haunches, removing his fingers and tongue from my body. My body burned where his teeth and lips had been, both in pain and in yearning. He was rock hard against the fabric of his underwear, his chest rose and fell quickly, his eyes were on fire like molten sapphires.

"Are you sure?" he asked but he was already pushing his boxers down past his thighs, revealing his large length. I nodded, my heart in my throat, my skin ablaze. His large hand gripped himself, working it up and down as his eyes burned into mine. "I mean are you *absolutely sure*? If I fuck you, you're *mine*. I'm not joking."

"I'm not either," I breathed, lifting my hips just barely off the surface of the bed. His seething, emerald eyes caught the movement, and his hand gripped the inside of my thigh painfully. "I don't fuck gently, Ophelia."

It was a warning and it chilled me. There was a moment before he entered me where he placed his massive hand on my stomach, and I reveled in the size difference between us. The expanse of his hand nearly crossed the width of my entire abdomen, and I realized how easily Tristan could hurt me. It was a fleeting moment, interrupted by Tristan angling himself to my opening and pushing himself inside of me. Pleasure ripped through me, sending electricity out from my center to every point of my body.

I gasped and gripped the bed sheets as he drew his hips back and then drove himself harder into me. He stayed back on his haunches, leaving me naked and open for him to see every part of me. His large hands had a vise grip on the inside of my thighs, pushing them far apart so that they touched the bed on either side of him. Suddenly self-conscious, I wrapped my arms around my chest, and he glared.

"Move your fucking hands," he growled at me. "I want to see every part of you." Before I could move, he grabbed both of my wrists in one hand and pinned them to the bed above me. He pushed deeper into me, and I cried out both from ecstasy and pain. Each thrust caused his body to slap against mine, it felt like my insides were tearing apart. His other hand forced me to look into his eyes. "You're *mine.*"

"Y-yes," I squeaked.

"You gonna go out with another man again?"

I shook my head. My body tightened around him, and he let out a deep growl.

"Fuck Ophelia, I want you so bad. I hate what you do to me."

He reeled back suddenly and grabbed my right hip; with a flick of his arm, he flipped me over onto my stomach. The world around me spun from my sudden velocity but I barely had time to register my new position before he gripped my hips and pulled me backwards, up onto my knees and onto him. He pushed my legs further apart with his knees and let go full force. My skin burned where his body connected with mine.

His hand fished into my hair and gripped tightly, forcing me to extend my neck backwards. His fingers dug into my hip; my skin tore under his nails. The pressure in my body was building greater and greater. I circled my hips and pushed back against him, invoking a swear from him.

He released my hair and encircled my throat, pulling me up so that I was kneeling on my knees, my back against his stomach. His other hand reached between my legs and spun circles against my clit. I cried out and moved in rhythm with his hips against me.

With a sharp tug, he pulled me by my jaw so that I was turned enough for his lips to find mine. His full lips engulfed mine, his tongue filled my mouth as if he too experienced the feeling of coming up for air. He pulled back and looked at me fiercely. His jaw flexed under tension, but his eyes were longing, hurting.

"If you fuck another man, I'll kill you."

The words made my stomach leap into my throat. The hunger in his grip, the way his body threatened to tear mine in two…I knew he meant it with every part of him. His hands worked faster against my clit, and I approached the precipice. My eyes rolled into the back of my head, my moans came faster and louder as it built. "Do you love me?" His voice was like gravel in my ear.

"Yes," I moaned.

"Tell me," he barked. I gasped and gripped his thighs behind me as the dam finally broke and my entire body seized violently. He held me firmly against him as he slammed into me harder.

"I love you!" I cried out. His hips hitched and a deep growl escaped him as he found his own cliff. He slammed me onto my stomach, his hips pushing out the last of the explosion until his body melted and he collapsed on top of me.

My breath came in gulps, soothing the painful burn in my throat from his hold as little quakes shook my body. The entire room around us was stifling hot, our skin stuck together and sweat pooled between where our bodies met.

Tristan's heaving breaths pushed against my bare back; his hand still held my hip while the other kept his full weight from crushing me. Neither of us spoke as we fought to catch our breaths and still our hearts. As our skin cooled, it became uncomfortably cold in my room. As if reading my mind, Tristan reached behind him and pulled my comforter over the both of us and pulled me deeper into him.

He planted soft kisses along my shoulder to my neck and back again. I couldn't stop the wide smile that lit up my face as he pressed his lips to my hair and hugged me tightly. I had wanted this moment so badly since I met him, and I couldn't believe we were here. This beautiful, obviously broken, and fierce man was *mine* and I was his.

Entirely.

Ophelia

12

The next morning, I cracked my bleary eyes open against the early morning light that streamed through my window and sliced across my bed like a knife. I attempted to roll over but something massive and heavy was weighing me down. It took me a moment to realize that Tristan was asleep on top of me, both arms wrapped tightly around my sides, his face in my stomach. I smiled at the memory, my thighs pulsated sorely, and I bit my lip. The sun glistened against his tan skin while I marveled at him.

The mountains and valleys between the muscles of his back, the long and slow curve of his lower back to where the blanket draped lowly across his hips. He had the word "Lawrence" tattooed in loopy writing across the expanse of his shoulders, down his left side extending from near his armpit to his hip was the word "California" in cursive. I ran my fingers through his dark hair and noticed an ugly scar that cut deeply across the back of his neck. I frowned as I softly ran my fingertip over the puckered skin. I hadn't noticed it before.

Tristan let out a soft moan and rolled off me and onto his back, stretching out his massive arms and chest. Taking the opportunity, I threw my leg over his hips and straddled him. He let out a soft chuckle but kept his eyes closed.

"Morning baby," he hummed. I ran my hands up his stomach to his chest, admiring him. I trailed my fingertips across his chest to his nipples and gently brushed them. His body came alive beneath me, pushed against the apex of my thighs at my touch. I smiled and continued my examination.

More tattoos here, the word "Reckless" across his stomach, a female Gypsy head over his left peck. I traced the interlocked "ML" over his throat and followed the gold chain down to his collarbone. At the end of the necklace was a gold disc with a crab on one side, the symbol for the zodiac sign Cancer on the back. The disc lay over another large scar, this one in the center of his chest. It appeared to splash across his chest to his right peck, it was older than the one on his neck.

I glanced up and startled when I noticed his eyes watching me closely, gauging my reaction. Being this close to him I could see hairline scars across his right cheek, just above where the rose tattoo peaked out from under his stubble. I traced the thin scar through his left eyebrow and let my finger trail across his high cheekbone to his straight nose.

"What're you thinking?" He whispered, his voice rough.

"Wondering how you got all of these scars," I whispered back. His face hardened but there was deliberation in his ocean eyes.

"Some are from boxing, some from being an asshole teenager…some from work."

"The garage?" I frowned, not understanding. He sat up suddenly, moving me off him by picking me up by the tops of my arms. He set me down on the bed next to him and leaned forward, his elbows on his knees. There was a battle waring inside of him, I could sense it in the way his eyes glared holes through my dark TV screen, our reflections staring back at him.

"What is it?" I whispered. I leaned forward and pressed my lips to his hard shoulder. He sighed and his body relaxed slightly. He turned and pressed his forehead against mine, closing his eyes.

"Sometimes how we accumulate our cars isn't under very legal circumstances."

I thought about what that meant for a minute.

"Okay," I decided in a soft whisper. He looked up at me, his eyes searched my face with a twinge of surprise in them. There was another emotion there, in the way he held his mouth, the way his eyebrows furrowed slightly. It almost seemed like sadness.

"I love you," he breathed. A thrill went through me at the words.

"I love you too."

He bent over and kissed my nose softly. "Let's

feed you."

Tristan helped me up out of bed and to my surprise, he helped dress me. He took the sweats out of my hands and held them open for me to step into and even pulled them up for me. Before I could find a shirt, he pulled his black t-shirt out from his black hoodie and held it out for me to put my arms into like a child. It absolutely engulfed me, but it smelled like him like honey and something carnal. He tugged on his jeans from the floor.

"There you are," Crystal greeted as we emerged. She was standing next to the square dining room table, one bare foot placed on the rung of one of the stools next to it. Her eyes flashed behind me to Tristan and balked. I suddenly remembered he was shirtless next to me as her eyes quickly raked across his body.

"I forgot about your roommates," Tristan bent to whisper in my ear. Steven walked around the corner from the kitchen with a steaming pan in his hand.

"Whoa—bro you're, like, really handsome."

The tension in the room evaporated as we all laughed at Steven's unexpected response.

"Thanks, my guy but I'm taken," Tristan laughed as he wrapped an arm around my waist. Crystal's eyes flashed down to the movement and back up to my face. There was something there that I couldn't pinpoint.

"You want coffee?"

I nodded and he gently pushed me toward Crystal.

I perched on a bar stool beside her so that I could watch Tristan move around my small apartment. He was light and gold where everything else was gray and brown. He was a good couple of inches taller than Steven but twice as wide. They chatted in the kitchen, Tristan brewing a pot of coffee while Steven made breakfast. I couldn't help the beaming smile on my face as I watched them interact.

"So…he's new," Crystal tried to sound casual as she took her seat next to me. I remembered my attempt at telling Crystal about Tristan back when he saved me from getting ran over and the way she blew me off.

I ignored her. Crystal let out a puff of annoyed air. Tristan brought me coffee and a bowl of cereal but pulled me off the stool so that he could sit in my spot and pulled me into his lap. His strong arms wrapped around me tightly.

"Thank you for the breakfast," I smiled. He smiled back and kissed my cheek. Crystal watched our encounter with that same, strange look on her face. She smirked then and cleared her throat as if to make an announcement.

"I'm surprised Ophelia can even walk straight today; you guys were pretty noisy last night." My face burned and Tristan's body tensed into stone beneath me.

"Yeah," Steven laughed. "I wasn't sure if she was getting her cheeks clapped or her ass *beat*."

I dropped my gaze to my coffee cup, embarrassed. Hearing couples having sex was common for roommates, but it felt taboo to talk about.

"Well, that's fucking inappropriate," Tristan scoffed, his voice thick with disgust.

"What?" Crystal blinked. My heart skipped to a quick tempo. I wasn't worried about Steven; it was obvious who would win if it came down to a fight between the two. But I didn't want it to get there. Tristan leaned toward Steven, ignoring Crystal.

"I don't know why you think it's okay to put her on blast about having sex with her boyfriend when we obviously didn't realize you two were home. *Especially* in that fucking context. That's fucking rude."

My heart thrilled at the word *boyfriend*. I told myself that now was not the time to focus on details. Crystal's head snapped back and forth between Steven and Tristan. Steven had been walking to the table with his plate of eggs but stopped short when Tristan snapped at him. He looked dumb, standing in a half-stride with his mouth open.

"We…we weren't trying to be rude," Crystal sputtered.

"No." His sharp eyes focused on Crystal. "You were trying to embarrass Ophelia and that's not fucking happening."

Crystal scoffed and pushed her stool back sharply. She made a gesture to Steven, and he awkwardly set his plate down on the table and followed her out of the front door, which Crystal slammed behind them.

"You don't like your coffee?" Tristan asked suddenly.

"Tristan," I hissed, turning slowly to stare at him. His eyebrows shot up his forehead, his face confused. "You can't talk to my *roommate* like that."

"Like what?" He was truthfully clueless about what he did wrong. He reached in front of me and took a bite of my cereal, his brows furrowed in confusion. Scoffing, I slid down from his lap and faced him with my hands on my hips.

"She pays half the rent; this is *her* apartment, and I can't afford for you to scare her off."

"Oh!" He realized suddenly. He rolled his eyes and waved a hand at me as he took another bite. "Pfft, fuck them."

"No! Not *fuck them*," I snapped. "Crystal letting me live here is what gives Hunter and I a place to live."

"So? Move in with me," he shrugged, licking a drop of milk from the spoon. My mouth fell open at his flippant behavior.

"I'm taking a shower," I announced. I turned around sharply as I retreated. "*Alone*."

I was fuming as I showered. Though I was flattered that Tristan immediately stood up for me the moment he felt like I was being disrespected, he had no tact. This was technically Crystal's apartment; she could kick Hunter and I out and then we would have nowhere to live. I let the water run cold, happy that I got even a few minutes of warm water. Then I took my time brushing my teeth and combing out my hair. I kept my eyes down as I stomped from the bathroom to my bedroom and sharply closed the door behind me.

I dressed in a pair of jeans and a cropped black t-shirt. I threw on a black pleather jacket and went to find Tristan. I skidded to a halt when I spotted him. He stood on the back patio, one hand stuffed into the front pocket of his jeans, the other was down at his side, holding a lit cigarette. He was facing the patio door, but his head was craned back as he slowly blew out a billowing cloud of cigarette smoke.

The way my heart skipped at his appearance was embarrassing. The sun shone through his ebony hair, bringing out flecks of red. The light hugged each curve of his body, enunciating each mound of muscle. He lowered his head then and I watched as his eyes searched for me.

He flicked his cigarette over the ledge and slid the patio door open with a simple flick of his wrist. I opened my mouth to say something, but he cut me off.

"I'm sorry," he started. "You're right. What I said was justifiable, however, I get why you're upset. You're worried about how what I said could affect you and your son. I get it."

I chewed my lip, thinking. His emerald eyes watched intently as I did.

"So, you're my boyfriend, huh?" I finally blurted.

He shrugged his shoulders. "If you'll have me. I already told you that you're mine, there's no backing out. I belong to you like I need air to breathe."

My cheeks pricked at the intensity of his words, thrown off by how casual and easily he said something that made my insides feel like Jell-O. He smiled when he saw how overwhelmed I was.

"In short, yes. I'm your boyfriend."

"Okay," I nodded, which made him laugh.

"Alright tough guy, I'ma grab my sweater and let's stop by my place. I want to shower too, and I need to go to the shop." He pushed past me towards my bedroom, and I whirled around, suddenly nervous.

"I'm going with you?"

"Duh." He rolled his eyes and disappeared into my room.

I was too distracted by trying to mentally prepare myself

for going with Tristan to the shop, meeting all his coworkers officially–the only other time I had encountered them was the evening Tristan saved my life. So much had changed in such a short time. It was these thoughts that stopped me from noticing the truck parked in the street or Tanis standing in the middle of the parking lot, right in front of Tristan's car.

"Uh…hey."

"Tanis!" I gasped and skidded to a halt, so close that I nearly plowed right into him. Tanis's suspicious eyes darted between Tristan and I, taking in this large and beautiful man standing so close behind me that I could feel him breathe. "W-what are you doing here?" I was suddenly hyper aware of Tristan, the way his body stiffened as he realized what was going on.

"You said you weren't feeling good last night," he shrugged but I could see the disappointment in his face as he put two and two together. "I was just coming by to check on you. I tried calling…"

"Her phone is dead." Tristan's deep voice reverberated off my back. His arm snaked around my hips. "We got a little…caught up last night. She must have forgotten to charge it. Who are you, again?"

Tanis looked away from Tristan's hand on me and nodded.

"No one." He turned to walk away, and I tried to step after him, but Tristan pulled me backwards into his chest.

"Ophelia…" His voice was so low, I could hardly hear him, but the warning was clear.

"Stop it," I snapped and pushed his hand away. "He deserves an explanation. I'll be right back. Tanis–wait!" I hurried after him, relieved when he stopped. Pissed, Tristan stalked over to his car and got inside, slamming the door loudly behind him.

"It's okay O," Tanis sighed. "It's not like we were a couple or anything."

"I know but…" I looked down at my feet and bit my lip, unsure of where to go from here. I decided on the truth. "Listen. Tristan and I had just met and were talking…when he went to jail. I didn't know he was gone, I thought we just sort of fell out. He got out last night and told me what had happened. I'm so sorry, but I owe him a chance."

Tristan's Cutlass revved loudly, making Tanis flinch.

"Jail," Tanis's eyebrows raised. He blew the word out like a sigh. He glanced over his shoulder, though Tristan's windows were heavily tinted, we both knew he was watching us closely, the engine purred like a dangerous lion waiting to pounce. "Okay, well…that's that then. You're really an awesome girl, O but it sounds like you made up your mind. I'll see you later. And no hard feelings. I promise." He smiled sweetly at me though it didn't reach his eyes and got back into his truck. I watched him drive away with a sinking feeling of guilt. With a deep breath, I got into Tristan's car.

Tristan didn't speak for a stretch of time and my thoughts raced. He was clearly angry–the way the tendons in his jaw flexed, his vice-like grip on the steering wheel. The air between us was charged, my skin prickled and my heartbeat loudly.

"I don't understand why you're so upset. You were gone for a month, and I had no idea where you were." My voice came out low but did not waver. His fist clenched harder on the steering wheel; his icy eyes focused straight ahead. I watched him for a long moment, the quick rise and fall of his chest as he deliberated.

Suddenly, the car jerked to the right and came to a screeching halt. Tristan appeared to collapse, his body melted, and he dropped his head, pressing his forehead into the steering wheel. I watched him, the way his golden necklace had slipped from his shirt and swung like a pendulum against his chest.

Finally, he spoke. "I hate how I feel about you," he whispered. His words cut me. Before I could wallow in self-pity, he added: "I barely know you and you've already ruined me. I've worked so hard to be a better person, but you make me want to rip out the throat of any man who even looks at you. Eventually I'll either end up in prison or dead for you and I'll be happy to do so."

I blinked at him, stunned into silence. Every part of me wanted this man. Tristan turned to look at me, his head still resting on the steering wheel. The pain in his grassy eyes made my heart leap. Without thinking, I reached forward and held his face between my hands and pulled him close to me. I ran my hands through his hair and held him to me, willing him to understand.

"You have all of me Tristan," I whispered. His eyes searched mine, the sorrowfulness burning away into lust. With a sigh, he wrapped his arm around me and pulled me flesh against him, crushing me in his powerful grip.

"I won't live without you." His lips crushed against mine, ravenously. With a growl, he pushed me away sharply, his eyes on fire. "Let's get you into my bed."

Tristan drove us too quickly but with such ease it was obvious that this was how he chose to drive all the time. The rumbling of the engine purred as we coasted down the narrow streets of the trailer park.

Most of the trailers looked like they had been abandoned, weeds grew freely around the properties. Seedy looking men hung out in groups outside of a few, throwing suspicious glances over their shoulders as we passed. A few nodded their heads in greeting to Tristan and he lifted a hand back to them. I quickly relaxed my expression, hoping that my unease and trepidation of this place wasn't too obvious. Finally, Tristan pulled into the awning of a single trailer.

The white paint looked newer than its neighbors, a small patch of grass in front of the end of the trailer below a window. It looked more maintained than the others. I moved to open the door to get out, but Tristan's hand flashed across my body and slammed the door closed. I turned to question him, but his burning face was inches from mine.

"You don't touch doors in my presence. That's my job. Understand?"

I nodded dumbly.

"Good girl." He got out and was at my side quickly. I got out a bit shakily and took his hand for support. He slammed the door shut and suddenly pinned me back against it, pushing his body into mine and eliciting a fiery response from my body. His lips were on mine, warm and delicious. I sighed and pulled his waist into me, moaning when the electricity in my stomach brightened.

He was already hard, pushing against me and my heart pounded. Excited, I bit his bottom lip and he moaned, intoxicated. He pulled back sharply, breathing heavily. My head spun.

"I need you—*now*." He grabbed my hand and roughly pulled me after him into the trailer.

The door had just closed behind us and he was on me. He shoved me roughly against the kitchen counter and ripped my jeans and underwear down. I yelped as he slapped my ass hard. His hand caught my hair at the root, and he pulled my head back until my neck arched.

"I'm going to make you cum so hard that you see stars," he growled into my ear. "Your body is *mine.*" He slapped me again, in the same spot and I cried out as my skin burned. I gasped as he dropped to his knees behind me and spread me open. His tongue, hot and wet, caressed every inch of me. My panting breath escaped me in huffs, my cheek pressed against the laminate counter. His tongue swirled in sweet circles around my clit, the scruff of his stubble scraped me.

His tongue continued in an up-and-down motion from my very front to my very back, his fingers dug into my ass cheeks. He let go of one side and grabbed the back of my thigh and hoisted my leg up so that I was partially sitting back on to his face while the other hand kept me pinned to the counter. A small, coherent, part of my brain had the sense to wonder how he was able to support most of my body weight above his head with just his hands. Then the hand that had been holding my ass cheek apart released me before roughly shoving two fingers inside of me.

I cried out, my hands desperately clawing at the cold counter. He pushed his fingers deeply inside of me, his knuckles crushing against me. He pulled his fingers back to their tips and reinserted with a third finger and my body collapsed. He moaned in response and curled his fingers inside of me, making my hips buck.

"Beg for me," he growled.

"Tristan," I breathed.

"Do you want me inside of you?" He bit my thigh, his teeth cut through my skin.

"Yes!" I gasped. He pulled his fingers out of me and released my legs so suddenly that it stung. I staggered backwards and he caught me, shoving me once again against the counter. His hand encircled my throat tightly, cutting off my air flow. Blood pooled in my face, it made my lips burn and my eyes bulge.

"*Beg me,*" he hissed. His body crushed mine into the ledge, making it impossible to take a breath of air around the vice grip of his hand around my throat.

"Please!" The word choked out of me in a tiny squeak. With a groan, he kicked my feet aside and held them apart with his knees. The movement made my hips drop and he used it to shove himself into me. My eyes pinched shut as pleasure flooded my body, unable to make a sound as he tightened his hold on my throat. Pain exploded from my hip bones as they slammed into the counter.

My lungs began to burn from the lack of oxygen, and I clawed at Tristan's hand, desperate for relief. Black spots popped into my vision, I felt disconnected from my body. Just before I thought that I would pass out, Tristan released me, and I fell forward, gasping for air. The air rushed into my lungs like fire. Without warning, Tristan pulled out of me and spun me around sharply.

He removed my shirt and jacket with a quick swipe and picked me up and set me onto the counter. "Slide your hips forward," he barked.

I did as I was told, wrapping my legs around him and leaning backwards. He slid back into my body easily and I held onto him desperately. He wrapped one arm around my waist tightly and cupped one of my breasts in his free hand. I moaned as he kissed and licked the bruises forming on my throat.

"Fuck," he growled into my collarbone before he bit down onto my shoulder. I cried out and he moaned louder. "I want to see you naked in my bed." He pulled back away from me and quickly removed his shirt and kicked his pants off the rest of the way.

With too much ease, he scooped me off the counter and cradled me against him. I tightened my grip around his waist with my legs as he carried me towards his bedroom. Taking the opportunity to be in charge for once, I kissed the hollow of his throat and ran my tongue over his Adam's apple hungrily.

"Ophelia," he growled in warning. Heart pounding, I bit his massive shoulder as hard as he had bit me. With a huff, he slammed me up against a wall. Tristan pumped into me so sharply that it made my skin burn, icy pain tore through my stomach. I shrieked and tried to push myself upwards, using his shoulders for momentum but it was no use. Tristan rammed me so hard that I felt nauseous.

"Tristan, stop!" I gasped. He peeled me off the wall and stormed into his bedroom. Without warning, he dropped me onto my back onto his bed. The cool, silk sheets felt refreshing against my hot and burning skin. Tristan loomed above me, his eyes wide and burning. Sweat beaded over his heaving chest.

"Play with yourself," he ordered.

"What?" I balked, deeply self-conscious. He gripped himself in his large hand and began to pleasure himself, his eyes dancing.

"I want to see you play with yourself," his voice was breathy, rough. He forced my hand between my legs and left it there, leaving me to do as he said. Glaring up at him, feeling extremely exposed, I pulled my feet onto the bed and let my knees drop to the side, giving him a clear view of me. His emerald eyes flashed down to my hand as I worked on myself, swirling circles and then back up to my face. I played into it, moaning loudly as my free hand caressed my body, trailed up to my breast and tugged at my nipples.

"Tristan," I breathed, and his jaw flexed. I continued my hand upwards to my throat and mimicked his threatening grip. My back arched, pushing my hips into my exploring hand and I cried out. My eyes rolled backwards, and my eyelids fluttered.

"Keep your fucking eyes on me," he panted. A blush had been burning my face, but it was turning to pleasure as I watched him work himself faster, his breath came in sharp bursts. It got to be too much, and Tristan growled and was suddenly on top of me, sliding himself into me. His mouth found mine eagerly, our kiss a fight for control. He reached up between us and used his thumb to pull my bottom lip down into his mouth.

He bit my lip a lot more gently than I expected, and I moaned. He reared back onto his haunches and lifted my hips up off the bed. My lower stomach tightened, the pleasure building. My back arched and my breath came in desperate gasps. "That's right baby, cum on my dick."

At his words, my body released intensely.

I didn't try to stifle my cries. Spasms rocked through my body as I gripped at his bed sheets, attempting to hold onto the earth before I slipped away. With a final thrust, Tristan joined me in my implosion. His hands grabbed at me desperately, trying to hold me impossibly close to his body. He caught himself on one hand, barely holding himself up as he panted above me, his sea- green eyes electric. I reached up and caressed his cheek, marveling at how devilishly handsome he was. An unreadable expression filtered across his face, and he turned his face to kiss my palm.

"I'm going to go shower then let's head out." He kissed the tip of my nose and removed himself from me with a smile.

After he had left the room, I got dressed and let myself explore his house. His bedroom was to the left of the front door, the kitchen just a few steps inside. A small living room took up the space between his bedroom and kitchen: a tan couch, a large mirror propped against the wall and a TV on top of a TV stand. There was an impressive stereo system in the spaces of the TV stand, but I didn't understand any of it.

To the right of the front door was a small bathroom where I could hear him showering, a stacked washer and dryer across from that and at the very end of the short hall passed the bathroom was another bedroom.

I cracked the door open and peered inside, what I saw made my heart shatter. This was obviously meant to be his daughter's room–Tristan had told me everything about his split from Katherine and how she kept Millie from him. It had been so hard for him to tell me about them, it was evident in the way he hesitated, the way his voice broke. Years of painful regret had bled through his voice.

This small room was a shrine to what could have been. A small bed with a white frame, a matching dresser and toy chest overflowing with girly toys dominated the space. Soft, pink curtains hung from the one window, an old wooden rocking chair in the far corner. Tristan had said they had left when Millie was just a baby, but this room was meant for an older child. My throat tightened when I realized that he must have updated the room over the years, preparing for her return even though it may never happen.

I went into the tiny kitchen in search of something to drink. Opening one of the cabinets, I gasped. A heavy black gun rested on the bottom of the cabinet in front of a metal safe with a spinning lock. More intriguing than the gun was the row of orange pill bottles on top of the metal safe. I squinted to read the labels, all prescribed to Tristan: Zoloft and Lithium. They were both completely full and apparently very past their expiration dates. The shower shut off suddenly and I quickly closed the cabinet and found the one with drinking glasses.

I filled up a cup of water and chugged it down as Tristan came into the kitchen, a cloud of steam wafted after him. I couldn't help but freeze when I saw him. His raven hair looked much darker when it was wet, his waves flattened and slicked backwards. He had shaved off his stubble, the sharp angle of his jaw more visible, the rose tattooed there seemed to shine. Water dripped from his round chest and down his flat stomach. He had a towel strung around his hips, gathered into one hand at his side.

"What time do we have to pick up Hunter?"

Something about his concern made me smile.

"At three."

Tristan nodded and glanced at the time on the little clock on the microwave.

"We gotta while then. You ready to meet the crew?" "Not at all."

He laughed loudly and went to his bedroom to change.

During the drive to the garage, Tristan seemed lighter. He had changed into a thick, gray t-shirt and black jeans, a Boston Red Sox hat with a flat bill was placed backwards on his head. He rolled the windows down, the smoke from his blunt streamed out of the car in clouds. He turned the music up to a deafening level, singing along with each song. The hand that wasn't holding the blunt held mine tightly and he alternated between singing and kissing my hand. The streets grew increasingly more nerve-wracking, homeless people staggered around like zombies; questionable characters walked in groups down the dirty streets. Of course, I knew this area because this is where the BART station was that I took to work and school. Tristan drove us into an industrial area under the overpass, chain linked fences lined the streets.

Tristan didn't turn down the music as we approached, announcing his arrival to everyone in the shop. A faded sign above the gate said L&L Auto Body. We waited as the gate slowly creaked open, and the car rolled into the parking lot. My hands trembled in my lap; I was suddenly feeling extremely self-conscious. Sensing my tension, Tristan pressed his lips to the back of my hand and said: "They're just a bunch of goofs, you've got nothing to worry about baby."

I nodded, not the least bit comforted. The roll-up doors that lined the front of the building were all open and bodies milled inside, hunched over, or standing under hoisted vehicles. They stopped and turned as the monstrous Cutlass rolled through. Tristan parked and winked at me as he exited the car. I waited awkwardly inside, remembering his earlier words about not touching any doors while he was around. A thin, gangly guy with shaggy black hair led a group of guys over to Tristan.

They greeted each other, slapping Tristan's hands or pounding him on the back. I realized that he probably hadn't been back here since he got out of jail. Tristan motioned for them to hold on and he circled around the front of the car with long strides to open my door for me.

"You listened," Tristan smiled in surprise as he pulled me by my hand.

"I've been known to do that from time to time," I said. He laughed loudly, freely with his head thrown back. He took my hand and squeezed it tightly, reassuringly as he led me over the group waiting for us.

"This is my girl Ophelia," Tristan introduced me to the guy with shaggy hair that I vaguely recognized. "Ophelia, this is Donovan."

"Nice to finally meet you—for real," Donovan smiled. "Tristan's been driving all of us crazy with how much he talks about you."

I blushed and glanced up shyly at Tristan, but he just winked at me and made my blush deepen.

"That's Tony, Greg and Louis," Tristan motioned to the group of guys behind Donovan but didn't go out of his way to name each person. I smiled and lifted a hand.

"It's nice to meet you all." A movement caught my eye just behind the group, at the opening of the first rolled up door. I recognized Cherry immediately by her ruby-red hair that hung down to the back of her knees. She had her arms folded across her chest, a look of disgust on her face. Tristan's moved smoothly between us, blocking her view of me and mine of her without breaking the conversation he was engaged in with one of the other guys.

"You going with us tonight?" A big, bald guy with a lazy eye asked Tristan. Tristan glanced down at me and back to him.

"Naw, it's my first day out. I'm gonna spend it with my girl."

"Better not let Charlie see you then," Donovan mumbled, shuffling his feet. A tense moment passed wordlessly.

"I gotta pick up my money from him, that's why we're here." Tristan's voice was tight. The group of guys behind Donovan suddenly became very interested in getting back to work, they hurried off into the garage.

"Uh, T, that may not be a good idea with–" Donovan glanced down at me and back up to Tristan. "I mean, you know how he gets."

"Fuck him." Tristan spat the words out and reached into his pocket for a cigarette. Whoever Charlie was, there clearly was unspeakable tension between him and Tristan. I followed the two into the garage just as it began to rain.

There were three stalls behind three roll-up doors. Two had vehicles hoisted above while guys worked on their underbellies doing who-knows-what while the third had a vehicle with the hood open. There was a low steady stream of music pouring out of speakers somewhere in the shop, two black leather couches were to the far left on either side of a wooden coffee table. A fridge stood behind the further couch next to an array of different types of tires and shiny rims. The air smelled like oil and weed smoke.

Cherry had thankfully ducked away somewhere and was out of sight. Tristan took me on a tour of the shop, explaining that the garage is obviously where they do most of their work.

I tried to ignore all the eyes burning into our backs as he led me passed the vehicles to a door in the back next to a rack of different types of motor oils. The room was pitch black, but Tristan flipped a switch, and it took my eyes a moment to adjust. It was a large room, the walls painted black, the fluorescent lights above hummed and put out a dull orange light. In the center of the room was a lifted, square platform with ropes around each side.

Gym equipment was stuffed into the sides of the room, and I assumed this is where Tristan spent his time gaining the sheer amount of muscle that he had. Tristan motioned for me to crawl up the platform, which I did with his help. He hoisted me up and pulled the ropes apart for me to duck through.

"I used to train in here for nine hours a day," Tristan said, his voice low as his eyes swept over the familiar ring. The floor was old and faded from the years of feet pacing back and forth. The center of the ring had the ghost stains of dried blood. "I really thought that I was going to make something of myself in here."

I watched him as he remembered a past life. He looked back down to me and quickly rearranged his face. "C'mere." He motioned at me with a smile.

Cautiously, I walked over to him, and he nodded at my hands.

"Put your hands up like this." He held up two fists, his body sank into a familiar stance, his hips bent slightly and feet apart. I tried my best to mimic him, and Tristan laughed. "You look like you're holding up a sign, try this." He closed my fist tighter and placed one hand near my face. "You gotta keep one hand up to block your face."

"I don't plan on changing careers any time soon," I rolled my eyes.

"You're a beautiful woman, Ophelia, you need to know how to protect yourself." The seriousness in his tone made butterflies dance in my stomach. "Most people have a *tell*, a warning sign that they're about to hit. It might be a look or the slightest constriction of their body. If you're able to see that, you're able to protect yourself."

Testing him, I braced myself and threw a punch as hard as I could at his shoulder. Disgustingly easy, Tristan slapped my feeble fist away before it was anywhere near him. I shook my hand, trying to rid the pain of his slap. Annoyed, I tried again and once more he easily blocked me.

"Stop moving!" I snapped when he stepped away from my third attempt. He laughed and a wicked look came over his face. I swallowed and took a step away from him as he sank low into a crouch. "Tristan…" I warned as I took another step back.

He was too fast; he lunged for me and caught me around my middle. He swung me around his body onto his back and rolled. The momentum spun my entire world around, but I wasn't the least bit injured, protected by his strong arms as he rolled me beneath him and pinned me to the floor. I laughed loudly, startled, and exhilarated by his speed and strength.

"You cheated!" I laughed.

"You're just slow," he laughed and planted a gentle kiss on the tip of my nose. Light flooded the room, blinding us both as another larger light came on. Tristan groaned and pinched his eyes shut. I craned my head back to see what had changed and spotted a man watching us. From my upside-down view, I could only make out that he was an average size man with curly, brown hair. He wore dirty jeans and a white wife-beater. Tristan's entire body stiffened around me; his face became frightening.

"If you're done fucking around, I need to talk to you. In private." The man said flippantly, already turning to walk away.

"You can talk to me in front of Ophelia," Tristan growled. He stood and pulled me up to my feet after him too sharply, I stumbled against him. The man turned back to face us, his eyebrow cocked and an unreadable expression on his face.

"I don't think you want your new *girlfriend*," he drew the word out sarcastically, "to hear what I'm about to say."

Tristan pulled the ropes apart and motioned for me to get down. I did as I was told, waiting for him to follow me but instead he lightly jumped over the ropes and landed easily on his feet next to me. The man shrugged and continued speaking: "Whatever, she probably won't be around much longer anyways."

"Fuck you Charlie, you better watch your fucking mouth," Tristan growled. I shrank away from the level of his voice, the venom in his words. Tristan flexed his hands at his sides, his knuckles popped audibly. The door swung open between them suddenly and Donovan appeared. Donovan glanced between the man named Charlie and Tristan.

"Get her out of here, Don."

I didn't hesitate or wait for Donovan; I hurried out the door and into the garage. Once we were free of the garage, I spun on my heel to face Donovan.

"Shouldn't you stop Tristan?" I shrieked. Tristan was at least twice the size of Charlie and in our short time together, I already learned about his temper. I briefly thought of the two medication bottles in his kitchen.

"Tristan?" Donovan looked at me, puzzled. "Tristan won't hit Charlie…but Charlie will probably kick Tristan's ass."

"Why not?" I frowned.

"Charlie is Tristan's dad; Tristan wouldn't ever hit him." Donovan shrugged casually. I was taken aback. The obvious hatred they had for each other, the way they spoke and apparently fought didn't seem familial at all. I could see the resemblance though. The same sun-kissed skin. But Charlie's nose was round where Tristan's was straight, his lips thin and Tristan's full. "Tristan looks like his mom. Apparently." Donovan said, reading my mind.

"What do you mean apparently?" I asked. Donovan looked at me, his turn to be confused.

"Aren't you two like star-crossed lovers or some shit? Tristan didn't tell you?"

"I mean he told me that he grew up with his dad…" "Long story short: Tristan's mom was a junkie. She OD'd while she was pregnant with Tristan and his twin brother. The twin died; Tristan was born with a hole in his heart. His mom died a few days later. Despite being born premature, and his heart fucked up, Tristan grew into a fucking tank anyways."

"Jeez," I sighed, my shoulders sank. "What was her name?"

"Evelyn," he said.

"He and his dad obviously don't get along…" I threw a nervous glance towards the back door of the garage. It felt like they had been in there forever.

"Charlie is the fucking devil," Donovan said. "Tristan and I grew up together. He used to crawl through my bedroom window late at night to get away from his dad. Charlie has a drinking problem and has always treated Tristan like a damn punching bag. Eventually, Tristan's grandma got custody of Tristan when he was in high school."

"Then he dropped out." I nodded.

"Yeah." Donovan also nodded. "Then she died of cancer—took her really fast."

"Let's go."

We spun around to see Tristan just a yard behind us. I blushed, nervous that he had heard our conversation. His face was tight, his eyes murderous. Tristan held the door open for me without a word, his face turned away. I got in silently and jumped when the door slammed closed.

I stared at Tristan as we drove away from L&L Auto Body, the name made sense now: Lawrence & Lawrence Auto Body. Tristan puffed heavily on a rolled joint; the embers ate away the white paper with each inhale. I studied his face, the sharp angle of his cheek bones, his square chin and perfect nose. It was hard to see the little kid in him beneath the hard exterior that he had been carved into.

I imagined him at Hunter's age, with wavy brown hair and bright, innocent blue-green eyes. How could someone ever imagine hurting him? It was no surprise that Tristan had grown up into the man he was now; furious. But under the hard coating of anger that protected him, he was thoughtful, sweet, and very affectionate.

Tears welled up in my eyes as I thought of the damage that must have been done to him by both his mother and father to turn him into such a hard individual. His grandmother had tried to help, tried to save him but when she ultimately passed away, Tristan was once again alone.

Then Katherine had hurt him again, stolen away their daughter and left Tristan behind. His fierce protectiveness and possessiveness over me suddenly made so much sense. I unhooked my seatbelt and Tristan glanced down at me, wondering what I was doing. It was the first time he had looked at me since we had left L&L.

I sat up on my knees and took his face in both of my hands, gently turning him towards me. He kept his narrowed eyes on the road, his jaw tight in my hands. I smoothed his face like I did whenever Hunter got into a screaming fit and fought my attempts to console him.

A bruise had begun to bloom over his left cheekbone, I gently ran my thumb over the reddened skin. Tristan's breathing became quicker as I bent my head and softly kissed the split through his bottom lip, tasting his blood. I pushed his hat upwards so I could run my fingers through his hair and pressed my forehead to his.

The car jerked roughly to the left and Tristan threw the car into park and wrapped his large arms around me, crushing me to him. He buried his face in my chest, and I held him tighter, tucking him into me. His entire body shook in my arms both from the adrenaline and from the hatred. Hatred of Charlie, of his life and his past. I smoothed my hands over his wide back and kissed the top of his head. Tristan pulled back after a moment, when the tremors ceased to rock his body and he looked up at me, his face soft.

"Thank you."

"For what?" I frowned down at him.

"For being you," he shrugged. He sighed and pulled away from me, his body melting into the seat. "I have to go back to the shop, Charlie paid me, but I have to go on a run tonight."

"A run?" I echoed.

Tristan was silent for a long minute.

"Does this have to do with whatever Charlie talked to you about earlier?"

He nodded, still staring at the roof of the car. After a long pause, he groaned and dropped his hands into his lap.

"I'm scared that if I tell you the truth that you'll leave."

My heart squeezed and I reached out to grab his hand.

"You don't know how much you mean to me."

"Tell me," I whispered, then added: "I'm not going anywhere."

His face crumpled at my words, and he took a deep, steadying breath before he continued.

"You know how I said the way we get our cars and stuff wasn't exactly legal?" He glanced at me, and I nodded silently. "That's part of it. We boost cars, Donovan is in charge of getting me in and out of a spot. Tony will pick me up in a truck sometimes if it's too risky for me to drive the car out of there. Greg is in charge of stripping the car if we're not selling the car to a high paying buyer. Louis is freakishly good at changing VIN numbers and license plates so these cars can be bought and registered without getting back to us. I do all the boosting and driving because I'm our best driver and can get out of a…situation if I find myself in one."

"What does that entail?" I asked carefully.

"My history with boxing has a lot to do with it," he said. I mulled over what he had told me as rain began to pelt the car.

"Have you ever hurt anyone?" My voice was flat, careful. The rain outside began to really pour over us, it wavered over the windows as if we were submerged in a river. He glanced at me and away quickly and my shoulders sank. "How badly?"

His words came out in a rush: "Look, if it means me being killed or getting out–I'ma get the hell out of there."

I brought my feet up onto the seat and hugged my knees to my chest as I thought this over. This was not the life that I had wanted for myself and definitely not for Hunter. I had divorced Jimmy to get away from a dangerous life, though Jimmy's was centered around drugs, he was often in trouble with the law, and I was constantly worried about our safety. Was this any different?

"Can you leave?" I asked.

"To do what, Ophelia?" He snapped. "I'm a high school drop out with a rap sheet facing my third strike and doing life in prison. What else is out there for me?"

I bit my lip and rested my chin on my knees. He was probably right. As if reading my mind, he snatched the tops of my arms and pulled me upward so that I was looking directly into his face. His eyes were wide, sincere. "I can protect you baby, you, and Hunter. You won't ever have to worry about being safe–or money for that matter. I make a decent living doing this. I can take care of us."

"How do you know that?" I glared.

"We're a careful team, we've been doing this for years now and we're smart enough to not get caught. We lift cars from lots that we don't have any connection to."

"But you've *killed* people, Tristan."

His eyes searched mine desperately, trying to read the future in them. He let go of me sharply, his face hardened.

"And I'll kill anyone I have to if it fucking means *my* life or the life of my crew and it sure as fuck means I'll hurt anyone I have to in order to keep you and Hunter safe. You two are my *life*." His booming voice shook the small space around us. "I've done bad things, I know, but I'm not a bad man. I love you."

"I love you too," I resolved with a sigh.

His eyes brightened and he kissed me softly.

"Put your seatbelt on, we have to pick up Hunter."

Tristan

13

It was like I hadn't been gone this last month at all, everything and everyone fell back into place the moment I walked back into the garage. We closed the shop, rolled down the garage doors, cleaned up equipment and swept up the mess from the day and threw the rags into the wash. Then we sat down to discuss business. We took our usual seats around the table in the shop: Donovan on my right, Tony on my left. Greg and Louis sat on the couch across from us and Charlie stood to my left with his arms folded across his chest.

"We're going to intercept a shipment tonight," Charlie started.

"Tonight?" I frowned at him. "That's not enough time to prepare. We usually give it a couple of days."

"Kinda hard to iron out details when our only driver is in the fucking pen," Charlie spat, and I clenched my jaw. He laid out some maps and pictures on the coffee table. He stabbed his finger on the map and said: "There's a shipment meant to go to the Harley Davidson store in Union City coming from Emeryville. We're going to tail it down the 880 highway and grab it at the exit for 29th Avenue."

"There's a roundabout type of deal right beneath the exit Donovan and I can wait for them there," I nodded, picturing the map in my head.

"What's the plan?" Donovan asked, squinting at the pictures of loading docks, and marked boxes. "Are we stealing the truck or the shit inside?"

Charlie shrugged. "The truck would give us the most."

"Also be the hardest to get away with," I pointed out.

"Be the hardest to hide," Louis added.

"Some good parts on a semi though," Greg countered. Charlie deliberated and rubbed the stubble on his chin. He looked older, more tired than usual.

"Do you think you could get it out of there?" Charlie asked, lifting one bushy eyebrow at me.

"Probably but not if anyone comes after me. Shit is too big to maneuver down the highway exchange."

Charlie nodded again. Deciding, he clapped his hands together.

"All right. You and Don are going to stop the truck and unload what you can into the Jeep but leave the truck."

"How many drivers are we talking about?" I asked, ashing the burnt end of the blunt onto the floor before passing it to Don. Charlie picked up a paper off the table and squinted at it. His eyes were going bad, but he refused to wear glasses.

"Since I last talked to my contact at Harley, it should only be one."

I rolled my eyes. Charlie had "men" everywhere, they were usually our intel on these types of jobs. When it came to "smash and grabs" like when I broke into lots and boosted the cars, we did our own research.

Everything was set up as well as it could be on such short notice. I felt uneasy about the whole thing, it felt rushed. Most jobs took around a week to really plan out, to make sure we had the right manpower; recruiting some of the regular shop guys in case we needed more bodies. I knew most of the highways and interstates that cut through the Bay Area as well as I knew my own dick, I wasn't worried about that. I hated taking the Jeep on runs because it was top heavy, but it could fit a ton of crap into it. I kept my worries to myself and drove the heavy Jeep down the 880, pissed about how cold it was in the open car.

Donovan followed behind in the Saab and I glared at his lights in the rear-view mirror as my hood ripped and tore around me from the harsh wind. *It better not fucking rain*, I thought to myself. My burner phone beeped on the dashboard, and I snatched it up with numb hands.

Unknown: Target just hit the 880 exit comin ur way in 20

The text was from Louis, he had been following the truck since it left the warehouse in Emeryville on its way to Union City which was usually only about a thirty-minute drive. I took the exit for 29th Avenue, screeching around the bend in front of the AT&T store as I slammed my brakes. There was no one around to see me maneuver the Jeep back over a curb, through the hole in the chain-linked fence and into a patch of dirt directly under the overpass. I cut the lights and backed up as deep into the space as I could, facing the roundabout.

I rubbed my hands together to warm them and lit a cigarette. It was well after midnight, creeping closer to 1 AM so I knew that Ophelia was already asleep. I pictured her in her bed, dreaming peacefully, her dark brown hair draped over her pillow. The way her chest rose and fell in her sleep, her full lips parted slightly, and I felt my dick harden against my pants.

I was thinking of heading to her house in the morning when another text came through my phone.

Unknown: In place with the strip

This text was from Donovan, he was just a few yards above and passed me. Hidden away in the shadows, his job was to throw a spike strip across the road just as the truck passed. It would blow out the tires, forcing the truck to stop. It was dangerous, too easy for the truck to careen and crush Donovan. I knew he would get out of there in time, but my stomach churned nervously.

Donovan had been my closest friend growing up, had seen me at my worst and bailed me out more than once. It made us both nervous when we went on these jobs, worried about the other getting hurt. He had been distraught when I was shot a few months ago, everyone had thought I was for sure going to die–me included. Donovan took it the hardest.

I checked the time; the semi-truck would be approaching any minute. I tossed my cigarette out the window and sat up straight with my hand on the ignition, adrenaline pumped through my veins. The air around me seemed to still, my senses sharpened as I listened.

The sound of mammoth sized brakes screeching to a halt and an explosion made me jump into action. I cranked the ignition, the Jeep roared to life just before I slammed the accelerator down. The Jeep bounced over the curb; the tires screeched as they connected with the asphalt. I fishtailed around the roundabout heading for my exit. The Jeep lurched up the on-ramp, the air whipped me.

The taillights of the semi-truck were just a few yards away, they had turned their hazard lights on. They blinked softly, unknowingly like beacon. There was no sign of the spike strip or Donovan–good, he got out okay. The Jeep screeched to a halt behind the truck, I jumped out the driver's side door and ran around the front of the cab as two men jumped down.

Fuck. I pulled the gun from my waistband and pointed it at their surprised faces.

"Aw shit," the first man groaned.

"Give me the keys to the engine," I demanded. My voice wasn't the least bit concealed behind the black ski mask. The men stepped back in unison, flinching away from me. The second man tossed me a pair of keys and they landed at my feet. I scooped them up without moving my eyes off them. I hadn't expected there to be two of them, Charlie had said only one. Having two meant I couldn't turn my back on either of them, Donovan should've been with me. Blood rushed through my ears as I jerked the gun to the side, gesturing for them to go around the back.

We only had a few minutes before traffic would be coming through this area and it would be a bust. "Unlock the back and start filling up the Jeep." I barked.

They hesitated, throwing nervous glances at each other. Irritated, I cocked the gun and pointed it at them again, showing that I wasn't fucking around. They jumped and the second man began to unlock the back, they usually divided the keys so that they could keep the engine running while the back was being unloaded. It saved time or some shit—I didn't know. The first man glared at me while the second man swung open the heavy doors.

"The fuck you looking at bruh?" I shouted.

"Nothin'," he shrugged. He turned slowly and hopped up into the truck of the bed and started passing heavy boxes to the second guy. They were moving too slowly. I was getting antsy as cars passed beneath us on the underpass. I hated that I was out here alone with these two fucks, we really should have two men on each boost, but we didn't have the right manpower.

The second man turned to drop a heavy box into the Jeep, grunting and sweating under the weight. I had turned slightly to watch him and took my eyes off the first man just for a brief second. The explosion of a gun made me jump just as a bullet shot passed me and hit the side of the Jeep.

"Fuck!" The second guy shouted, ducking away. The first man lined up his gun and took another shot before I could react. This one grazed my thigh and pain erupted through my body, nearly knocking me off my feet. He took aim once more, but I whipped my gun around and fired. The bullet missed but the man's attempt to dodge it made him lose his footing and he fell from the back of the truck, flat onto his back. The sickening sound of his skull connecting with the asphalt made my stomach lurch.

"Oh Jesus, oh fuck!" The second guy screamed, his hands on his head as he watched his friend lie motionlessly.

"Shit," I hissed. The second guy was too busy screaming to pay me any more attention, so I hobbled painfully around the Jeep and got in. The tires screeched loudly as I took off going the wrong way of traffic. I tore through the underpass, nearly lost control of the Jeep as I hit the roundabout and slammed the on-ramp going north.

The Jeep struggled under the weight of the new load, but I pressed the pedal down as hard as I could. The pain in my leg was gnawing, the blood seeped slowly from the wound into my sock, but it was slow, it hadn't done too much damage. But fuck it hurt. I darted between cars and shot through the exit for 23rd Ave. The Jeep was full of stolen contraband that was like a beacon to cops, especially the high speeds I was driving.

I forced myself to slow down, to slowly let my foot off the accelerator as my heart hammered painfully. I tore the ski mask from my face and gulped in fresh air. With shaky hands, I typed out a text message to Donovan's burner phone to let him know I was on my way back. I stayed on 23rd Ave, taking it to where it merged with

E 1^{2}h Street and took a left on 1st Ave. My anxiety didn't lessen as I crept along at the speed limit, desperate to get back to the shop and not attract any attention. Cops crawled this area of Oakland pretty thick and were all too happy to pull someone over.

I breathed a sigh of relief as I bounced into the parking lot of the shop and into a loading dock, the door clanking shut heavily behind me. The boys came jogging up, ready to unload the Jeep while Louis quickly swapped out the license plates from the fakes to the originals.

Grunting, I slid out of the jeep and landed on my good leg a little unsteady.

"You good, man?" Donovan glanced at me over the top of a large box.

"Yeah man, all good," I nodded. I limped over to the couch, snagging the First Aid box off a back shelf on my way. My chest heaved with each breath, taking longer than usual to calm down as I set up a spot to clean my leg. The jeans I wore were already ruined so I tore them.

"Let me help you." A small hand brushed mine, Cherry kneeled in front of me. I stiffened but she rolled her eyes at me, her long fake eyelashes brushed her eyebrows. She took the kit and rifled through it until she found a small brown bottle and a pack of gauze. She poured the frothy liquid over the cut, and I winced. "How did it go?"

I shrugged watching the blood swirl and mix with the cleaning solution. "Wasn't really prepared…"

She nodded, pursing her big lips together.

"Charlie's been hurting while you were gone," she dabbed at the gash with the gauze. Her voice was low, solemn. "We all were."

"It's gonna be a while before we get a turnaround for the parts," I nodded towards the large pile of boxes now on the floor of the shop. Eventually they would be hidden away somewhere in the shop, waiting to either be pieced out and sold individually or purchased as a wholesale to some buyer.

"That's not what I meant," she whispered. Now that the wound had stopped bleeding, she put a clean pad over it and taped it down. I watched her long fingers hesitate on my leg when she finished taping it down. She placed both hands on my thighs and slid them up to my dick.

"Cherry, stop," I groaned. I was so tired of this cat and mouse bullshit with her. No matter how many times I told her to fuck off, she kept coming back like a drug addict. The adrenaline was wearing off and I was getting a pounding headache, my entire body was fucking exhausted.

"But I missed you," she pouted. She didn't give a shit that everyone could see us, I think she got off on it. She lifted the bottom of my shirt and planted soft kisses along my stomach just above my waistband. I shivered and she took it as an invitation and slid her hand down to undo my button. Her warm breath and wet kisses made my body respond despite myself, my dick stiffened under her hand, and she smiled. "I know baby, you missed me too."

My zipper slid down audibly, fighting against the girth of me pushing against it. She hummed happily and ran her fingertips over my dick against my underwear, teasing me.

"Fuck, Cherry get the fuck off of me." I grabbed her face and shoved her back into the coffee table, it screeched a foot away from the impact. She looked up at me from the ground, her eyes wide and full of hate.

"Fuck you, Tristan! Fuck you!" She crawled up onto her feet and ran away from me with her face in her hands. I groaned and rubbed my eyes; it was late, and my body felt depleted. Donovan walked over to me with a blunt in his hand and landed heavily in the spot next to me.

"That was a pretty big haul," he said, handing me the blunt. I took it happily and pulled a long drag off it. My lungs burned from the weed, a welcome feeling.

"Fucking better be man, my leg fucking kills me." He laughed and took the blunt from me. It was customary after a boost for the crew to party, but I was too tired. I melted into the couch, high as shit as the boys blasted music over the speakers, smoked and drank.

Charlie joined in, already wasted. Some of the guys brought chicks over to get wasted and I grimaced. It was like they had something to celebrate—what was it? Donovan and I were the only ones who stuck our necks out for this shit and yet they got to reap all the benefits. Charlie would sell off the shit and each of them would get a cut. Granted, I got the biggest portion after Charlie, but it never seemed like enough.

My head lolled backwards, too stoned, and too exhausted to be held up. The bass vibrated through my body; smoke drifted across my eyes like a muslin blanket. Someone was fucking on the couch across from me, but I didn't care. A heavy hand patted the top of my head, and I blinked an eye open.

"Good job, boy," Charlie smiled.

"Man, fuck you." My words were garbled. He laughed and walked off with a forty ounce of beer in his hand.

It had been two days since I saw Ophelia last, and I was getting fucking anxious. I wasn't stupid, I knew this shit wasn't healthy, but I couldn't help it. She was just so insanely beautiful, she genuinely made me laugh—something not many people, let alone a chick, could do. I loved how smart and dedicated she was to bettering her life for her and her son. Part of me felt guilty, like I was distracting her from her goals, but I couldn't fucking help it. I thought of her in class, texting me but also of the other dudes in her class. They got to spend more time with her than I did–I fucking hated it.

"Dude, you grabbed the wrong wrench," Donovan snapped.

"Fuck you bitch, I grabbed the right one–you *asked* for the wrong one."

Donovan turned his head slowly to look at me, alarmed. My vision focused and I noticed the guys had all stopped what they were doing. Worse yet, there were customers in the shop. All eyes had turned to stare at me. I relaxed the fists I had unconsciously made at my sides. A beat later, everyone went back to what they were doing.

"¿Qué pasó?" Donovan nodded at me when everything returned to normal.

"Lo siento, man," I apologized. "Solo estoy distraído"

"Distracted by what?" Donovan frowned. I sighed and rubbed my eyes; they were dry, and my head throbbed from lack of sleep. My body felt like it had been cut open and filled with ants, my skin crawled, my insides buzzed.

"What day is it?" I frowned.

"Wednesday…why?" he asked. I wiped my hands off on the rag from my back pocket and tossed it to Donovan who caught it easily.

"Me tengo que ir," I ducked under the car we had hoisted above us. "Cover me, okay?"

"What? Tristan!" he called after me, but I was already jogging away towards my car.

I still had Ophelia's location programmed into my phone, so I found her at school easily. I had no intention of going inside the building until I was there. It felt weird being inside of this building, it was just a junior college, but it was something I never would have stepped into if it wasn't for my girl. The green dot that marked her proximity on the screen of my phone blinked like a beacon, pulling me closer. I hesitated outside of the door, listening to the sound of a man's voice echoing through it.

I eased the door open and slipped inside quietly. It was one of those auditorium-type classrooms with the rows of seats extending downwards like at a theater. I slipped into the closest empty desk next to a blonde girl and scanned the large room.

Shit. This class was a lot bigger than I had expected. Which was good, I guess, for not being spotted. Then I saw her, and it was like the sun came out from behind a dark cloud. She was busy taking notes, by hand and not on the computer or an iPad like the other students.

Her head was bent forward, listening in earnest, her hair spilled over her desk. My heart raced as I watched her, a prideful smile tugged at the corners of my mouth. My attention was pulled slightly by the sudden whispering to my right, by the girl next to me.

"Uh…hi," she leaned over towards me, her elbow rubbed against mine.

"Mm-mm, no," I shook my head and leaned away from her, craning my neck to get a better view of Ophelia. The girl scoffed and snapped back in her seat. Ophelia raked her fingers through her dark hair and pulled it over her left shoulder, exposing the right side of her bare neck.

My breathing picked up as I stared at the smooth skin, the way her neck flexed as she bent forward over her notebook. Thoughts of my lips on the hollow of her throat, my teeth on her shoulder made my zipper tighten on my jeans. A guy to her right leaned over suddenly, so close that their face was just inches apart. Ice singed through my veins watching them whisper to each other, their faces too close.

Their encounter was brief, just a few seconds, but I was seething. The skin over my knuckles was white, my fists shook on the small desk. They pulled away laughing and my face burned. *What the fuck were they talking about? What did they think was so funny?* My teeth grit so hard they creaked. I stormed out of there, letting the heavy door slam loudly behind me.

Not much longer after that, class was dismissed, and they all filed out. I watched them, hunkered down in my seat, my grip on the steering wheel threatened to crush it. My entire body was trembling, I swear my car shook around me. Ophelia appeared, bouncing down the steps with her backpack slung over one shoulder. The small smile that had formed on my lips when I saw her evaporated as the same dude from her class came bounding down the steps next to her to catch up.

He was a short, lanky dude just a head taller than Ophelia with scarred skin but a bright smile as he spoke with her. My teeth gritted watching them. They spoke briefly, Ophelia waved and headed toward the BART station.

Part of me wanted to follow her, offer her a ride but instead, I watched the guy she had been speaking to. He walked over to an old, blue Toyota Rav4 and threw his backpack into the back seat. I pulled out of my spot as he left his and followed two cars behind. I followed him through the northside of Oakland onto the 24-highway going east. It was late evening, after seven, the sun had long sunk behind the Berkeley hills. Music vibrated in my chest, a plume of weed smoke snaked from my lips as I seethed.

Who the fuck was this guy? I thought, furiously. *Some chummy-ass dude getting too close to my girl, that's for sure.* Making her laugh, following her close behind. The car between us turned right as we entered the dark highway, not many cars in sight. I sped up to chase him through a stop light, not giving a fuck that the light had turned red as soon as his car cleared the intersection. His car struggled up the on-ramp while mine purred effortlessly. All of us on the crew had souped up engines, especially mine.

I had dumped a majority of my cut into this thing, making it a fucking beast. My Oldsmobile Cutlass lurched forward and clipped the bumper of his car. His head snapped up in shock, his eyes frantically searching his rearview mirror. His hazards flashed, he had intended to pull over but instead, I rammed his car again letting him know this shit was intentional—not an accident.

His Rav4 leveled off on the top of the ramp and he shot forward into the traffic. The 24 was surprisingly sparse of traffic, God himself giving me the green light. I smirked and pressed on the accelerator; my car gained on his easily. I rear ended him again, this time harder, causing his car to fishtailed slightly. He craned his neck around to see me, but my windows were too dark, it would be like looking into an abyss.

I jerked the steering wheel, my tires screeched as I switched to the lane beside him and brought my car close to his. He nervously tried to drift into the next lane, but I followed, less than a foot from him. My engine revved in warning. His window rolled down as he leaned his head out.

"What?! What do you want?" He was clearly afraid.

Good.

My passenger side window rolled down and I hoisted my 9mm gun up at his face. His face went white, and he smashed on the gas. I laughed and followed as he attempted to lose me through the Caldecott, a system of tunnels through the Berkeley Hills. The eastbound tunnel was narrow and decrepit. My car sped up to follow him.

Orange light and gray cement shot passed as I tailed him. The entrance was uneven, it caused my car to bounce and sway as it gained traction. I rolled my front windows down enjoying the deafening sound of my engine bouncing off the cement around us. I pulled up beside him, this time on his right and jerked my steering wheel—my car slammed into the side of his and forced him against the wall. He screamed something but I couldn't hear him. Metal sparks exploded as he pulled his car forward and out of the tunnel. Everything around me quieted.

With one last ram, this time against his rear corner panel, his car spun out of control across the highway. It crashed into a cement barrier, coming to an abrupt halt with a grating explosion. His door swung open, and he collapsed onto the asphalt on his hands and knees. My tires screamed as I came to a sharp stop behind his car and kicked my door open. He heaved heavily; vomit spewed from his mouth onto the asphalt. Gross. I grabbed him by the back of his sweaty neck and yanked him effortlessly to his feet. Tears streamed down his face; his body trembled as I slammed him up against the side of his Rav4.

"W-what do you want?" he gasped.

"What's your name, homie?" I towered over him, dropping my head so that my face was inches from his. He winced and turned his face away from me. I grabbed his chin and forced his face back to mine.

"Matt," he stammered.

"Okay, *Matt*," I nodded, my eyes burning. "You got a thing for trying to fuck another man's girl?"

"W-what?" he stammered; his brown eyes wide. "I don't know w-who—"

My skin was on fire. Red pulsated in my vision; it shook my entire body. I slipped the gun from my waistband and held it up to his temple.

Tristan

14

"When can I see you again?" I blew out a cloud of cigarette smoke into the cold air and shrugged deeper into my heavy coat. The air smelled like rain; the dark, heavy clouds were slung low in the sky under its weight.

"I'm actually taking Hunter to see my mom tomorrow," Ophelia said, and I frowned. I thought their relationship was strained. "Then I have to work after." My hand tightened around my phone; the plastic groaned in protest. I worked to get my voice under control.

"So, I won't see you all week?" Despite my effort, my voice came out flat and disapproving. She sighed heavily.

"I know, I'm sorry. I miss you." The frustration subsided slightly. She missed me. She obviously didn't miss me enough to not make time for me though. Was she lying to me? Did she have some *other* guy from school she was entertaining?

"Can I come see you now?" My body trembled with this…*need* for her. I had never experienced this before. It was like she had stolen a part of me that I needed to survive.

"Um," she paused, and my body stiffened. "I just got Hunter to sleep."

My free hand flexed, the joints popped loudly.

"Cool." My voice was flat, my blood began to boil. I didn't even attempt to hide my disapproval. I smashed the *end* button on my phone until the screen went black. I took one last, long drag of my cigarette while I stared at the glowing light that spilled from her living room onto her wooden patio. My hands had long since grown numb as I stood out here, leaned against my car. I had no idea how long I'd been out here.

Steven's car was parked a few spots down and I gritted my teeth as I eyed it. I closed the distance between it and myself with a few long strides, simultaneously pulling my knife out of my pocket, slipping it out of its leather pouch. I wanted to dismantle the vehicle, smash the replaced windows a second time. Instead, I made do by slashing both rear tires. A satisfying hissing noise erupted from the rubber as the blade sliced through them.

Back at the shop, a police cruiser was parked out front. I pulled up slowly, my mind busy running through a list. I didn't have any current warrants so they shouldn't be here for me. Shouldn't be. Unless Matt spilled his guts about our encounter.

The garage doors were all pulled shut, closed for the night but the police clearly were inside speaking to someone. I took my time rattling my key in the door, signaling my arrival to not spook whoever was inside; getting shot again was the last thing I needed right now. As I entered the dimly lit front room where customers entered, two police officers slowly turned to face me.

One was a tall, skinny guy with a stereotypical cop mustache. The other was a short, curvy woman, her hair slicked back into a tight bun. Charlie stood behind the counter across from them, his arms folded tightly over his chest.

"Hi there," the female officer greeted me. "My name is Officer Torres; this is Officer Chadwick."

"What's up?" I nodded to Charlie, but his eyes hardened.

"There's been a string of robberies," Officer Chadwick sniffed, eyeing me with a sour look on his face. I fought the urge to roll my eyes. He removed a black and white picture that had been on the counter and held it out for me. I didn't take it.

Officer Torres spoke up: "Most recently was a delivery truck with motorcycle parts bound for a Harley Davidson's shop in Union City four days ago."

"Is that right?" I cocked an eyebrow. "Sorry, ma'am, I don't know anything about it." I shifted my weight casually and the female cop's eyes flashed to my hands. I smiled at her.

"You sure?" Officer Torres squinted up at me.

"The boy told you he don't know nothing," Charlie groaned, leaning against the counter.

"But if I hear anything, I'll be sure to call you," I said softly, focusing on her. A blush bloomed softly under her brown skin. The female cops always tried to be the hardest one in the squad car, mostly because they were seen as weak by their counterparts and those they tried to impress the law upon. In my time I've learned that the female cops are no joke, they're more dangerous as their dick-swinging partners.

I usually got further by being charming with them than I would if I fought against them. I stepped closer to her and lowered my voice, sweetly. "Do you have a number that I can call?"

"Yeah," she retorted. "It's 9-1-1." I
laughed despite myself.

"You gentlemen have a good night," Chadwick nodded, clearly tired of being here. "We'll be seeing you."

"I *sure do* hope so." I eyed Torres as she pushed by, her shoulder connecting with my arm. We both waited until they were in their cruiser and gone before either of us spoke.

"Take care of that," Charlie pointed after them with a lit cigarette.

"*Me?*" I scowled. "The fuck am I supposed to do?"

"Figure it out." He took a long drag of his cigarette and went into the office behind the counter.

"Stupid prick," I spat.

Ophelia
15

I stared at the dull screen of my laptop, it was old and could barely hold a charge longer than twenty minutes. I sat crisscross on the floor in front of the coffee table, bent forward and scribbled my notes onto a notebook beside it. This semester I was taking Microbiology, and it required a lot of group work, unfortunately. Something that I hated. Something about the collaboration of a mixture of work ethics that didn't meld properly drove me insane.

I usually ended up doing the most and I hated it. I chewed on my pencil, trying to make sense out of Professor Whitmore's crude explanation of serial dilution. Tristan's large hand brushed along the length of my shoulder to my neck and back, his touch faint and thrilling. I shivered under his touch but tried to push him from my mind so that I could focus.

The battery on my laptop beeped and I lunged for the charger before it could die. Tristan caught my hips between his hands as I bent forward on my knees, he ran his hands over my ass slowly and the warmth between my thighs sprang to life.

"Stop it," I snipped but my voice was light. I sat back down and tried my best to focus. He chuckled softly; the sound made me shiver. Tristan sat up on the couch I had been leaning against suddenly and threw one long leg onto each side of me so that I was between his legs. "What're you doing?" I asked, his fingers raking through my hair.

"Shh," he hushed me. With a gentle tug, he pulled my hair free from the elastic that had been holding my hair out of my face. It cascaded around me in a dark wave, and he groaned. He fanned my hair out across my back and began lifting sections of my hair on top of my head.

He twisted the wefts between his fingers, sliding his fingers up near my temple towards where he gathered them in his hands. His touch was delicious, it melted me into a goosebump mess. After a minute I realized what he was doing.

"Are you braiding my hair?" I laughed.

"Mm-hm," he hummed softly. I leaned into his left leg; his thick thigh supported my weight effortlessly. When he was finished, I felt the perfect French braid he had managed to tie my hair into.

"Where did you learn that?" I smiled but a darkness crept into my thoughts. What if he braided his last girlfriend's hair?

"My daughter, Millie, she had the longest hair I've ever seen on a little kid." He smiled at the memory, but it didn't reach his eyes. "I used to braid it for her every night before bed to keep it healthy. It took me a while, but I finally got the hang of it."

My body stilled; I didn't know how to respond. He very rarely spoke of his daughter outside of mentioning that he even had one.

"Does she have dark hair like you?" I whispered. He nodded and reached into his pocket, he removed his phone and quickly swiped to a picture of her. It looked recent. It showed her profile as she sat on her knees in a long tuft of grass, playing with a plastic tea-set. She wore a smock-type of dress, it was white with pink edges. Tristan was right, she had very long hair for a little girl. It swam around her waist in dark waves, just like her father.

From this angle, you could see her long, black eyelashes as they curled upwards away from her childish cheeks. Just on the edge of the picture was the lower half of a woman sitting in the grass with Millie. She wore ripped jeans, but there wasn't much in the frame except for two hands that extended towards Millie, her skin was heavily tattooed.

"That's her mom," Tristan answered my silent question.

"Your daughter is beautiful," I chose my words carefully. I hated the jealousy that I felt, I tried to remind myself that they were long since over. That Katherine had done her damage and wasn't coming back. However, part of me hoped, for Tristan's sake, that Millie did. He smiled sadly and placed his phone back into his pocket. Something dawned on me. "Is that what the ML on your throat stands for?"

"Yeah," he absentmindedly touched the tattoo there. "I send money to Katherine's account every week–for the last 5 years–but I don't get to see or talk to my daughter."

"You can't find out where they are?" I frowned. He shook his head and pressed his palm against my cheek. I kissed his hand and he smiled softly.

"Katherine and I had been together a long time, almost ten years, she knows all my tricks to find her. Plus, her dad is a retired Sheriff."

"What does that have to do anything? I mean…besides what you do for a living."

He was silent for a long moment; his searching eyes studied my face.

"He knows about it, which is partly why he hated us being together. Plus…" He hesitated; his face tightened. "Katherine got me arrested for domestic violence when she was pregnant–but it never fucking happened. The bitch got mad at me for not wanting to stay in the house with her throwing a fucking fit, so I left. The police showed up at the garage and arrested me. Doesn't look good if I tried to fight for custody. Amongst other things."

I placed my hand firmly over his hand on my cheek, holding him there.

"That doesn't seem right, you have to have some legal rights as her father."

"Again, what would I have to show them? My busted trailer in the ghetto? My rap sheet and the fact that my paycheck shows a fraction of what I *actually* make?" He propped his elbow up on the back of the couch and dropped his face into his hand, tired. I hated seeing him like this.

Quickly, I pushed the hem of his long white t-shirt up and planted a soft kiss on his stomach. I moved an inch over to the left and placed another soft kiss. He sighed but didn't move. I pushed my breast against his crotch as I bent to place a warmer kiss below his belly button. I felt him snap his head down to look at me as I ran my hands up his sides and gently raked my nails down his side.

"Ophelia," he shivered. "What about your roommates?"

I shook my head and licked a trail down his hip bone, he groaned.

"She won't be home tonight."

At my words, Tristan let out a guttural moan, the sound made my heart race. I went to his other hip bone and licked a matching trail down to his waist band. Despite my best effort, a blush had seeped across my cheeks, and I smiled up at him, my hands working to undo his belt buckle. His eyes were glazed over, half open as he watched me.

I tugged at his jeans, forced to use most of my strength. He chuckled and lifted his hips so that I could slide them out from under him. His impressive length was fully exposed before me. I glanced up at him as I slowly wrapped my lips around him, and he moaned loudly. I started slowly, focusing on his tip, sucking, and licking.

He gasped and grabbed my shoulders in his crushing grip. I wrapped one hand around his base and used the other to prop myself up on the couch cushion. I worked my hand in the opposite direction of my mouth, tears sprang to my eyes as I took him in as far as I could.

"Oh baby," he groaned, a growl rattled in his chest. "*Fuck.*" I flattened my tongue against him and trailed the tip of my tongue up and down his length. His hand snaked into my bra and cupped my breast as I picked up the tempo, squeezing my hand tightly around him. The warmth between my legs began to throb, spurred on by each of his moans. Most guys wanted to be macho during sex, so they didn't moan–Tristan was not like that. He let me know exactly how much he was enjoying it.

I twisted my head side to side and sucked his tip deeply. He made a painful, pleasurable sound in his throat. "I want to be inside of you."

"Mm-mm," I hummed around him, and his hand clenched my breast.

"Please baby, I miss you. I need to be–" his stomach tightened like a python then, his hands froze on my body. "Oh fuck, I'm gonna cum," he breathed. I sucked harder on his tip, pumping my hand down his shaft quickly as he filled my mouth, warm and sweet. I smiled shyly up at him, swallowing him down inside of me. His face hardened, his eyes flashed and suddenly his hand was around my throat. His lips connected painfully with mine as he squeezed. His tongue searched my mouth, tasting himself inside of me. He snapped my head back, away from him and glared at me.

"Don't ever tell me that I can't fuck you, again," he growled. He pulled me up to my feet, the lack of oxygen made my lungs scream. Then his hand was gone, and I was suddenly airborne as he bent and lifted me up by my legs and threw me over his shoulder. He sat me down gently on the high dinner table. I was only wearing pajama shorts and a tank top, both made of thin fabric that barely could contain the heat in my body. Tristan pushed my knees up to my chest and his electric eyes locked on the wetness between my legs. "Oh baby," he groaned. He pulled my thin black shorts to the side, exposing me to the cool air. My heart hammered excitedly.

He softly ran his finger tip up and down my opening, eliciting a moan from my lips as my back arched off the table. With a shrug, he threw my legs up and over his broad shoulders and I marveled at the sight. He sank one finger inside of me and curled it against the ridges just inside of my opening. An immense pressure burned deep inside of me, too sharp and too wonderful.

His free hand grabbed the top of my white tank top and pulled it down roughly to expose my breast. He gently pinched my nipples until they formed little peaks and removed his finger to the tip. When he reinserted it, he added two more fingers, and I cried out. "Oh god," I moaned. My heart felt like it was going to burst right out of me.

"I want you to cum in my mouth, baby," he breathed hoarsely. He bent and pressed his lips to my mound, kissing me softly. My hips lurched, searching for his tongue in anticipation. He chuckled and gave me what I wanted. I gasped loudly and gripped fistfuls of his hair as he worked his tongue over me, eagerly. He moved his fingers inside of me to the tempo of his tongue on my clit. My muscles tightened as I approached the cliff, panting heavily.

I glanced down and the view of my legs draped over his behemoth shoulders, fingers intertwined in his ebony hair did me in. I cried out and pulled him down closer to me, damn near lifting my entire body off the table as my body came undone under his lips. He straightened, wiping his mouth with a wicked glint in his eye.

"Good girl," he purred, and I laughed. He helped me down off the table, catching me when I staggered. I was attempting to catch my breath when my phone rang from somewhere on the couch. Tristan watched me closely as he pulled his pants back up and fastened his belt.

"I need you to take Hunter," Jimmy demanded. I checked the time on my phone, it wasn't even ten in the morning, I wasn't supposed to pick up Hunter for another five hours.

"Jimmy you can't always do this," I sighed, and Tristan straightened.

"Well too fucking bad, I'm outside and I have to work." The phone went dead, and I glanced up nervously, Jimmy's silhouette was outside of the front door. Tristan was at my side immediately.

"What is it?" he breathed but his face was hard, his eyes were zeroed in on Jimmy's shape through the blinds.

"Stay here," I said sternly. I glanced around the room; I didn't feel like Jimmy seeing my nipples through my tank top. I located my sweater on the floor and roughly tugged it on over my head. I took a deep breath and grabbed the door handle but stopped to glance back at Tristan, my face serious. *"Stay here."*

I opened the door quickly and slipped outside, hastily slamming it closed behind me. His hazel eyes glanced over my shoulder to the door. I had never not let Jimmy in the apartment before. I ignored him and grabbed Hunter out of his arms, he squirmed excitedly when he saw me.

"Hi baby," I smiled widely as I cradled him to my side. I slipped the diaper bag off Jimmy's shoulder and tossed it inside, again slamming the door shut. "Jimmy, we need to talk. If you can't hold up your end of the custody agreement, then I think we need to go back to court."

"I have to *work!*" he snapped. He brushed his greasy brown hair out of his eyes and threw his arms up. "I have bills to pay too dude."

"What *bills* do you even have, James?" I rolled my eyes. "I paid for your—*my*—car in cash. Your rent is two hundred dollars and you're on food stamps."

"Whatever." He threw up his hands and stomped down the stairs.

"Go ahead and ditch your kid again you fucking loser!" I shouted after him. This argument between us occurred every other month or so but rarely did it happen in front of Hunter. I knew it was wrong as I was shouting but I was just so exasperated, so completely fed up with Jimmy and his lackadaisical parenting. I'd much rather have Hunter full time than rely on him—he couldn't even afford diapers and, more often than not, he would choose to buy drugs and alcohol instead. I just needed a signed court order to make it happen and I couldn't do that without Jimmy signing over his parental rights.

"Shut up bitch!" he shouted up at me.

The front door to my apartment exploded open, slamming into the side railing of the staircase with a massive boom. Tristan's huge frame shot out the apartment and halfway down the stairs before I even realized what was happening. He shook with rage; his fists were balled tightly at his sides.

"The fuck did you say, bitch?" he shouted, and I flinched. Jimmy stared up at Tristan with large eyes full of surprise. He composed himself slightly and offered a weak grin.

"I'm talking to my wife, bro," he smirked and waved a hand toward me.

"If she's your wife then why is she up here with *me* bruh?" Tristan shook. "You can come say that shit to my face motherfucker, I'll break your fucking jaw."

"Who is this guy?" Jimmy asked me.

"I'm her fucking man," Tristan bellowed. "She's *my girl*, you ain't gonna talk to her like that you feel me?"

"Whatever," Jimmy huffed and moved to open his car door. I caught Tristan's shoulder before he could charge after him.

"You guys stop!" I shouted.

"The fuck you say, bitch?" Tristan halted at my touch, he trembled beneath my hand.

"Tristan that's enough–get inside!" I snapped. Tristan didn't move. He continued to breath so heavily that his shoulders rose and fell. He stared down Jimmy as he got into his car and drove away. Once he was gone, I spun on my heel and hurried into the house, clutching Hunter to my chest.

I set Hunter down on the couch and covered his little face with kisses. He was too little to completely comprehend what had happened, but he knew when adults were yelling because they were angry. His bottom lip wavered, and I choked back a sob.

"I'm so sorry," I told him and smoothed his face. "It's okay baby. I missed you so much, did you have a good time with daddy?" Hunter nodded; his brown eyes wide. The screen door slammed shut and I spun to see Tristan. He was at my side in an instant, his eyes still alight with fury.

"Man, fuck him," he growled. He came to a sudden stop and grabbed my hand, placing it on his chest. His heart hammered frantically like a bird in a cage. "Fuck him. I'll be your ride or die, baby."

"Tristan, Tristan, stop," I hissed, glancing down at Hunter. Tristan's face snapped out of it as he realized that Hunter was in the room.

"I'm sorry," he sputtered. "I-I need a minute."

"I'm going to give Hunter a bath and feed him lunch." I nodded, pushing past him.

I forced myself to focus on Hunter as I bathed him and not think about what just happened. It wasn't like Jimmy didn't deserve it…it had been a long time coming that someone put him in his place. Jimmy was like a cockroach that kept surviving despite what life threw at him and it made him cocky.

I wasn't one to hold my tongue when it came to how I felt about my ex-husband, neither behind his back nor to his face. But time and time again, Jimmy showed me just how little he cared. I couldn't hide it, I was thrilled. I also deeply regretted that any of it happened in front of Hunter.

Hunter splashed in the warm, soapy water and laughed. I laughed with him as I smoothed his hair into a short mohawk and blew bubbles in the air above him. His chubby hands slapped the water and sprayed me. I smiled sadly as he played with his toys in the water, pretending the car was a dolphin. Being a mother made me feel fulfilled. Being Hunter's mother was enough for a lifetime, but I needed to finish school and land a good career to take care of us. Never again would I put him or myself in a situation to rely on another person. I kissed his chubby cheeks. I would gladly die for him if it came down to it.

"Mama! Dolphin!" Hunter shouted as he shoved his toy car back under the way and shot it up into the air.

After his bath, I lathered him up in lotion and diaper cream and changed him into a fresh set of clothes. Hunter was such a good baby, he was so easygoing, nothing I did ever seemed to bother him. He busied himself with studying his toes as I placed a new diaper on him and swatted at my hair as I tugged shorts on him. When we finally made our way back into the living room, Tristan was still on the back patio. I eyed his shirt and jacket draped carefully over the back of a bar stool. He was shirtless outside, the sun glistened off his back as he blew out a plume of cigarette smoke.

I didn't make any sort of movement or noise to catch his attention, but he glanced over his shoulder the moment I stepped out of my bedroom. He flicked his cigarette over the ledge and slid the glass door open.

Wordlessly, he went to the small kitchen sink and washed his hands carefully, all the way to the elbow. He ran his wet hands through his hair, slicking it back and sucked a handful of water into his mouth. He rinsed his mouth and spat into the sink before he turned to face me. I cocked an eyebrow as he tugged on his shirt.

"I didn't want to have any cigarette smoke on me for him," he explained almost sheepishly. He stepped over to where Hunter stood beside the coffee table playing with a drink coaster and crouched low next to him. "Hey little man."

"Hi," Hunter chirped without looking up at Tristan. Tristan smiled and ruffled Hunter's wet hair.

"I'm your mommy's friend, my name is Tristan. I'm really happy to meet you."

"Meet you," Hunter mimicked, still more interested in his newly found toy. Tristan chuckled and gently knocked his knuckle under Hunter's chin and looked up at me. What I saw made my throat tighten. Hope twinkled in his beautiful eyes. Wordlessly, Tristan cupped the side of Hunter's head and gave him a soft kiss on his hair and stood up. Tristan wrapped his arms around me suddenly and pulled me close against him, tucking his face into my neck. My hands grabbed eagerly at his jacket, twisting it into fistfuls. Something exchanged, wordlessly, between us.

Whatever it was, it was full of promise, and I hugged him tighter. I hadn't realized how much I wanted a partner, someone to shoulder the world with, to make decisions for Hunter with until this moment. My chest tightened and I swallowed hard. I knew Tristan must be feeling something similar, a yearning for a family that was stolen from him–twice.

Tristan

16

I could finally breathe. A weight has been lifted off me, my chest felt lighter, the days seemed worth it. Now that we had got through the awkward initial introductions between Hunter and I, I spent every free moment with him and Ophelia. As soon as I wrapped up at the garage, I went home to shower and headed over to Ophelia's. I physically ached being away from her, my stomach was in knots the moment we were apart. I didn't even mind Charlie being a dick as per usual, it didn't matter now that I had my girl and our boy.

"The guys at the shop been talking about you," Donovan started. We were in line at In N Out, waiting for our order to be ready. I glanced down from the corner of my eye at him, but he was smartly not looking at me, working to keep his pale face neutral.

"Number forty-four," a girl called out from behind the counter, and we walked up to grab our food. I waited until we found a plastic, red and white booth to sit in before I replied.

"Not news," I rolled my eyes and huffed as I tried to fit comfortably into the booth. I was just too damn big. "About what?"

"Nothin' crazy. You just seem…happy." Don shrugged one shoulder, studying his cheesy burger intently, working to peel it out of the wrapper. I had ordered a fucking mountain of food, but it wasn't anything outside of my norm: two cheeseburgers, protein style, with grilled onions, two fries and a strawberry milkshake. *Gotta eat big to get big.*

"I am," I stated nonchalantly.

"Yeah, it's fucking weird," Donovan laughed but his face suddenly turned serious. "It's cool man, no one's really seen you happy for a while." His eyes flashed down to the large, ugly scar on the inside of my forearm. Ophelia finally asked me about it, guess it took her a while to work up the courage. She had trailed her finger over it gently and cried when I told her the truth. It killed me to see her so upset at the thought of my pain, of what I tried to do to myself. Even now, it made my throat burn.

"Keep being happy for me, I'ma fall in love with you too," I winked, and he laughed. We didn't talk much more as we scarfed down our food like two hungry dogs. Once we were finished, I stretched out and winced. My knees felt tight from being crammed into this booth for so long, I needed to get up and move around. My phone beeped and my heart leapt in hopes that it was Ophelia. I frowned when I saw it was just Charlie.

Charlie: Need u in the office

I rolled my eyes and stuffed my phone into my jacket. "Charlie's *requesting* me."

"He's been pretty burnt with you for bailing so often lately," Donovan patted his full stomach.

"I'm tired of carrying you motherfuckers on the crew, it's about time someone else got shot and stabbed." I was only half joking, but I elbowed Donovan in the ribs playfully, not wanting to hurt his feelings. Donovan winced and rubbed his side.

"We've been holding try-outs after the shop is closed."

"No takers?" I laughed loudly. It was such an odd feeling, this lightness in my chest. I was almost always smiling for no fucking reason. No one could ruin my mood, not even Charlie's dumb ass or Cherry pouting at me constantly. Luckily, she had been staying away since I turned her down, but this was our usual game. Soon enough she would be back trying to get me to fuck her or confess my dying love for her. Never going to happen. No wonder her and Katherine had been such toxic friends–I stilled.

For the first time in five years, I had thought of Katherine and my skin didn't crawl, my bones didn't threaten to completely shatter. I forced myself to turn over my car's ignition and threw it into gear so that Don wouldn't notice but the shift was monumental. I needed to see Ophelia–*now*. She was at work but getting off soon, I was supposed to pick her up like I had been the last few weeks, but I wondered if she would dip out of her shift early for me. I hit all green lights on the way back and my excitement grew, I was closer to seeing my baby.

I dropped Donovan off at his mom's house, a small blue house that should've been condemned a decade ago and headed for the garage. When I got there, I B-lined for the office to find Charlie. The shop was closed now, all the padlocks in place and the dryer in the back was going–readying the rags for the next day. I frowned at an unfamiliar car parked out front of the office, a newer red, Chevy Malibu.

I threw open the door, the bell above jingled, and I stopped short. Charlie was in his usual spot behind the counter, slouched on the bar stool with his arms crossed. A short woman was in the room with him, but I ignored her.

"You wanted to see me?" I nodded to him. Charlie's eyes flashed down to the woman and back to me quickly.

"You got company," he smirked. The woman turned slowly, and my frown deepened. She looked vaguely familiar, Hispanic with dark curly hair that hung in waves just passed her chin. "You remember Officer Torres?"

"Torres?" My eyebrows shot up my forehead. I completely didn't recognize her out of her uniform, she now wore a navy-blue button up and slacks, she had a brown purse slung over her shoulder. "Uh–what can I do for you ma'am?" I was caught off guard. I looked at Charlie, but his thin lips were pressed into a hard line, fighting a smile.

"Tristan," she licked her lips and smiled. Something in the movement had warning bells screaming in my head. "My partner and I were here a couple of weeks ago questioning about your involvement with a robbery of a semi-truck hauling Harley Davidson' equipment. The robbery in question took place in the early morning hours." It wasn't a question though she stated it as if it were.

"I thought I answered your questions?" I sighed, already annoyed.

"Yes. You had said that you didn't know anything about it–correct?"

"That's what I said–wasn't it?" I never really had a good poker face, but Torres was really starting to piss me off. She nodded; her black bob bounced against the collar of her shirt. She rummaged into her purse briefly and removed a clear plastic bag with a large piece of red tape over the top. It was labeled EVIDENCE.

My stomach hit the floor. Inside was a pack of too familiar Marlboro reds with my favorite Zippo lighter tucked into the cellophane. The one with my fucking name engraved into it, it had been a gift from my grandmother.

"This pack of cigarettes and lighter were confiscated from the scene of the robbery," her voice rang clear. "Is your name not Tristan Kyle Lawrence?"

"What? Did you and your dirty fucking partner pick that off me the last time you were here?"

That was it.

My third strike. I was facing life in prison. The gear that I stole that night was well worth one hundred grand, easily. Another felony. The end of any possible life with Ophelia. "You dirty fucking pig." I spat at her shoe, but she didn't flinch.

"Calm down, boy," Charlie rolled his eyes, finally uncrossing his arms. "She's here to make you a deal."

"No, no it's okay Charles," Torres said without looking at him. Her brown eyes were focused on me, a familiar glint in her eyes. The fuck was going on here? "That ferocity is exactly what I'm looking for."

I looked between them; Charlie looked bored of this conversation already.

"Someone going to tell me *what the fuck* is going on here?" I demanded.

"I have a…proposition for you," she smiled slowly. "You spend the night with me…and I'll give it back to you. You can have the evidence that links you to the robbery. Or–you can get your third strike and spend your life in prison."

I gawked at her; a laugh burst through me.

"Are you fucking serious? You want me to fuck you in exchange for my freedom?"

"That's right," she folded her arms across her chest, her tone cool and even. Her face was even, well composed though she was fucking high–she had to be. I turned on Charlie.

"What're you, my fucking *pimp* now?" I shouted.

"It's what's best for the crew," Charlie shrugged. "You screwed up, now you fix it."

"What's to say she won't come after us for something else even if I do this?" I said.

"Nope, I will do my part to keep the station off of you and your *crew's* tail." She drew the word out, condescendingly. I turned my back on them, needed to get their fucking faces out of my sight for a moment. I cracked my jaw and flexed my neck, the loud pop did little to soothe the tension. Without another word, I spun around and grabbed Torres roughly by her elbow and shoved her ahead of me towards the office. Charlie chuckled as I elbowed him out of the way and slapped the door open. I threw Torres inside, not sparing any roughness as she fell.

She wanted ferocity and she was going to get it.

She picked herself up and smoothed her shirt down, cool as ever. Inside the small office was a wooden desk, a file cabinet, and a small bed that Charlie sometimes used to sleep one off. It was old and filthy.

"You like this shit? You like being fucking manhandled?" I didn't try to keep my voice low, I let it bellow and my vision pulsated. Torres's face tightened but she lifted her chin defiantly. I wheeled and threw my fist into the mirror on the back of the door, it shattered with a loud explosion. Glass fell to the floor in soft tinkles. I whirled back around and closed the distance between us with one long stride. I loomed over her.

She had to crane her neck back to look me in the eyes. Using two hands, I gripped the collar of her shirt and tore it apart, the buttons shot off with a protestant groan. She flinched in surprise.

"You had a lot to say out there when you were being tough," I glared.

"I'm being patient–waiting." Her voice didn't waver. "Take your clothes off."

I couldn't move immediately; my muscles were so locked into place that it prevented me. Finally, I pulled off my shirt and jacket. I let them fall to the floor behind me. Her breathing hitched as her eyes slowly looked me over, took in my body, my scars, my tattoos, everything. Slowly, she reached out with both hands and placed them flat against my stomach. A shaky breath escaped her.

Heat flashed through me, and I grabbed her roughly by the throat. She gasped, her eyes wide as I shoved her backwards onto the bed, landing on top of her with my hand around her neck. I squeezed tightly and sank my teeth into her shoulder, breaking skin. She slapped at me, and I pulled back, releasing her. She gasped for air and coughed but her eyes were bright, excited. I swung my arm and the back of my hand connected with her cheekbone with a sickening smack. Her head jerked to the side; her black hair sprawled across her face.

"You like this shit?" I spat at her. Her bare breast heaved as she pushed the hair from her face and smiled at me. I fucking hated her. It took me just a second to pull down the slacks from her wide hips and throw them onto the floor. Her hips were already moving in anticipation.

"Take your pants off," she demanded.

I ignored her and only unbuttoned my jeans and pulled myself out.

"Take them *off*," she repeated.

I rolled my eyes and worked them off all the way. She let out a moan as she stared at my naked body.

"Shut the fuck up, pig." I got back onto the bed and slapped her hand away as she reached for me. "Don't fucking touch me."

"Kiss me," she snarled.

I slowly crawled over, letting her anticipation build. Her hips moved faster; her eyes thrilled. Instead, I grabbed her chin and turned her face away from me and kissed her neck. She sighed and wrapped her arms around me tightly. She smelt of jasmine. Part of me wondered if she had prepared for this, showered, shaved every part of her body and sprayed perfume just for me. I trailed kisses and bites down her large chest and sucked her nipples into my mouth. Her breath sucked in with a hiss and she arched against me.

I circled my thumb over her clit, and she moaned loudly. Hella loudly, she wouldn't shut the fuck up. I know Charlie was outside, gloating and could hear her. I slapped my hand over her mouth, but it only made her moan louder.

My blood had turned to acid, burning my veins, filling every part of my body until I was rock hard against her. I hated it, I hated myself for it. Images of Ophelia flashed behind my eyes, and I winced. I would kill Officer Torres and Charlie for this shit. I withdrew from Torres roughly, shoving her away from me as I leaned back, breathing heavily. I grabbed her hips and spun her around onto her stomach so that I wouldn't have to look at her. She yelped as I lifted her hips into the air and back onto my dick as hard as I could.

It was the roughest sex that I ever had. I intentionally tried to hurt her. Any time I touched her, I gripped her as hard as I could until she cried out in pain. I ran my fingers into her thick hair and made a tight fist in their roots and pulled as hard as I could. I snapped her head back so that I could look into her face. She had tears pouring down her hot cheeks.

"Is this what you wanted?" I hissed in her ear.

"Yes!" She cried out and I pushed her away from me in disgust. I rammed myself into her, feeling the end of her opening fighting me. The pressure was building, and I knew she was close to finishing, so was I. I wrapped both hands around the back of her neck and squeezed as hard as I could. I didn't care if I killed her in that moment. She bucked and jerked away from me, but she wasn't strong enough.

Her hands clawed at mine, but I didn't feel it. All the hate I ever felt for the police, for Charlie, for this fucking bitch poured of me. I hated her. I hated myself most of all for doing this to Ophelia. For being so fucking weak that I would choose this way out even though it meant I could go home to her.

Torres's face was turning purple, her eyes were wide with panic.

"You stupid fucking bitch!" I hissed through clenched teeth. Her body spasmed and I felt her juices flow over me just as I finished into her. I collapsed next to her on the bed, breathing heavily. Torres rolled away from me, struggling to catch her breath. She coughed and gagged, and I thought she would throw up. As soon as the fire in my lungs subsided, I rolled across her and out of the bed. I dressed quickly and threw her shirt at her. She didn't catch it, it hit her in the face.

Her purse had landed on the floor, its contents still inside. I snatched it off the ground and fished the evidence bag out. I stormed over to her, and she recoiled from me. I grabbed her by her cheeks, forcing them together as I made her look up at me. I held the evidence bag against her face.

"Stay the *fuck* away from me." I pushed her back down on the bed and she laughed. A chill swept through me. She continued laughing as she brushed her hair out of her face.

"Thanks for that Tristan, I haven't came that hard in years."

My stomach churned and I got the hell out of there.

I stormed out across the parking lot, not bothering to pull my shirt back on. My heart was pounding, shame burned through me like white hot flames. My knees gave out and I crumpled onto the cold, dark asphalt.

Brianna Gustafsson

"FUCK!" The scream tore through my throat. My fist beat the ground, but I didn't feel the crack of my knuckles, the tear of my flesh.

I pulled myself up to my feet and stumbled over to my car. I drove silently. I didn't turn on any music, I didn't roll up any weed to smoke as I drifted through the dark streets. It didn't take long for me to reach Charlie's place. It was a squat, dark brown building with wild rose bushes that grew chaotically up the sides. My body was numb as I pushed the unlocked door open, it swung open lazily into the dark house.

This had been my childhood home, passed down from my mom's parents after they had died. When my own mother passed, Charlie just never left. It wasn't a romantic gesture, his effort of preserving his dead girlfriend's ghost, instead it was out of convenience. It meant the mortgage was paid and he didn't have to move.

There were two bedrooms and one-bathroom shared Jack-and-Jill style. I nudged open the first door on the left which had been my bedroom. My old twin bed was still there, just a box spring on the floor. Charlie had taken my mattress away when I was eight and I spent a handful of years on just that box and a too-small blanket. I don't even know why he had taken it, to teach me some sort of lesson I'm sure or to let some junkie crash on it. A stack of crates had served as my dresser, to the right of the room which I had an old TV balanced precariously on top of.

The rest of the room was stuffed full of garbage: porn magazines, trash bags, stale laundry, car parts and other crap. This would have been my twin brother's room if he had survived but it was just me in this room. A memory flared then. I was about six years old, lying in bed reading some comic book when Charlie came home, drunk and in a rage.

I don't know what he was angry about but whatever it was, he took it out on me. He stormed into my bedroom, screaming, and swearing about something. I tried to jump up and run away but his large boot connected with my stomach and knocked me down. He kicked me in the stomach until I threw up and he left without a word.

For an entire month after that incident, my bruised ribs throbbed with every breath. It took me hours to fall asleep each night because of the pain. I was sure that he had broken a rib—it wouldn't have been the first time he broke one of my bones.

I blinked heavily to banish the memory. Fury tore through me so suddenly I didn't have time to prepare for the mental shift from despair. I spun and punched a hole through the wall, tearing a large gap into the old wallpaper. I raised my first and punched again…and again…and again. I stormed down the hall, shaking, towards Charlie's bedroom in the back. He had a large bed, the dirty sheets crumpled at the foot.

A hulking solid wood entertainment center took up most of the room on the right wall. I grabbed the old baseball bat from behind the door and swung it as hard as I could at the TV. The connection with the bat sent a jolt up my arms as the screen exploded. I pulverized it before I turned and smashed the glass mirrors built into the headboard. Glass sprayed across the room, lost in the bedsheets.

I moved throughout the house, swinging the bat into any surface that I could. I kicked over the fridge, it landed with a huge boom onto the kitchen floor. My teeth grit with each swing, each hit and kick. My body was exploding, ripping apart at the seams in anguish. I fucking hated Charlie. Everything bad in my life had happened *because* of him. First, he got my mother on drugs. Then she died and left me with this abusive drunk. Everything since had been downhill, my path clear to all those who knew me. But then Ophelia came into my life, and I thought I finally had something good—a chance to be good.

How was I supposed to look her in the eye now? To see all the love and acceptance she felt for me in those big, green eyes? To hold Hunter and hear his little squeals of laughter knowing what I did? Ophelia would never forgive me. I think Charlie knew that too. I had been unfaithful before in previous relationships, but this was different, this was coercion—I wouldn't have ever done it if it didn't mean the future of my crew.

The shattered bat clattered noisily against the filthy floor at my feet. I was numb, no longer furious or seeing red. I stood amongst the mess that I had made destroying my childhood home. I left as quietly as I had staggered in.

I blinked my heavy lids groggily; it had taken me hours to finally drift off to a restless sleep. The barrel of a gun pushed harder against my temple, pushing my head back into my pillow.

"Get the fuck up," Charlie growled. My vision snapped into focus, and I could see Charlie as he leaned over my bed, shoving his 9mm against my temple. I tried to slap his arm away, but he shoved me roughly.

"What the–"

"You think you're fucking *funny* boy?" Charlie seethed. Flashes of me shattering his home came back to me. He gritted his teeth; spit speckled his chin as he spoke. His fist slammed down against my cheek bone, sending pain and stars bursting into my vision. I jumped off the bed and shoved him away from me.

"You think what *you did* was funny?" I bellowed. "Forcing me to fuck that cop bitch?"

"Do you wanna go back to jail–prison for the rest of your fucking life and drag the shop down with you?" he retorted.

"You only give a shit because we make *you* money."

"I don't know why you're so burnt anyways." Charlie stuffed the gun back into his waistband. "So, what–you got your dick wet, it didn't sound like you weren't having a good time." He laughed and I charged him, grabbing him by the front of his shirt, slamming him back into my bedroom wall. His hands grabbed at me as I lifted him above my head.

"One day I'm going to fucking kill you," I hissed through gritted teeth and dropped him to the floor.

Charlie pulled himself up and brushed his shirt off. He turned to leave but stopped and looked at me steadily.

"It's gonna be me or you, boy."

Ophelia
17

School had taken a stressful turn these last few weeks. Matt had suddenly dropped from our Physiology class at the end of the semester a few weeks ago, but I wasn't sure why. I thoroughly enjoyed my Microbiology class. Learning about different diseases, how to identify their cell types through different testing methods and how that was important for antibiotics or antivirals. I had these class three days a week in which two of those days were two-hour lectures and the third day was a two-hour lab class.

Today I sat in the large lab room at one of the long black top tables that each had a sink built into the surface. Professor Whitmore entered the room then, struggling under the weight of a heavy box that was full to the brim. A boy from class that usually sat by the door jumped up to help Professor Whitmore carry the box to his desk at the front of the class.

"Thanks David," Professor Whitmore huffed. He was average height with a large belly that stretched his sweaters to their maximum. Santa Clause-style hair and wire rimmed glasses, he looked like a stereotypical science teacher, and he spoke in a nasally, monotone voice. I let my eyes linger on his helper for a beat longer than I should have. He was a good-looking guy, tall with shaggy brown hair and high cheekbones. He turned around to walk back to his desk and his eyes met mine briefly. I dropped my gaze back down to my notebook, embarrassed.

Professor Whitmore rubbed his hands together excitedly as he addressed the class.

"Okay everyone!" He drawled. "Today we are going to start our next module of experiments. You and *one* partner," I groaned, "will work together at home outside of class on this project. It will be your *only* homework assignment for the entire semester, it'll be one, large project broken up into six parts. You and your partner will collect a bacterial sample from your item of choosing. You will grow the sample on your petri dish and bring them to class so we can run a series of tests. During the next few weeks, you will work together to figure out what the sample was that you collected, and you will write one paper together."

I glanced around the room, awkwardly. I never really spoke to anyone in class outside of Matt but since he unexpectedly dropped from the school–a stupid thing to do, whatever program he was applying to would see the withdrawal on his transcript and most likely reject his application–my pickings were slim.

As I glanced around, my eyes landed on a pair of brown eyes gazing back at me. David was turned halfway on his stool, staring at me from over his shoulder. I thought of glaring at him, sending him a message but also remembered that I didn't have a partner. I smiled politely instead and looked away. Professor Whitmore clapped his hands loudly, causing me to jump.

"Go! Be free and pick a partner!" The class shifted as everyone got up and moved about, finding new seats next to their lab partner. I noticed a pretty redhead leaned forward toward David, but he shook his head and rose to his feet. Warmth crept up my neck as David walked towards me with a soft smile.

"Hi there," he breathed. He had a slight Boston accent. "My name is David Lombardi, what's your name?" He sat down next to me on the empty stool without permission.

"Ophelia Black," I replied.

"Nice to meet you Ophelia," he smiled and bumped my shoulder with his. "So…lab partners?"

"Sure," I chuckled. "You have an accent?"

"So do you," he teased. "I just moved here about a year ago from Boston–good ol' golden California."

"Everyone wants to be here," I said sardonically. "Despite the insane cost of living, homeless population and drug problems." "At least there isn't any traffic," he winked, and I laughed. "So, listen…since we're gonna be lab partners the next few weeks and have to work on this outside of class, we should exchange phone numbers." Though I knew he was right, we needed to be able to get into contact with each other, I couldn't help but be nervous. I thought of Tristan, *how would he feel about me working with an obviously attractive guy from class?*

"You're right," I concluded. He picked up my phone off the table before I could stop him.

"Whoa, is this your guy?" His eyebrows shot up as he turned the phone towards me to show me the shirtless picture I had taken of Tristan. He looked otherworldly, massive, and dangerous.

"Oh–yes," I balked and snatched my phone away out of embarrassment. David rattled off his phone number and I entered it into my phone. Professor Whitmore came around then with a thin folder of instructions and a box of supplies for us.

"Mr. Lombardi and Ms. Ophelia, this will be an interesting team," he smirked. He threw an overdramatic glance over his shoulder and leaned in towards us. "You two are the smartest in the class, I'm not worried about your project." He chuckled; his belly bounced with each laugh as he moved on to the next table.

"No pressure," I mumbled, and David laughed, the awkward moment passed already.

"The compliment was really for my benefit," he teased, and I smirked.

David and I had agreed to meet later that evening to get a head start on the project. I had the brilliant idea to get our sample from the bottom of my work shoes–who knows what kind of bacteria I stepped in during those 8-hour shifts? Which was exactly why I never wore my work shoes into my car or house. I always kept a change of shoes in my trunk.

I picked up Hunter from my mom's, deciding to stay long enough to eat a quick dinner with them.

"How's school going?" Tamara asked. She had made her famous Shepherd's pie for us. I shoveled a spoon full of mashed potatoes into my mouth before speaking.

"Good! This is my last semester before I am finished with my associate degree and can apply for nursing school."

Hunter squealed as he spread his hands through the mashed potatoes I had plopped on his highchair.

"That's great, baby," she smiled. She was still dressed in her work clothes—a silk blouse and black trousers but her blonde hair had come undone from its clip and now cascaded down around her shoulders. "Won't be too much longer before you're a nurse. Anything else new going on?"

I bit my lip and busied myself wiping Hunter's hands free of mashed potatoes.

I didn't want to tell her about Tristan. Tamara was not one to hide her disdain for my choices, mainly over Jimmy and I knew she wouldn't be too happy with me being with Tristan. He didn't check the boxes she was looking for.

"Jimmy has been better about keeping Hunter for the full time," I replied.

"Good," she nodded and folded her arms across her chest. "I've noticed since you hadn't needed me to pick Hunter up last minute for a few weeks."

"Sorry about that," I grumbled. "But I really appreciate it."

We finished up dinner and it was time to get Hunter home and in bed so that I could meet David. I sighed a breath of relief when I saw Steven's car parked out front, we wouldn't be alone. Hunter was already sleepy by the time we got home so I quickly brushed his teeth and got him in pajamas.

A soft knock startled me out of my reverie. I gently laid Hunter into his little bed next to mine and made my way out of the room. Steven had beat me to the door and had opened it for David. I had been grateful for him and Crystal being home, but I was suddenly insecure about David coming over.

"'Sup bro?" Steven leaned out of the door instead of opening the door wide for David.

"I'm here for Ophelia." David didn't sound intimidated by Steven. "I'm a friend from school."

"Ophelia?" Steven glanced between the two of us and chuckled. "Oh, *you know* he ain't gonna like this shit." He continued chuckling as he went back into Crystal's room. No doubt telling her that I had a *boy* over.

I was suddenly nervous. Standing in my living room with a backpack slung over his shoulder, David was undeniably handsome. He wore a gray thermal shirt that clung to the contours of his round chest and broad shoulders. The sleeves were bunched up around his elbows, showing off the hard form of his forearms. Part of me worried that Tristan would appear suddenly, but he had told me that he had to go out of town for work tonight. *I'm being stupid*, I thought to myself.

"Are you thirsty or anything?" I asked to break the silence.

David shook his head without speaking, his dark eyes trained on me. I swallowed hard and motioned to the couch. He sat down on it and pulled his bag across his lap. Attempting to sit as far away from him as I could, I opted to sit on the floor in front of the couch between the coffee table.

David slipped down to sit beside me.

"Um, I went ahead and collected the sample," I stammered. I pulled the petri dish out of my bag and handed it towards him. David's hand brushed mine as he took the dish and my skin prickled where he touched me. He held it above his head into the light and studied the underside. My eyes drifted down to his sharp jawline, his strong throat before I had to force myself to look away. I was making this so much worse.

"Wicked," he chuckled and placed the sample onto the coffee table. "So, we just wait?"

"Um," I rifled through my bag for my copy of the instructions and opened to the first page. "We're supposed to research what are the common bacteria found in the location we're testing."

"Shoes?" He frowned and I chuckled.

"No not necessarily but the care home that I work at."

"You work at the one by the school? Sunset Ridge or whatever?" His dark eyes studied me carefully and I felt the warmth return to my neck. He had a soft way of speaking, almost so that I had to lean closer to hear him. It wasn't necessarily like a whisper, but it made you listen harder.

"Yeah, how'd you know?" I frowned. He shrugged one shoulder and pulled his laptop from his bag.

"I drive by it every day, I just figured that's where you worked since you go out of your way to go to Berkeley City College."

Well, he's not wrong, I thought to myself.

"I work at the lumber yard off of the Berkeley Marina."

"You had to drive kind of far to come over here," I frowned. "I could've met you in the middle or something."

"I don't mind," he shrugged again and suddenly he leaned in close. "You said you had to get your son to bed. Why would I make a young, pretty mom stay out late doing *homework*?" He rolled his eyes at the last word, and I blushed. I tapped his laptop on the table, changing the subject.

"We need to look up common bacteria in nursing homes," I reminded him. He hesitated, still staring at me. Then he smirked and started typing.

After some time, the awkwardness passed, and I grew more comfortable with David. We got a good portion of the first part of our project completed. We found the top five most common bacterium types in nursing homes, both of us groaned at *C. diff*, and began drafting our section of the different make ups of each. I learned that David moved out here after a bad breakup, he moved in with an aunt and was still living there. He said when we graduated, he would be applying to a Radiography Technician program in Southern California.

"Warm beaches," David sighed. "Mad different than what we have in Boston. When I'm all set up, I'm gonna move my little sister out here."

"How old is she?" I asked. I had made us a cup of coffee; he was also a late-night coffee drinker.

"Seventeen, she's a few years younger but she doesn't get along with my step-ma," he said. He pronounced most vowels like *a* as *ah* or *o* as *oh*. I found his light accent charming. He stretched then, the bottom of his shirt rose up and bared the hard skin of his flat stomach.

"It's late," I realized, suddenly nervous. Tristan said he was going out of town, but he usually dragged himself into my apartment in the early hours and collapsed into bed with me. David yawned and nodded in agreement as he got down off the stool to gather his things. I followed him into the living room, watching as he packed his bag.

"Thanks for being my lab partner." David smiled down at me as he slung his bag over his shoulder. Without warning he bent and kissed my cheek. I stiffened but he didn't notice. "I'll see you next week."

I nervously glanced at Crystal's bedroom door, but it was still closed. They hadn't come out once since David came over. I rushed into the shower, scrubbing away the butterflies in the cold water. There was no doubt that David was handsome, but I didn't feel for him like *that*, I was very much so in love with Tristan. He was just a boy from class but the way he looked at me made me uncomfortable. I also felt guilty–for what I don't know. It felt like I had done something shameful.

By the time I got out of the shower and into one of Tristan's large shirts, I was no longer worried. David was my lab partner, and he was just overly friendly but that's probably how they were in Boston. He knew about Tristan, and I knew that I would never let anyone jeopardize what we had. I fell into bed next to Hunter, my mind tired of overthinking. A few minutes later, I heard the familiar rumble of Tristan's Cutlass.

Ophelia
18

I woke up later the next morning feeling more refreshed than usual. I stretched across my empty bed, groaning as my muscles stretched and the joints popped. Cloudy sunlight filtered through the window and across my bare stomach, Tristan's shirt was bunched up around my chest. My right hand reached out and felt for Hunter, but his bed was cold and empty. I sat up as if a rod of lightning hit me, in a panic as I looked about the room. My own bed was empty of a very large, very tattooed man as well.

Before I could panic further, faint laughter trickled in through the door. I sighed in relief and went to investigate.

Tristan held Hunter on his right hip as he stirred something in a bowl on the counter. My heart squeezed as I watched them, a warm feeling swept over me. This moment was all I ever wanted for Hunter, a man who loves him and his mother, who treats us well. But this moment was also tainted. How many of these types of moments did Tristan get to have with Millie before she was taken by Katherine? How many did he imagine?

Tristan dipped the tip of his finger into a can of frosting and held it up for Hunter to lick, which he did with excited shrieks. Tristan's booming laugh echoed at Hunter's excitement, he threw his head back to laugh and that's when he noticed me.

"Aw you caught me," Tristan chuckled sheepishly as he brushed the remnants of frosting, the evidence, off Hunter's mouth.

"Frosting for breakfast?" I smirked as I walked over. Tristan shrugged and leaned over to kiss me around Hunter.

"Wait until mommy sees the cupcakes we're making," Tristan stage-whispered to Hunter. Hunter clapped his chubby hands for me, and I took him down from Tristan. "What's on the agenda today, mama?"

I bounced Hunter around the dining room, pretending to bite at his fingers which made him squeal.

"I have to go to work this evening, so I'm supposed to bring Hunter over to Jimmy's." Tristan stiffened, pausing as he went to fill the cupcake tin with the batter.

"We're still dealing with that prick?" he growled.

"He's Hunter's dad, Tristan," I sighed. "We have a court order."

"Fuck the court order, dude!" Tristan slammed the metal mixing bowl into the sink with a loud clatter. I jumped from the sudden crash, clutching Hunter to my chest. "Jimmy's a piece of shit babe, he doesn't give a fuck about you or Hunter. He's only doing it, so he doesn't have to pay child support."

"Tristan!" I snapped. Hunter had begun to cry loudly. I hushed him and bounced Hunter on my hip but Tristan didn't back down.

"I don't know how you don't fucking *see that*, Ophelia!" He stepped closer to me, gesturing wildly. "We need to just take Hunter and let the man fuck off."

"We?" I gaped.

Tristan looked just as caught off guard as I felt.

"I mean, shit Ophelia, if we aren't going in that direction then what the fuck is the point?" He was exasperated and he had a point, what were we doing? Having a good time but then what?

I knew that every part of me wanted every part of Tristan, even the dark parts. My skin burned where he touched me and when he was gone it was as if he took my heart with him. Then why was I nervous? Why were there alarm bells ringing in the back of my mind? The skin on the back of my neck prickled in warning. Anger flashed through Tristan's emerald eyes at my hesitation.

"¡Necesito que te decidas qué es lo que quieres!" His balled-up fist connected with the cabinet beside him making me jump. His entire body trembled as he breathed heavily, towering over me.

"You need to lower your voice," I hissed. "I don't know what that means."

Hunter had tucked his face into my neck and was crying. I rubbed his back and bounced him on my hip to calm him. Wordlessly Tristan stomped around me to the bedroom. A moment later, he stormed out of my bedroom, tugging on his shirt.

"Where are you going?" I called after him.

The door slammed behind him and a moment later I heard the roar of his engine.

Fighting tears, I placed Hunter on my bed with some of his toys so I could give myself a moment. I couldn't process what just happened I didn't even understand what our fight had been about. Tristan clearly hated Jimmy, I mean so did I, but I didn't have the option to just take Hunter away from him.

Was Hunter even safe with his dad? Flashes of memories of Jimmy passed out on the couch came to mind. Too often I had walked into the living room during our marriage to see Jimmy passed out fully clothed on the couch. He would take my car and disappear for hours, drinking and doing drugs with his friends only to crawl back when he was done. I went to bed alone most nights, fighting with him to stay home *just this once*. He never did. He would be hungover and miserable the entire next day, his hands shook as he rubbed his bloodshot eyes. Jimmy would get overwhelmed quickly with Hunter and pass him off to me, yelling and pissed off that he couldn't get Hunter to calm down.

Whatever went on in Jimmy's house was not something I was aware of, and it made me sick to my stomach. During our divorce I had brought Jimmy's arrest records, his court-ordered rehab judgments that he never attended and records from previous DUI's but the judge didn't care. I had the feeling that the judge looked at the both of us and saw trash. Jimmy had once been handsome and now he looked as if he had the life force drained from him.

His hazel eyes were dead, his skin dull and his teeth chipped. I was a young mom fighting a loser ex and we had a child in the middle. The judge all but rolled his eyes at us when we entered the courtroom. I didn't have the money to hire a lawyer and fight for Jimmy's rights to be revoked–he wouldn't allow it anyways. Part of me wondered if it was because we were both awarded more on our food stamps because we had a child, and he didn't want to give it up or if it was control. Control over me.

Within the hour, Hunter and I were at Serena's. Alicia was in school, so it was just the three of us. Hunter busied himself playing with Alicia's play kitchen set in the living room while Serena and I sat at her fold-up card table she used as a dining room table in her small kitchen.

"Well, what *do* you want?" Serena asked. She also spoke Spanish which came in handy for translating whatever Tristan had yelled at me earlier. I sighed and stared down at the cup of hot coffee between my hands.

"I love him," I nodded. "But I mean, what future can we truly have? He has a record. What happens if we applied to rent a place together–would we be denied because of that? His job...doesn't seem like a long-term option. And his *temper* is exhausting!" A headache had bloomed in my temples.

"Nobody is perfect," Serena shrugged her bare shoulders. She was wearing a green silk dress that made the gold in her skin stand out. "It's about what you're willing to put up with." My phone chimed and my heart leapt hoping it was Tristan.

WORK: Ophelia Black, PM shift–canceled

I frowned. A shift being canceled happened time to time due to staffing levels but that also meant that was $200 I wouldn't be receiving on my next paycheck. That was my car payment, bills, gas, or clothes for us down the drain. Serena saw my shift and grabbed my hand.

"Let's go out tonight–my treat."

Serena always had the ability to talk me into going out when I really didn't want to. Originally, I had wanted to wallow and stay home reading a book but Serena whipped me up in her infectious energy. We made our way to The Sugar Room in downtown Oakland, alcohol from the shots we took in Serena's car burning through our veins.

It was cold and damp out, but we still sported short dresses and high heels, weather be damned. We bounced from side to side in line to enter the club attempting to shimmy some warmth into our numb bodies. My phone beeped, signaling that an email had come into my school account. It was quickly followed by a text.

David: Hey love! Just letting you know that I emailed my portion of the project to you just now.
David: It's just a rough draft.
David: Hopefully we can get together this week to work on it? (:

It took me much longer than necessary to get my numb hands to work out a response.

Me: Thanks! Yeah, sounds good.

The heat of a large room packed with bodies hit us as we entered the club. Serena grabbed me by my hand and led me through the shimmering wave of bodies to the bar. We both ordered a shot and a mixed drink and knocked back our first shot. I laughed as I wiped the spilled alcohol off my exposed cleavage.

Normally these places would have sent me into a panic attack–too many people and the music was so loud that we had to shout directly into each other's ears, but the alcohol lubricated the overstimulation.

We made our way to the dance floor with our drinks and moved our bodies to the beat. Flashing lights darted above our heads before they crisscrossed and fanned out over the crowd. It repeated this dance, taking on new patterns as the beat shifted. Part of me worried about Tristan coming to look for me and finding me here but he had no way of tracking me. Noticing my empty hand, Serena took my glass and motioned for me to stay put so she could order us another drink. I agreed and kept twirling and dancing in my spot.

A body slid up against mine, a hard crotch against my ass and lips at my ear.

"You're gorgeous, what's your name?" a male voice shouted.

"Mm-mm," I shook my head but met the sway of his hips. He chuckled and wrapped an arm around me, pulling me closer. The music vibrated across my skin; it shook the blood in my veins deliciously. The lights and people around me were already doubled in my drunken vision, my better judgment gone. I closed my eyes and leaned my head back on his shoulder enjoying the weightless feeling in this moment as we danced together. His hands gripped the tops of my thighs, pulling my ass harder against him.

Somewhere in my brain, I vaguely wondered what was taking Serena so long. The feeling of the hem of my dress being gently pulled up higher brought a trickle of cool air to my hot flesh and I relished in the brief feeling. My hem kept moving higher until I'm sure the crotch of my underwear was exposed. The man's hands cupped the inside of my thighs and my spine straightened. I planted my elbow into his side to give myself leverage to turn and pull out of his grip. I was about to tell him off and that's when a fist went flying over my head and directly into the man's nose.

The sickening crunch of his nose and spray of blood dazed me.

Did I punch him? I stood there wondering, stupidly. The man's head snapped back, and he lifted his hands to guard his face, but it did little to stop the fierce blows that landed with a sickening packing sound. I stumbled backwards as my double vision snapped into a singular view of Tristan suddenly in front of me. He was so fast; he had delivered the first punch to the guy's nose then two more with alternating fists before the man could even react. The man fell to the ground with Tristan on top of him. By then, chaos had broken out in the club. People were screaming, yelling at Tristan to stop, to get out or to fuck the guy up in encouragement. "Tristan, stop it!" My voice squeaked out, but it was lost in

the shouts. Tristan straddled the guy I had been dancing with, his fist slamming into the guy's face one after another. My own fists beat pathetically on Tristan's wide back, but he either didn't notice or didn't care.

Tristan stopped hitting the guy and began choking him.

The man looked up through swollen eyes in alarm, kicking his feet under Tristan's large body. *He's going to kill him*, I thought frantically.

Bodies surged forward, knocking me out of the way as they grabbed at Tristan. I recognized Donovan and Greg pulling at him desperately. Tristan fell backwards on top of them on the ground, nearly flattening Donovan, and Greg under him. Donovan's arm was wrapped around Tristan's throat, but Tristan didn't seem to notice. His face was absolutely murderous, his eyes glazed over.

The expression on his face terrified me. Gaping, I turned stiffly to look at the poor pulverized guy. A pair of familiar brown eyes stared up at me in shock and disgust. Tanis had been one of the ones to help get the injured man away from Tristan before he could choke him to death. Tanis looked at me now as if he was seeing me for the first time, the repulsion in his face made my stomach churn.

Serena appeared then, fighting to get through the crowd over to me. She threw her arms around me as if to pull me away, but I steeled myself.

"You need to get out of here," I said. My voice was stern and demanding. Donovan and Greg were already roughly pulling Tristan to his feet, trying to shove him towards the door before the police showed up. Tristan's eyes were focused on me, easily ignoring the hands that grabbed him. Wordlessly, he held out his large, bloody hand to me. I pulled out of Serena's arms and took Tristan's hand.

He towed me roughly through the crowd, Donovan's hands pushed at my back to move me along faster. My heart pounded in my ears as I focused on not tripping over my feet and falling. Greg was in front of Tristan, pushing people out of the way that tried to stop him from leaving. We exploded into the cold air but didn't linger.

Sirens pierced the air.

"Take the Saab!" Donovan shouted as he tossed the keys at Tristan. Tristan in return tossed his keys to Donovan without breaking stride. We ran for the black car, my high heels threatening to break my ankle as I wobbled. Tristan threw the passenger door open, and I dove inside. In second, he was in the seat next to me, gunning the engine to life. I barely had my seatbelt on before the tires were spinning, and we shot out of the parking lot.

I was thrown against the door as we fishtailed onto the street and shot forward. We raced through a red light, cars honked and darted away to avoid hitting us.

"Tristan!" I shrieked as a car narrowly avoided colliding with my side of the Saab. Tristan's jaw flexed and he threw the car into gear. Suddenly red and blue lights lit up the interior of the cab, a siren wailed.

"Fuck," Tristan groaned. I craned my head to see a police car's headlights through the tinted black window.

"Sit back." His bark made me flinch. I sat back in my seat and pulled my seatbelt tighter.

Tristan cranked the steering wheel, throwing me against the door again as the car made a half-circle turn to the left and shot forward. Tristan shifted again, releasing the clutch quickly and we were propelled impossibly faster. In the side mirror, the police car was still tailing us but much further behind now.

"Suspect is in a black Saab," a voice came through the black box on the dashboard. *"Heading south on Lake Merritt Blvd, requesting back up."*

I squealed and pinched my eyes shut as Tristan darted around traffic much too close to the other vehicles. Acid burned my mouth, and I wondered if I was going to throw up. All the alcohol from earlier had evaporated, leaving fear in its place. A blinding light cut through the dark interior of the cab, dazing me.

"This is chopper 5-Delta-Max we have eyes on the suspect heading East on Foothill—negative make that North on 7th Ave."

"I hate helicopters," Tristan grumbled. I sank lower in my seat and covered my face with my hands. We were silent as Tristan raced to beat the police chasing us. What was going to happen if we got caught? Tristan would be arrested for assault as well as from fleeing from the police. What would happen to me? I prayed for Tristan to go faster.

I was thrown against the door for the fourth time, this time pain stung my arm. I peeked through my fingers and saw the world spiraling by. The 2-ton vehicle was expertly spinning in a long arch around a wide roundabout like what I had seen at the sideshow those handful of months ago.

"Suspect is headed for the 580," the helicopter officer rattled. The Saab came to a screeching stop, throwing me against my seatbelt and then slamming me back into the chair. Tristan slammed the clutch and threw the gear shift simultaneously. The car lurched backwards, bouncing sharply as Tristan backed the car into a space between a broken chain linked fence. It took me a moment for my eyes to realize where we were. Tristan had driven us under a highway overpass, the 580 I assumed, and hid us between two fences.

He cut the headlights off and stared straight ahead. Our shaking breaths filled the cab, Tristan's chest heaved with each breath. My hands trembled in my lap. *Please, please, please,* I begged silently. Now that the engine was off, the sound of the helicopter blades was loud. My stomach clenched as they grew louder, and a beam of powerful light scanned the road ahead of us. My eyes stung as the light flickered across the roundabout we had just escaped and sliced through the highway just above. The helicopter lingered for a minute, sweeping its massive light back and forth.

"We no longer have eyes on the suspect," the voice crackled. *"Suspect must have traveled south on the 580. Calling off search."*

Ophelia
19

Tristan gave me my space and went to smoke a cigarette on the hood of the car. I stayed inside the cab for a long time, staring at his large back. My emotions were in turmoil inside of me: anger, shame but also understanding and love. I replayed the events of the Sugar Room over and over inside of my head. If Tristan hadn't shown up, I would've told the guy off and went to find Serena–no big deal. Sure, he had been grabby, but he had smelled of alcohol and he didn't fight me when I had pulled away.

Tanis's expression had felt like a hot blade slicing through me. I knew exactly what he was thinking and that's where the shame came from. Earlier that day had I not had a conversation with Serena about my trepidations with Tristan–our future? It felt like everything had boiled down to this moment, this insane blow out on the dance floor. It had summed up most of my worries and put them on display. Yet I still chose to go with Tristan.

The sound of the car door popping open was the only sound out here but still Tristan did not turn. After the police stopped chasing us, we drove silently for a few minutes up to Berkely. Tristan took us to my favorite spot, Grizzly Peak, which overlooked the Bay Area. I stepped around the car to Tristan but didn't turn to him, instead I looked out over my hometown. Since it was nighttime, you could see millions of lights from the cities below.

Martinez was to the left, Berkeley to the right, Oakland straight ahead and San Francisco just passed that. The Bay Bridge connecting Oakland to San Francisco was lit up in a spectacular light show that made it look like waves cascaded down the side of the bridge. Across the bay loomed the Golden Gate Bridge with its dotted lights.

I stood silently for a long time soaking in the sight and shivering in the breeze. Wordlessly, Tristan pulled me between his legs against the hood of the car and wrapped his thick arms around me. I leaned into his heat and sighed heavily. He fought me momentarily as I grabbed his right wrist, but he let me win. Turning his hand toward me, I studied the cuts that sliced through his knuckles, the chunks of skin missing on the middle knuckle. His fists were slightly swollen and bruising already, dried blood splattered across his forearms. I turned in his arms slowly and he dropped his head to hide his face, but I placed my palms gently on his cheeks.

His sad eyes broke my heart. It was as if he was a little boy who had been caught stealing and he knew his punishment was coming. Except he wasn't a little boy, he was a grown man who hurt someone else.

"You can't act like that," I frowned.

"Act like what?" His voice was hard. "Like a jealous boyfriend? I am. You let some guy dry hump you and expose your underwear to everyone." He pulled his face from my hands. My face burned as I realized just how much he had seen.

"I was telling him to fuck off when you showed up," I snapped.

Tristan rolled his eyes and moved me aside so he could slide down off the hood.

"How did you even know where I was?"

"I don't fucking get how you're so comfortable letting men touch you like that." He ignored me. His eyes flickered over me, taking in my short dress and heels which I instantly regretted. "You seemed pretty okay with it."

"Fuck you for insinuating what you're trying to say." I stepped after him. Those familiar warning bells in the back of my head sounded again but I ignored them. I was tempting the bear, and I knew it, but I didn't care. "You don't *own* me; I'm allowed to go out with my friend and have a good time. I'm sorry some guy got too handsy with me, but I was handling it."

Tristan's jaw tightened; his hands flexed at his sides causing the joints to pop. I hated when he did that. It was like a snake making a striking warning.

"You're so *fucking naive*, Ophelia," he snapped. "Two half naked girls out in Oakland getting fucked up and dancing with random dudes is how you get snatched up."

"Snatched?" I snorted. "I'm not going to get *kidnapped* Tristan."

"They don't gotta take you like that," he glared at me. "All they gotta do is take you to the backseat of some car. Pull your panties to the side–you make it too easy."

Heat flared through me then.

"Fuck you," I spat. "I'm not easy."

Tristan's scarred eyebrow shot up as a dark look overcame his eyes. I swallowed hard but stood my ground.

"Fight me off then." Without warning he strolled over to me and caught my face painfully in his hand. I tried to scream but couldn't open my mouth as he squeezed. I slapped at him, but he hardly seemed to notice as he pushed me back against the hood of the car. His knees pushed my legs apart and the short hem of my dress shot up around my hips.

His hot palm ran up and down my crotch, burning where he touched me. I tried to kick him, but he easily pushed my leg down and pushed against my knee, making it impossible to raise my leg. He pushed his hard dick into the thin fabric of my underwear, and I struggled to get free.

His pointer finger hooked around the thin fabric and pulled it aside, exposing me to the cold air and I gasped.

"This is just one way that I could take you," he breathed. He pushed himself against me as he spoke. His free hand grabbed the front of my dress and yanked it down so that my breast fell out the top. His hot tongue lapped up my breast and spun circles around my nipple. My hand was momentarily free, and I brought it down with a sharp slap across his cheek. Tristan jerked away from me; his eyes furious. My heart hammered my ribs. His breath escaped him raggedly before he gripped my hips and spun me around, slamming me down against the hood of the car.

"Tristan!" I hissed now that my face was free.

He shoved my dress further up so that my entire ass was out.

"Someone could drive by."

"It's too dark to see us," he growled. His fingers sank into me easily and I yelped. I pushed my hips back against his hand and he groaned. He withdrew his hand long enough to unzip his pants and then he buried himself inside of me. I moaned as he separated me deliciously, his nails dug into my hips as he brought me roughly down on top of him again and again. The hard metal of the car slammed into my stomach, forcing the air out of me painfully. Tristan suddenly jerked my head back, nearly tearing the hair from its roots.

"You let another man touch you," he growled into my ear. "I almost killed him because of you."

A shiver passed through me, and he moaned.

"He touched my thigh." My voice came out in bursts as the air was slammed out of me. Tristan's hand slid down to my face, and he squeezed my cheeks together, forcing my lips into an O shape.

"I'd kill any man for just fucking looking at you," he hissed. "I would gladly go back to jail for you."

"Prison," I corrected, my voice full of venom. "That would be your third strike." I had meant to hurt him but as soon as I said the words, I regretted it. My face slammed forward suddenly; pain erupted across my cheek. Tristan held my head against the windshield of the car, flattening my cheek against the cold glass as he pushed himself impossibly deeper inside of me.

"Fuck you," he groaned. Just when I felt like he would tear me into two from the inside, his breath hitched, and I felt his release into me. As soon as his body stilled, he pulled out of me and zipped his pants back up. He let me stumble backwards awkwardly, no longer being held up by his sheer strength. I fixed my underwear and tugged my dress back down. I spun around to yell at him but suddenly he was grabbing me up in his arms, much more gently. He picked me up and carried me over to the fallen tree trunk across the gravel lot. It had been there for years; I remember climbing it as a child. At some point, someone came through and spray painted the tree.

Tristan set me down on the trunk carefully and covered my face in kisses. Initially, I resisted him, but the warmth of his body and his familiar smell broke my resolve. I met his lips and kissed him back hungrily, pulling him down to me. He fell to his knees without breaking our kiss, his hands grabbed at me hungrily. He broke his lips away from mine to leave a trail of kisses along my cheek.

"I'm sorry," his breath fanned across my cheek. He kissed the hollow under my ear. "I'm so sorry Ophelia. I love you so much." His hand reached up and cupped my left breast, pushing it up and into his mouth. I moaned and ran my fingers through his hair. He used both hands to push my dress up higher, again exposing me.

"Lean back baby," he whispered. Without hesitation, I leaned backwards slightly over the fallen tree trunk, struggling to hold myself up as Tristan pushed my thighs apart. He kissed my knee and my head dipped back; my hair brushed my hands holding myself up. He licked the inside of my thigh and I shivered. He softly bit the inside of my skin near the V of my thigh, and I moaned.

He took my answering moan as an invitation and pressed his lips gently to the thin fabric of my underwear. My breath caught in my throat, but he removed his lips, turning his face to plant a small kiss into my hip. His fingers reached up and gently swirled circles over me and I burned, eager for the feel of his flesh on me.

He continued his trail of kisses and bites up my other thigh and I moaned in protest as his lips moved further away. He chuckled and I growled. I gasped as he suddenly pulled the fabric aside and licked me deeply. He slowly dragged his flat tongue up the front of me, flicking the point of his tongue against my clit. I was already swollen and ready from his assault a few minutes ago which made this contact brutal. He caught my clit gently between his teeth and sucked hard. My entire body jolted, threatening to collapse around him.

"That's it baby," he breathed against me as he inserted his fingers inside of me again. "Cum in my mouth." He drove his two long fingers down deep inside of me as he continued to suck on me. Blood rushed from my head down to my crotch, causing me to swell impossibly further. My hips rocked gently against his tongue, asking for him to go deeper.

He slowly pulled his fingers out of me and reinserted with a third. The stretch of me around him was unbearable. I grabbed at the back of his shirt to hold myself up as the pressure built to ungodly heights. Tristan moaned against me and drove his fingers in and out of me faster.

My release was brutal, it rocked my body and caused me to cry out. Stars bloomed in my vision against the night sky. My hands grabbed fistfuls of Tristan's hair as he refused to let up on me, still sucking and licking and driving his fingers into me. I cried out and shoved him away from me. He finally let go of me but caught me as I collapsed forward into his chest. His booming laugh echoed in his chest as the world swirled in front of me.

"You taste so good," Tristan sucked on his fingers that had just been inside of me and I blushed.

"Stop it," I smacked his arm. My body quaked and throbbed making it impossible to catch my breath. He adjusted my clothing for me, covering me back up. His expression changed suddenly, no longer amused but now troubled.

"What is it?" I asked.

He glanced up at me from under his lashes and my heart broke at how beautiful he was.

"I've said it a few times, but I mean it, you're going to be the death of me," he whispered. "I can't imagine my life without you–I don't want it if I don't have you and Hunter."

"You have us," I reminded him, but he shook his head.

"I really don't think you get it," he laughed dryly. "Some guy touches you and I *lose it*, in front of a whole club. I didn't know my boys were there, they had followed me when I went to look for you. I didn't know *who* was in that spot, it could've been anyone– with a gun. I didn't think–I *don't* think when it's about you. I just react. I'm not ashamed of my behavior." He shrugged. "I would break the jaw of any man who thought it was okay to touch you. I would burn this whole fucking world down for you Ophelia, but I don't think you want me to."

"You don't have to." I frowned. "I'm not going anywhere. I love you Tristan, but I think you need help."

His sea-colored eyes flashed to me, hard and unsure.

"What do you mean?"

I sighed and brushed my hair out of my face. My body had cooled down and now I was freezing again.

"These fits of rage aren't healthy," I pointed out. "You're so volatile. One minute you're up and the next you're down. I can't keep up with when you're going to be happy or suddenly angry. Then you have sex with me to distract me."

"I'm not trying to distract you," he said. "I was trying to prove a point–which I did by the way."

I folded my arms across my chest, shivering. Tristan caught the motion and shrugged out of his jacket. He placed it across my shoulders, and I sank into the heat happily.

"That's really not the point," I said.

Tristan sighed and looked up at the night sky, his face unreadable.

"This is who I am, Ophelia, I'm explosive but I have a lot of feelings–I just don't know how to control them all the time. I've been through some shit you don't even know about. You're lucky I didn't let it all get to me, lucky that I've put in work on myself over the years. I used to be fucking miserable to be around, fly off the handle any time I thought someone was trying to pull some shit." He strode over to me and took both of my hands in his. "I'd do anything to protect you. Is that not enough?"

I bit my bottom lip and studied our hands together, the way his enveloped mine. He released one hand to trail his knuckle softly across my cheekbone. I sighed and turned to softly kiss it as it made its path back and forth over my cheekbone.

"It's enough to start." I smiled up at him.

We went to his house. I showered and changed into one of his oversized t-shirts that hung down to my knees. Tristan had gone out and purchased bathroom necessities for me, to my surprise. He had them waiting in a little pouch on the back of the toilet for me. The small gesture was surprisingly overwhelming, it was so considerate. It had a razor, toothbrush, a pack of tampons, toothpaste, and hair ties in it. He had acted nonchalant about it, but I could see the slight blush darken his cheeks.

When I was done changing, I gathered my clothing and my cell phone fell out. I picked it up and sat in the middle of Tristan's bed as I read through the texts.

David: What're you up to?

Another text 10 minutes later had come from him.

David: I can't sleep.

There was a string of texts and missed calls from Serena. I bit my lip wondering what in the world she was thinking and what I would say to her. Quickly, I typed out a message:

Me: I'm okay, I'm at Tristan's. I'm so sorry for tonight.

I glanced out the bedroom window that overlooked the street and saw Tristan standing on the front patio smoking a cigarette. My phone buzzed in my hands.

Serena: I'm just glad you're okay. Call me when you get home.

She was rightfully concerned about me and tonight's events. I really couldn't blame her, especially since our conversation in her kitchen had been a perfect predictor for tonight. The door bang closed as Tristan came back inside. I listened to his footfalls as he cut across the trailer to the back of the house toward the bathroom. A moment later I heard the shower start. My phone buzzed again, and I frowned at the screen.

David: I can't stop thinking about you.

Oh no, I thought. I didn't have the mental capacity to deal with this right now, I felt completely empty. My emotions had been on such a rollercoaster tonight that it left me dry and exhausted. I quickly swiped his text thread to the left and deleted the evidence. But as soon as I did, guilt washed over me. I hadn't done anything wrong. I didn't even know where this was coming from but having those words in my phone felt like a betrayal. Like I was sneaking around behind Tristan's back.

I groaned audibly as I imagined *that* conversation. I turned my phone on silent and placed it on the bedside table to charge as Tristan came back into the room.

"You good?" He quirked an eyebrow at me. *Shit*, I thought. I obviously didn't have a poker face. I shrugged and busied myself crawling under the blanket.

"I'm just tired, it's been a long night." It wasn't a lie. Already my eyes were heavy as my body sank into his bed. It smelled of laundry detergent and Tristan. He pulled on a pair of basketball shorts and got into bed with me, turning out the light on his way. His silhouette was illuminated by the streetlight through the window. The curves of his broad shoulders, the lines of his arms as they wrapped around me. I sighed heavily and wormed deeper into his chest. His body was stiff around me.

"You good?" I mirrored back at him. I felt him nod softly above me, his chin brushing my hair.

"I just love you." He tightened his arms around me as he spoke. "I just don't know how to show you how *much* I do."

"I think that's pretty obvious," I smirked. My eyes were closed, I was already drifting to sleep.

"I would die for you," he whispered so softly I almost didn't hear him. "I'm already dying."

"Don't say that." I frowned, brought slightly out of my slumber.

"It hurts to love you as much as I do, I've never felt this before. I don't know how other people do it."

I yawned and relaxed back into him. I hushed him and hugged him tighter as sleep took over me.

Tristan went with me to pick up Hunter from Jimmy's the next morning. Tristan had another surprise for me, he purchased a car seat for Hunter for his own car. Except it was in the Cutlass so we had to drive the Saab back over to the shop to switch back. I was smart enough to leave some clothes at Tristan's for this exact sort of scenario. I wore a pair of jeans, slip on canvas shoes and a hoodie. Since Tristan bought me bathroom supplies, I was able to brush out my wild hair and tie it up. I was pleasantly surprised that I looked half decent. It helped slightly as I knew I was going to face Donovan and Greg at the shop after last night's mishap.

We bounced over the familiar gate entrance into the shop but the roll-up doors were half closed against the rain and wind. Tristan pulled up close to the roll-up doors so that I could jump out and avoid the rain while he went and parked the Saab in the back. I stood there awkwardly as the shop bustled with work. A couple of customers were standing in the front office, talking animatedly with Charlie from behind the counter. Each lift in the shop had a car being worked on, it was a busy day for L&L.

"Hey, O!" I looked up to see Donovan jogging over to me, a bright smile on his face and his black hair bouncing. He came to a halt in front of me with his fist out. I laughed and hit my fist against his. "Sorry about last night. Hopefully T didn't lay into you too hard…"

Flashes of being bent over the hood of the Saab on Grizzly Peak came to mind and I blushed.

"No, no I'm sorry about last night." I shook my head. "It was just a misunderstanding."

Donovan shrugged and twisted the dirty rag in his hands.

"T tends to overreact, doesn't think things through enough. Glad you guys patched it up though, you're a cool girl."

"Don!" A deep voice barked out. I glanced behind Donovan to see Greg's bald head peeking out from around the hood of a yellow car. "Oh, sorry Ophelia, I didn't know you were here. Glad to see you though." He gave me a stern, knowing nod and I smiled back. Donovan grinned at me and hurried back to whatever it was he was working on with Greg.

Movement in the back of the shop near the door leading to the gym caught my eye. Cherry's eyes were trained on me, narrow and full of hate. Just then, Tristan's arm wrapped around my shoulders. I returned Cherry's hard gaze and reached up to pull Tristan's face down to mine. I smashed my lips against his, felt the surprise in his face before he quickly kissed me back. After a moment, he pulled away, his face hard.

"Not in the shop," he corrected me, and I felt my face burn. "I got the keys, you ready?"

I nodded my head, embarrassed, and followed him back out. It wasn't until we were inside of the Cutlass that he turned on me.

"The fuck was that about?" He quirked an eyebrow at me as the engine gunned to life.

"Cherry!" Her name exploded out of me in exasperation. I slapped my hands against my thighs. "I'm so tired of her *glaring* at me any time that I'm around. She clearly wants you."

"She does," he shrugged. The rain came down hard, it made a river across the windshield before Tristan turned the wipers on. "Cherry is harmless. She's all bark and no bite baby. But that doesn't mean we need to make out like a couple of horny teenagers at my job." He gave me a knowing look.

"What is she even doing there all of the time?" The Cutlass bounced over the gate as we left L&L and hit the street.

"She works there." He looked surprised that I hadn't gathered that by now. "She does paint and ceramic wraps on the cars."

"Of course, she does," I grumbled, and he laughed. "Why is it that when you get jealous you almost choke a guy to death but when I'm jealous about some *broad* who clearly wants you, you think it's funny?" Anger pumped through me. Tristan leaned back comfortably, plopping one wrist on his steering wheel, and using his other hand to hold my trembling hands.

"Firstly, I'm capable of doing a lot more damage than you," he winked, and I glared. "Secondly, Cherry doesn't mean shit to me babe. She's had a crush on me for years but that's all it is."

"Have you ever fucked her?" I countered.

"No." His voice was tight and signaled the end of the conversation. I huffed and turned to look out at the rainy city as we drove through.

Something in the dynamic of our relationship shifted last night but I couldn't quite say what it was. Undeniably, we felt a lot closer as a couple. It was almost as if I could read his thoughts and he could read mine. It had already been hard to say goodbye before, but I was absolutely dreading it now.

We picked Hunter up without incident. Jimmy tried his hardest to advert his eyes from Tristan who was gleefully staring us down as I gathered Hunter in my arms. I immediately smelled urine and knew his diaper was full. Instead of making an argument that I knew would turn physical, I grabbed the full diaper bag and hurried out of the rain. When we got home, I immediately went to clean Hunter up. I gasped when I pulled back the heavy, soiled diaper and saw the large blister on Hunter's bottom.

"You okay? I heard you gasp," Tristan hurried into the

bedroom and skidded to a halt when he saw the angry diaper rash on Hunter's bottom. It was angry, swollen and obviously very painful. Hunter twisted away from me as I tried to blot gently at the stale urine on his skin, anger boiled inside of me.

"He needs a bath to soak the urine off." My voice wavered. I wadded up the old diaper and handed it to Tristan. "Could you throw this away for me please?" Tristan's eyes grew wide as he snatched the diaper from my hand, startled by the weight of it. I looked up at his face, searching. Tristan's hard eyes flicked down to Hunter, crying and squirming on the bed and back to me.

"I'll kill him." He spun on his heel and stormed for the door.

"Tristan!" I shouted and sprinted after him. Miraculously, I made it to the door before him. "You can't do this right now, not after last night."

"How long do you think Hunter was in this diaper for?" Tristan held it up as evidence. It had turned gray. "That shit *burning* his skin? I'll make him fucking eat it." He moved to step around me, but I countered. Hunter's cries began to wail from the bedroom.

"Just let me call him!" I begged.

The sound of a door creaking open made us both look up. Crystal and Steven were standing in the doorway looking alarmed.

"Everything good you guys?" Steven asked, taking in Tristan's furious posture and my begging eyes.

"Call him, I'm going to give Hunter a bath." Tristan whirled around and stormed back into the bedroom, not before he tossed the diaper into Crystal's surprised hands.

"Jimmy…" I explained sheepishly as I took the diaper back and scrambled to pull my phone out of my back pocket. The couple exchanged looks and slinked back into their bedroom.

Jimmy answered after a couple of rings.

"What?" His voice was thick and slow, he was clearly drinking. It wasn't even noon.

"James," I snapped. "Why does Hunter have a blister on his butt the size of a golf ball? His diaper was *soaking wet.*"

"Maybe if you gave me some fucking diaper cream, he wouldn't have a rash," he argued.

"Gave you some? Why can't you go buy some diaper cream? You could've avoided this by just changing his diaper!" I was basically screaming at this point.

"I don't have the money to buy him diaper cream." He hiccupped and I heard him take a long drink of something.

"But you have money to get drunk!" The line clicked off then, he had hung up on me. Tears slid past my lashes despite my best efforts. I stomped over to the kitchen sink and splashed cold water on my face. I took a few shuddering breaths before I went to find them.

Tristan was sitting on the closed toilet lid, his head in his hands when I walked into the bathroom. Hunter happily splashed in shallow water. The air smelled faintly of soap and urine.

"He just gave me excuses."

"I heard." He spoke to the ground, not moving from his stiff position to look at me. I kneeled beside the tub next to Hunter and sadly petted his soft, golden hair.

"Mama! Bubbles!" Hunter laughed as his splashing caused little bubbles in the soapy water.

"Good job baby," I smiled. I picked up a rag and began to gently scrub every inch of Hunter, hushing him softly when he protested me washing his hair. The entire time I bathed him, Tristan sat motionless.

"I'm trying really hard," Tristan finally whispered.

I turned halfway to face him, keeping Hunter in my line of sight as I ducked my head between Tristan's hands to see his face. I hadn't realized he had been shaking.

"I want to be good for you Ophelia, but I just want to rip his fucking throat out. I'd make him swallow that filthy fucking diaper whole."

I sighed and pressed my forehead to his.

"I know you do. I appreciate how upset you are about Hunter, I am too."

Tristan made an annoyed sound and pulled away from me. Tristan's lips were pressed into a hard line, fighting back from saying something. He looked at Hunter then back to me, with a shake of his head he stood up.

"I can't be here right now, I'm too pissed. I'll see you later." Without stopping, he called out over his shoulder: "I promise I won't do anything stupid."

The door slammed violently behind him.

As I listened to the sound of Tristan driving away, there was a loud crash from the living room. I pulled the plug on the drain and wrapped Hunter in a towel to go see what happened. Steven and Crystal already stood in the living room, confused. Lying on the floor was a brick with a piece of paper attached with a rubber band. I stupidly wondered how it got in here then I noticed the gaping hole in the glass window behind the couch. Cold air blew lazily through it, moving the thin curtains like a ghost. "Get it," Crystal elbowed Steven. He opened it carefully as if it were a bomb and read the note written in black ink.

"It just says 'whore' on it," Steven frowned. Crystal and I glanced at each other, both of us wondering who the whore was.

"Wrong apartment," Crystal said and went back to her room, leaving Steven and me. We glanced at each other, and Steven shrugged.

"I'll get the vacuum and then I'll patch up the window."

Tristan
20

I promised I wouldn't do anything stupid, but I didn't know how long I would be able to hold onto that promise. Voices screamed wildly inside of my brain, telling me to hunt Jimmy down and break his neck, another told me to stay away from him. A war raged inside of me pulling me towards each side. I headed for L&L without thinking about it.

The doors were rolled shut so I parked in the back and went through the back door. Music rumbled through the building; the smell of pot smoke met me before I opened the door. Inside was the usual scene: clouds of weed smoke, people stuffing the shop to the brim, falling over each other drunkenly, some having sex on any flat surface they could find and dudes getting head on the couch.

L&L was never really on the up and up but once those doors rolled shut, it was a completely different place. I walked past a girl doing a line of coke off another girl's neck and was intercepted by Tony.

"Ay bruh," he slurred, his eyes thickly glazed over. He stumbled over too close to me, bumped into my chest, and staggered back a step. I frowned down at him already annoyed from the events earlier. "Charlie wants you to meet him at Ballards, Donovan and Cherry are already with him."

"Thanks," I grumbled. I wasn't in the mood to deal with Charlie let alone get involved in whatever he was trying to pull on some unexpecting sop. Charlie and I were killer at playing pool, we took money from anyone who tried to bet against us.

I *definitely* didn't have the patience to deal with Cherry's bullshit.

I got to Ballard's an hour later hoping I was too late to get caught up in whatever Charlie was planning. Charlie's '69 Chevelle with its sparkly gold paint and black racing stripes was parked next to Cherry's brand new, hot pink Dodge Challenger. Cherry wasn't usually invited out for any kind of…meeting unless she was being dangled as a prize. I couldn't stand the bitch but it also fucking disgusted me when Charlie treated her like bait.

Inside Ballards was similar to L&L, minus the sex and drugs. The lights were dim inside, the music too loud and the air was heavy with smoke. Glancing around, I spotted Donovan standing at the pool table, holding a cue nervously. He was shit at pool, something Charlie and I relied on when we were trying to get guys to come over.

"Sup?" I elbowed Donovan in the side. He looked up at me, relieved.

"It's not the usual game tonight," Donovan replied. He nodded toward the back wall with the small built-in tables and bar stools. Charlie was animatedly talking to someone. "But Charlie's up to something, he's been trying to stall until you got here."

"The fuck for?" I frowned down at him. Donovan shrugged just as Charlie noticed me and waved me over. Grudgingly, I made my way over to him.

"Sup?" I repeated, not trying to conceal my irritation. Charlie clapped me proudly on the shoulder and gestured to the guy he had been chatting up.

"Barry this is my son Tristan," Charlie shouted over the music. Dude was getting old. Barry was close to my height but nearly twice as wide. Older than Charlie, he had cropped gray hair and arms so long he looked like an ape. His eyes twinkled when he saw me, and my gut churned. "Hands down the best fucking driver I know."

"Nice to meet you, son." Barry held out his hand.

"You too," I said as I shook his hand. Barry stretched out his hand dramatically as if I had crushed it and I further fought the urge to roll my eyes.

"Woo-wee!" He hollered. "Charlie told me you were a big sumbitch, but I didn't believe him. How tall are you?"

"Six foot five," I retorted. Barry's eyes widened and he held up two fists, shadow boxing the air near my shoulders.

"Man, you must've been fucking terrifying in the ring!" He dropped his fists and laughed loudly. *Homeboy keeps talking, I'ma have to lay him out,* I thought to myself. My temper was flaring.

"Barry here is in the same…autobody business," Charlie tilted his beer towards Barry. "He's looking to form a partnership. We could always use more bodies."

I glanced between the two old dudes; the line had begun to form.

"You call me here for a vote?" I snarled. Charlie laughed but there was an edge, a warning. Barry presented an opportunity for Charlie to make more money, that was the endgame here.

"Charlie was saying that maybe you could teach my boy how to drive like you," Barry said. The glint in his eye was growing, I'm sure all the old dude could see was money signs. Without turning, Barry waved eagerly at someone. "C'mere Micah." A gangly, sheepish guy walked over with his eyes downcast. He had a very young face but the thick, black stubble across his jaw made him look older.

"Hi," the guy lifted one hand quickly, his eyes darted up to look at me and back down.

Is he retarded? I thought darkly.

"Your kid?" I asked. "How old is he?"

"He's young," Barry shrugged. "But he's smart, sharp as a nail and he's a quick learner. Take him on a few runs and I'm sure he'll be driving *circles* around you." Barry laughed loudly and affectionately shook Micah by the shoulders. Micah laughed awkwardly as Charlie's hand tightened on my elbow in another warning.

"When is this supposed to go down?" I asked.

"In a few weeks," Charlie took a long swig from his beer. "We got some details to iron out."

"We *sure do.*" The way Barry dragged out the words made my head snap back to him. His eyes were trained on something behind me, I knew what had his attention before I even turned around. Cherry was bent over the pool table, reaching with the cue stick to make a shot. Dressed in her usual fucking style, her tits were all but spilling out of her top. Her long red hair spilled over the pool table like a red wave of blood. "There more of *her* at your shop?" Barry licked his lips.

"Plenty," I rolled my eyes. In fact, the shop was full of attention seeking, half-dressed women. Most of them were already high or had a dick in their mouths. There was never a shortage of snatch at L&L. Cherry was always jocking on my shit, but she didn't open her legs for everyone that Charlie dragged through the shop. She might here and there but it was because that's what *she* wanted. I hated when Charlie paraded her around. Acting as if I was just shifting my weight, I blocked Barry's view of Cherry.

The conversation drifted so I broke away to find Donovan. He was stuffing his face with a piece of greasy pizza and held up a second plate with a slice for me. I laughed and took it gratefully, I was starving. We hung back and watched Cherry kick Barry's ass at pool which was hilarious. Luckily Charlie didn't plan on scamming anyone other than Barry tonight, so I wasn't expected to play. Feeling bad for the kid, Donovan called Micah over and they began talking off to the side. *Always one to take others under his wing*, I smirked.

"Hey Tristan," Cherry purred at me. I nodded to her; my mouth full of pizza. She made a point to bend over in front of me for her next shot, pushing her ass out far enough to brush my crotch. I chuckled despite myself and moved away. She sank her shot and jumped up and down cheering. Her tits bounced wildly in her top, every guy around her stared hungrily.

I caught Donovan's gaze and raised an eyebrow. He looked away bashfully. It was no secret that Donovan had a thing for Cherry so I couldn't help but give him a hard time. Donovan was *well* aware of the times Cherry blew me but for whatever reason, it didn't deter him.

Cherry sauntered over with a wide, cocky smirk on her face. "Feel like I haven't seen you in forever."

"Just at the shop the other day." I shrugged nonchalantly. She sighed heavily and dramatically fell into my chest.

"Whatever you say lover boy," she hummed. "Oh! I wanted to show you something." She jumped up quickly and pulled her phone from her back pocket. She swiped through pictures of a recent paint job she did.

"Wow Cher, these are amazing." I was genuinely impressed. Cherry knew her shit that's for sure. Her hand painted work was amazing, she didn't need anything other than two hands to make some of the cleanest line work I've ever seen. "You could get a spot at a real shop and make good money; I don't know what you're doing slumming it at L&L." The fair skin of her cheeks turned pink, and she looked down at her phone bashfully.

"I don't know," she shrugged. "Just hoping things change I guess." She looked at me with her large, blue eyes with hope. I stiffened.

"Things don't change, Cher."

Eventually it was time to go. Charlie was hammered, much to no one's surprise. Him and Barry hung onto each other, laughing boisterously as they stumbled out of Ballards. Charlie tripped and lay on the dirty sidewalk, laughing so hard that no sound came out.

"That was a blast, man," Barry chuckled. "Charlie gimme a call sometime next week and we'll get the ball rolling."

"You bet!" Charlie rolled onto his stomach and struggled to get up. Barry threw a couple of jabs that he considered fast in my way and winked.

"I'll be seeing you, Mountain." He continued laughing as he stumbled into the parking lot towards his car, Micah following quickly behind. I rolled my eyes and stepped over Charlie.

"Get up," I snarled. I grabbed him by his upper arm and hoisted him up to his feet.

"Whoa!" He laughed as he struggled to get his feet under him. "What? You mad that you can't get any *bigger*?" He pinched his eyes shut as laughter rocked his body.

"You need any help?" Cherry asked.

"Nah, you guys' head on out, I'm good."

I dragged Charlie to his Chevelle, ignoring his protests along the way. I tossed him into the passenger seat and gunned the engine. The only thing I ever wanted from Charlie was this fucking car. He had it since I was born, and he put countless hours into maintaining it. Pretty sure it was the only thing Charlie actually owned or gave a shit about. It was supposed to be a high school graduation gift from my grandma, but Charlie never got there. She gave him the car anyways. Nan was a pushover.

Five minutes into the drive Charlie was passed out. Not much longer after that we pulled up to the house. The passenger door swung open, and Charlie tumbled out onto the driveway. I briefly contemplated leaving him there but decided against it. I already owed him money for the repairs on the house. I hefted him up and over my shoulder like a hunter carrying their kill home and walked him inside of my childhood home.

I tossed him onto his bed, but he still didn't wake up. I rolled him on his side and wedged a pillow behind his back to keep him in that spot in case he threw up and left him there. He was snoring loudly. The house was dark and smelled of fresh paint. Charlie had hired a crew immediately to clean up my mess. I flicked on a few lights as I walked around, checking out the repairs. Even though I knew better, I toed the door of my old bedroom open.

All My Life

The garbage had been hauled out, as well as the box spring that had been my bed, the crates and old tv. The small room was now filled with paint cans, tarps, plaster, and other shit. I don't know what I was expecting, it's not like he would have preserved my bedroom, or hell, made it better. Not like I did with Millie's bedroom…

My chest squeezed unexpectedly, and I stomped away from my childhood bedroom. I went into the living room and collapsed on the couch. The price tags were still attached. Charlie's snores echoed down the hall, a familiar and unsettling sound. I hadn't visited this house much after moving in with Nan as a teenager. If I could have, I would have burnt it down. I don't know why I was here now; all I knew was that I needed space from Ophelia, and I didn't want to be home. Didn't want to be around Millie's ghost that lingered there.

Despite the years of abuse in this house, I just wanted something familiar. But her ghost was here too. With a sigh, I pulled my cell phone out of my jacket pocket.

Ophelia: I love you, goodnight.

As pissed off as I might be at her and her inability to tell Jimmy to fuck off, I loved her so much it hurt. All I wanted was a life with her and Hunter, but I didn't see how that was possible with Jimmy around. *I could kill him*, I thought. Wouldn't be the first time and by now the crew and I had gotten pretty good at hiding bodies. Guilt gnawed at me, I knew that if I did that and had to lie to Ophelia and comfort her when she heard the news, it would kill me. But I was still too heated to reply to her. I tossed my phone on the floor along with my keys as well as Charlie's and fell asleep.

I was seven years old again, riding in the back of Charlie's Chevelle with Donovan. Donny's dad had split a year prior, so his mom was more than happy to let him spend the summer at my house. They didn't live far in a small, blue house just a few blocks over. We were on our way down to the beach early in the morning before the summer heat settled in. This summer had seen record highs that made people's AC units run double time until they gave out.

Charlie had all the windows down in the Chevelle, his cigarette smoke blew wildly in the cab. Donovan and I had turned around in our seats, sitting on our knees so we could play with our mini, green Army Guys on the back of the seat.

"Pew-pew-pew!" Donovan mimicked a machine gun, jabbing his Army Guy at mine.

"Ahh!" My Army Guy flipped backwards dramatically before it landed with a small thump on the brown leather. "You killed me!" Donovan threw his head back, his shaggy black hair fell away from his pale, round face as he laughed.

"No one can defeat Captain Mustard's army!" He cheered.

"You're my best friend, Donny," I told him. It wasn't a heartfelt pouring of emotions; it was the simple exchange of young children. But I knew Donny and I were closer than most friends, he was more like a brother to me. Donny was my age but very small forhis age, the clothes Charlie gave him–hand me downs from when I grew out of them–were much too long for him.

"You're mine!" He shrugged and we went back to playing Army Guys.

I woke from my dream in a cold sweat It was early morning, the muted light trickled in through the front windows illuminating the room around me. The daylight burned away the veil that the nighttime had casted over this house, and I shuddered. I didn't want to be here. I jumped up to my feet and spun around when I heard Charlie behind me.

He looked like shit. Still wearing yesterday's clothes, down to the boots, he dragged his withered body into the living room. A cigarette dangled from his thin lips, the smoke bothering his eyes as he handed me a cup of coffee.

"Thanks," he grumbled.

"You look like shit." I took the cup of coffee and sank back down onto the couch. Charlie groaned as he plopped down onto the La-Z-Boy recliner.

"I feel like it."

We sat in silence for a while, both sipping coffee and watching the morning news. The sense of discomfort in the smoky air between us slowly eased as the coffee warmed us up and the sleep fell away. I was still feeling on edge from my dream, still trying to shake the remnants from my mind. I tried not to remember the nights I slept on the couch because Charlie had a girl over and they were fucking loudly in the back bedroom, keeping me awake. Or the nights I couldn't handle being home anymore, so I snuck out to Donovan's. Donovan's mom would drive me home the next day without a word.

Eventually Charlie went to shower as I rolled up a blunt on the wooden coffee table. He had told me to get one ready for when he got out of the shower and provided the weed, so I agreed. Charlie was shit at rolling anyways and free weed was free weed. I packed as much dry, dank weed as I could into the blunt wrapper, forcing it to roll closed. I enjoyed rolling, it was a process that didn't take much thought or concentration, allowing my mind to float free and wonder.

I thought of Ophelia. The way her dark brown hair cascaded down her back, the voluptuous curves of her hips and the thickness of her thighs. The curve of her lips and her green eyes, the way they were flecked and yellow in the center. They reminded me of the grapes I ate on the beach during the summer as a child. She made me laugh which wasn't something easily brought out of me. There wasn't anything I wouldn't do for her, she had me wrapped around her finger tightly. I found myself missing her the more I thought of her, sorry for my earlier behavior.

My phone had died since I didn't charge it last night. It was a Wednesday which meant she had work, maybe I could go see her and my great grandma this afternoon. I hadn't seen my great grandma in a while, it was time I went to check on her.

Charlie came back into the living room and plopped back down on his recliner, nodding at me to spark up the blunt. We sat silently for a while just smoking and getting higher while we watched the news.

"That cop chick might come in handy," Charlie said offhandedly as he exhaled a cloud of smoke.

"Bitch is a freak," I ran a hand through my hair. "Not happening."

Charlie chuckled and stretched until his joints popped.

"Let's get going, we gotta open the shop."

"For sure, I gotta swing by Ballards and scoop up my whip though." I stubbed out the roach on the table and left the mess for him to clean.

The sun was just edging over the roofs of the houses on the quiet street, painting everything in a subdued hue as we emerged from the house. My shoes clomped loudly on the broken cement steps as I walked through the overgrown weeds towards the driveway. I hesitated for a moment, taking in the way the morning glow reflected in the gold paint. Charlie's Chevelle had always been gold, but Cherry had recently revamped the paint and it looked killer.

Something was off. The Chevelle sagged awkwardly to one side, it took me a moment to realize what I was looking at.

"The fuck?" I frowned. I hurried over and bent to inspect the driver side tire. A deep gash sliced through the black rubber; someone had slashed all four of Charlie's tires.

"What the fuck?!" Charlie bellowed, running up behind me. "What the fuck?!" He repeated.

I stood up and met his confused glare.

"Who did you piss off–last night?" I said. There wasn't a lack of people that Charlie might have fucked over but for this to happen suddenly, without warning, was startling. How many times did the crew get into shit because of Charlie or because we backed each other up? Usually there was some kind of buildup, some sort of tension between a known target and us. Things had been chill for a while, maybe we were due.

"Fucking no one." Charlie shook his head. "I don't know who would've done this. Did anyone follow you last night?"

"No." I answered quickly. I had a habit of checking my rear view and noticing cars wherever I went, a bit of occupational hazard. "I'll call Don, give me your phone."

After a quick call to Don, he showed up about thirty minutes later in the Jeep with new tires. A perk for working at the shop. With the three of us, we changed out the tires like some sort of Nascar pit crew and had the Chevelle ready to go in a matter of seconds.

"Man, that's personal." Don shook his head. "Coming after a guy's car."

"When I find out who did it, they're dead." Charlie spat as he threw the last shredded tire into the back of the Jeep.

"Must've been some punk ass teenagers acting tough," Don said.

Charlie mumbled under his breath and walked away.

I drove with Donovan back to Ballard's to get my car. Now that we were heading back to pick it up, I was anxious to see Ophelia.

"Ay, you have a charger in here?" I asked, looking through the empty console.

"Like this is *my* car." Don said. "You worried about your lady friend?"

"Yeah." I didn't try to hide my anxiety or act tough, not in front of Don. Honestly, the way I felt for Ophelia was so fucking obvious I knew the entire shop was well aware of how bent I was over her. My searching came up empty and I groaned, slamming the glove compartment closed.

"Can you drive faster?" I snarled. Donovan laughed in response which only made me more heated. The Jeep noticeably decelerated on the highway.

"I'm just kidding," Don laughed again as he pushed down on the accelerator. I punched him softly in the shoulder, and he winced. His face grew serious suddenly.

"Mom isn't doing too well," he sighed. "She keeps getting pneumonia, doctors don't think she has very long left."

I didn't answer immediately, instead I studied him. Donovan was still very much a kid at heart despite the cards that life had dealt him. He never lost the sense of humor, the glint of hope in his eye. Five years ago, his mom, Tasoula, was diagnosed with breast cancer and she deteriorated quickly. The cancer spread to her heart and lungs and rendered her completely bedridden. Honestly, he should've let her go a year ago, but he spent all of his hard-earned money on keeping her alive.

I couldn't really blame him. She was the closest thing I ever had to a mother and all she ever did was give me a place to crash and made me pancakes on Saturday mornings. She did bail me out of jail the first couple of times when I was a teen though…

"What do you need?" I asked. Wind whipped through the Jeep, flattening Don's shirt against him and flinging my hair into my eyes. He shrugged and pulled off the highway onto our exit.

"It would be nice if you came by," he said without looking at me. It was another minute before I could answer. I reached out and put my arm around his shoulders and pulled him towards me. I rested my forehead against the side of his head and sighed. Donovan was really the closest I would ever get to having a brother. I could feel his pain. Our embrace was quick but the unspoken message between us made my chest tighten.

"Tonight," I nodded and looked away.

My hands trembled as I cut off the engine of my Cutlass. Nighttime had fallen, coating these familiar streets in a blanket of darkness. The light posts did little to light the streets, the county didn't do shit to maintain them in the ghetto. I was parked outside of Donovan's house, but I didn't want to go inside. Not yet. I pinched my eyes shut as waves of crushing dismay washed over me. Could I really bring myself inside to see Tasoula?

Brief memories of her long, strawberry blonde hair brushing across my face as a child came to mind. The smell of her perfume, the way she painted her face up every day. She had been so beautiful before the sickness took her. She had been a young mother, lost and without guidance. She worked a number of odd jobs to provide for Donovan but wasn't ever able to elevate their living situation.

A few times, she had packed me a lunch for school when Charlie wasn't home or didn't give a shit. She had run her fingers through my hair and patted my back the first time Katherine and I had broken up. She had driven Donovan to the hospital when he was too distraught to after my attempted suicide. I completely abandoned her when her sickness became too real for me, when her hair began to fall out and her cheeks became hollow. I had already lost one mother that I didn't get a chance to know, I didn't see how I could say goodbye to another.

But she's Donovan's mother too, I realized. I hadn't just abandoned Tasoula, I had also abandoned Donovan. I left him to deal with everything. After a few more seconds, I steeled myself and got out of my car.

I didn't need to knock. Though it had been some time since I had been here last, this house was still my second home. The thin front door creaked open, and I was immediately catapulted back to when I was a teenager. The front of the house was dark, the only light came from the back of the house where Tasoula's bedroom was.

I stepped inside slowly, almost nervous to disturb the silence of the place. I went to the kitchen and scrubbed my hands in the small, silver sink with scalding hot water. I washed all the grease off that had accumulated from work earlier. Even after my hands were as clean as they were going to get, the water ran clear, I kept scrubbing.

And scrubbing.

A hand gently grabbed my shoulder, and I lost it. I collapsed onto the counter; heavy sobs racked me. Tears poured hot and quickly down my cheeks as I rested my forehead against the counter. Donovan's hands grabbed at me, turning me away and I threw my arms around him, crushing him to me. He held me silently as I cried into his shoulder. Cried for not being here for her, for not helping him when I knew that he needed me. Finally, I stilled, and I pulled away, wiping my face.

"Let's go see mom." He clapped me on the back. I didn't know what death row felt like, of what walking to the gallows felt like but I assumed this was close. Donovan's arm was wrapped around my shoulders reassuringly and I hated that he was the one comforting me. I entered her bedroom and my breath caught in my throat. No longer were there red scarves draped over the lamps to cast a sensual glow, no longer did she have the golden, loopy bed frame. Instead, everything seemed sterile. Her bed had been replaced by a hospital bed.

The scarves were gone to allow bright light into the room. Two IV poles were placed beside her hospital bed, the room smelled of disinfectant. The only thing that was the same was the llama blanket folded carefully over her lower half. One of the machines beeped quietly in the background.

Tasoula had been curvy and beautiful just a few years ago. Now she was frail, gray, and sunken in. Just under 50, she looked much older and much more fragile. Tubes and medical lines ran from the machines and into her body. She was on a ventilator; the tubing was taped into her slack jaw and her eyes were closed. Her head was covered in a silk cap. Donovan gently ushered me into the room when I hesitated and led me over to a fold up chair beside the bed. I sank down heavily into it, the metal groaned beneath me.

"Hey mom," Donovan greeted her. I watched as he bent over her hospital bed and placed a hand on her shoulder. She didn't move. "Tristan is here." Donovan glanced at me expectantly and I swallowed the lump in my throat.

"H-hi mom," I stammered awkwardly. I don't know what I expected but when she didn't open her eyes, my shoulders slumped. I inched forward on the small chair, leaning my elbows onto my knees. "S-sorry I haven't come by sooner, just been busy."

"He met a girl," Donovan smirked, elbowing me to continue.

"Yeah, I did. She's great, she's going to school to be a nurse and she has a little boy." My voice caught in my throat. "You would really like her." My throat constricted then, and I couldn't go on.

Donovan caught the look in my face and picked up for me.

"She's really great," he added. "They met because Tristan saved her life."

Despite myself, I laughed. I hadn't thought of that night since it happened—too enthralled with getting to know Ophelia instead.

"Yeah, I guess I did, she wasn't paying attention and almost got flattened by a truck. She's clumsy." I suddenly remembered earlier, and my eyebrows shot up. "Charlie's tires were slashed earlier this morning."

"Crazy," Donovan shook his head.

"We don't know who it did but–you know how Charlie is." Again, I chuckled, enjoying the weight that was lifted from my shoulders. Before I knew what I was doing, I reached over and took her hand in my own as if it were any other day. I could feel the brittle bones beneath her thin skin. "I'm sorry this is happening to you, mom. I wish I could take it all away, I hope it doesn't hurt. Luckily you have Donny here taking such good care of you all this time. He's a really good kid."

"She already knows that." Don elbowed me with a smirk.

Seeing Tasoula lying there, one of the few good people in my life—someone who treated me with actual kindness was too much. Panic rose up like a wave inside me until I couldn't stand it anymore.

"I have to go." I stood up quickly causing the chair to shoot out from behind me. I turned as I reached Tasoula's bedroom door. "I'll come back…just…just let me know if you need anything."

Donovan nodded knowingly and I left.

Ophelia
21

Something clinked against my bedroom window, but I ignored it, it was probably from something falling from a nearby tree. However, the second and third time snagged my attention. I stilled as I listened for the *plink*, Hunter was fast asleep in his bed next to mine. Homework was sprawled across my bed, they fluttered gently in the breeze from the box fan in my window.

Crystal and Steven were in the living room having one of their smoke-out parties, so I had turned the fan on full blast and stuffed a towel under the door. The box fan was loud, thumping in its plastic container but the sound of something bouncing off my window was still detectable. When it came again, I stood on tiptoes on my bed to peer out the dark window.

The street was empty. I squinted, peering at the row of parked cars but when a full two minutes passed and nothing happened, I gave up. As I turned to sit back down, another *plink* came from outside. I groaned and spun around quickly just in time to see a dark figure standing in the street. My heart leapt at the sudden intrusion. Maybe it's just a coincidence, I tried to calm myself. That thought was quickly shattered as I watched the figure lift its hand and throw another rock at my window. He was deliberately doing it, but I couldn't tell who he was. I flipped him off and quickly lowered the plastic blinds.

The sound came again. A rock bouncing off the window.

Then again.

And again.

Quicker in succession now. He was antagonizing me. My heart pounded painfully as I grabbed for my phone.

"Hey babe!" Tristan greeted; he had answered on the first ring.

"Tristan, there's some guy standing outside of my bedroom window throwing rocks at me." The words came out in a rush, I wasn't sure he even understood what I had said. There was a brief pause on the other end.

"Turn your light off so he can't see inside. Are you home alone?" There was a crashing sound from his end of the line, then it sounded like he was running. I jumped up and clicked the light off just as another rock hit the window, much harder this time. I glanced at Hunter nervously, but he was sound asleep.

"No Crystal and Steven are home." A car door slammed in the background, followed by a second door slamming. Assuming Donovan was coming with Tristan as backup, I relaxed slightly.

"Can you still see him?" Tristan's voice was tight, careful. I tiptoed back over to the window and pulled apart the blind to peer through it nervously.

"No," I whispered. The street was empty.

"I'm coming baby, just close your blinds and back away from the window." Doing as I was told, I crouched on the floor next to Hunter's bed. He snored softly; the sound was calming.

A few minutes later I heard the roar of Tristan's engine rumbling outside in the parking lot. My heart pounded loudly in my ears as I listened for any commotion outside, but none came. My bedroom door flew open, and I jumped with a loud gasp.

Tristan's eyes scanned my bedroom and found me quickly in my spot crouched beside Hunter. Relief washed over his face and his shoulders relaxed. I hopped up and ran over to throw my arms around his waist.

"Don and I didn't see anyone outside," he reassured me, his large hand smoothed my back. "Probably just some asshole teenager playing a prank on you."

"Didn't look like a teenager to me," I grumbled. Tristan chuckled and pushed me back to look down at me.

"I'm glad you're careful but you get scared too easily."

Not long after Tristan showed up, Crystal and Steven ended up going to Steven's house. It was evident that they didn't like Tristan and I was glad, it meant I didn't have to hide in my bedroom anymore. Donovan and Tristan hung out for a few hours to see if my visitor came back but there wasn't a sign of him.

Maybe Tristan was right, and it was just some kid playing a prank. Nevertheless, they scared the crap out of me. I snuggled into Tristan's side on the couch as the three of us watched a movie and I realized how nice this was. Donovan was sprawled out on the loveseat while Tristan and I were on the couch. I felt safe. Something I never felt with Jimmy. I dozed off during the movie happily.

I was exceptionally sleepy today. I nearly dozed off on the BART train heading to school which would've meant that I missed my stop. We were due to turn in the first portion of our Microbiology project today and I had the materials, so if I had missed my stop, it would've hurt David's grade as well. I dragged myself off the train and into school, barely registering my surroundings. David was already perched on the metal stool at our lab table when I walked in.

"You sleep, okay?" He eyed me.

"Think I slept *too* well, actually," I smirked. Flashes of Tristan's head between my legs last night, his hand over my mouth to keep me quiet on the couch made my body flush with heat. An unreadable expression flickered through David's eyes, and he looked away just as Professor Whitmore entered the room.

I rifled through my backpack to pull out our first

assignment and handed it over to David to look through.

"Looks good." He nudged me with his shoulder. "Glad I got you as a lab partner."

I laughed and settled into my stool as Professor Whitmore came around to collect the papers. Professor Whitmore began his lecture then about anaerobic and aerobic microbes and I hurriedly jotted down notes. My hand began cramping after about an hour, just in time for Professor Whitmore to call for a ten-minute break.

"Man, that stuff went right over my head," David groaned. He leaned his elbows onto the desk and dropped his head into his hands dramatically.

"It's okay, I'll help you understand it for the next section of our project," I laughed.

"Speaking of." David said. His brown eyes were searching, but for what I didn't know. "If we get a jump start on the next section, we can get it done pretty quick." I glanced down at the schedule on the front of my binder that had each due date highlighted. He was right, we should probably want to get moving on the next section.

"Okay, sure. When do you want to come over again?"

"Tonight?" A hopeful gleam flickered across his face and my mind immediately went to the late-night text I had received from him. My stomach knotted nervously. Before I could answer, my phone rang, saving me from the embarrassing moment. I answered without looking at the caller ID.

"Hello?" I breathed. A robotic, pre-recorded voice came on the other end.

"This is a call from an inmate at Contra Costa County Jail—"

"Ophelia? Can I come over tonight?" David ducked his head closer to mine.

"Do you accept the charge?" The robotic voice continued.

"Uh, sure," I replied to both.

A moment later, Jimmy's voice was on the other end.

"Hey O, it's me," he said quickly.

"Jimmy," I groaned and dropped my head into my hand. "You're in jail again?"

"Yeah, they're trying to pin another DUI on me," he continued.

"A DUI?" I frowned. "Jimmy! You were supposed to pick up Hunter tonight. Were you going to pick him up *drunk*?"

A couple of heads turned to look back at me as my voice rose. I struggled to lower it.

"I wasn't drinking *today*," Jimmy snapped. "I was drinking last night. Anyways, listen. I need you to bail me out. It's $750."

"$750? Absolutely the fuck not. I don't have that money, Jimmy."

"Come on, O," he begged. "I don't want to stay here."

"Fuck you." I hung up and squeezed my eyes shut tightly against the headache that had begun to pound.

"You, okay?" David whispered.

I shook my head and quickly began dialing my mom.

"Mom!" I shrieked when she answered, no longer caring who in my class was staring at me. "Jimmy is in jail again—can you pick up Hunter from daycare? I won't make it in time if I leave now."

"Oh baby," my mom crooned. "I'm sorry but I'm out of town all week remember?"

"Oh, that's right I forgot about the convention for your work. It's okay! It's okay! Gotta go!" I quickly hung up and dialed again as Professor Whitmore came back into the classroom.

"Hey baby! Aren't you in class?" Tristan greeted.

"Yes, I am and that's the problem. Jimmy just called—he's in jail, he was supposed to pick Hunter up in thirty minutes from daycare. I won't make it there in time."

"I'll get him." His voice was even, too calm. I didn't have time to focus on what he was possibly thinking or feeling, I just needed my son picked up from daycare. "I have the access code for the gate and the car seat in my trunk already. Do you need me to come get you too?" I glanced at the clock on the wall and bit my lip. By the time Tristan picked up Hunter and made it to me, it would be over an hour after class was out. Thinking about waiting outside in the dark next to the homeless encampment made me nervous.

David, overhearing, leaned in and whispered: "I can take you; we have to work on our project anyways."

"Um, no it's okay. My lab partner offered to take me home."

"Cool," Tristan's voice was tight. Professor Whitmore clapped his hands together, signaling that break was over.

"Thank you so much Tristan, I have to go. I love you; I'll see you soon." I hung up before I could hear his response.

I could hardly focus the rest of class, too riled up from everything that happened in the last ten minutes. Jimmy and I had been on a good roll these last few months, he kept Hunter when he was supposed to and didn't ask me to pick him up early. I knew that, largely, it was due to Jimmy being scared of Tristan.

Good, I thought darkly. One of these days I was going to let Tristan do whatever he wanted to Jimmy. David stayed silent but continued to peek at me from the corner of my eye when he thought that I wasn't looking.

I sighed again and rested my chin on my folded arms across my papers, no longer able to focus. I didn't even notice when Professor Whitmore excused the class until David stood up.

"You ready?" He smiled down at me. I jolted up right and began stuffing my things into my backpack haphazardly. Silently, I fell into line behind David as we exited the building. I followed him over to a royal blue Firebird.

"This is your car?" I couldn't help but smirk. "What? Are you supposed to be the hot guy in a teenage romcom?" I laughed.

David's eyes grew wide as he halted to a stop at the driver's side door. He barked out a laugh.

"That's actually really funny," he laughed again. My cheeks blushed when I realized what David might have heard in my statement even though it was a joke.

"It's unlocked."

The inside was black leather and smelled like mint. My phone buzzed as a text came in.

Tristan: I have Hunter we're at your house

As David fired up the engine and pulled away from the school, I realized suddenly that it might not be a good idea for Tristan to meet David. *He's just my lab partner*, I argued silently. Still, my stomach churned nervously the closer we got to my apartment. "You've been really quiet," David pointed as he pulled off onto my exit. *I'm worried about my temperamental boyfriend…* I thought. "Just upset about how today turned out," I said instead.

David nodded knowingly as we made a few turns and pulled onto my street. My heart leapt when I saw Tristan's large, white Cutlass parked in the parking lot. I suddenly regretted having David take me home, it might have been better to brave the homeless encampment in the dark.

I guided David on how to park in the haphazard parking lot and got out nervously. From the distance it took for me to walk from David's Firebird to my front door, I tried desperately to think of an excuse to send David away or for what I would say to Tristan to calm him down. My mind came up blank.

My hand trembled as I twisted the doorknob, David stood just a foot behind me. The door slowly creaked open, and we stepped inside. Tristan glanced up; his indigo eyes met mine for a fraction of a second before they flashed up to David behind me. When his eyes met mine again, they were hard. I swallowed.

"Hi baby," I smiled at Hunter, trying to convey ease as I tossed my bag onto the couch. Tristan had Hunter in his lap, trying to soothe him to sleep. I was pleased to see that Hunter was bathed and in a fresh pair of pajamas.

"I fed him dinner." Tristan stared passed me straight at David as he spoke.

"Thank you." I kissed the top of Hunter's head and leaned over to kiss Tristan's cheek. He didn't move or look at me. "Tristan, this is David, my lab partner. David, this is my boyfriend, Tristan."

"Nice to meet you," David said. Tristan didn't respond, didn't take his eyes off David.

"I'm going to put Hunter to bed," I mumbled. Hunter was already half asleep when I had walked in. I scooped Hunter out of Tristan's arms and carried him quickly to the bedroom. My heart pounded loudly in my ears as I tucked Hunter into his little bed.

"Night mama," Hunter yawned, his eyes already closed.

"Night baby." I smoothed his blonde hair until he began to snore softly. Grudgingly, unable to stall any longer, I went back into the living room. Neither had moved from their spot. Tristan continued to stare at David, his eyes ablaze, his jaw set tightly. I stood there awkwardly, unsure of what to do.

Crystal's door swung open, and Steven walked out. He fell back a step before he could plow into me and followed my eyes to the awkward standoff in the living room.

"Uh, who's this?" Steven frowned at David.

"Ophelia's lab partner." Tristan finally spoke, still without looking away from David.

"Lab partner? Oh, the guy you had over the other night?" Steven glanced at me. A chill spread through me as if someone had dripped ice down my spine.

"What?" Tristan's head snapped to me, and I flinched. Steven groaned softly, realizing his mistake.

"David came over to work on part of our project," I explained quickly. "It's a huge project worth 50% of our grade."

Tristan's face was unreadable, but a hint of hurt darkened his fiery green-blue eyes.

"Fuck this." Tristan pushed past me towards the door, and I hurried after him.

"Tristan!" I hissed, grabbing for his arm. Tristan pulled out of my grip effortlessly. The door slammed behind him so hard that the glass rattled. A few seconds later, his engine roared to life, and I listened as the sound diminished as he drove away. Tears stung my eyes. It wasn't fair, his behavior, the way I had to tiptoe around his temper and jealousy.

I hadn't told Tristan about David because I wanted to avoid this reaction but me *not* telling Tristan made it seem as if I was hiding it which was worse. After a few deep breaths, I composed myself enough to turn around to face David. Steven had slunk away back into Crystal's bedroom, thankfully. I might have ripped his head off if I laid eyes on him.

"I'm sorry," I blurted.

David shrugged and smiled.

"No worries, I get it. Do you need a minute?" He ducked his head to meet my gaze and I forced a grin.

"N-no, I'm okay," I replied, though my voice shook. "Let's just get started."

I sat crisscrossed on the couch as far to one side as I could while David sprawled out on the end of the other. David ended up doing most of the work while I sat there, numbly staring off into space. Occasionally, I would nod my head and agree with whatever he said, no longer giving a damn about the project or my grade. I felt like I had been deflated, shrunk, and shriveled up under Tristan's glare.

David graciously let me melt into my despair without a word, trying his best to make me laugh. After a couple of hours, I was exhausted and had no idea what we had accomplished.

"I'm beat," David sighed, leaning back heavily away from his laptop and sinking into the couch. He rubbed his red eyes. I glanced down at the clock on my phone and saw that it was almost ten pm…and that Tristan hadn't tried to contact me.

"We got a lot done," I mumbled. I had crossed off items on our to-do list for this section as David instructed me to do. I stared down at the paper in my lap without really seeing it. "I'm tired too."

David nodded sleepily and began to pack up his work. We stood at the same time, my knees popping from having been bent and smashed under me for the last couple of hours. I winced as the blood flowed back to my toes. David stretched his arms up over his head with a groan, the hem of his shirt lifted to expose a deep V line between his hips. I looked away quickly.

"Guess we really don't have to meet for a while," David said, his voice glum. "Since we got so much done tonight."

I nodded quietly as I followed him to the door.

"Sorry I'm such a crappy lab partner…and for earlier." I bit my bottom lip, fighting back the urge to cry. David turned as he reached the door and gently lifted my chin with his knuckle.

"Listen Ophelia, you don't deserve that," he said softly, his eyes searching mine frantically. "We aren't doing anything *bad* here, just homework. There's no reason for him to act like that."

I pulled my chin out of his hand and shook my head.

"Tristan's past is…complicated," I said. "He gets hurt easily."

"How fair is that to you?" He frowned. When I didn't answer, he smiled softly. "I'll see you next week. Let me know if you need anything."

I had to call out of work the next two days in a row because Jimmy was in jail, my mom was out of town and Tristan wouldn't respond to me. Missing work meant that certain bills wouldn't get paid. I sat on Serena's couch with the calculator app on my phone and a notebook while Hunter and Alicia played in Alicia's room.

"I can't fucking believe that." Serena shook her head as she walked back into the living room. She handed me a plate of mole poblano that she had cooked for us. The kids both ate their small servings but were too excited about playing, their plates were left to cool on the table. Serena had offered to watch Hunter for me but with her own work schedule, I would have missed most of my shift anyways. "Sounds like your man has some serious anger issues."

I took a bite of the smothered chicken and set it aside to cool as I mulled over if I should tell her something.

"A few months ago, I found prescription bottles of Lithium and Zoloft at Tristan's house."

Serena stared at me silently for a moment before she pulled her cell phone out and began to Google. "He has anxiety…and he's bipolar."

"I know what they're for." I leaned my head back onto her couch and stared up at the ceiling. The fact that he had mental health disorders didn't deter me but instead made me worry for him. He couldn't *help* how his mood fluctuated or how easily he was set off, coupled with a hard past with Katherine–I couldn't blame Tristan. "But he's also *not* taking them."

"Which he should! He's obviously not managing them well on his own." Serena gestured wildly and I rolled my eyes. I attempted to go back to my notebook to see what I could afford to skip this month to pay other bills like my gas and rent. I clicked out a few numbers on the calculator and quickly hit the clear button. It took me four tries before I calculated correctly.

"I need to tell my case worker that I'm missing work," I grumbled. "Maybe they can help me out more this month." Suddenly irritated, I slammed my notebook closed. I pulled my plate over and began to shovel food into my mouth.

"Can you pick up shifts at work to make it up?" Serena suggested. I gulped down the last bite and stood to take my plate into the kitchen.

"If they need me then I probably can." I continued talking

as I dumped my plate into the sink and began scrubbing it clean. "But I have this huge project for Microbiology that I need to work on." I chewed my lip, thinking about the events of the other night. David didn't look surprised at how upset Tristan had become, and honestly neither was I. I hadn't even told Tristan about the text message from David.

I hated this so much.

I hated having so much on my shoulders and being the only one able to carry the burden. It was moments like this that I resented Jimmy for not growing into the father that I had hoped he would. I wanted the family I thought I would have. Tristan had already proven to be a better father to Hunter than Jimmy, but the rollercoaster of his volatile emotions was exhausting.

He was possessive. Though a small, stupid, part of me was thrilled at the thought of his jealousy, it really made my life increasingly difficult.

Alicia and Hunter came running out of Alicia's room giggling. "Mama, we sleep here?" Hunter's big brown eyes looked up at me hopefully.

"I think that would be fun," Serena said as she entered the kitchen with her own empty plate.

"Yes!" Hunter's little fist shot up in the air and we laughed. The kids both ran away back to play.

"I'll just grab his pajamas and a toothbrush," I said. It was already Hunter's bedtime. I headed out of Serena's apartment to make the short walk down the pathway to the stairs that would lead me up to my own apartment. My eyes immediately flicked across the parking lot out of habit and my heart leapt when I saw the clunky Cutlass. Tristan stood leaning against the side, smoking a cigarette. After a short pause, I continued walking forward. Tristan flicked his cigarette aside and walked towards me. Wordlessly, we fell into stride next to each other as we made our way up to my apartment.

Tristan waited until we were inside to say anything.

"You don't have anything to say to me?" he grumbled. "What do you want me to say?" I put my hands defiantly on my hips. "Sorry for having a *male* lab partner?"

"Whatever," Tristan said and turned to leave but I hurried

across the living room and grabbed his arm.

"I don't understand you!" I snapped. Tristan pulled back, looking at me in surprise and with distaste that I raised my voice.

"A *dude* doesn't just come over to some chick's house late at night only to do homework, Ophelia," he hissed at me. My cheeks burned at the implication of David's intentions but also with embarrassment that he might be right, and I had missed it. Tristan's eyes searched my face, seeing the blush there. "You didn't realize that? You're so fucking naive."

"He wasn't being inappropriate." I shook my head.

"He knew you had a boyfriend, yeah?" he challenged. I

nodded my head silently.

"Mm-hm and yet he still came over before on another night, I'm assuming it was late? That's *inappropriate*."

"I'm sorry." My shoulders slumped. "My only intentions were to work on our project. Steven and Crystal were home the entire time."

He hesitated a moment before his resolve broke and he dropped his arms with a sigh.

"I know, baby, but that's the naivety he was hoping for." He wrapped his arms around me and pulled me into his chest. I hugged him tightly, breathing in his familiar, intoxicating scent. The heat and hardness of his body, the way he engulfed me. My body responded, a warmth spread across me, and I wanted him desperately, but Serena was waiting for me, we didn't have time for that.

"It's just weird that this guy pops up and all this weird stuff starts happening," Tristan said, his voice muffled as he pressed his lips to the top of my head.

"What stuff?"

"Well, someone was throwing rocks at your bedroom window and someone slashed Charlie's tires the other night."

"They did?" I pulled back in surprise to look up at him. He was staring straight ahead, his eyes seeing something far away in his mind. "You think it was David?"

"He would be fucking stupid if it was," he growled. "I'll rip his fucking throat out if it is him."

I shook my head slowly as I pulled out of his arms.

"The brick," I gasped, my spine straightened. Tristan's eyes flashed down to mine, his raven hair fell forward. "Someone threw a brick through the window the other day, it had a note attached to it…"

"What did it say?" Tristan frowned.

"Just the word *whore*." My mind was racing. "David doesn't seem…crazy."

Surprisingly, Tristan simply rolled his eyes and brushed my hair back behind my ear, my skin tingled where he touched me.

"You don't know this guy. Just be careful baby." He bent forward and kissed my nose. I lifted my face as he straightened and caught his lips in mine. At the heat from his soft, full lips a moan escaped my throat. Tristan stepped forward, closing the distance between us and kissed me deeper. I stood on tiptoes to wrap my arms around his neck and smashed my body to his, relishing in the surge of electricity between us. Tristan groaned and grabbed my hips, pushing himself against me. Suddenly, he pushed me away so that I was arm's length away, I frowned.

"Where's Hunter?"

"Serena's." I nodded towards her apartment. "I came up here to get us a change of clothes, we were going to sleep over."

Tristan nodded and released me, the fire cooling.

"Go on then, go have fun with your friend. I'll see you tomorrow." He turned me around to face my bedroom and slapped me once, hard on my ass. I yelped and threw a glare at him over my shoulder, but he was already walking out the door, laughing.

Tristan

22

This girl is going to fucking kill me. In another instance, I would probably welcome it, but her ignorance was fucking insane. Ophelia had been through so much shit in her childhood and again during her relationship with dumbass Jimmy, but it was like she had no idea how shit works. If her *lab partner* had any respect for her, he would have waited until it was daylight to come over to work on their project.

"Stupid ass fucking project," I said out loud. My entire body trembled with rage so bad I struggled to light the blunt in my hand. I didn't have any proof that he was the one who sliced Charlie's tires or threw a brick through Ophelia's window so I couldn't handle this situation like I had done with Matt months ago. It would be too obvious now that Ophelia knew that I was pissed about David.

I could ask one of the homies in the crew to handle him, Greg, Tony or even Louis would get it done for me if I asked. Donovan was too levelheaded to break the kneecaps off some sleaze ball, he would try to talk me out of it.

Honestly, regardless of who did it, Ophelia wasn't *stupid*, she would know it was me. Ophelia loved me but I don't think she would be able to handle that. The week that followed the run-in between David and I, I kept tabs on both of them. David pretty much worked every day with long hours at a lumber yard in Martinez. I sat in my car for hours, waiting for him to come out.

Finally, when his shift was over, I followed him to his house in Rodeo about twenty minutes from the lumber yard. He lived in a small, boxy house with a metal stair railing, a window on each side of the door was framed with white shutters. His was the only car parked out front, a blue Firebird, but I could see the TV light flickering inside. Someone was home–but who? Maybe he had a girlfriend.

However, as the days went on, I didn't see any sign of who the person may be, and he never left the house with them. David didn't do much outside of going to work and school, it seemed. *Fucking loser*, I thought to myself. A dark thought dawned on me before I could squash it–maybe Ophelia needed to be with someone boring like David, someone ordinary. He clearly was going to school for something which meant he had goals and potentially a career ahead of him. In comparison to David, what could I offer Ophelia?

I shook the thought away. If he ever crossed a line again, I wouldn't need one of my boys to do my dirty work for me. I didn't give a fuck how much I scared Ophelia.

When I wasn't stalking David, I kept an eye on Ophelia. The person throwing rocks at Ophelia's bedroom window never returned. She went to work like usual, even picked up an extra shift now that Jimmy was out of jail and her mom was back in town. I didn't see her come out of her class building with David. From the looks of it, they were both behaving appropriately. But that didn't mean they weren't texting each other…

"Fuck." I placed a hand over my face, too tired to go down another rabbit hole. The thought spiked a whole new wave of anxiety over me. I had sworn to myself that I would trust Ophelia, that I wouldn't ever go through her phone but now I was anxious to check myself. The shit that happened with Katherine was flooding back in painful glimpses. The evidence in her phone was how I had caught her cheating on me the *first* time. Dumb bitch didn't even delete the pictures.

Nothing hurt more than when I walked into the too familiar, dark house and caught her myself. I didn't want that with Ophelia.

"What're you still doing out here?" Donovan said, startling me. It had just rained, leaving the air smelling crisp but the setting sun was lingering in the horizon, hinting the end of winter was approaching.

"Just trying to clear my mind," I frowned down at the smoldering blunt in my hand. I held it up to my lips and took a long drag. Wordlessly, holding the smoke in my lungs, I handed it to Don.

"You seem pretty burnt lately." Puffs of smoke snaked out of Don's mouth as he spoke. He kept the blunt and hit it again, I didn't care enough to give him shit about it. "Charlie is trying to get Barry to the shop to work out some sort of deal."

"He's tryna pimp me out again," I said. "He wants me to get Barry's kid into driving, thinks we will be able to pull twice as many runs."

"Sounds dangerous," Don nodded.

"Sounds fucking stupid…sounds like Charlie." I snagged the blunt back with a smirk as Don tried to pull back, but I was too fast. "Barry is probably blowing him off because he knows Charlie is a crook."

"How's paying him back going?" Don raised an eyebrow at me, and I rolled my eyes.

"He's been taking almost everything I've been making. We might need to go on a run soon so that I can finish paying him off for the damages to the house and move on."

Louis popped out just then, his face flushed and sweaty. "Yo, T, I need your help. I can't get this fucking bolt out of the engine block on the Impala and it's driving me crazy."

I nodded and took one long, last drag off the blunt and handed the rest to Don. I followed Louis inside and it wasn't long before I was able to crack the warped bolt off with a head bolt socket. This engine must have overheated often for a while to warp the head bolts this bad. The shop was pretty busy this late in the evening, probably people trying to get their cars worked on before summer hit when the prices would go up and we would be the busiest.

Good, I thought. The more money I made, the quicker I could pay off Charlie and he could fuck off for a while. Things had been going smoothly between work and things with Ophelia until this shit with David popped up. The thought of some prick showing up and messing things up for us—for having the fucking balls to think he could even try—really pissed me off.

The fact that I couldn't just go and handle the situation made sitting around the shop even worse, knowing some creep was out there harassing my girl. Usually, work was pretty good at occupying my mind, the smell of grease and the struggle of working on a complicated project but my mind was going a mile a minute.

By the time we closed the shop and cleaned up, I didn't feel any better. I thought of heading to the back and working out for a bit, to get some of this pent up shit out of me but my back ached and the old boxer's break in my right hand was acting up. Making a fist killed my hand, pain shot up the underside of my arm like electricity. I doubted I had the grip strength to jack off let alone lift a weight.

"Ay, yo T!" Tony shouted to me. "Wanna go for a cruise?" Tony, Greg, Louis, and Donovan were standing in a circle outside, waiting for me to join them. I glanced over at the Cutlass, contemplating surprising Ophelia at work but I knew my sour mood would just make us fight.

"I'm down, c'mon Donny." I nodded my head towards the Cutlass and Donovan followed obediently. We usually went on late night cruises during the summer, but I welcomed the distraction. Don quickly busied himself gutting and rolling up a blunt from the bag of weed in his pocket as I revved the engine loudly. The deep roar of the engine shook the cab like a wild animal waking up.

I had put so much work into this Oldsmobile Cutlass, this shit could smoke anyone in a race. Usually, our cruises ended up in a sideshow, wangin' doughnuts or racing each other. Typically, it ended with us trying to ditch the cops, but it was a good ass time, a good way to take your mind off the bullshit.

"For once you gotta let me drive," Don smirked as we fell into line with the other guys. Usually, I liked to run the cruise, lead from the front but tonight I motioned for Greg to pull ahead of me in his candy red El Camino. "People are gonna think we're a couple if you keep making me the passenger princess."

"You fucking wish I was your man," I laughed loudly.

"You're not my type." Donovan smirked as he held the flame of his lighter to the end of the blunt. "Shut

up or I'll kiss you on the mouth." Donovan

laughed and handed me the blunt.

We drove in silence, the music thumping loudly enough to rattle the windows, weed smoke filled the car and blotted out the windows. The weed seeped into my brain, dulling the anxiety that made my hands tremble as we drove aimlessly with the others.

There was something about driving, especially with the crew, blasting music and smoking a blunt that was cathartic. Donovan and I didn't speak much, both just enjoying not having to run off adrenaline during a run, of busting our backs and hands trying to fix up these shit cars or deal with dying moms. The crew all had our own shit to work through, demons to fight but at the end of the day, these dudes would take a bullet for each other. This world had been cruel to all of us. When Louis's wife had kicked him out, he had stayed at my place until they worked it out.

When Greg couldn't afford his electric bill (running it 24/7 for an illegal weed growing setup) we all had pitched in to get it paid off. Tony's sister had killed herself from a drug overdose a few years ago so the crew paid for her funeral. The crew also took turns checking on Tasoula, making sure she got the care she needed.

I owed my crew my own life, I put it in their hands each time we made a run. Whether it was Don making sure I got into a spot safely, or Tony or Louis making sure I got the hell out of there safely–I depended on them. Lights of the Bay Bridge cut through the rolled down windows and I stuck my hand out to feel the cool breeze coming off the ocean. I felt weightless, happy even.

Ophelia
23

After my conversation with Tristan, I wasn't sure how to act around David and I sure as hell didn't know what to say to him. We had four more portions of this project left to work on together, my grade and future depended on it. I took a deep breath and held it as I entered the classroom, but seeing David wasn't there yet, I relaxed slightly. My anxiety turned into confusion as Professor Whitmore entered the classroom to begin the lecture but there was still no sign of David.

I checked my phone, but he hadn't texted me in a few days. Professor Whitmore began walking around the classroom, passing out the graded submissions for our project and my confusion turned into panic. Before my panic could hit a crescendo, David shuffled in with his bag slung over his shoulder and head down. I sighed. He sat in his seat next to me wordlessly just after Professor Whitmore handed me our paperwork.

"So far we're right on track," I told David. He nodded silently but didn't turn to look at me. I frowned at the side of his face. "What's with you?" I whispered.

David's head whipped around, and I gasped. His right eye was swollen almost completely shut, the skin was an angry purplish red and a deep slice ran through his bottom lip.

"Leave me alone, Ophelia," he snapped. A few people turned to look at us and my face burned. I ducked my head and leaned closer to David.

"Was it Tristan?" I whispered.

David's hands slammed down onto the blacktop table with a loud slap, and I jumped. He stood up quickly, his metal stool scraping backwards. Wordlessly he snatched up his backpack and stormed out of the classroom. Everyone's heads snapped up as the door slammed. A sob caught in my throat as I hurriedly gathered up my things and hurried after David, but his car was gone.

My car bounced over the gate entry into L&L auto shop. The lights were off in the office, the doors pulled shut, but everyone's cars were still out-front including Tristan's Cutlass. I parked my car in a hurry and stormed inside of the building through the unlocked side door. It was bright inside the shop but quiet. I stormed around the corner and saw them standing in a large circle, all dressed in black.

It didn't dawn on me that they were getting ready to go for a run, I didn't care. My eyes landed on Tristan instantly, it was easy being that he was head and shoulders above the rest. Everyone's eyes darted to me the moment I stormed inside, but it took Tristan a second longer to realize.

"What're you–"

"I need to talk to you," I cut him off. An uncomfortable silence fell across the shop, all eyes on Tristan. I didn't wait for his response. I spun on my heel and stalked across the shop towards the office, slapping the door open with my palm. Tristan's long legs caught up to me quickly.

"What did you do?" I demanded.

"What are you talking about?" He frowned.

"David!" I shouted, throwing my arms out. "He showed up to class today and it looked like someone beat the shit out of him. He refused to speak to me."

Tristan's eyes darted between mine, not a single hint of knowledge in his deep green-blue eyes.

"Though I'm glad someone whooped his ass, it wasn't me," he said finally.

"He hinted that it was you, he told me to leave him alone." "Doesn't mean it was me," Tristan replied. "Dude's just embarrassed the girl he's into has to see him looking like a chump."

"You didn't see him," I said. "He was really upset with me."

"Whatever," Tristan said. He lifted his large hands with his palms facing down to show me the back of his hands, his knuckles. "I don't have a single mark on me. Trust me baby, if you let me get my hands on that chump, my fists would be bloody stubs."

I frowned down at the tattooed and scarred skin of his hands, but he was right, there wasn't a single fresh mark on him.

"I'm so confused." I covered my face with my hands, my skin turning red. Tristan gently took my wrists and pulled my hands from my face.

"Who do you believe, baby?" His hauntingly beautiful face was inches from mine. His eyes were wide, earnest and my heart shattered.

"I'm so sorry," I sobbed. "I'm just so confused."

Tristan's lips pulled up at one side into a crooked smile and I was so relieved that he wasn't mad.

"You just read too much into the situation baby girl. Thought the worst immediately instead of talking to me about it first." His voice was sweet, but his eyes turned hard, and my stomach churned. "You storm into my shop like that again and I'm gonna have to show you a thing or two." His lips crushed into mine hungrily, desperately. His hands released my wrist and spread up the back of my neck into my hair and locked into their roots. I grabbed a fist full of his hair and gripped him to me, my lips just as hungry against his.

"What're you going to do about it?" I whispered against his lips, and he groaned. The sound made my heart flutter. His right hand released my hair and slid down my side to my ass, he squeezed me against him. Electricity shot through me as he pressed himself into the apex of my thighs.

"I want you so fucking bad," he growled. "Stay up and wait for me?"

"Mm-hmm," I hummed. He crushed me to him once more before he released me sharply, my lips burned. His chest rose and fell quickly, his eyes were on fire. "Be safe tonight. Come home to me."

He stooped forward and kissed the tip of my nose gently.

"I love you," he said.

"I love you too."

He hesitated for a moment, his face unreadable before he turned and went back into the shop, back to whatever danger waited for him tonight.

Ophelia
24

I drove home feeling stupid for how I acted but also comforted in knowing that Tristan hadn't been the one to attack David. Headlights flared in my rearview and I squinted from the glare. I had pulled off onto my exit and was on a backroad not often taken by other traffic. Whoever had pulled off with me must also live out here. Their headlights were on full blast, illuminating my entire car.

"Fuck off!" I squinted through the pain of the lights. Black spots filled my vision, causing me to swerve. Then the car suddenly turned down a street and disappeared. "Asshole."

Hunter was with Jimmy tonight which meant I could go home and fall right to sleep. Today's events had drained me mentally and emotionally, I was ready to close my eyes and forget it all for a few hours.

Steven's car was parked in the lot when I pulled in. Hopefully they weren't having one of their parties so that I could shower and sleep in peace. I was thinking of the hot water and my cool sheets as I staggered into my apartment. A large suitcase was lying open on the coffee table with garments hanging loosely out of it.

"Oh hey!" Crystal greeted me with more enthusiasm than she ever greeted me with before. She had a bundle of clothes in her hands that she tossed haphazardly into the suitcase.

"You going somewhere?"

"My sister is in labor so we're going down to LA to see her and the baby," she smiled. She was in a good mood, but a brand-new baby would do that to anyone. Steven walked out of the bathroom then with a large toiletry bag bursting at the seams.

"If we leave now, we will get there around two in the morning," he said.

"Long drive," I nodded.

"Yeah, so we gotta get going!" Crystal took the bag from Steven and tossed it into the suitcase and zipped it up. "We'll be gone for a few days, probably just the weekend."

"Drive safe, see you later." I sidestepped out of their way as they hurried excitedly out of the door. I sighed in relief as I thought of having the apartment to myself tonight. I hurried into the bathroom, stripping my clothes off as I did. I cranked the hot water all the way up to better hog the hot water from the rest of the apartment and connected my Bluetooth speaker. Music poured out into the little bathroom loudly, something I never did when Crystal was home because I was worried about annoying her.

My shower was gloriously hot and long. I excitedly exfoliated and shaved every part of my body in anticipation for Tristan's arrival tonight. I wrapped a towel around me and brushed my teeth sleepily. I pulled on one of Tristan's large white t-shirts and a pair of cotton shorts. I turned the speaker off and was plunged into an eerie silence. The apartment felt too still. Suddenly uncomfortable, I tossed open the bathroom door and hurried out.

I skidded to a halt; a scream lodged in my throat.

David stood in the middle of my living room.

"David!" I gasped. "What're you doing here?"

"I tried calling you," he explained. My cell phone was stuffed into the pocket of my jacket that was on the floor of my bedroom too far for me to grab… His bruised face was relaxed, open but alarm bells screamed in my head. "The door was unlocked so I just let myself in."

"You can't do that," I snapped, trying to sound braver than I felt. He held up his hands as if in surrender.

"You're right, I know that," he nodded. "But I needed to see you."

"You could've waited until tomorrow, David," I glared. "This isn't okay."

He nodded and took a step towards me, but I quickly stepped back. He stopped.

"Your roommates are gone." It wasn't a question. He took another step towards me.

"Tristan is on his way over," I lied.

"No, he's not," he shook his head. His eyes glinted wickedly, and I swallowed hard. "Him and his *boys* are going out on a run, aren't they?"

"How do you know?" My voice wavered despite my best effort.

David rolled his eyes and took another step towards me.

"I've been watching him from time to time," he shrugged nonchalantly. "I knew guys like him back in Boston. You know–I really don't get what you see in him." He laughed dryly.

"David, you need to leave." I forced an edge to my voice.

"You know I thought someone like you would be too smart to fall for a guy like Tristan. You know he's garbage, right? He's just white trash. Being with him reduces you to nothing but a whore."

I flinched at his words, the malice in them. My eyes flickered behind him to the window that Steven had repaired the other week.

"Was that you? With the brick?" My voice squeaked.

"I was just trying to get you to *wake up*!" He shouted and I jumped. "Do you think good guys just go around beating up their girlfriend's lab partners?" He gestured to his bruised face.

"Tristan didn't do that." I shook my head frantically. "I asked him, and he said he never touched you."

"Oh sure!" He rolled his eyes. "Believe the criminal! I tried to intervene when and where I could, to get you two to back off each other but you're both so fucking stupid."

"What do you *want?*" I said. *If I screamed, someone in the complex ought to hear me.* My hands clenched into fists at my side. Without speaking, David stomped over to me and grabbed me roughly by the face and smashed his swollen, cut lips to mine.

I cocked my fist and punched him as hard as I could in his bruised eye and shoved him backwards. I tried to run past him to the front door, but his hand snaked out and snatched me by my hair. I cried out in pain as the roots threatened to rip from my skull. He pulled me backwards into his chest sharply.

"Ophelia just stop!" he shouted. I opened my mouth to scream but his hand clamped over my mouth tightly. "You're being ridiculous!" He hissed into my ear; his breath hot on my neck. I struggled against him as his other hand reached around to my front and cupped my breast. I felt him spring to life in his pants against my lower back. He groaned into my neck as his hand continued to rove over my body, feeling the plane of my stomach beneath the shirt.

"Stop," I tried to say but his hand crushed my lips against my teeth.

"Oh Ophelia," he breathed. His hand dipped between my thighs and cupped me, and I gasped. My vision blurred as he spun me around and gripped the tops of my arms. "I just need to feel you, you should be mine not his."

His lips crushed against mine but this time he held my wrists down at my sides. I bit his bottom lip as hard as I could, tasting blood. A sharp blow landed on my cheek, forcing me to let go as stars erupted in my vision. A blow landed on my chest, knocking me backwards onto the floor between the coffee table and the couch, my head connected sharply with the ground.

He was on top of me, forcing my legs apart with his. I slapped wildly at him, trying to kick out my legs but he was too strong for me. He pinned my arms above my head with one of his hands and my hips with his.

"God, don't you see what you do to me?" He said as he pushed his hips into me, showing me how hard he was in his jeans.

"David please stop!" I cried.

"I don't get what your problem is!" he shouted back; his face twisted with fury. With his free hand he gripped the collar of my t-shirt and pulled down. The fabric tore with a loud rip. He shoved his hand into the shirt and grabbed at my breast hungrily. He moaned and planted a line of kisses up and down my neck, licking and biting me along the way.

"David, I don't want this! Get off me!" I shouted, bucking my body forward in an attempt to get him off of me. Instead, he pressed himself harder into me. His hand snaked between our bodies, his fingers hooked on my shorts and pulled them roughly to the side. "David! Please stop!" Tears collected in pools in my wet hair. David ignored me as he struggled to undo the button of his jeans single handedly. There was a soft pop as the button came loose followed by the metallic clink of his zipper pulling down.

"I just want to show you that you don't need him," he huffed excitedly. He spit into the palm of his hand and reached down to himself between us.

"No! Get off me!" There was an explosion as I screamed, muffling the sound. Suddenly David was gone with a yelp.

"*The fuck are you doing?!*" Tristan bellowed. He had David by the throat, pinning him to the couch easily with one hand. His green-blue eyes were on fire as they swept over my crumpled and crying form on the floor. A sob rocked through me as I pulled my knees to my chest and wrapped my arms around them. Tristan's eyes zeroed in on the tear in my shirt, the handprint on my cheek.

"Tristan," I sobbed, my voice breaking.

"*What did you do?!*" Tristan roared; his hand tightened on David's throat. Already his face was turning red, his eyes bulged. "*What the fuck did you do?!*"

"Tristan, he-he tried…" I couldn't answer, another sob shook me. The movement was quick, I didn't even see Tristan reach into his waistband for the gun. He released David for a fraction of a second, that's all it took for Tristan to grab a pillow from the couch and hold it over David's head. The sound of the gun firing was muffled, blood sprang from David's head across the couch.

I blacked out.

"Ophelia–Ophelia baby, stay with me," Tristan shook me gently. My eye cracked open, I was so tired. "Where is your roommate?"

Tristan had set me sideways into the front seat of his car.

"LA," my voice slurred. "All weekend."

Tristan nodded and said something into his phone. A moment later he was smoothing my hair backwards, out of my face gently.

"Oh baby, baby," he cried. His hands felt good on my hot skin. "I'm so sorry, I'm so sorry. Did…did he…?"

"Mm-mm," I shook my head slightly. "He tried…but…I fought him hard." My head felt like it was full of black water, my eyes refused to stay open.

"*Fuck!*" He screamed and punched his steering wheel multiple times. I sleepily wondered if he would break it. "Fuck! I knew I shouldn't leave you without someone being with you. Oh fuck, oh Ophelia I'm so sorry baby."

"Doesn't matter anymore," I said, and he was silent. A few minutes later, someone pulled up next to us and Tristan got out of the car to talk to them. I could hear them outside of my window but didn't care to listen, it felt better under the black water. Tristan was suddenly beside me, crouched next to me.

"Ophelia baby, Donovan and Cherry are going to take you to my place. I have to stay here and clean up."

"Clean up," I laughed.

"Keep an eye on her, I think she's in shock or something," Tristan told someone, his voice full of concern. "I got some clothes for her, they're in the backseat, Cherry."

The car roared to life, and we were moving.

I must have fallen asleep because the next thing I knew, I was in Tristan's bed, curled up on my side.

"What do we do?" It was Donovan, I recognized his gentle voice.

"You go outside and wait for Tristan to call," Cherry ordered, her voice was stronger. "I'll help her in here."

The bedroom door clicked softly behind him as Donovan left. There was a long pause where I think I might have drifted again. Finally, Cherry sighed and softly touched my ankle.

"Hey girl, I'm going to help you change. I doubt you want to stay in these clothes."

"Mm." I struggled to sit up. I pulled my shorts off, and Cherry helped me get my feet into the gray sweatpants and pull them up my hips. There wasn't any shyness or discomfort between us as she pulled the torn t-shirt over my head. We didn't speak but whatever tension usually lingered between us was gone for now. She tugged a fresh t-shirt over me and called for Donovan to bring a wet rag.

A minute later she gently wiped my face, and I flinched as she rubbed the bruise that was blooming over my cheek.

"Sorry," she whispered. My legs suddenly felt too weak to hold me up any longer and I plopped down onto the bed. A sob racked through me, shaking my entire body before I could stop it. Wordlessly, Cherry sat on the bed next to me and put an arm around my shoulders.

Her gesture was small but so welcoming that I collapsed into her, resting my forehead onto her neck as the sobs continued. She held me like that for some time until the tears finally dried and my body sagged exhausted. Cherry pulled Tristan's blankets back on the bed for me and I crawled in eagerly. I was asleep in seconds.

I don't know how long I slept, it could have been days or minutes.

Some time had passed before soft hands brushed my hair back.

"Keep sleeping baby." It was Tristan. "I just wanted to tell you that I called Jimmy, he's going to keep Hunter for another night, and I'll get him tomorrow. I didn't want you to worry about him."

I reached out blindly and felt Tristan's face. His beard stubble pricked my hand. He turned his head and gently kissed my palm. He sighed and leaned his forehead against mine.

"I love you," he whispered. "Everything is taken care of. I'll be right here when you want to wake up." I

nodded and fell back into the waters.

It hurt to wake up. My body felt like it had been trampled, my muscles were sore. The skin around my wrist burned, my face felt swollen. Slowly, I allowed myself to wake up bit by bit. I wiggled my toes and flexed my ankles. I made a mental list of things that hurt as my body slowly defrosted.

My head pounded the worst. I groaned as consciousness brutally entered my mind. The bed groaned as someone shifted.

"You waking up?" Tristan whispered. His fingertips brushed the curve of my ear.

"No," I groaned, and he chuckled softly. I blinked my eyes open and winced at the bright light. He let me adjust slowly to the awake world around me. I licked my chapped lips. "Thirsty."

"I got you, here." He helped me sit up and I winced again as the pain shifted with me. He handed me a glass of cold water and I gulped it down, aware that he was watching me closely.

"Thanks." I looked around the empty room, disorientated. "What day is it?"

"It's Saturday," Tristan responded.

"Hunter?" I frowned, vaguely remembering what he had said before.

"I picked him up from Jimmy earlier. He's bathed and fed, he's with Don and Cherry in the living room."

"Good," I nodded but it hurt so I stopped. "Thank you."

Tristan didn't reply, instead he watched me closely, his face full of pain.

"Ophelia...are you okay?" he whispered, ducking his head so that I had to look at him.

"I don't know," I whispered back. "You killed him?" His face turned serious, stoic and he nodded once.

"Okay."

Tristan's brows puckered but he didn't respond. "What did you do with him?"

"No." Tristan's face was hard, careful. "That's not something for you to worry about. The guys and I took care of it." "The guys?" I balked. My eyes felt like two eggs, swollen and dry in their sockets. I pressed the back of my hands against them. "Who?"

"Everyone." I felt him shrug. "No one is going to find out, Ophelia. When Crystal gets back from her trip, she won't be able to tell anything happened." I dropped my hands into my lap and sighed.

"Okay." Tristan gently placed his hands on either side of my face, gingerly to not hurt the bruise on my cheek.

"Baby I need you to do something," he said. "I need you to go to school and work just like usual. If someone asks you why David isn't in class, I need you to act like you don't know." I nodded silently; I figured as much. That I would have to keep my mouth shut and carry on like usual. Butterflies batted gently against the walls of my stomach, but I was too disconnected to pay them too much mind.

Ophelia
25

Tristan's strong arms were wrapped around me tightly, the sound of his heartbeat rhythmically, calmly in his chest beneath my cheek. My body felt like jelly but was getting stronger minute by minute while my head raged. I was too scared to close my eyes, to see the blood spraying again and again. Tristan breathed evenly; the sound of his breath was muffled by my hair as he pressed his cheek against the top of my head.

We stood this way for a long time, not caring about the people passing by on the bustling platform. The air had a warmth to it, the sky was blue today as winter came to an end. California really never had a true spring season; it just jumped from one extreme to another, which meant that in a few weeks it would be blazing hot again. Which felt oddly metaphoric for the closing of a chapter of my life.

I had to work today, back to reality though I didn't know how in the world I was supposed to help old folks to the bathroom, feed, and dress them while my insides were shattering. My train rolled slowly onto the platform and my heart lurched, my hands clung desperately to Tristan's shirt.

"Tristan," I whimpered. The corners of his mouth attempted to pull into a reassuring smile, but they faltered.

"You'll be okay baby just keep your head down and go about your day like usual," he said. "I'm just one phone call away if you need me."

The doors opened and people began to shuffle forward, if I wasn't fast enough, I would miss my train. Tristan and Donovan had agreed that I needed to act business as usual and continue riding the BART train instead of Tristan dropping me off. I was scared to be away from him. He had become the calm center of my world, holding me together when all I wanted to do was fall apart. Tristan's face suddenly crumpled, and he lifted me to smash his lips to mine.

There was something that I couldn't quite name in the urgency in which he kissed me, drinking me down like he didn't want to forget how I tasted. Like he wanted to hold onto this moment. It did little to squelch the rising panic in me, if anything my heart thumped nervously as he set me back down on my feet.

With a gentle shove, he pushed me toward the filling train cart. I craned my neck to see him over the bustling people shoving me toward the already full train but lost sight of him. The doors slid closed with a *thwunck* sound, and I saw him, as he stood with one hand on his chest, his face hollow, his eyes dark as the train began to pull forward. I called out his name though he couldn't hear me. The cart picked up speed. Just before I could no longer see him, Tristan's head dropped, and he turned his back to me.

Work dragged on impossibly slowly. My hands trembled as I brushed one resident's hair, helped feed another in the dining room. I avoided Maria, the friendly nurse, ducking into the laundry room or into a resident's apartment if I saw her approaching. I didn't want to exchange pleasantries right now, to have to throw on a fake smile or try my best to not burst into tears.

I dragged a load of laundry into the laundry room and threw it into the washer. I sighed heavily as I wiped sweat from my brow and pulled my phone out of my back pocket. A picture of Tristan, Hunter and I was my screen saver. Usually, our smiling faces brought me a token of peace but now it just made my stomach churn. There weren't any missed calls or incoming texts from Tristan. I swiped my phone open and typed out a simple, quick text.

Me: I love you

The rest of the shift became so busy that I didn't have a chance to check my phone again and I was eager to do so. Tamara was going to pick up Hunter from daycare for me this evening after she got off work and I was to pick him up from her after I was done with my shift. Business as usual.

Finally, it was time to clock out and I hurried for the back locker room. I tore my black apron off and tossed it into my locker, slamming it closed. I whipped my phone out of my pocket once more. Still nothing from Tristan. His previously planned run the night of…I pinched my eyes shut tightly against the memory.

The run had been canceled due to "bad intel" Tristan had said which was why he was at my house hours before I had expected him. Thank God it had been canceled, I didn't want to think of how far and how bad things could have gone if he hadn't shown up. *They did go badly*, I reminded myself and I shuddered as the sound of a muffled gunshot burst through my thoughts.

I got into my car after getting off BART feeling low. I wondered if he and the guys had been put on a last-minute run or something and that's why I hadn't heard from him, but it was just speculation. The look in his face as I peered through the grimy train window sent a chill down my spine. I've never seen anyone, let alone a mountain of a man like Tristan, look so desolate…so broken and helpless. Absentmindedly, I touched my lips thinking of the fervent way he had kissed me goodbye.

The lights at Tamara's were off, the reflection of the TV in the living room flickered across the dark lawn as I pulled up. I opened up the back door and made my way inside quietly, having done this routine countless times. Tamara was perched on the edge of the couch as usual in her favorite pink robe, her hair tied up on top of her head.

"You look beat," she frowned. I couldn't even imagine how I looked.

"It was a long shift," I shrugged and looked away. My breath caught in my chest as I watched the late-night news play across her flatscreen. The male news anchor was speaking about a series of robberies in the area, of home invasions but there was nothing about David or Tristan. I tore my eyes away, blinking quickly. "H-how was Hunter?"

"A total angel," Tamara smiled. "He didn't want to eat dinner, so I let him have an avocado instead. Ate the whole thing right up."

"Teething, his molars are probably coming in," I nodded, distractedly. This conversation felt so oddly ordinary, so mundane compared to the last 72 hours. "Thanks for getting him, I'm going to hurry up and get us home."

"Okay baby, same time tomorrow?"

"Yeah, but I have class tomorrow, so it won't be so late." I pushed away a flare of panic as I thought of going to class tomorrow, of feigning to not know what happened to my lab partner. I stumbled into my mom's dark room and scooped Hunter up into my arms.

I hadn't returned to my apartment since the event. Tristan swore that him and the guys cleaned it up so that there was no sign of what happened, but I wasn't sure how that could be possible. There had been so much blood.

Steven's car was absent from the parking lot but the lights inside of the apartment were on. Excitement propelled me from the car, unhooking Hunter quickly and up the stairs to my apartment. I hadn't seen Tristan's Cutlass in the parking lot but that didn't mean Donovan, or the other guys hadn't dropped him off.

If we were supposed to be acting normally then he should be here. The front door popped open with a groan as it unlocked and swung open, but it was empty. My eyes revolved around the small space of the living room; my breath stilled in my chest as if I was waiting for a ghost to pop out.

Tristan was right. There wasn't a single sign of what had happened–of what he did. The couch looked the same as it always did, the cushions were in their usual places. I glanced down between the couch and the coffee table where I vividly remember a splatter of blood, but it was spotless. By the time we entered my empty bedroom, my excitement had completely vanished. I could hear the low sounds of Crystal's TV in her bedroom, signaling that she had returned from her trip.

After showering and dressing in one of Tristan's large shirts, I crawled heavily into bed next to Hunter and pulled his little body close to mine. I buried my face into the small space of his neck and shoulder and breathed in the familiar scent of him. Tristan had given him a haircut a few weeks ago which had made him look so much older than two and a half. His third birthday was approaching in a few months, and I would need to plan something for him. I groaned and pushed it off for now, putting it into a mental to-do list.

It was late when I finally drifted off to a restless sleep.

The next morning, I still hadn't heard from Tristan. I had woken up in an empty bed, fully expecting him to have crawled into the covers in the early hours. The crushing pain in my chest was severe when I saw that it was empty.

Me: Are you okay?

I threw my phone into the top of my hamper, angry and hurt. Hunter slowly woke up, whining as he searched for me.

"Good morning baby," I sighed and picked him up.

"Morning," he yawned. "Mama me hungry."

I was buckling Hunter into his highchair when my phone pinged. I slid the tray in securely around Hunter and handed him his bowl of oatmeal before I sprinted into my bedroom.

I exploded through the door and lunged for the hamper, my heart pounding. I fumbled with my phone, dropping it twice before I got the screen unlocked.

Serena: Hey, haven't heard from you in a few days. Dinner tonight?

Disappointment flooded through me. *Act normal*, Tristan's words echoed through my head.

Me: I don't think I can, I have class tonight and have to pick up Hunter from my mom after. Maybe this weekend?
Serena: Sure! Love you

I let my phone fall to the floor, but I did not move. I stared straight ahead out the window, my body slowly stiffened into stone. Alarm bells were ringing somewhere in my mind, but I couldn't tell what for.

Like a Band-Aid, I thought as I pulled open the classroom door. Everything was normal. There was chatter from the other students as they waited for Professor Whitmore, no one looked up at me as I stumbled into my seat. I dropped my backpack heavily onto the black top table and rested my head on top of it. A sour taste filled my mouth, but nothing happened. Police didn't break down the door. A helicopter didn't hover just above the roof top.

David didn't walk in.

Tristan didn't text me.

Whatever Professor Whitmore said in class was completely lost on me. I tried my best to pretend to take notes, to pay attention and look attentive but I couldn't hear over the blood rushing through my ears. Then class was over, that was it. I jumped as the other students stood up. I stuffed my notebooks back into my bag and stood up unevenly.

Walking out of the classroom felt like a breath of fresh air. I tried to keep my pace natural, but I wanted to sprint away from the building. No one had questioned David's absence, no one really even looked my way for the full two hours. By the time I stepped off of the BART train, I felt dirty.

I don't know how Tristan could do this, to kill a person and act as if nothing happened. *Comes with the territory*, his deep voice echoed in my head. I wasn't sure how much I believed his nonchalance; he was still a human with emotions, and I wondered how deeply he had to bury his feelings to go about his life like nothing happened.

Just how many people had Tristan killed? Were they always just casualties related to the job? Obviously, David hadn't been. Tristan hadn't hesitated at all to remove his gun from his waistband and pull the trigger. He snuffed David's life out as easily as flicking a light switch. The entire weekend that he spent glued to my side, nervously watching my every move, he didn't show a single hint of it bothering him. Sure, David was a monster who had every intent to hurt me, but didn't it bother him…at all?

By the time I gathered Hunter up from Tamara's and fed him dinner, I was absolutely exhausted. To save time, I showered with Hunter, something we hadn't done in ages. Then I dressed him in pajamas and pulled Tristan's shirt back on. I had been wearing it for a few days now almost like a talisman, a homing beacon to summon Tristan to me.

My skin vibrated like my body was full of bees, making it impossible to sleep. I fanned my hands out over my cool bed sheet, searching for my phone. It didn't even phase me when I saw that I still hadn't received a response from Tristan. I swiped to my call history and hit *dial* on his name.

Immediately I could tell that something was wrong. The other line didn't ring, instead it clicked. A short pause.

"Error. The caller you've attempted to reach is no longer in service. If you believe this to be an error, please reach–" I smashed the red button to end the call. I stared at the dark screen for a moment before I tried again.

"Error. The caller–" I tried again…and again…

Tristan
26

February

March

April

May

Lights swirled in colorful loops and dots across my blurred eyes. The edges of the people around me blurred into whisps, coming into focus to show doubles. My head lolled heavily backwards onto the couch, too much for me to hold up right. With my eyes closed it felt like I was on the Gravitron, spinning…spinning…I clenched my jaw against the nausea that sprang to life, and I sat up, too uncomfortable to sit here anymore.

I lurched awkwardly to my feet and stumbled as my legs tried to keep up with my body. I pitched forward and fell, catching myself on someone's arm, nearly knocking them down in the process. They shouted something to me over the music, but I couldn't tell what they said. They pushed me back upright, steadying me on my feet. My eyes slid through the pool to see who had helped me up, it took me a moment to realize the four eyes I was staring into was Louis.

"Hey…thanks," I slurred. Louis frowned and said something, but I shook my head, still unable to hear him.

"You good, man?" Louis shouted louder. I winced and staggered backwards away from him; his hands shot up to catch me but my feet found their ground beneath me before I could fall.

"Fuck no," I laughed. I shrugged away from his hands and stumbled out of L&L.

There were too many people in here, the air was thick with humidity and smoke. Something was crawling through me, attempting to get out. It dug its claws into my throat, squeezed my heart but I fought it back as I fell through the door to the outside. The air here was much cooler and I gulped it down, holding onto the door so that I didn't fall.

It took a few tries to get my cigarettes out of my pocket, but I finally was able to get one free from the pack. The first one I lit the filter instead.

"Fuck." I flicked it away and went for another. This one I was able to light correctly though I could hardly see it clearly. It finally made it to my lips, and I sucked down the familiar burn, pushing away whatever was threatening to break out of me. Music from inside pounded against the door behind me and all I could think of was getting away.

I didn't have a real plan, I just kept walking forward to the best of my abilities, stumbling a few times. Everything inside me was on fire, burning and turning to ash. Nothing left behind after the embers smoldered and went out. I wanted to die, and I had been here before. Everything I ever touched had turned to ash beneath my hand, anything good I ever had in my life had been reduced to nothing and it was all because of me. I was a cancer on those around me.

There was a time when I thought that maybe *just this once* I could have it all. A girl and a kid that were all mine. That I could keep them safe, tucked away from the blackness that I caused but in time it found them too. It was only a matter of time before the truth came out. I was forced to stand there and look at our lives for what they were: she had promise and I had nothing.

I would continue to bring her down until there was nothing left of Ophelia. Then she would hate me, resent me for ruining her life. It wouldn't just be her; it would also be Hunter and any other children we might have had in the future. They would be reduced to this petty life because of me. I had nothing to offer her but dead bodies.

The hole in my center tore open then and it was too much. I stumbled forward and collapsed onto the sidewalk under a streetlamp. My knees burned but the alcohol soaring through my veins numbed the pain. I pressed my forehead to the ground as the sobs tore violently from my chest.

"FUCK!" I screamed again and again, punching the ground with each guttural yell. Pain sliced through the numbing effect the alcohol had but I didn't care. I did it over and over. Tires squealed from somewhere behind me followed by the sound of pounding footsteps.

"Tristan!" A voice called but I ignored them. Hands grabbed at me, attempting to turn me over. My bloody fist struck out at whoever it was, connecting with a sharp smack to his jaw. Donovan had dodged it in time, only getting the tail end of my punch.

"Aww man," I pinched my eyes shut. "I'm sorry, I'm sorry." I shoved Donovan's chest away roughly which caused his grip on my shirt to slip, and I fell backwards. My head connected with the cement with a sickening sound, but it was nothing compared to the despair that pulsated through me.

"Tristan, what the fuck man?" Donovan grabbed for me again, but I rolled away from him, the small rocks in the cement bit at my skin.

"Leave me alone," I muttered.

I didn't care that Don was seeing me like this, he had seen it before, but I knew I was scaring the shit out of him. I hated myself more for it. He struggled under my weight, and I really wasn't helpful as I couldn't get my feet under me. He grunted and huffed as he got me into the Saab.

"Are you *drunk*?" He frowned, shocked.

"I ruined everything." My voice came out a whimper. Donovan clipped me into my seatbelt and shut the door, but I continued. "I ruined everything. I ruined everything."

My eyes snapped open as the nausea came flaring back and I opened the car door just in time to vomit all over the asphalt outside. When I was done, I blinked up at the bright lights as my trailer came into view.

"No!" I shouted, slamming the door shut.

"What man? You haven't been home in weeks, sleeping at the shop. I thought–"

"No, I don't want to fucking be here!" I shoved him roughly and pointed at the windshield. "Get me the fuck out of here."

Donovan ended up taking me to his house. I tried my best to walk freely without his help, holding onto the side of the house to steady myself. He took my elbow and lead me to his bedroom in the back of the small house. I tripped over my own feet and fell forward onto the side of his bed. I slid down to the ground, miserable. Donovan sighed heavily.

"Just call her, Tristan," he said. "I don't know why you're doing this to yourself."

"She's not cut out for this," I shook my head, the effort making me dizzy. "You didn't see the way she looked at me." My voice was just a whisper. My hand had begun to throb, dried blood covered my knuckles. Donovan sighed again as he bent down to help me up onto the bed.

"I knew this would happen," he muttered. "I tried to warn you."

"Fuck you."

Don managed to get my shoes off and tossed my hat onto the floor somewhere. After he got me settled, he went and grabbed a large bowl for me to throw up into in case I needed it and a large glass of water.

"Sit up, asshole," he demanded and I shakily obliged. I gulped down the cold water eagerly, it dribbled down my chin and neck.

"Thanks," I hiccupped. "I love you."

"You're a dick but I love you too, go to bed." Donovan had made a bed for himself on the floor and crawled into it. He paused momentarily and looked up at me with alarm. "Swear to god if you puke on me in your sleep, I'm going to kick your ass."

Despite myself, I laughed and fell asleep.

Donovan woke me early with a cup of coffee and a shitty rolled joint. I groaned against the morning light and flung my arm across my eyes. They felt raw.

"Can't do it," I groaned. The smell of the coffee was too strong, my stomach churned.

"Then at least hit this, it'll help." He shoved the joint back into my face, and I took it grudgingly. Don was right, after a few minutes the weed took the edge of the hangover off enough for me to sit up right. My mouth tasted like sandpaper, my head throbbed, and my hand was on fucking fire. It was swollen and angry, I wouldn't be surprised if I rebroke the old boxer's break I got years ago. Great.

"I don't know how people drink," I groaned, blinking down at my feet.

"Well, you seem to be doing a good job of trying to figure that out," Donovan retorted. He was right. I had been drinking almost daily since I left Ophelia at the train station, but I didn't know what else to do. It was that or rip my own fucking throat out.

"You look like shit."

"Fuck you." I winced as pain sprang through my head. Eventually I staggered into the bathroom to take a shower. I stood in the hot water for as long as the heat could hold out. The shower head only reached my shoulder, so I had to duck to rinse my hair which was welcoming after last night. I scrubbed the dry blood off of my hand the best I could, but it killed. Charlie was going to be pissed.

I dressed in the same clothes from last night, glad that I hadn't puked on my shirt. Donovan was a good foot shorter than me, and fifty pounds lighter, there was no way that his clothes would fit me. By the time I was dressed and chugged the now cold coffee, I was feeling marginally better.

"You still look like shit," Donovan smirked as I collapsed into the Saab. I tossed an elbow lazily at him.

I dreaded going into the shop today. The sun was too bright, the air too hot inside of the shop. Everything was back to business as usual; cars were lined up outside of the shop to be worked on. I walked in behind Donovan and every head turned to look at us. Concerned eyes darted between us and I groaned. Without a word, I turned on my heel and stormed into the office. "There you are," Charlie snorted. "Someone's here to see you."

There was a moment before she turned around that the earth stilled. My breath caught in my throat in anticipation. I hated how every part of me wished desperately that it was Ophelia. Instead, who was standing there nearly knocked me onto my fucking ass.

Tristan
27

Hey Tristan," Katherine greeted, her eyes careful. I couldn't speak right away; my brain was scrambling to catch up with a reality that I couldn't believe. Katherine didn't look much different than when I saw her last.

Short and thin, her brown hair was shaved closely on one side, exposing the tattoo of a rose on her skull, the rest of her hair was brushed to the side and hung down to her pale shoulders. Her thin eyebrows were furrowed slightly over piercing blue eyes, watching me closely. Almost every inch of her skin was tattooed, she exposed it proudly wearing a cropped tank top and shorts.

I staggered backwards, like she had just sucker punched me in the stomach. I couldn't speak.

"W-what are you doing here?" I choked out.

Charlie cleared his throat and muttered something before he ducked out. I stared at his back as he retreated, wishing that I could disappear with him. Katherine folded her arms across her chest and shifted her weight.

"I need money," she said matter-of-factly. "I need eighty grand."

"Eighty *grand*?" I blinked at her. "The fuck for? I send you money every week."

"We're moving–Millie and I are."

The sound of my daughter's name made me recoil. It was onslaught after onslaught. I needed to sit down, to catch my breath. I shook my head and rubbed my tired eyes. This had to be a dream, a fucking nightmare.

"*Where*? I don't even know where she is now!" My voice was rising, my temper flared dangerously. Her icy blue eyes watched me nervously. "Let me see my daughter."

Katherine chewed on her stupid lip ring for a moment. She had to know that I would demand to see Millie, she wasn't stupid.

"Give me the money and you can see her."

She must be desperate.

"Sure," I scoffed. "You can't do this shit Katherine. You can't keep her away from me for *five years*, take my money every week without a fucking word and then show up on my god damn doorstep demanding *fucking eighty thousand dollars*." My body shook from fury, our entire relationship came flooding back in crushing waves. I was fifteen, seventeen, twenty-five again trying to shout some sense into her thick skull. Begging her to be a decent fucking person while I broke and crumbled in front of her.

"Whatever," she said and turned to walk away. I lurched after her without thinking and caught her by her wrist. Her eyes flashed down to my bruised and bloody hand wrapped around her wrist and back up to my face. "You haven't changed at all."

"Just–just wait a moment!" I begged. I took a deep breath and covered my face with my hands, trying my hardest to calm down. "Just…let me see her, okay? Please? I'll get you the money but please let me see her first. Please Katherine."

Katherine glanced out the window and back to me.

"Meet us at Diamond Park in an hour."

"Thank you," I breathed. Without looking at me, she hurried out the front door, but I chased after her. "Wait! Katherine."

"What?" She hesitated before turning around.

"Where are you moving to?" I asked desperately. Her lips pursed into a thin line. "*Please?*"

"Vallejo." She quickly turned back around and climbed into a large white truck and was gone. Vallejo. That was only a thirty-minute drive without traffic.

Hope sprang to life in my chest. Katherine couldn't move Millie that close to me without expecting me to burn the entire fucking city down looking for my daughter. Even knowing what I knew about Katherine, I'd go to the ends of the earth for Millie. Over the years I had my suspicions on where they might be living, one of those was Las Vegas. Greg and Donovan went with me as I tore through the flat, hot city in search of my daughter.

I went to all the bars and casinos I could get into to demand answers. We spent two weeks in the desert but came up with nothing. Katherine had a sister who lived in Vegas, but she had no clue where Katherine was, they hadn't spoken in two years. Or so she had said. I had definitely made my intent of finding my daughter clear to her sister which might have tipped Katherine off.

We came home empty handed again that time. But I wouldn't this time.

I had never been so nervous in my life. I had gone to the trailer to freshen up, get the stale cigarette and alcohol smell off me. I changed into a fresh black t-shirt and jeans and shaved the stubble off my face. I jumped into the Cutlass and hurried across town to Diamond Park on Hanly Road with my heart in my throat. On the seat next to me was a stuffed unicorn that I had bought for Millie a year ago.

Since Ophelia and I had gotten together, I had stopped buying things for Millie. It wasn't much but little things here and there that I thought she might like. Going into her old bedroom had been unreal, knowing that I was just minutes away from seeing my daughter.

Relief washed over me when I saw Katherine's truck at the park. She hadn't lied. She was definitely dangling Millie in front of me, enticing me like an Anglerfish before trapping me in her jaws. But I didn't give a shit. I wiped my sweaty hands on my jeans and grabbed the unicorn, taking a deep breath as I got out of the car. Diamond Park was huge with lots of trails and shit, but I figured they would be at the playground.

I finally spotted Katherine sitting on the low cement wall that encircled the park and I froze. My heart hammered, my entire body trembled with its force, and I suddenly felt stupid. Millie would be almost 9 now, did she even like unicorns? I looked down at the stuffed animal in my hands, suddenly self-conscious. Would she even know who I was? Did she even remember me?

She had been just three years old when Katherine took her away. I swallowed the lump in my throat and took another deep breath. Katherine's back was to me, she hadn't spotted me yet but from this small hill I could see the playground clearly. The ground was made of a rubbery, blue AstroTurf, the structure itself consisted of a plastic blue slide, held up by red poles and other areas for kids to run and play.

Suddenly it was like the sun beamed down onto one little girl running around the playground. Her raven hair glistened beautifully in the sun, it was long and wavy like a princess's. I tried to not notice that her hair was slightly curlier than mine. That the tip of her nose slightly rounder. I could hear the sounds of her tinkling laughter as she ran around with two other kids. My heart seized and for a fraction of a second, I thought of leaving. An invisible force propelled me forward down the small hill to the edge of the playground, coming to a stop just behind Katherine.

"You made it," Katherine said without turning to face me, her voice full of accusations. I ignored her, refusing to look away from the little girl.

"Millie! Come here!" The sound of Katherine's voice made me flinch. The little girl I had been watching stopped running in her tracts and skipped obediently towards us. My body stiffened.

"Yes mommy?" her little voice chimed.

"There's someone I want you to meet." Katherine looked over her shoulder up at me. "This is Tristan."

Millie's large green-blue eyes flickered up to me, having to squint in the light. My knees buckled and I sat down heavily on the cement next to Katherine.

"Hello," Millie said. Not a single ounce of recognition in her wide eyes. It killed me. Pain seared me but I forced a smile.

"Hi Millie," I breathed. I remembered the stupid stuffed animal. "I found this the other day and I thought maybe you'd like it."

Millie shrugged and took the stuffed animal.

"Sure, thanks."

I studied her closely, soaking up as much of her as I could. She wore her hair in a half-up style, pulled away from her face but the rest cascaded down her back. She had my sun-kissed skin tone, the sharp shape of my lips but her mom's chin. Millie wore a light pink dress with tiny flowers. I looked desperately at Katherine for answers, for help.

"Millie, I have a surprise for you." She broke her eyes away from my face and forced a smile. Millie looked up excitedly, already forgetting the unicorn. "Tristan isn't just an old friend he's…he's actually your daddy."

"You are?" Millie frowned and my heart broke. It took me a few tries before I could find my voice.

"I am, baby." I smiled sadly. "I've been wanting to see you for a very long time."

"Where were you then?" she challenged. She wasn't even 9 yet but she was smart. There was so much I wanted to tell her, to blame her mother for taking her away but I understood why.

"I've been right here waiting for you," I said finally.

Katherine seemed to relax slightly, and I realized this was difficult for her too.

"Oh," Millie said simply. "Thank you. Can I go back to playing, mom?"

Katherine nodded and Millie ran back to her friends, still holding the unicorn. I released a heavy sigh that I hadn't realized that I had been holding.

We sat silently for a while watching our daughter play happily. My mind raced with the possibilities. Maybe I could have her on the weekends if Katherine agreed. That way her school schedule wouldn't be interrupted and maybe over breaks like spring and summer…I was deep in my plans for the future when Katherine spoke.

"So…how've you been?"

We both chuckled at the awkwardness.

"Surviving," I shrugged. "Why are you moving?"

"Better environment for Millie," Katherine said cautiously. There was more she wasn't telling me. I wouldn't push it right now. "We're going to rent a house with a yard so she can play."

"Maybe I can get her a dog?" My thoughts shifted to picking out a puppy for her, already ten steps ahead.

"Can't have pets," Katherine shook her head.

We didn't say anything again for a while, enjoying this weirdly pleasant time together. Without a doubt there was tension between us, we both didn't know how to navigate this part of our lives together. But we would have to figure it out because now that Millie was back in my life, I'd be damned she would be taken away again. Katherine knew that.

Suddenly Katherine stood up and brushed her shorts off. "Millie, time to go!"

"Already?" I scrambled to my feet. "We just got here."

"No, *you* just got here. We've been here for over an hour already." She wouldn't look at me.

"But you told me to be here in an hour at the shop," I glared. I felt tricked.

Millie bounced over then and Katherine took her hand.

"You got to see her." Katherine pushed past me, and I hurried after them.

"What, so, almost a hundred grand buys me fifteen minutes?" I hissed.

Katherine ignored me and continued towards her truck. "Just wait!" I stepped in front of her path, and she skidded to a halt, her face annoyed.

"I'm not comfortable, Tristan," she growled. "The restraining order is still in place."

Millie looked between us, her wide eyes alarmed.

"I know, I know," I rushed. I ran my hands through my hair. I didn't know what to say to make her stay longer, I didn't know what to do. "I just need to be in her life, Katherine. She needs to know me, and I want to be there. Please just give me a way to reach out to you."

Katherine chewed the loop through her bottom lip again.

"Hold on." She tugged Millie after her and stomped over to the truck. She instructed Millie to climb in as she rummaged through her purse, handing me a card to the Motel 6 they were staying at. "When you get the money you can call me here, the room number is on it."

"You're staying at this dump?" I frowned. "You can stay at the trailer, as long as you want. I updated the room for Millie, I don't have to be there." I stepped eagerly towards her, and she stiffened. Her white-blue eyes darted behind me and whatever she saw there made her face twist in anger.

"I have the room for only a week. Call me when you have the money." Then she turned and climbed into the truck. I studied the card in my hand, committing the number to memory. I walked numbly back to the Cutlass, wondering why her mood had soured so suddenly. I froze when I saw it.

Hunter's car seat was still in the back seat of my car.

I fidgeted anxiously; my nerves were on fire but everyone else was moving too slowly. The shop had closed an hour ago and everyone was doing their due diligence cleaning up and resetting everything for the next day, but I was too distracted to help.

Slowly the crew started making their way over to our usual meeting spot at the couches. Cherry joined though she never really took part in doing the runs, she mostly waited at the shop in case anyone–mainly me–needed to get stitched back up afterwards. The crew was all here but we continued to wait until Charlie finally dragged himself out of the office.

"Well, you called the meeting, so start," Charlie grumbled. He perched on the edge of the couch and took a cigarette from Louis. Energy was racing through my veins, damn near causing me to bounce in place.

"I need to make a run–*tonight*, I need eighty grand."

"Per person?" Charlie balked. During our usual deals we usually got a couple of grand each with Charlie getting the majority, very rarely did we ever smack a total like that for *each* person.

"No…uh." I shook my head. "I need to come up with eighty grand as soon as possible. Katherine and Millie are back." A hushed silence fell over the crew then as each person exchanged knowing looks. Cherry stiffened but her expression remained neutral, no doubt she was already aware.

"What do you mean they're back?" Louis frowned.

"They're moving back to the area and Katherine needs money to help with the move." The words came out in a rush, my tone annoyed that we were wasting time on details.

"Lemme guess, you help her, or you don't see Millie?" Donovan's face hardened.

"Who cares?" I shouted. "The point is–I have a chance to be a father to my daughter finally and I need your help." I looked at each of them, desperately pleading with my eyes.

"Tonight, can't work," Charlie finally spoke up. "There's not enough time to gather information, let alone even find a target."

"So, find one!" I shouted. "You have your people all over, I'm sure one of them can come up with something."

"I agree," Greg spoke up but avoided looking at me. "Shitty planning means someone dies or goes to jail, and I don't want that to happen. We need more time."

"I can't believe this," I shook my head, the excitement evaporated from my body. "We've pulled runs last minute before."

"But it also means finding a *buyer* Tristan," Cherry chirped, and I shot an evil look at her. She dropped her eyes to the floor.

"They're right," Donovan spoke up. "We know how badly you want to be with your daughter, man. But these things have to be set up beforehand."

"You know we're all down to do whatever it costs to get you to your baby again," Tony nodded, his face sincere. "I can't imagine what you're going through. But dude…we gotta be smart about it."

"Man, you all–" I began, my face hot with rage but Charlie stood up.

"Enough," he barked. "We will get you your money but it's not worth losing one of the crew. Give us a few days and we will figure it out."

Charlie motioned for everyone to leave and slowly they all made their departure. Greg, Louis and Tony all threw sympathetic glances my way as they hurried out and away before my temper could get the best of me. Cherry turned on her heels and stalked away without another word. Donovan lingered at my side.

Charlie finally turned to look at me squarely. If there was ever anyone, I've ever come across who was never afraid to stand up to me it was him. Only because I wouldn't ever hit him back.

"I'm not risking their lives for you," he said flatly. "This is why you aren't running the crew, you're too impulsive–too immature. You don't think before you act."

"Like you're any fucking better," I spat. "You send *us* out– mainly *me* to do your dirty work so you can do what? Sit up in your trash ass house smoking weed all day and collect money off our backs? How many times have you been shot or stabbed? You want me to show you my fucking scars?"

Donovan grabbed my arm and tugged me backwards. I hadn't realized that I was towering over Charlie, my fists clenched at my sides.

"This is exactly why you lost Katherine and Millie in the first place," Charlie rolled his eyes. "You're all fucking temper and no thoughts in your fucking brain. I can see that you're hurting, that you want to do whatever you need to see her again, but you need to *think*."

"What about Barry? He has a crew. He's trying to collaborate with us, let me work with him."

"Barry is in Oregon for his kid's graduation." Charlie shook his head. "We're supposed to meet in a few weeks to get his kid on board with us–it doesn't work."

"T, man it's not happening tonight," Donovan said, and my body stiffened. "We're all down to back you up but your dad is right. We need to plan."

My chest tightened but I dropped my shoulders. I knew they were right. I would die for my guys if the roles were reversed but it was selfish to expect the same in return.

"I'll look into it," Charlie nodded, seeing my resolve. "I'll try to find something for you before the end of the week."

Donovan followed me around like a puppy dog for the next two days. Every time I turned around, I would catch him looking away from me quickly. I tried to not let it bother me, to remember that he meant well but never in my life had I ever wanted to punch the motherfucker in the mouth.

"I'm not going to try to kill myself again," I blurted after I almost plowed him down because he was underfoot again. Hurt flashed through his face and I regretted it. I had put him through so much during our friendship, it really wasn't fair. The shop was full today and everyone looked over at us and my face reddened. Silently, I stepped around him and went back to what I was working on.

I didn't drink again, not after I puked my guts out and wholeheartedly contemplated attempting to hurt myself again. If Donovan hadn't followed me and found me lying in a crumpled mess on the side of the street, I most certainly would have thrown myself over the railing to the swiftly moving water below. The idea of being a father to my daughter again, better this time around, was the only thing that made me open my eyes every morning. But knowing that I had abandoned another child, just like his own father, made me want to close my eyes forever. It was a confusing fucking time.

I called the number at the motel to check on Millie, but Katherine only allotted me a minute or two to speak to our daughter each time. I tried to be patient, to see things from Katherine's perspective but it was getting increasingly more difficult each day. Sure, I had done my damage in our relationship, had put her in unsafe situations but she had also done her own to hurt me in return. I thought of Jimmy and my blood turned to acid. The stupid fucker had everything, and I hated that I was jealous of him. If we could change places, I absolutely would. I would change everything and get back to Ophelia and Hunter.

I had been so focused on getting the money for Katherine that I hadn't had time to think about much else. Their names stung like someone had ripped a Band-Aid off, taking layers of flesh away with it. Anxiety ripped through my stomach, and I hurried outside of the shop to catch my breath.

You're fucking cruel, I thought. I wasn't religious by any means but if there was someone to blame, someone to point fingers at, it was Him. Nothing in my life had ever been easy. When Katherine told me she was pregnant, I suddenly didn't hate life so much. When Ophelia came into the picture, I thought that I had found my purpose. It was a cruel, sick joke to have both taken away from me. Maybe He wanted me to try again…to remove myself completely this time around. *Keep trying me, fucker, and I fucking promise that I will.*

Tristan
28

Sweat dripped from my brow as I wiped oil from my hands on a dirty rag. It was fucking stifling inside of the shop. The Bay Area "spring" was in full effect, over 90 fucking degrees out and no air conditioner in the entire building. Charlie wouldn't let me go shirtless, so I was condemned to sweat to death. A sharp whistle made me look up to see Charlie staring at me, poking his head out from the office. He gestured at me and I grudgingly obliged.

I followed Charlie around the front desk to his back-office space, which is where I had been sleeping for the last few months. "I located a job to get you your money," he said. "I don't have a lot of intel on it, but it can be worth nearly one hundred thousand tops."

"Great," I nodded. "When can we go?"

"Just slow down." Charlie gestured at me as if stopping traffic. "I'm telling you that I don't have a lot of intel. What I *do* know is that there is a pawn shop out of Stockton that keeps a fairly good amount of cash on them at all times. They have the most of their cash in hand on Thursday nights before the manager takes about half of what's on hand to the bank."

"That's tonight," I said excitedly. "It'll take an hour to get out there without traffic."

"Get your guys together, shouldn't take many of you, it's a small shop. You could probably get it done with just Don, there should only be the store manager there at closing time." My mind was racing, a checklist already forming. We usually didn't hit stores, we kept it mostly to cars and parts but in desperate times… I hurried to the door and stopped abruptly after a second thought. I looked back over my shoulder.

"Thanks Charlie."

An hour later we were on our way to Stockton with the address Charlie provided, ski masks, guns, and duffle bags. If we got pulled over it was right to jail for both of us. I was in a lighter mood than I had been in years. The weather was nice, we cranked the windows in the Saab and blasted music as we drove down highway 4 around Mt. Diablo.

Charlie said it should be an easy job, in and out. His information came from an ex-employee who owed him a favor. I was touched that Charlie had been on the lookout for information to help me out without looking for a cut himself. This was also new territory of us, hitting up a pawn shop, so maybe he didn't want a part in it after all. Whatever got me to Millie was all that mattered.

We got to a little store called Vinny's Pawn Shop, a little after six. The shop closed at eight, so we had time to check out the area, plan our best routes out of there and whatnot. The shop itself was a single, small building that was a standalone on a weed-filled lot. There was a small parking lot in the back with plenty of access. The highway entrance was only a hundred yards away and from what we could see through the windows, there was only one employee—probably the manager. So far, it seemed like an easy deal.

Don and I grabbed a bite to eat at the Sonic a few streets over, no sense in letting our blood sugar tank in the middle of a robbery. I stared out of the windshield absentmindedly, my mind raced with different scenarios of how this would go. I might have been desperate, but I wasn't dumb enough to forget that if we got caught, that would be my third strike which meant life in prison. The sun slowly crawled across the vast expanse of the blue sky towards the mountains in the west, painting the sky a golden orange.

"Do you remember when we were little," Donovan began, staring out at the sunset. "My mom took us to Pacifica that one year with the really bad heat wave?"

"Yeah," I chuckled, I didn't have to think hard. "That one beach trip where she fell asleep?"

"Yeah, that one," Don chuckled, nodding. "She fell asleep instead of watching us and we went to play in the water. We both almost drowned but some nearby mom saved us."

"She was really pissed at your mom," I said. "Then when we got back all of your pet rats had died from the heat."

"The fish practically boiled in their tanks." Donovan and I both laughed really hard at that, at remembering coming home to all of his pets roasted to death. It was really fucking awful but also disturbingly funny.

"Listen," I cleared my throat when we finally stopped laughing. "I don't think I've ever told you…but thank you for your help, man. From everything when we were kids, to the shit with Katherine…saving my life and now, helping me get my daughter back." I stared out the driver's side window as I spoke, I found it unnecessarily difficult to speak those words out loud. Also uncomfortable, Donovan looked out his own window.

"That's what brothers do," he shrugged. I elbowed him softly and chuckled.

The sun dipped further, the sky taking on a deep purple color and my adrenaline began to pick up. The clock hit eight and it was time to roll. I maneuvered the Saab slowly down the street towards Vinny's Pawn Shop, making sure the traffic got ahead of me and drove past before I cut the headlights and pulled into the parking lot. The Saab hitched and bounced over the unpaved lot to the back where there weren't any cameras. Charlie's connection had given us a lot of information about how to hit this shop the best. According to the ex-employee, it was only the manager who closed up shop and the only gun in the store was a revolver under the cash register. The safe was in the back.

I reached under the seat and pulled out the Remington 870 12 gauge sawed off shotgun and laid it across my lap. It was heavy. Donovan had his 9mm and we both had a black duffle, gloves, and a ski mask. I tugged my mask over my head and rolled it down into my shirt collar to conceal my tattoos and looked at Donovan. His large brown eyes were calm, ready.

I went first, using my size and massive gun as an intimidation factor. I kicked open the front glass door and aimed my gun at Vinny. He was a fat dude, Charlie's age with a thick black mustache.

"Hands fucking up!" I shouted.

Don slammed the door closed behind us, locked it and flipped the *open* sign to *closed*. Vinny's eyes shot wide with surprise, but he raised his hands obediently.

"Hand over the gun under the register–now!"

He jumped and hurriedly made his way over to the register. I shadowed him, keeping my gun on him and watching his hands carefully. My heart pounded, blood rushing through my ears. Vinny grabbed the butt of the pistol and laid it on the counter. Don scooped it up and stuffed it into his waistband.

"W-what do you want?" Vinny stammered. "I have watches, jewelry–gold even! You can have whatever you want!"

"I don't want your garbage," I snarled. "Take me to the back where the safe is." Confusion flickered across his face, and he hesitated. No doubt he was wondering if someone had informed me or if I was bluffing. He was about to find out. Thinking better, he turned quickly and shuffled towards the back. I leapt over the glass counter and followed him closely, shoving the barrel of the sawed off into the back of his neck. He was sweating profusely.

He pushed open a door and there it was. A large green, safe with a keypad and a silver, 3-spoke handle. Vinny halted suddenly without turning but I shoved him forward. He stumbled against the safe and looked up at me, pleading in his eyes.

"Open it."

Vinny sighed and punched in a code and spun the handle, a satisfying *clunk* sounded, and the door popped open.

I tossed both duffels at him. "Fill them up–quick."

Vinny kneeled in front of the safe and began shoveling money into the bags, the first one filled quickly. I snagged it toward me and kept the gun level with him, urging him to fill the next bag.

"Hurry it up, man!" Donovan yelled from the front. We had allotted five minutes. Five minutes to be in, out and on our fucking way. Time was ticking. Vinny was moving too slowly; my nerves were on edge. I kicked his foot hard to get his attention.

"Keep it fucking pushin' old man," I snarled. "I have no problem blowing your brains all over this shop."

Vinny tucked his head and shoved handfuls of loose cash into the second bag. Finally, the second bag was full.

"Now what?" Vinny whimpered, his hands raised and his eyes on the floor.

"Pick the bags up, take them to the front."

Vinny did as he was told, struggling to grip the weight of both bags as he waddled towards the front with them. He grunted as he hefted them up onto the glass display case that cut the store in half. I leapt easily back over the counter to join Donovan and slid the strap of the first duffle over my shoulder and slid it off of the counter. The weight pulled on my shoulder, but my adrenaline was pumping too hard through my veins for it to phase me. Holding the bag and the large sawed off was difficult so I backed away first and unlocked the door while Donovan held his 9 on Vinny.

Hate poured out of Vinny's wrinkled eyes as I popped the glass door open.

"We're out," I hissed at Donovan and dipped out the door. I had left the Saab running with the headlights off, it took my eyes a moment to adjust to the dark to find the car. I sprinted for it and threw the heavy duffle into the trunk with the shotgun. I threw open the driver's side door and turned, waiting anxiously for Donovan. He backed out of the shop with his gun pointed at Vinny, when he was sure he wasn't going to move, Donovan turned and began to jog back to the car. Excitement pounded through me, my hands trembled on the door, ready to get the hell out of there.

An explosion rang out and I recoiled away from the blast. It was so sudden and blaring that it caught me off guard. Donovan faltered, stumbling forward slightly. There was a sickening moment where Donovan's wide, scared brown eyes met mine and I realized what had happened. Before I could move, another gun blast tore through his chest, and he pitched forward. I snatched the shot gun out of the trunk as a third blast shook the space between us.

I pumped the shotgun and fired, the power of the explosion bit through my arms but I didn't care. I stalked forward simultaneously pumping the shotgun again and fired a second time. Vinny's large body shook with the impact, blood sprayed like in a movie but still I advanced forward, pumping and shooting. Crimson filled my vision, my eyesight tunneled into a small pinpoint and all I saw was Vinny. He collapsed backwards; his abdomen was a gnarled, bloody mess. I kicked the revolver from his hands and pointed the gun down at his face. The next blast exploded his head into a bloody mess all over the cement.

I loomed over Vinny's dead body, breathing hard, unable to process what just happened. A small, wet cough made me spin on my heels and race back to Donovan. He was face down, choking. I rolled him onto his back and gasped in horror. I tore the ski mask from his head and groaned. Donovan's face was pale, molten with blood splatter across his skin. His lips gaped open like he was trying to drink the air as gasps rattled through him.

"Oh fuck, oh fuck," I cried. "Donny, no, no, no!" A broken howl escaped me as I clung to him. His body already felt weak in my arms. I hoisted Donny up, cradling him in my arms while I simultaneously slung the duffle over my shoulder. I sprinted towards the Saab like they were weightless.

Moments later, I tore out of the parking lot and headed for the highway. The tires hit the asphalt with a screech, the back end of the car fishtailed dangerously but I quickly got control and slammed the ramp onto the highway back home.

"Shit Donny!" I tore the ski mask off my sweaty head and threw it in the back seat. He leaned back against the doorframe, his brown eyes stared at me for help. Keeping one hand on the steering wheel, I pulled his shirt down and blood sprayed my face. Half of his neck was gone. I couldn't even see where else he had been hit but without a doubt the neck wound would be fatal. Somehow, I managed to pull off my black hoodie without crashing the car and pressed it hard against the flowing blood. Donovan's hands grabbed for my wrist; I knew he was panicking.

"Just hold on dude, just hold on. I'll get you help." Donny's hand gripped mine with surprising strength and his eyes pleaded.

If I took him to the hospital, they would automatically call the cops since it was a gunshot wound and if he survived, we'd both end up in jail. He wasn't going to survive without medical help, more than what Cherry could do in the garage.

Donny was going to die, and he knew it. Tears streaked my hot face as I slammed down on the gas. By some fucking miracle, I didn't get pulled over doing well over 100 miles per hour out of Stockton back to Oakland. Donovan held on the entire drive. The Saab bounced wildly over the gate entrance, and I laid on the horn, alerting everyone inside to come out. The tires screeched to a halt, clipping the edge of a cement barrier and shattering the left headlight.

"What is it?" Greg shouted, running for us followed by the rest of the crew.

"Fucking Donny, man!" I shouted as I put my arms under Donovan's and hoisted him out. "He's been shot, it's fucking bad."

Everyone froze, unable to process what was happening.

"Get him inside!" Cherry shouted from the opening of the garage. That kicked everyone into gear. Greg and Louis ran to the car to get the guns and cash out while Tony ran ahead to clear a long table as I carried Donny inside.

How many times had I been laid up on this same table? Getting stitched up by Cherry and once even came close to dying myself last year when a bullet took out the back of my own neck. But this was different because this time it was Donny and it looked bad.

Cherry used a pair of scissors to cut Donny out of his black hoodie and I winced. He had been shot in the back twice, both were clear exits as his chest was ripped to shit. His ruined chest rose and fell rapidly, fighting for air, the breath made a squeaking sound through his gaping mouth. Cherry froze and her eyes flashed to mine, uncertain.

"Oh, Donny I'm so sorry, I'm so sorry," I collapsed forward and wrapped my arms around him the best I could. I pressed my forehead to his and he was ice cold. He lifted his right hand shakily; it swayed in the air as he fought to control it but it fell back down to his side.

"This is all my fault; you didn't deserve this."

A loud cough racked through his body, and I jolted upright as blood sprayed from his mouth. It splattered across Cherry's chest, and she jumped back. Donny continued to hack, his throat filling with blood. I desperately turned him on his side but there was nothing that I could do to clear it for him. A spasm seized through him then.

Nothing.

Everyone froze as an eerie silence fell across the room. A whimper squeaked out of me. I didn't want to look; I didn't want to know but I could feel that his life was gone. Shaking, I slowly rolled Donny onto his back. His brown eyes were glassed over, staring unseeingly straight ahead. My knees hit the ground; my body slumped forward.

Today I had to get shit done. I rose slowly to my feet letting the blood move sluggishly against gravity. This house felt so much smaller than it did when I was a kid. The bathroom was just a step past the door frame of the bedroom I slept in. I turned the knob for the shower and water sputtered out slowly. The smell of vanilla filled the room just before gentle hands touched my back. I didn't need to turn around to know it was Cherry but still I turned to face her.

Her green eyes were soft, sad as she took in my appearance. It had been three days since Donny was killed. His dry blood still covered my skin and clothes. Wordlessly, she took the hem of my shirt and began to work it up my body. I helped her remove it and let it fall to the floor at my feet. She began to undo my belt buckle but there was no sensuality behind it. The metal tinkled softly in the silence as she gently pushed my dirty jeans down my legs.

Slowly she lifted her hands palm up and placed them softly on my chest. I sighed at the warmth in her touch and my face crumpled. I wrapped my arms around her and pulled her into me, burying my face in her hair as pain gnawed in my chest. Her small hands smoothed my back, caressing me and pulling me against her. She waited until the quiet sobs stopped shaking through my body before she lifted her chin up towards me. Without thinking, I planted my lips onto hers. Cherry opened her mouth and licked my bottom lip, but I recoiled. Her face pinched but she didn't respond. She let me pull away and step into the small shower. I expected her to leave but instead, I heard her undressing.

A moment later she joined me in the shower.

"Cherry…" I groaned without turning to face her.

"Shh." She hushed me and put a fresh rag to my back. I sighed tiredly as she washed the blood and sweat from my body. "Turn around."

I did as she said, and she reached up on her tiptoes to reach my hair. She purposefully pressed her large breast against me, but my body didn't respond. I was too exhausted. I was too tall for the shower head, so she cupped the water in her hands and poured it over my hair until she was satisfied that I was clean.

She flattened her feet, raking her naked body against mine as she did. I looked down at her, water dripped down my face as I studied her. She was gorgeous, she had a beautiful body. Another time, I would have been tempted to take her right then. We stood in the shower stream for some time, my hands on her hips and her fingers tracing patterns over my stomach. I sighed and gently moved her towards the edge of the tub. She got out and wrapped a towel around herself, holding one out for me and I wrapped it around my hips.

"For you," she motioned to a pile of clothes folded neatly on the toilet seat with a toothbrush with toothpaste and a hairbrush on top. "Thought you wanted to feel human today."

"Thanks Cherry." I hesitated but leaned down and kissed her softly on the cheek. She smiled up at me as she began to dress again.

Before I left, I stopped in Tasoula's room. I lingered in the doorway for some time just watching her breathe. Donny had been her only caregiver so what would become of her now? We would never let her just fade away, we would have to pull together and find a way for her to get care now that Donny…My brow pinched together. I could barely bring myself to think about it. I swallowed hard and went to her side. The machines beeped softly in the background.

"Tasoula," I sniffed. I gingerly touched my fingertips to the back of her hand. I didn't even know if she could hear me, but I remembered Donny speaking to her as if she would respond. There was no black phone for Donny. "Donny died three days ago; he was shot."

I don't know what I expected from Tasoula. To wake up and tell me what a piece of shit I was? That I never should have tainted Donny's life? For her to pass away from grief? Tasoula continued to lie completely still with the exception of the gentle rise and fall of her chest.

I squeezed her hand and left.

Donny and I had cleaned one hundred and twenty grand off of Vinny. The crew had counted it all while I was out. Before I left, I handed Cherry a band of ten thousand for making arrangements for Tasoula. Then I stopped at the shop and gave Charlie another ten thousand to finish paying off the remainder of what I owed him for house repairs. I tossed the money in his lap and walked away without a word. Katherine needed eighty which left me with $20,000 I didn't know what the fuck to do with. Having that amount of cash on me made me nervous but I couldn't just go deposit it in a bank, it would look suspicious. I would have to make small deposits over time until I could stash it all away.

My knuckles wrapped quickly on the hotel door. A few moments later, Katherine answered. She didn't speak, just leveled me with her eyes. I wasn't in the fucking mood. I pushed past her into the hotel room, but she didn't protest. Millie was sprawled out on the second small bed with a coloring book. A wave of relief washed over me, of feeling like life had a purpose and that Donny's death wasn't for nothing. Millie glanced up and I watched as the recognition filled her eyes for the first time.

"Oh hi," she squealed with a small smile. Wordlessly, I put my hand gently on the top of her head and sat on the edge of the bed with her, dropping the duffle by my feet. Katherine eyed the hefty bag and hurriedly shut the door.

"Did you get it?" There was surprise but also excitement in her voice.

"Donny's dead," I blurted, my voice full of venom. Katherine faltered in her step; her eyes were wide with surprise. She knew what that meant for me.

"Oh, Tristan," she whimpered.

When I could finally speak, I glared at her.

"I want my daughter," I said.

Katherine's face was sincere, her eyes soft.

"I want to know where you guys live. I want to have her when she's not in school. I want her to know me. I'll keep sending you money every week for anything she needs."

Katherine looked between Millie and me, the room was tensely quiet.

"Can I, mom?" Millie sat up on her knees, eagerly.

Katherine chewed her lip ring and glanced at the large duffle bag.

"Okay," she sighed.

Millie bounced excitedly on the bed and threw her little arms around my neck. I melted. I knew it wasn't that she was excited for *me*, she knew nothing about me. She was more excited for something new, but it still made my heart ache.

"C'mon Millie." I patted her arm and stood up. Millie jumped off the bed and quickly tugged on her sandals. Katherine followed on our heels out of the hotel to my car, rattling on about something but I didn't pay attention. I opened up the car door and folded the seat forward so Millie could crawl in. I directed her to sit in the new booster seat next to Hunter's car seat. Once she was safely buckled, I popped open the trunk and handed Katherine a second booster seat.

"Put that in your truck," I said. She took it with a confused look on her face. "Millie is too little to ride in a car without it–that isn't safe."

"O-okay," Katherine stammered. "T–wait!"

I stopped before I could close the driver's side door and looked up at her.

"I'm going to take her for the day, I'll bring her back tonight before bedtime."

"That's fine but. . .let me give you my number just in case." Surprised, I handed her my new cell phone so she could program her number in. Katherine wasn't stupid, she knew we had the ability to track her location with her phone number. She was trusting me.

"Thanks." I slammed the driver's side door, and we were gone.

I finally got to be a father to my daughter. I convinced Katherine to stay a little longer, letting them stay in the trailer while I continued to crash at the shop. Millie was excited to see her bedroom all set up for her with new toys, I couldn't help but feel a swell of emotion seeing her in her room.

Millie came to the shop with me most days and she loved it. The crew spoiled the shit out of her, sneaking her candy when I wasn't looking, letting her hold tools like she was helping. My heart was broken and full at the same time. It was hard to grieve when I was so fucking happy. Katherine went to Vallejo a few times that week to finalize things on the new place and let me keep Millie all to myself. She told me about school and her friends, the teachers she didn't like and the lizards she found on the playground. Her favorite class was computers and she hated math though she was good at it.

"Mom never lets me stay home," Millie pouted. "She said school is important."

"It is important, baby girl, you can do whatever you want in life, but you have to go to school."

She didn't like that answer. She frowned down at the bolt she was rolling between her hands.

"Did *you* go to school?" She sneered.

"Of course I did," I held my arms out wide to display the grease all over my clothes and arms. "I'm a doctor." Millie's nose wrinkled and then she laughed loudly, throwing her head back.

"A doctor for cars!" She laughed.

I took her to Six Flags and we rode as many rides as we could, she was surprisingly brave eight-year-old. We watched the orcas and dolphins jump through hoops and the tigers leap up high for chunks of meat. I watched her as she skipped through the butterfly exhibit, her hair turning into a frizzy mess from the humidity. She rode the small, dragon roller coaster over and over. When we were done, I carried her all the way up the steep hill to the car as she snored on my shoulder. The sun had gone down hours ago, but the air was still warm. A handful of stars blinked lazily in the inky sky above us. I laughed quietly as she patted my back softly in her sleep, her hands sticky from cotton candy.

"I missed you so much Millie baby," I whispered into her hair.

Katherine had asked if Millie could come stay with her until we figured out a new schedule and I agreed. It was hard taking Millie back to her mom, but I also knew it wasn't forever, that it wouldn't be like last time. Katherine came out when she heard my car pull into the wide driveway just a few minutes later and waved me inside. I carried Millie in and followed Katherine to her new bedroom. It was an older house but was surprisingly spacious with a big back yard, three bedrooms and two baths.

"Three bedrooms?" I raised an eyebrow and Katherine shrugged.

"Thought maybe you could sleep in there when you wanted to come up…or it could be a playroom for Millie." She avoided my eyes, but I couldn't help but put an arm around her shoulders.

"Thank you, Katherine." I pressed my lips to the top of her hair and felt her body stiffen. "This is all I wanted."

"We need to discuss how we are going to coparent," she stated.

"We will," I nodded.

We didn't have a funeral for Donny–couldn't risk there being an investigation due to the gunshot wounds. Instead, we took his body and buried him in the Muir Woods just a hundred feet from the beach under a massive redwood. We weren't strangers to having to bury dead bodies, to get rid of evidence but this wasn't a routine burial. This was Donny, one of our own. We took our time and were gentle with him even though I shattered over and over the entire time. Cherry had suggested that I let the others handle it, but I couldn't do that to Donny.

Greg's headlights were steady in my rearview on the way home, not letting me get too far away. I had a feeling that they were all going to continue to watch me closely for a long time.

Ophelia
29

I hated how weak I was. How destroyed I was. It had been months without a word from Tristan, but his message was clear, he didn't want me. Every night I wracked my brain to figure out *what I did wrong*, but I couldn't pinpoint it. Tristan was an emotional rollercoaster, it was exhausting but after…David, I felt like we had been closer than ever.

Jimmy even noticed the change in me and mentioned something when I picked up Hunter. I just shrugged him off and we never spoke of it again. With Tamara, it was a different story. I cried loudly on her bed while Hunter played in the living room.

"Oh, sweet baby," Tamara patted my back as I sobbed. My mother had never been a maternal person, never one to share a lot of emotions but she let me ache. Of course, I didn't tell her about David and what had happened to him. I kept it short: I was dating this guy and now I wasn't. "Your first break up after your divorce must be hard."

"It isn't just that." I shook my head. "He made me fall for him…so hard." I wiped my face on the back of my hands. Tamara didn't respond, just looked at me pitifully but I didn't expect her to. This wasn't just a normal break up, but I couldn't tell her that.

I barely passed Microbiology. Which could have ruined my chances of applying to the nursing program, but I scraped by with a B.

"Where's Mr. Lombardi?" Professor Whitmore had asked me as he handed me back my paperwork. My throat tightened, so I just shrugged.

"Oh well, you'll just have to complete the project on your own," he said.

Which I did, turning in the final piece just before midnight when it was due. The organism I had collected off the bottom of my work shoe was simply *Staphylococcus aureus*, a rather common and benign organism unless it gets inside of your body somehow. Done with Microbiology, it meant I was done with my degree, and I would be applying to the program in the next few weeks.

Though I was excited to finally be done, it was hard for me to focus on the future and to be proud of myself. Then Crystal dropped a bomb on me.

"When our lease is up, I'll be moving in with Steven," she announced. My mind instantly began crunching numbers: that meant I had one month left until I either had to find someplace else to move or pay her half of the rent. Which meant an extra $700 a month, which I did not have.

"O-okay," I stammered. One month wasn't a lot of time to save up money to move or get a second job to cover her portion of the rent. Now that I wasn't in school, I had more time to pick up shifts at work but if I got into a nursing program, it was full time…It felt like Crystal had punched me in the gut and knocked the wind out of me.

She left me alone to panic after that. What was I going to do? Hunter and I were about to lose where we lived.

I stomped down the stairs outside the apartment to my car, slamming the door behind me. The anger was a nice reprieve from the dread that had taken over my body these last few months. It was nice to feel something.

I pushed my old, crappy Toyota as fast as it would go. Hunter was with Jimmy for the next two days, freeing me up to lose my mind. Exit signs blew past me on the highway, I darted around slow cars across the boiling asphalt. I took my exit sharply, the little car clung to the road as I flew around the exit too quickly. By the time my little Toyota bounced over the gate entrance to L&L, my heart was pounding.

The sun had begun to lazily dip in the horizon though it was still easily 90 degrees out. The doors to the shop were all rolled down, closed early tonight but I knew he was in there. His clunky, white Oldsmobile Cutlass was parked in its usual spot out front. Music vibrated through the wood as I approached but I thought little of it as I kicked the door open.

I marched inside and skidded to a stop.

The air was thick with cigarette and weed smoke, it nearly choked me. But what made me halt so quickly were all the naked people having sex. Well, mostly naked women being humped roughly by familiar faces. It was clear that these weren't regular girlfriends but just hook ups, shamelessly being railed in front of others.

Worse still, were the lines of drugs on almost every flat surface. I don't know what I expected but this definitely wasn't it. A few heads snapped up when I stormed in, first confusion on their face slowly replaced by alarm.

"Where is he?" I demanded, my face burning hot. Louis was on his knees next to the coffee table, a dollar bill in his hand that he had intended to snort the drugs with.

"Uh…" He glanced towards the office. With that, I spun on my heel. "Ophelia, wait up!" He shouted over the music, but I ignored him.

The office door banged loudly against the opposite wall as I slammed it open and froze in my place for the second time. Cherry was completely naked and, on all fours, her large breast swinging heavily beneath her. Her wild, red hair pooled onto the thin bed beneath her like blood. Tristan glanced up, his face flushed with exertion from behind Cherry, his knuckles white from gripping her sides.

"The fuck?" he shouted when we locked eyes. "Oh shit!"

I glanced down at the pile of Tristan's clothes on the floor and spotted his black gun wedged into his pants. Without thinking, I lunged for the gun and aimed it directly at him. Cherry screamed.

"*Are you fucking serious?*" I screamed; my face hot as tears poured down my cheeks. Tristan detached himself from Cherry and held his hands up, his face a mask of shock. Cherry scrambled to cover herself.

"Ophelia what—what are you doing?" Tristan growled.

"After everything?" I continued, ignoring him. "After you killed David and *abandoned me*—you're off *fucking* her?"

The explosion from the gun sent a shockwave up my arm, the blast deafening in this enclosed space. Cherry's red hair exploded as the bullet shot passed her and impaled the wall behind her. They both froze for a millisecond before Tristan lunged off the bed toward me, grabbing the gun from my hand. Cherry tore out of the room, naked and crying with her clothes clutched to her chest.

Tristan wrestled the gun too easily out of my hand despite my best effort, shoving me backwards into the wall as he did.

"What the fuck are you doing?" He screamed. He switched the safety on and tossed the gun onto the bed. He had tugged his boxers back up, covering himself but his skin was dewy with sweat. I slapped him hard across the face and he grabbed me roughly by the top of my arms, his face burning with rage.

"You *abandoned* me!" I screamed back at him. His grip relaxed slightly on my arms. My fist collided with his chest, shoving him further away from me until he was backing away. He couldn't look at me.

I didn't care, my palm connected with his cheek, stinging my hand painfully as he tripped backwards onto the bed. His face crumpled as he curled up onto the bed, burying his face in the messy sheets. I stood over him, breathing hard as the anger slowly dissolved out of me. Tristan's body trembled, his fists balled up tightly at his chest and I realized he was crying.

Regret seeped through me as I stared at him. Tristan turned his head to look at me, pain radiated through his bright eyes.

"I'm sorry," he breathed. "I didn't know what to do."

"How do you think *I felt?*" I hissed. "You left me when I needed you the most."

A tear slipped free from his eye and trailed down his straight nose. His large hand reached out and gripped me by the back of the neck and he rested his forehead against mine.

"I didn't want to destroy you," he whispered.

"I don't understand," I glared. He stood suddenly, angrily gesturing towards the garage.

"Do you think this shit is *normal?*" He spat; his eyes hard. "You think this is a place you would bring Hunter to?"

I winced at my son's name. He knew I wouldn't be okay with it.

"He wouldn't be around this," I disagreed.

"That's just part of it Ophelia!" Tristan was shouting now, the veins in his neck bulged as his flesh darkened. "Do you *like* leaving a trail of dead bodies? Of looking over your shoulder wondering when the police were going to take you away?"

"You'd keep us safe." I shook my head.

"I can't protect you from everything!" he snarled. "Donny's dead. Shot in the fucking back doing a job for me. We couldn't even have a fucking funeral for him. Do you know what we did with his body?"

"Stop," I pinched my eyes shut hard.

"I buried my best friend in the fucking woods," he shook me as he spoke. "In an unmarked grave–where's the fucking dignity in that? Are you going to help me bury the next body? You're not made for this life, Ophelia," his voice was soft, begging me to understand. "I left because I didn't know what else to do. If I stayed around, then harm would continue to come after you and Hunter. I refuse to be the reason your lives are ruined."

"Our lives have been better *because of you*," I sniffed. "We were a family."

He gently brushed his hands over my shoulders. I sighed at the familiar sensation, my body aching for him.

"I've died every day without you," he said finally, his voice breaking. "I was just trying to do the right thing, no matter how much it killed me."

I turned slowly, calming myself as I looked up at him.

"I just want to be with you, I understand the risks," I said.

"You don't know what you're saying," he whispered, his brows pulled together.

"But Tristan, I *do*," I urged. "I know exactly what it means to be with you, to be in your life. But I also know that you would do anything to protect Hunter and I." My mouth soured and my stomach churned as I remembered the scene that I had walked into just minutes ago. I pulled back as if he had burnt me. "I just don't understand why…*her*."

"Cherry was just a distraction, a way of driving the wedge between us further. I thought if I got with her that it would be the final straw for you…for me." His eyes dropped shamefully to his feet as he spoke. "It was a boundary that I thought I had to cross."

I frowned at the bullet hole in the far wall. I had never even held a gun before I was firing it at Cherry. Tristan's eyes flashed across me and whatever he saw must have startled him because he quickly pulled the rest of his clothes back on and pulled me out of the office.

The moment we were out of the office, I began to gag and dry heave. Tristan's large hand smoothed my back while the other held my hair back in case I vomited. When I could finally catch my breath, I straightened and smoothed my hair away from the clammy skin of my face and neck.

Inside Tristan's rumbling Oldsmobile Cutlass, I couldn't stop touching him. I sat as close to him as I possibly could on the blue, leather bench, both arms wrapped around his and my head on his shoulder. It was like if I let go of him, he would disappear into a cloud of smoke.

"The trailer might be a mess," Tristan warned as we pulled into the narrow driveway. "Some of the guys have been crashing here the last few days and I haven't been home since…" his voice broke slightly, and he cleared his throat. "Since I thought we were done."

I nodded and kissed his shoulder softly.

I followed Tristan up the three small steps inside of the trailer and steeled myself for whatever was inside. The trailer was still surprisingly clean just not the way Tristan usually kept it clean. Tristan hurried around the trailer picking up dirty towels, plates and clothes while I stood awkwardly at the threshold.

"Let me just go shower really quickly," he said. "Make yourself comfortable baby, I'll be back." He took a small step toward me but seemed to change his mind and headed for the bathroom. I busied myself by making a pot of coffee and poured myself a cup in my favorite orange mug while the shower ran.

I sat at one of the bar stools tucked under the counter and sipped my coffee while I waited. The adrenaline of confronting Tristan and ultimately shooting at Cherry had taken its toll on me. The fact that I didn't even feel bad about almost killing Cherry was unnerving but the weird, unspoken jealousy between us had finally come to an end. Tristan might have fucked her but in the end, I made it abundantly clear that whatever they had was over and I was here permanently.

"What're you thinking about?" I jumped as Tristan's deep voice broke my train of thought.

"A lot to take in," I shrugged. A twinge of shame flickered through his face, but he quickly hid it. He nodded silently and went into his bedroom to change. He emerged a few minutes later in a black t-shirt and dark jeans, the red Boston Red Sox hat backwards. His dark hair was longer than it was when I last saw him, the curls more prominent as they hooked around the edges of his hat. He had small diamond studs in his ears that I hadn't seen before. I reached up and gently touched one and he smirked. "They were a gift from Donny a few years ago, I never wore them." A hint of sadness touched his eyes and his lips pressed into a flat line.

"Tell me what happened?" I said softly.

Tristan slumped onto the barstool next to me and leaned back against the counter. His breathing hitched and I watched as he swallowed hard and the muscles in his arms twitched.

"We had bad intel on a hit," he began. "We were told by an ex-employee that the manager only had one gun in the place." Tristan took a large, shuddering breath and shook his head. "Turns out there were at least two–fucker shot Donny in the back." His voice broke on the last word, and he dropped his face into his large hands. I slid down off the barstool and wrapped my arms around his broad shoulders the best I could.

"I'm so sorry, I'm so sorry." I repeated the words like a mantra as Tristan cried, his large shoulders shuddered under my arms while I fought to hold him to me. He pulled his hands away after a minute and wiped his wet eyes on the backs of his arms.

"I've missed you so much," he whispered. "It felt like I didn't have anyone left after Donny."

My chest burned at his words, remembering how empty I had felt without him. Silently, I lifted my face and kissed his cheek. The feel of his warm skin, the scent of him triggered something and I kissed him again, desperately. Tristan turned his face to meet my lips, cautiously at first then with more urgency as the hunger grew in both of us. His hands grabbed at my hips, crushing me to his side until he turned and pulled me between his legs and against his chest.

I wrapped my arms around his neck and steeled myself against his body impossibly tighter. His tongue roved into my mouth and twisted deliciously against mine. I moaned softly and his fists tightened on my hips. Then I pulled away sharply, shoving my hands against his chest as I struggled to catch my breath. His brilliant blue-green eyes burned intensely but his eyebrows knitted together in confusion.

Still not speaking, I reached down and took one of his hands in mine and pulled gently. His face smoothed as realization settled in and he rose to his feet. My heart pounded excitedly as I led Tristan across the living room to his bedroom.

His room was, for the most part, as I had remembered it. A bed without a headboard between two small nightstands, a black entertainment stand with a large TV, two large speakers stacked on top of each other and red drapes over the singular window. The bed was a mess, something I had never seen Tristan leave behind before–the remnants of whoever had been sleeping here in his absence. I didn't care.

I turned to face him, and I met his gaze evenly. He raised his scarred eyebrow silently as we stared at each other. I raised my arms above my head making Tristan chuckle as he lifted the baggy t-shirt up and off me.

It landed at our feet. To save me the effort, Tristan tossed his hat on the entertainment stand and pulled his own t-shirt off. The sheer *size* of Tristan was astounding let alone the defined muscles that rippled through his body like a bag of ropes. My palms skated up the *Reckless* tattoo across his stomach to the large scar on his chest opposite of the female Gypsy head tattoo.

I leaned forward and planted a soft kiss onto the ruined skin, and he sighed. Then I reached up and took his face in my hands, gently beckoning him to lean forward so that I could kiss the small scars on his cheek above his rose tattoo on his jaw, the thin scar that cut through his left eyebrow.

Tristan ran his long fingers through my hair, cupping the back of my head and forcing me to look up at him. His tormented eyes searched mine for a long moment.

"I love you," his voice was quiet but fierce. A knot formed in my throat, blocking my voice so that all I could do was nod. Tristan's face crumpled and his lips returned to mine hungrily again, fervent. I stepped back until I felt the bed behind me and pulled him down on top of me. Tristan maneuvered himself so that he was between my legs and sat back on his haunches.

His expert fingers grabbed at my waistband and unhooked the button in a matter of seconds while my hands fumbled with his belt clumsily. I lifted my hips so he could tug my shorts off me and toss them on the floor. He stopped for a moment to admire my body, running his large hands over the expanse of my stomach before he bent forward and kissed my sides.

I sighed heavily as his hot lips made a trail to my hip bone where he bit it softly and I yelped. He groaned against my flesh, and I broke out in goosebumps. Tristan kicked his pants off and pulled me down sharply towards him.

"Wait," I gasped, and he froze, his eyes excited but his face cautious.

"Are you okay?" He asked breathlessly and I knew that he was worried about pushing me after what happened with David. I nodded as I scrambled up onto my knees, so we were almost face to face.

"Lie down," I demanded. I shoved against his massive shoulders, but he didn't budge.

"Why?" He frowned.

"Just do it," I laughed and pushed him again. This time he let me, and he laid down on his back, watching me carefully. "I want to do this differently…" I trailed off, biting my lip nervously. "But…with Cherry…did–did you…?"

"I was safe baby, I promise."

"Okay." I crawled on top of him, straddling him as I watched excitement fill his face. He was already hard, and my body burned for him, so it was easy to set myself down on top of him. Tristan moaned, his eyes rolling backwards as pleasure erupted through my core. He had always been on top before and never let me be in control. I watched joyfully as Tristan struggled to relinquish control to me as my hips rocked and swiveled against him.

A few times, he tried to reach up and pull me down to kiss him, but I refused and swirled my hips faster until his hands fell to his sides. Sex with Tristan was always deliciously rough, I left smarting and bruised each time, but I wanted this time to be different.

I leaned forward, smashing my breast against his chest and his strong arms snared around me, crushing me tighter against him. His hands were in my hair, smoothing it back and gripping me all at the same time. His lips entangled with mine deliciously, his soft moans echoed in the chambers of my mouth. Something shifted in him, and his need quickly turned into something softer, something sadder.

His hands on me were no longer gripping but caressing, holding me to him as if he was trying to memorize the curves and valleys of my body. I pulled back enough to look down at him and his eyes were much softer, longing and pain swirled in their iridescent pools. When I bent to kiss him again, my own lips had turned sad and longing. Echoes of our time apart reverberated through me.

Tension built in my core, building wonderfully to the precipice. When it exploded, it shook my entire body and I collapsed with a cry on top of Tristan. We lay like that for some time, until our bodies cooled and stilled, our hearts quieted in our chests. He propped himself up on his elbow and looked down at me, his eyes moving over every inch of my body with an unreadable expression on his face.

"What?" I reached up and pushed his ebony hair out of his face. He turned and pressed his lips to the inside of my wrist, and I shivered.

"I feel selfish," he admitted with a shrug. "I'm not stupid Ophelia, I know how bad I am for you—that us being together is a mistake. But I can't help but be so fucking happy that you came back…and that you don't hate me for trying to keep you away."

"I couldn't hate you," I whispered. Then added jokingly: "Though I definitely tried."

"I promise that I only did it to protect you and Hunter." He faltered to a halt, and something flickered across his face. "Where is he?"

"With Jimmy."

Tristan smirked and was suddenly flipping over me and off the bed. He tossed my clothes at me.

"Let's go get our boy."

When Tristan emerged from the bedroom his eyes were downcast as he came to stand an arm's length from me.

"What?" I chuckled nervously in an attempt to break the tension.

"Are you sure?" His deep voice was even but guarded. I searched his turquoise eyes for understanding but all I saw was a blank wall. His devilishly beautiful face was blank, expressionless and suddenly it clicked. He was giving me a way out. After everything this last year together and especially after today, I thought we were passed this. I scowled up at him.

"Absolutely," I challenged. The corner of his broad lips twitched as he fought a smile. He glanced down and then back up at me through his long, black eyelashes, his molten eyes blazing and a smirk on his lips and my heart skipped a beat.

"If you're *really* down for me, I want you to have this." He held out a small, black square.

"A cell phone?" I scrunched my nose and a deep, booming laugh erupted from him.

"No," he continued laughing. "I mean, yeah, it's a phone but it's what we give someone important to let them know…if something happened to us."

"Oh." My voice dripped with disappointment as I turned the sleek phone over in my hand, the battery was dead, but it felt like a snake in my hand. It was going to come alive and dig its fangs into my flesh. "So…if something happens…?"

"Keep that charged and on at all times," he nodded to the phone. "In the event some shit goes down and I'm taken out, someone will call you on this to let you know then you destroy it. But it's not *just* a phone, Ophelia." His voice was suddenly serious, and he ducked his face to be level with mine, snagging my attention. "We have an agreement that whoever we give these phones to also gets our cut of whatever deal comes after we die. Forever."

"'After we die'," I echoed absentmindedly. "You sound so sure."

"Comes with the territory baby," he shrugged. I grimaced down at the phone again and that's when Tristan gently reached out and took my left hand in his. My brain had been a storm of *what-if*'s so it took me a moment to note the sudden, infinitesimal weight change on my fourth finger. It wasn't until Tristan ran his thumb over the gold band that it registered.

"What's this?" I gasped up at him. A blush bloomed gently across his cheeks.

"Whatever you want it to be," he whispered. "It can just be a promise if that's what you need right now. I would like it to be more than that, but I understand if you need more time before you marry me—"

"*Marry* you?" I couldn't help the way my voice shrieked, and he flinched. I closed my eyes and took a deep, steadying breath. "I just mean…I'm surprised."

"Why?" I could see the hurt darkening his eyes. "You're locked in with me baby. But I understand if you need more time."

I gaped at the simple, golden band around my ring finger and my thoughts flooded with all that the infinite circle meant. The silent cell phone in my other hand suddenly felt like an anvil waiting to fall on to my head.

"Okay," I whispered more so because I didn't know what else to say. Tristan's vice-like arms wrapped around me and squeezed me tightly.

Ophelia
30

Tristan was in a much lighter mood as we drove across town. He rolled the windows down and played music softly in the background, our hands locked together on the bench between us. He sang along with every song on the radio, and I was surprised at how good his voice was. I glanced into the back seat to check to see if he still had Hunter's car seat and frowned when I saw the second, bigger car seat.

"What's that from?"

"That's something we need to talk about…Millie's back." He saw the surprise in my face and his eyes quickly turned away. "Katherine popped up at the shop a few months back asking for money to help them move back out here. Long story short, we worked out some stuff and I get Millie on the weekends."

"Oh." I looked down at our hands on the bench and then out of the window. Part of me was thrilled that Tristan could finally have his daughter back, it was beyond evident how destroyed he was over not having her. I couldn't help but feel insecure about Katherine, after all, they had a very long and tumultuous relationship that resulted in their shared child.

"Oh?" Tristan raised an eyebrow at me. "Don't worry baby, Katherine and I are long done. That bridge is long since burnt, I just want my daughter."

"I know." I nodded and took a deep breath. "I'm excited to meet her."

Tristan flinched. The movement was so miniscule that I initially thought that I had imagined it.

"We might…need to ease Katherine into it." He grinned apologetically. "She's already very hesitant to let *me* back into Millie's life. Introducing her to my new girlfriend might freak her out."

"New girlfriend?" I scowled. "Is that all I am?" I pulled my hand out from his sharply. Tristan's jaw flexed and suddenly the Cutlass was careening sideways across traffic. I gasped and grabbed for the door handle as the inertia threw me backwards into my seat. Tristan slammed on the brakes, and I catapulted against the seatbelt and slammed back again. Tristan was on me in a flash, his hand gently but firmly gripped me by my chin, forcing me to look into his blazing, molten jade eyes.

"I'm not doing this shit with you again," he snarled through clenched teeth. "You wanna be mad about stupid little shit here and there–go ahead. But you're not fucking going anywhere again, I just got you back and you got me *fucked up* if you think I'm going to let you go again. Not with my grandmother's ring on your finger."

He released my chin with a small push and all I could do was stare at him. There was an obvious distinction between how he spoke to me and to his friends at the shop, with me he was much softer and with them he was very sharp and hurled swears and threats easily. Most of the guys in the Bay Area had a very similar way of speaking, especially when in a group of other men but Tristan never was so abrupt with me before. Sometime between Tristan slipping the ring on my hand and now, something in our relationship had changed.

I opened my mouth to say something, but he sighed heavily and crumpled forward, resting his forehead on the steering wheel.

His gold necklace slipped free from his black shirt and slowly swung between his chest and the steering wheel. How many times had I seen him in this exact position before?

"It'll fucking kill me," his deep voice was thick with emotion. "I swear to God Ophelia, I can't survive that shit again. I wanted to die when you were gone, so if you're back then be fucking *back*. Ride through this shit with me and I promise we will make it through it all."

"I never said I was leaving," I shook my head.

"I know but I can hear it in your voice—the disappointment. I will figure out Katherine, but I need you to be by my side supporting me as I do. She's a fucking handful."

"I will."

"That ring you're wearing—I mean it. Whole-fucking-heartedly." He turned to study me and whatever he saw there must have reassured him because he started driving again. "You're not allowed to take it off."

We approached Jimmy's apartment complex, and the row of small buildings was busy with people celebrating summer. Some barbequed on their front stoops, a gaggle of naked toddlers ran around between the parked cars while some lady sprayed them playfully with a hose and someone played music from a large speaker shoved haphazardly into a nearby window. I immediately grew suspicious that Jimmy wasn't perched on his own stoop with a beer in hand. He loved summer evenings because it meant he had more people to drink with and better weather to do it in.

I didn't voice my concerns as Tristan parked the Cutlass next to Jimmy's rusty Saturn. Tristan had gone with me multiple times to drop Hunter off or pick him up, he had even done the exchange himself when I was practically comatose after the David incident. I never had the chance to ask him how it went, and I was too deeply broken to ask Jimmy about it. Still, I didn't expect Tristan to get out of the car when we pulled up but suddenly, he was out of the car and I was scrambling after him.

Two guys were hanging out in the shade of their front porch as we walked by, and their eyes were glued to Tristan. Without a doubt they were trying to figure out who he was and what he was doing here. Someone Tristan's size didn't go unnoticed, but they were smart enough to stay silent.

"Tristan," I hissed as he pushed the unlocked door open. He ignored me and entered Jimmy's house. Luckily it appeared that his roommates weren't home, but Jimmy and Hunter weren't in the living room. Instead, a large dirt bike stood on a mount in the middle of the dirty carpet.

It was clearly being worked on but by the garbage that had collected on top of it, it also appeared abandoned. Tristan halted so abruptly that I almost ran straight into his back, I had to hop to the side to avoid a collision. I opened my mouth to speak but the words died in my throat when I noticed how stiff Tristan had become, his hands were balled tightly into fists down at his sides.

"Fucker," he spat and suddenly whirled on his heels and stormed loudly down the short hall towards Jimmy's room, leaving me to hurry after him. Tristan's large black shoe smashed through Jimmy's bedroom door sending it flying open with a loud bang as it collided with the opposite wall.

"W-what the fuck?" Jimmy called out. Tristan was crouched over Jimmy with one hand clamped firmly around his thin neck, pulling his face up to his.

"I fucking *warned you*," Tristan hissed through gritted teeth. "Mama!" Hunter cried and my focus blew open to my surroundings. Hunter was curled up at the foot of the bed wearing the same t-shirt I had dropped him off in two days ago. His face was red from crying. I reached down and scooped him up in my arms and hissed when the smell of stale urine from Hunter's overly full diaper hit my nose.

"How long has he been in this diaper?" I said. Tristan released Jimmy and closed the small distance between us with one long stride. With a quick movement Tristan released the filthy diaper from around Hunter and hefted the weight in his hands. His burning eyes flashed up to mine and what I saw there made me shrink away from him. Tristan whirled and launched the oozing diaper open side into Jimmy's face where it landed with a wet *thwunk*.

"Tristan!" I hissed but it was useless.

Jimmy scrambled to get off the bed, but Tristan shoved him back down onto the dirty, bare mattress and pinned him there under his knee.

"What the fuck did I tell you last time I was here?" Tristan shouted. I clasped my hand over Hunter's ear and brought his head down to my chest in an attempt to shield him from Tristan's booming voice. Jimmy stared defiantly up at Tristan which only angered Tristan further. Tristan leaned his massive weight onto his knee in Jimmy's chest and Jimmy clawed at his leg. "Huh? You feel like ignoring your kid is okay? Letting him sit in his filth for two days straight while he cries?"

"Get–get–off," Jimmy gasped but Tristan leaned down further. "C-can't–breathe!"

"Tristan, that's enough!" I shouted but he ignored me. I turned swiftly and ran with Hunter out into the living room where I had seen his diaper bag. Quickly, I changed Hunter's diaper with him standing in a spot on the dirty carpet. I gently but thoroughly wiped his skin down as the heavy packing sound of flesh on flesh echoed from Jimmy's room.

My stomach heaved at the sound, but I did my best to hide it from Hunter. Satisfied that there was no longer any urine or feces left on Hunter, I told him to stay put and ran into Jimmy's bedroom. A small scream escaped me before I could clamp my hand over my mouth. Jimmy was no longer in his bed but now was crumpled on the floor beside it in a bloody mess. Already his face was unrecognizable, swollen to twice its normal size and purple.

Blood splattered his thin, bare chest, his hands, and the wall behind him. My stomach churned sharply, and I gagged as the rusty smell of blood reached me. But Tristan was coming for him again, lifting his bloody shoe to stomp on Jimmy's head. With all of my might, I grabbed the back of Tristan's shirt and pulled backwards causing the fabric to tear slightly and to teeter Tristan off balance.

One large hand lashed out and slammed against my stomach painfully. Stars burst into my vision from the pain as it gripped my chest. My throat burned like someone had shoved a red-hot poker down it, leaving me gasping for air. Tristan hardly noticed. I watched in horror as he reached into the back of his waistband and pulled out his handgun.

"Tristan!" I screeched through the pain and to my surprise, he halted. His massive shoulders rose and fell quickly with each frantic breath and part of me was glad that I couldn't see his face. Seeing my opportunity, I spoke again: "Please–please don't do this. He's had enough, please–let's just leave."

The moment spanned into eternity as I watched him deliberate. Jimmy was half conscious on the floor, his skinny arms thrown up over his head, his hands were shaking.

"You have one week." Tristan spoke slowly, carefully to ensure that Jimmy heard him. "You have one week to get your pathetic ass down to the courthouse. You're going to file to relinquish your parental rights to Hunter. Do you understand me?"

"Please, Tristan…" I took a step towards him. Tristan threw me a look over his shoulder that was so cold, it froze me in my tracks. When Jimmy didn't answer, Tristan kicked him sharply in the thigh and I flinched at the sound of Jimmy crying out.

"Do you fucking hear me?!" Tristan towered over Jimmy; the gun pointed at his head.

"Y-yes!" Jimmy cried out.

"One week," Tristan repeated. He spat a large wad that hit Jimmy's cheek with a wet smack. "You fucking loser. He's not your kid anymore."

Outside was a completely different world. The children were still playing. The food was still being barbecued and the music still played. I fumbled with Hunter's harness, unable to see through the thick layer of tears in my eyes until Tristan slapped my hands away and took over instead. I slumped into my seat and dropped forward, resting my forehead onto my knees, and hyperventilated.

The Cutlass roared to life around me and we were gone.

We rode in silence, my heart hammering my ears was the only thing that I could hear. A sour taste had filled my mouth and I fought hard not to vomit. My stomach still burned from Tristan hitting me–I don't think he even realized that he had.

Wordlessly, Tristan gently put his hand on the back of my head, and I recoiled away from him. A small hiss came from him as he snatched my left hand and slapped it over his chest. His heart pounded like a wild animal caged inside of his chest.

"You're *my* family," Tristan said very matter of fact with a slight nod. The anger was gone from his face, but his words were tight. A warning. His thumb brushed over the gold band on my finger. "I *will* kill for either of you." I pulled my hand back like he had stung me and scowled silently at him.

My head was a war of what I wanted to scream at him, of images of Jimmy's blood body and Hunter's sagging diaper. But my heart ached for him, seeing him so fiercely protect my son. Underneath the shock and horror…I was touched.

Tristan

31

This hurt. I was genuinely uncomfortable. Every breath sent my heart into a frenzy, energy surged through my veins like electricity and made my hands shake. So many emotions raged through me at once, creating a chaotic storm inside of my brain that threatened to drive me insane. I thought that I had had it bad before but now…I couldn't even name it.

I was in love. So, fucking in love with Ophelia that it physically hurt me. The future suddenly was full of promise, of this new dynamic that I had prayed for ever since Katherine took Millie. Something inside of me had broken, quietly and gently when Ophelia accepted the wedding ring, and it unleashed this floodgate of happiness that I never felt before.

We didn't even need to go to the courthouse to make it official, she was my wife—forever. That simple band had glued us together, shifted the balance so that we were no longer two people but instead we were now one entity. Man, my fucking chest *burned* with pride. I was so pumped up that I wrapped my knuckles tightly and headed into the back of the shop to spar–something I hadn't done in years.

There wasn't anyone brave enough left in the crew to actually spar *with* me, so I was left with the old punching bag that smelt like mold. Each time my fist connected with the heavy bag, it created a hollow *thud* and the chain creaked loudly.

My lungs burned from the familiar exertion; my muscles thankful for the distraction. It was fucking stifling hot in the back of the shop, there weren't any windows or large garage doors back here to let in any air flow. The fluorescent lights above buzzed softly and cast a harsh, orange glow over the room. *Maybe I could teach Hunter how to box*, I thought.

It would be good for him to learn a few moves to defend himself if he ever found himself in a shitty situation. God knows that school kids could be mean. But he also had me as a dad now who would whoop the shit out of any of those kids' dads if I had to protect my kid. Jimmy had stuck to his word and filed to release his parental rights to Hunter a few weeks ago which only made us feel closer as a family.

I helped with the pick-ups and drop-offs from daycare and even kept him here at the shop with me when there wasn't anywhere to take him. I would set him up in a playpen near the couches and fill it with toys for him to play with while I worked. The crew loved him, they all took turns holding him and showing him how to work on cars–the best that a three-year-old could understand.

I even met Tamara, Ophelia's mom. She had come over to the apartment for Hunter's birthday party. It was a small event with just the three of us, Tamara, Serena, and her daughter Alicia. Tamara had been welcoming enough to me, shook my hand without hesitation but I didn't miss the way her eyes had gone wide when she saw me.

Crystal had moved out…early. After I beat the tar out of Jimmy, I had taken Ophelia and Hunter home. Crystal and Steven were in the middle of carrying some of her stuff out of the apartment and I just lost it.

"What are you doing?!" Crystal had screamed as I hurled her shit over the balcony. I ignored her and shoved past her to grab another box of her crap while Steven stood aside awkwardly. "Ophelia–fucking stop him!" That made me snap. I whirled and towered over her; she cowered in her spot.

"You don't get to fucking speak to her," I had spat. "You think giving a single mother less than a thirty-day notice is cool? You barely gave her a chance to prepare before you just fucking dipped."

"N-no," Crystal shook her head, her eyes wide with fear. "I gave her as much notice as I–"

"Shut the fuck up," I roared. "I don't want to hear your excuses *puta perra asquerosa!*" Steven's face stiffened and I realized he also spoke Spanish. Good. "*¡Di algo más y me voy al coche, voy a descargar el maletero en tu culo de perra!*" Steven looked down at his feet. It took no time at all to get Crystal cleared out of the apartment. Ophelia had snatched up Hunter and hid with him in the bedroom while I had my tantrum. They wouldn't call the cops on me; Steven might have been a punk ass bitch, but he wouldn't risk tussling with me. After the dumb bitch was gone, I stormed down to the little leasing office building and handed the lady behind the metal desk, a wad of cash.

"This should be enough to cover the next six months of rent for Ophelia Black," I had said. The lady had looked down at Jimmy's dried blood coating my hand but hadn't said anything as she took the cash.

Since then, things have been great. I had been able to convince Ophelia to take some time off work, so she had been hanging out at the shop a lot with Hunter. Cherry gave us a wide berth, keeping her eyes downcast any time either of us were around. I couldn't help but feel prideful of my girl.

She had seen something she wasn't cool with, and she shut that shit down–even almost caught her first body in the process. Of course, I felt terrible for Cherry. She had just gotten wrapped up in some bullshit and didn't deserve to get shot at. Eventually, I would have to find a way to apologize. But right now, I was *so fucking happy.*

A loud knock snatched my attention away from the bag and I staggered back half a step as I tried to catch my breath. My knuckles throbbed in a way that I hadn't realized that I had missed so much. My sides ached with the exertion, but I felt so fucking alive.

"C'mon," Charlie wagged two fingers at me, his eyes downcast. "Meeting time." I nodded and made my way to follow him back into the main garage. It was much more crowded than it normally was after-hours. Six new guys stood awkwardly in a loose circle, their hands clasped in front of them, and their chins held high trying to appear tough. I threw a quick glance around the room and saw that none of my guys were acting as tough and then I spotted Barry standing off to the side with Charlie and I rolled my eyes. Probably didn't help that Cherry was standing behind Tony with her tits half exposed.

The six guys all eyed me carefully as I casually strolled across the garage, purposefully cutting through their group to the small refrigerator near the far wall. I let them get an eyeful of my size, the battered boxing tape that hung in tendrils from my scarred fists as I reached in and grabbed a water.

"What's this about?" My deep voice wasn't loud, but it rang clearly through the garage to each person. When I reached the black couches, I turned and dramatically flopped down onto it, stretching my long legs across the entire length of the couch. I wasn't trying to be cocky, but I intended to let these dudes know I wasn't someone to fuck with. Like in jail, they always used to try the big guy—I wasn't having any of that shit.

Every head had turned when I spoke and now those eyes were boring into me. Charlie motioned with his head for Barry to follow him over to the couches. Louis, Greg and Tony quickly joined me, forming a sort of protective stance around me.

"Tristan," Barry greeted with an extended hand. "Nice to see you again son."

"What's this about?" I repeated, releasing his hand. Barry gestured to someone behind him without turning. Micah staggered over with his lips pressed into a hard line.

"You remember my son Micah," Barry wrapped an oddly long arm around the boy's thin shoulders. "I just picked him up from Oregon and he's come to stay with me. Thought maybe you could show him how to drive."

I got a good look at Micah, giving him my full attention unlike I had done when we first met at Ballards. "How old are you?"

"S-sixteen," he peeped, and I couldn't help but laugh.

"Don't you have fucking school or some shit?" I chuckled but Micah just shook his head.

"He graduated high school early, at the top of his class." Barry shook Micah proudly and Micah grinned.

"And you want him out here, running on a crew?" I wasn't laughing anymore. I looked at Charlie, but he wouldn't meet my eyes.

"He's a smart boy," Barry clapped him on the back and Micah flinched. "He learns fast, and he needs…a skill."

"Jacking off is a skill he might have more luck with." I scoffed. Micah frowned down at his feet but still didn't speak. I stood up quickly and the other guys took a step toward me, and I rolled my eyes. "You wouldn't last long." I warned the closest of the group next to me and pushed by him to step up to Micah. He was at least a foot shorter than me; his head barely reached my chest. He recoiled slightly the closer I got but I wanted a good look at him.

He had a sort of lopsided but sweet face, he was probably a good kid just a dork. He had short, messy brown hair, thick eyebrows, and black eyes. He was pretty pale, probably spent a lot of time inside playing video games. I could feel Barry's uneasy eyes on me, watching my every move.

"He's just a kid," I sighed, frowning at Charlie. Charlie shrugged.

"Gotta learn at some point," Charlie said. He sounded bored and I wanted to punch him in the throat. "You might be a jackass but you're the best driver that I know. He could learn a lot from you."

"Yeah, maybe where the dick is supposed to go," I grumbled. One of Barry's guys couldn't help but chuckle and he shot the guy a murderous look.

"That's enough," Barry snapped. "Like it or not, *boy*, our crews are gonna be running together for a while and my Micah is going to learn how to drive."

I made a face but held my hands up in surrender.

"I have my own announcement," I smirked. I glanced around at the remaining guys in my crew with a swell of pride in my chest. I purposefully avoided Cherry's eyes. "I proposed to Ophelia–I'm getting married."

Greg clapped me on the back proudly while the others said their congratulations and knocked their firsts against mine. "And I'm giving her the black phone, she's to be called if anything happens to me and my cut goes to her."

Cherry's eyes shot open wide, before she turned and hurried away.

With that, I tugged my shirt back on and followed Barry and his crew out of the shop. A bunch of new, black Ram 1500s were parked in the lot.

"What in the redneck hell is this?" I muttered. "Is this all that you have?"

"They all got V8 Hemis in them." One guy I learned that was named Mateo said proudly.

"I don't give a shit what those top-heavy ass trucks have in them," I snorted. "You try to dip from the cops in that and your shit is gonna tip like a drunk, fat bitch." My guys laughed but Chuck scowled at me.

"Whatchu got then, gangsta?" Javier sniffed and I rolled my eyes.

"Not this conspicuous-ass shit," I folded my arms across my chest. I whistled sharply at Micah and his head snapped up. At least he was obedient. "You know how to drive a stick shift?"

"N-no," he peeped.

My guys laughed and I smirked.

"'K so that means the Saab, Greg's El Camino and Louis's Mustang are all out," I said.

"Guess you gotta take him in the Cutty," Greg laughed, and I scowled. I wiped a heavy hand over my tired face and motioned for the kid to follow me. He hesitated slightly but followed me around the back as the others headed back inside of the shop.

I was fucking with the kid. I flicked the police scanner on and slammed that gas pedal to the fucking floor. His eyes shot wide as he was flung into the back of his seat, and I couldn't help but laugh. I whipped a doughnut in the intersection, throwing him against the door before we straightened back out, leaving tire marks behind us. One thing about the Bay Area–CalTrans didn't give a shit about repairing our roads. Potholes and dips turned our streets to Swiss cheese which made for a very bumpy ride for Micah as I gunned it over the steep hills.

At one point, I swung the car around, threw it in reverse and stomped on the gas. The Cutlass screeched as it took off backwards down a busy street.

"W-whoa!" Micah shouted, his fists white knuckling the doorframe. "Shouldn't you be looking?!"

"Nope." I was looking though, just at the rearview mirror instead of turning around in my seat. His hands flew up to cover his face and I pinched my lips together to keep from laughing. We blazed through redlights and stop signs, narrowly missing parked cars along the streets and even a homeless man staggering in the street–that was an accident. I hadn't seen him until it was too late, but the Cutlass chirped expertly around the tweaked-out dude just in time and we sailed past.

By the time we reached L&L, the poor dude was pale and shaking. His hands fumbled with the door, and I reached over him and shoved the door open while simultaneously unlatching his seatbelt. Micah tumbled out of the Cutlass onto the asphalt with a heavy thud, just in time to vomit loudly. The guys had hurried out when they heard us approaching at high speeds and got an eyeful of poor Micah vomiting. Charlie looked up to meet my eyes, his face hard. I shrugged. Barry's worried eyes flashed from Micah to me and back again before a deep belly laugh erupted from him.

"That must've been some driving, son," he hollered.

Ophelia
32

I was terrified of Tristan and yet every inch of my skin burned deliciously when he touched me. I couldn't get enough of him. Our lips twisted together ravenously, our tongues danced in each other's mouths as our hands grabbed and grabbed. He tasted of sunshine and hate. His large hands pinned my hips down to the mattress as he moved between my thighs, pushing himself into me deeper and deeper until I cried out. A low growl vibrated in his chest as he found his own release and collapsed on top of me.

We had barely been able to keep our hands off each other whenever we were near. It wasn't always from love or lusting after each other, more often than not it was possessive and hungry. Our dynamic had shifted since Crystal left and Tristan spent more and more time at the apartment with Hunter and I. We had even moved my bed and belongings into Crystal's old room. Tristan had bought me a proper headboard and bed frame. Hunter was excited to have his own room but more often than not, would end up in our bed by morning. I would lie awake and smile at the image of Hunter's small body almost completely enveloped by Tristan's massive arms, just a small foot exposed under Tristan's elbow, Hunter's cheeks squished against Tristan's chest. They both snored.

Most weekends Tristan was with Millie and usually slept over at the trailer. Doing his best to ease back into Millie's life without bombarding her, as he had explained to me one afternoon when I asked if I could meet her. Guilt had flickered through his ocean eyes.

"I just got her back, babe," he had sighed. "Let me get her comfortable with me, in being a family again before I introduce her to you guys."

"Is that for her benefit or for Katherine's?" I had snapped and immediately regretted it.

"I don't do shit for her," he spat. "Everything I do is for Millie." Then he had sighed heavily and pressed his forehead to my chest, his long arms wound around my hips. "Just be patient with me Ophelia."

I had run my fingers through his dark hair and breathed in the honey scent of him and let it go.

It was time to send out my applications for nursing school. My hands trembled as I put together my packet of transcripts, reference letters and other necessities into large manilla envelopes. I had spent most of my morning at Kinko's printing everything to have it ready to put together that afternoon after Hunter went to bed. I double checked and cross referenced my lists of needed items for each school I was applying to and the piles I had created on my dining table.

Each school required different classes and work hours to be eligible to apply, I didn't want to risk sending the wrong information and have to wait an entire year to apply again.

Being a nurse had been my dream since I was little and now it was just outside of my reach but quickly approaching. My heart hammered excitedly as I marked off items on my list and took a long sip of my glass of white wine. Tristan was out on one of his driving lessons with Micah, they were gone most nights now but apparently the kid was getting better so maybe Tristan would be home earlier soon. Hunter was fast asleep after dinner and a warm bath with promises of going to the Oakland Zoo tomorrow since I had the day off from work.

Music played softly in the background to break up the silence of the lonely apartment. I thought of texting Tristan but fear that I would be interrupting made me drop my phone back onto the table. After I sealed my final packet, I sat back heavily and sighed. My fingers were numb from shifting through papers, writing, signing, crossing off and double checking for the last few hours.

The doorknob jiggled and I sat up right, my heart hammered as I threw a wary glance to the floor of the living room just in front of the couch where…but it was just Tristan. He walked into the apartment, and I relaxed, my shoulders slumped as the tension left me. I opened my mouth to speak but the tight expression on his face told me not to. Heat twirled in my stomach as he crossed the living room quickly. His hand shot out and gripped my jaw tightly but also without hurting me as he leaned my face back and covered my lips with his. His kiss was deep, hungry. I had just reached up to wrap my arms around his neck when he pulled away sharply, his brows knitted together.

"What?" I breathed.

Wordlessly, he released me as his eyes searched the table. Still silent, he picked up the half empty wine glass and turned on his heel. He stalked to the kitchen, and I jumped as the glass shattered in the sink. His shoulders rose and fell as he breathed deeply, his back to me for a long minute. It took just two long strides for him to turn and reach me before his hand wrapped around my wrist and pulled me roughly off the stool and after him down the hall to the bedroom.

Sex with Tristan that night was different. Searching. Needing. Tristan seemed to be in pursuit of something with his lips, looking for an answer to a silent question. His grip was like a cobra around my neck as he thrust into me, the sound of flesh on flesh echoed in the small room. Stars filled my vision both from lack of oxygen and pleasure as the tension built dangerously.

His teeth sank into the spot between my shoulder and my neck, enough to make me shriek. His mouth traveled down my chest to my breast, leaving a trail of bites along the way and I was worried as he reached my nipple. Instead, he grazed his teeth gently over the goosebump flesh and my back arched into him.
He groaned softly and came undone.

Still without speaking, Tristan reached over the bed onto the floor to where he had dropped a fresh towel and began cleaning me. His eyes were somewhere far away. He used a clean end of the towel to wipe himself but as he turned away, my hands caught his face gently.

"What is it?" I frowned.

"I love you," he said, and my stomach tightened. "I had a dream."

"About what?" My hands were cold against his hot flesh.
He dropped his eyes and lifted my left hand, pressing the gold band against his lips.

"What do you think?" He asked carefully. "Would you be my baby's mom?"

My eyebrows shot up my forehead and I dropped my hands to my lap.

"You…you want to have a baby?"
His face was broken, a storm lashed in his eyes.

"I want a family with you," he said. "You're a great mom Ophelia, I would love to have a baby with you." I didn't know what to say. Instead, I leaned forward on my knees and smashed my lips into his. A few moments later, we were tumbling off the bed.

Tristan

33

I could tell by all the fucking black trucks in the parking lot at L&L that today was going to give me a fucking headache. I had woken up from a text from Charlie at midnight, telling me to get my ass to the shop ASAP.

Bleary eyed, I rolled into the shop with so much weed smoke in my car that I could barely see out the windshield. I hadn't wanted to leave Ophelia. Hunter hadn't crawled into bed with us yet so I had uninterrupted time to run my hands all over her naked body. The memory made my blood heat, and I gripped the steering wheel. That woman had a spell on me. Being around her made my veins feel electrified, my heart sped up with her every breath and I lost myself every time I felt her cum around my dick.

There wasn't anything I wouldn't do for her. If Ophelia handed me a blade and told me to stab myself in the heart, I would do so gladly and still apologize for getting blood on her shoes.

I hurried across the dark, wet parking lot, shoving my hands into my hoodie pockets as I made my way into the shop. The slick floor made my shoe slip as I entered but I caught myself and made my way to where the others were sitting. I plopped down on the leather couch next to Louis, not making eye contact with Barry or his crew. Charlie gave me an annoyed look before he cleared his throat.

"We're going on a run," Charlie declared.

"When?" Greg frowned.

"Tonight–now," Barry said, and I scoffed. Every eye turned to me.

"Oh, are we? Where? With what intel?" I shrugged and looked at Charlie expectantly, but he didn't make eye contact.

"We're hitting a liquor store–" I snorted but Charlie continued as if he didn't hear me. "Just a simple smash and grab. Barry wants to get Micah's feet wet."

"You should be worrying about getting his dick wet first," I said. "The kid ain't ready." I glanced at where Micah stood behind Barry, his eyes downcast.

Micah had taken to sleeping in the office and following me around like a lost puppy dog during the day, getting under my foot and always less than a few inches from my back. It was irritating. Apparently, Barry and Charlie thought it was a good idea for him to spend as much time with me as possible to learn about how cars work, they thought it would help his driving in the long run.

I doubted it. The kid was clueless, but he was eager to please which could wind up being bad for him.

"He's as ready as he's ever going to be," Barry glared at me. "Tristan you're driving, Micah is riding with you. Mateo scoped out a spot for us off of Seminary and Fairfax, the intel is good. Just hold them up, take what's in the register and bounce."

"All right, let's go." Charlie made a motion for us to get off our asses, but no one moved, my crew all threw apprehensive glances my way.

"You're fucking joking, right?" I snarled.

"You gotta problem?" Mateo stepped up and I was on my feet in an instant, towering over him.

"Yeah, I got a *fucking problem*," I spat. "We're supposed to just trust you *putas* off the bat like that? We don't fucking know you." Mateo puffed his chest up, ready to retort but Barry put his arm between us.

"That's enough!" He barked. "The intel is good, *boy*, get your ass in the fucking truck. He needs to learn how to drive in one of our trucks so you're taking mine." I looked over his head at Charlie, but he just shrugged.

"Whatever." I shoved my way between them and stormed off towards the door. Without stopping, I called over my shoulder: "Let's fucking *move* Micah!" I heard him stutter before he hurried after me.

Just a few minutes later Micah and I were in the Ram 1500, donned in black hoodies and ski masks. My 9mm was on the console between us, set snugly in the cup holder, which Micah continued to throw nervous glances at. None of this felt right. The truck was too big. Too loud. Something deep inside of me was screaming alarms but I was stuck. I chalked it up to the fact that I've never hit a fucking *liquor store* before, it seemed childish. Desperate.

"They keep large amounts of cash on them," Mateo had explained as he very briefly went over the details before we left.

"And usually just one gun," Javier had added.

"Usually," I snorted. None of them had seemed concerned, hands in their pockets and rolling their eyes nonchalantly. But it wasn't any of their necks on the line. I wasn't just driving tonight but I had to be the muscle and the lookout too. Mateo had said that they usually did these sorts of smash-and-grabs with one or two guys and as long as they got out of there quick enough, they never had a problem.

"Sitting ducks," Javier had laughed.

"Two strikes," I grumbled to myself now as I headed down Fairfax towards Seminary where Mateo had told me to hit the Valero there on the corner. Micah was a ball of nerves in the passenger seat. He bounced his right leg on the ball of his foot and tapped his knees anxiously, staring unseeingly out the window.

"My first run was a warehouse out in Hayward," I said. He broke his stare out the window and glanced at me. "I was 19 when Charlie sent me out with the crew."

"H-how was it?" Micah stammered. His skin was pale, sweat lined his upper lip.

"I was scared shitless," I chuckled dryly, and he cracked a grin.

"But you kept doing it," he pointed out.

"But I kept doing it…" I trailed. I took a deep breath and shook my head. "Didn't have a choice, there wasn't much else out there for me. There isn't anything else you would rather be doing?" "I don't know," he shrugged. "I thought about becoming a veterinarian."

I cocked my head and studied him for a long moment. Finally, I looked away and said:

"My girl is going to be a nurse." I don't know why I told him. Telling these outsiders anything about me and my girl felt like a violation, like I had lifted the curtain and exposed my vulnerabilities. Micah smiled but there wasn't any malice behind it.

"Might come in handy when you come home and need to be patched up." He chuckled lightly but his words banged around inside of my head and left a sour taste in my mouth. We didn't speak the rest of the drive.

"There," Micah said as we approached the Valero, pointing out the windshield to the large teal building that I obviously couldn't miss. "There's cars here."

"No shit," I growled as I pulled down an alleyway just before the parking lot. This is exactly why we didn't hit these sorts of places; they were always open which meant we could be discovered or interrupted at any moment. Mateo had said the cameras in the back of the building hadn't been working for the last two months. The truck continued bouncing and swaying over the unfinished road and I gritted my teeth.

This would be the way in but the road out would be the main road which was paved and smoother. Micah shouldn't have a problem getting us out of there. Part of me wasn't above pushing him out onto the street and leaving his ass behind if need be. But I glanced at him from the corner of my eye and something made my spine stiffen. His profile as he looked out the window, the dark hair, made my chest tighten. "Do I get one of those?" He nodded to my gun as I switched the safety off and stuffed it into the waistband of my pants.

"Not today, you get one of these." I reached into the back seat and pulled out a black duffle bag and tossed it at him. "The best thing we can do for a job like this is just get in and get the fuck out. Ready?"

"Y-yeah," he nodded fervently.

"We're about to find out, let's go." I pulled my ski mask down over my face, the familiar caress of the soft fabric over my skin was like taking a hot bath at the end of a long day. I got out of the car, one hand on the gun and swore under my breath. "*Your mask, pendeja!*" Micah froze mid stride and pulled his mask down over his face, struggling with getting the eyes lined up so he could see. His hands were shaking.

I led the way in, hoping to use the ambush and my size as a distraction to get whoever was inside to hesitate long enough for me to get the upper hand. I gripped the cold metal of the glass door and flung it open.

Glass exploded around me. I jumped backwards, the inertia causing me to slip and fall onto my ass as another shot blasted over my shoulder. I scrambled up onto my feet and grabbed Micah, shoving him forward behind a shelf of chips. Gunshots continued to ring out over our heads.

"What the fuck?" I managed to breathe as I pulled my gun out the moment we hit the linoleum. I whirled up into a crouch to peer around the rack as a bag of chips just inches from my face exploded. I recoiled and slapped the chips from my eyes. "Were they *expecting us?*" I hissed. Blindly, I stuck my gun around the rack and fired off two rounds not knowing who or what I hit. I just did it to give me enough time to figure out what the fuck was going on.

"Who the fuck are you?!" An older male voice bellowed from the other side of the room. The shooter. Well that answered one question.

"Fuck you man!" I shouted back.

"I've already called the cops!" The man shouted,

confirming my suspicions. "The moment I saw you two lowlifes pulling around back!"

The cameras. So much for Mateo's intel.

"Ayy man just let us go," I shouted. "I'll put my gun down and we will leave if you just let us go."

"Like hell you will!" Another blast tore through the thin fabric of the mask just missing my head. Micah shrieked. Swearing, I pulled the ski mask off and tossed it aside. I ducked and crouched over Micah, shielding him. The moment the small room was quiet, I gritted my teeth, seeing red and I stood to my full height and found the man behind the counter. He was probably in his late fifties with a large pot belly protruding out from between his suspenders.

Two strikes.

I fired off two shots in quick succession. They hit their mark in the man's shoulder with a wet packing sound. He cried out as he crumpled to the floor. I had to move.

"C'mon bro." I grabbed Micah by the front of his shirt and hauled him after me. The sound of sirens was faint but approaching. "Shit." I shoved Micah towards the truck and jumped into the driver's side. The large tires spit rocks as I gunned it down the uneven road back towards the street. The truck groaned in protest as it bounced over the potholes and broken cement before finally evening out as the tires connected with a screech on the street.

There was an explosion, and we were airborne.

The truck groaned like a massive whale as it rolled, crumpling and spraying glass. It finally came to a rest upside down. I coughed and blinked as the debris from the airbag flittered down around us. Pain erupted from every part of my body; my head felt like it was still spinning.

"Ugh, fuck," I groaned. I was still partly in my seat, stuck upside down. I pulled myself free and fell onto the roof of the car, knocking the wind out of me. Broken glass cut into my skin as I crawled through the destroyed windshield.

"Oh my god!" A woman screeched. "I didn't see you—you came out so fast!"

Blood dripped down into my eye, and I pressed my palm into my pounding forehead.

Micah.

He hadn't been in the truck when we landed. Straining to see while my vision swam, I hurried up to my feet and shouted his name. He didn't answer. I spun around, sucking in a lung full of air to shout again as the sound of sirens came closer.

"Mi—" my voice caught in my throat. Micah lay ten yards away in the street, his arm bent unnaturally behind his back.

"Oh my god is he—" the woman began screaming, her hands flew up to her mouth. The sirens were getting louder.

"Where's your keys?" I demanded.

"I-in th-the car," she stammered. Wincing, I ran over to Micah and scooped him up into my arms. He wasn't breathing. I laid him down in the backseat and had just turned the woman's Cadillac Escalade around when the police hit the street.

Tristan
34

Mica was dead. He had died before we made it back to L&L. Everyone had swarmed us as I crashed the Cadillac into the cement bollards that lined the back of the shop. The air bags had deployed. There had been so much yelling, hands that grabbed at me, but I couldn't speak. Barry was there, holding his head in his hands and screaming. I locked eyes with Mateo, and everything blurred. I was only partially aware of Greg and Tony pulling me off him while Javier and Louis grabbed at Mateo to separate us.

"The cameras! The cameras!" I just yelled over and over. Realization sunk in and Mateo's eyes had gone so wide I could see their whites.

I dropped my head, feeling the tension pull in my neck and shoulders as someone walked up softly, quietly next to me. I didn't open my eyes as she sat down on the curb next to me.

"He was just a kid," I groaned.

"I know," Cherry said flatly.

"He wanted to be a vet," I mumbled. Wordlessly, Cherry leaned her head onto my shoulder, not caring about the blood. I rested my cheek against the top of her head and looked out, unseeingly, across the lot. "I don't know how to fix this."

"You can't," she sighed.

Cherry was right. There was nothing I could do to take back what happened, that Micah was dead. But it wasn't entirely my fault. The whole job was rushed, we were given bad intel and didn't have enough men with us. If Donny had been there, none of this would have happened…Barry was obviously grieving but it caused a rift between him and Charlie, whatever deal they had worked out was evidently a wrap.

After a few days, when the dust had settled, everyone went back to work. Business as usual. Just like we did when Donny was killed–life kept moving. I clung to Ophelia in those following days, unable to express to her the ominous feeling that had crept into my dreams since Micah was killed. A few times I had awoken in the middle of the night gasping for air, my skin covered in sweat.

Once, I had grabbed Hunter up in my arms and pinned him behind me against the wall, my hand reaching to my waistband for an invisible gun. It scared the shit out of Ophelia. I didn't know how to tell her I was scared that I wouldn't be able to protect them. So far two people had died—one who was a brother to me, and I could do nothing to protect them. Sometimes I looked at that gold band on her finger and wondered what hell I had condemned them to.

Everything was tainted. The color of the world around me had been dimmed, turned down and I knew why. I didn't care anymore. Didn't care about the shop. About Charlie. About the crew. I was tired of death, tired of risking my own life to line Charlie's pockets, risking my third strike, and being taken away from Ophelia forever. It had been a few weeks since Micah died and apparently Barry got caught up in some mess because he was facing a six-month stint in jail. Probably distraught over losing his only son. The invisible knife twisted in my gut.

The shop was closing for the night, and I helped with the closing duties though I barely did shit at all that day—the last few weeks really. Charlie sauntered into the shop from the front office with some papers in his hands, a cigarette dangled from his lips.

"Okay guys, I got a new hit–"

"No." The word burst out of me before I could think. Everyone turned to look at me. Charlie raised an eyebrow; his eyes searched my face for a long pause before he spoke.

"No?"

"No." I tossed the rags into the washer and slammed the door closed loudly. "I'm done. I'm done with all this shit, get someone else to be your lackey."

Charlie lowered the papers in his hands and fixed me with an even stare.

"I don't think you know what you're saying," he glowered.

"No, I know exactly what I'm saying," I shook my head. It felt like something inside of my chest had finally snapped and I felt lighter. "I'm tired of risking *everything for you*. I have a life now—a family."

"A family?" Charlie scoffed. "That bitch and her kid are your family now? Not that long ago she was some other dude's piece of–"

My fist connected with Charlie's mouth. I threw my entire weight behind it, the fury boiled in my blood and poured out of me. For everything Charlie ever did to me. For stomping me in the stomach when I was a kid, for pushing me out of the window when I was 2, for burning me with cigarettes, for getting me wasted when I was 10 as a joke, for beating me with a baseball bat when I was 14, for fucking Katherine.

For the fact that Millie might not even be my daughter…but my sister. I ravaged Charlie, hitting him over and over for who he made me into. For this monster. For ripping away my future before I had even started. For shaping me into this man who wasn't worth Ophelia.

Hands grabbed me roughly and tore me off Charlie, the momentum causing us to fall backwards into a painful pile of knees and elbows. Charlie took the opportunity to lunge on top of me, his brass knuckles connected with my cheekbone with a disgusting crunch. Blood sprayed as his fist landed over and over. Finally, I untangled myself out of the limbs of my crew just as they got to their feet and pulled Charlie and I apart.

"You–you're *dead*!" Charlie spat a stream of blood at me, his face was twisted with fury. My face throbbed painfully; my heart slammed loudly against my ribs, but I felt light.

"I'm fucking done with you and this crew–I'm out." My chest heaved with each breath. Whoever had their arms around me shook with the effort to contain me, to hold me back.

"Good," Charlie fixed me with an even, hateful stare. "Finally."

Ophelia
35

I was worried. Tristan had come home earlier than usual one night, his face swollen and bloody, but his eyes were bright, wild as he grabbed me. He covered my face in kisses, leaving bloody lip prints on my skin. He refused to go to the hospital to treat his wounds or check for broken bones, so I was forced to clean him up in the tiny kitchen.

A pile of bloody paper towels made a leaning tower on the counter as I tried to staunch the bleeding. I gingerly pressed onto his cheekbones, trying my best to avoid the swollen and purple skin but I couldn't *feel* any breaks. His left eye was completely bloodshot, the blood pooled around the jade iris. Coupled with the scars on his face, and wicked gleam in his feral eyes, he looked lethal.

I swallowed hard as I dabbed Neosporin onto the cuts on his cheekbones, his split lip. The entire time I tended to him, he ran his hands over my body, gripping my hips and pulling me against him between his legs. The heat that grew in my stomach was defused with each dab of the wet paper towel against his bleeding skin.

"I'm out, I'm done," he breathed excitedly. The fire in his eyes made my stomach twist. "This won't happen anymore, I promise."

"Don't promise that," I whispered, lowering my hands. How many times had he told me that this life was all he knew? All he was capable of. But Hunter had woken up then, crying softly in his room and I hurried to settle him back down, to stop him from seeing Tristan broken and bleeding, his eyes wild.

It didn't last long, the burning excitement seemed to boil out of him. For days and days Tristan slept. I went to work, dropping Hunter off with either my mom or at daycare and when we returned, he was still asleep. The food I had prepared for Tristan left to rot in the microwave.

Each night after I tucked Hunter into bed, I would crawl across our bed to Tristan, but he wouldn't stir. I pressed a hand on his back to check that he was breathing before I curled up against his back and went to sleep. This went on for weeks. It was as if the weight of his entire life, of those he's lost had suddenly collapsed on top of him and it was too much.

More than once, I was awoken in the middle of the night to Tristan shaking in his sleep, making small whimpers. I would smooth his hair back and whisper that he was okay, that everything was okay, and he would eventually still and fall back asleep. I was beginning to worry. Serena came by a few times to ask if I wanted to go out to dinner or get the kids together.

"Um," I had stalled, biting my bottom lip as I glanced over my shoulder towards our bedroom where Tristan still slept.

"He's still in bed?" She had frowned.

"He's not well," I said. Serena sighed but understood and left.

I was drafting what I would say to Tristan on my way home from work. I had dropped Hunter off with Tamara earlier that morning and she had asked to keep him for the weekend. I figured this would be the best time to try to rouse Tristan out of his stupor. But when I entered the apartment, I was shocked to see the lights on.

The apartment smelled of his body soap, the humid air from the shower still circulated in the air as Tristan sat on the couch, his elbows on his knees as he ate the plate of food in front of him. He glanced up at where I had stalled in the entryway, the bruises barely visible on his face. He had shaved and cleaned up but there was something in his eyes, a distant look as he looked me up and down.

"You're awake," I blurted. He wore a fresh white t-shirt; his familiar honey and sugar scent filled the small apartment. He nodded quietly and went back to eating. My heart sank.

"The mail came," he said. I jumped up and hurried over, but he called after me: "It's not in there."

I ignored him as I tore through the stack, searching. He was right, there wasn't a single response from the applications I had sent out. It was too early; the application period was still technically open. It would be weeks before I heard back.

"Damn," I grumbled. Silently, he stood and washed his plate before putting it into the drying rack. "Let's go for a drive."

"Where do you want to go?" His voice was flat, his face expressionless. But he was talking, he was out of bed. I closed the gap between us and wrapped my arms around his waist, craning my neck to look up at his face.

"I just want to get out of the apartment with you. We can go wherever."

He nodded silently and grabbed his keys off the counter. "I'll drive."

The car smelled like him and I relaxed into the leather seats. The engine roared to life, and we eased out of the parking lot.

We drove the streets aimlessly, but I could feel him loosening bit by bit as the streetlights passed, their orange glow only able to penetrate our dark fortress through the windows. I watched the light dance across the smooth planes of his handsome face. His golden necklace sparkled under the collar of his t-shirt. I ran a hand across his wide shoulders, and he sighed heavily as if I was releasing the tension he kept there. He reached across to my other hand and lifted it to his lips.

"I love you," I breathed. He playfully bit my knuckles and lowered our hands to his lap.

"I love you more than you realize." His words made my heart leap. "We will figure out our new life together." He released my hand to reach back to my other hand on his shoulder and studied the gold band on my finger. "Have you decided?"

"I'd be happy to marry you." The words felt heavy in my mouth. I knew what it meant to solidify our lives together, the temper of his that would keep us awake for hours each night. The possessiveness that would stain my friendships. But I also knew the fierceness in which he would love and protect both Hunter and me. That he would do anything for us. Tristan stopped the car in the middle of the street, ignoring the cars that honked and swerved to avoid hitting us. His hands were in my hair, holding me to him as his lips devoured mine.

His scent filled my senses and I sighed heavily, intertwining my own fingers in his hair. His lips were urgent against mine like he couldn't kiss me fast enough, get enough of me. My body burned and it took everything in me to not crawl on top of him.

Red and blue lights flared through the tinted windows.

Tristan pulled back sharply, his eyes immediately on edge.

"They probably want to know why we're stopped in the middle of the street," I guessed, squinting through the tinted window to see through the glaring lights in the side mirror.

"No." Tristan's voice was hard as I noticed two officers snaking around the back of the Cutlass, their guns unholstered.

"Tristan Lawrence, get out of the car with your hands up!" One of them yelled and my stomach dropped. I turned to ask Tristan, but the car lurched forward, slamming me back against the seat. Words escaped me as we raced at illegal speeds through the streets, careening around slower traffic and pedestrians. I cried out and covered my eyes as we narrowly avoided a couple walking hand in hand through the intersection.

"Tristan!" I cried out but he ignored me, pushing the car faster. His jaw flexed, his hands gripped the steering wheel as those red and blue lights filled the rearview mirror.

"I need to drop you somewhere," he rushed. "As soon as we're out of their line of sight I need you to jump."

"Jump?!" I shouted.

"You'll be okay." The tires squealed as we hit a corner, but the police car was on our tail. A second pair of lights joined. Then a third. "Fuck, there's too many."

"Tristan–Tristan, what's going on?" I demanded. He ignored me, taking another turn too quickly, the back tires of the car swept sideways, but he righted the Cutlass and shot forward. "Just stop!"

"I can't!" he yelled. "I have to get you out of here."

I twisted in my seat and squinted as the lights battered my eyes.

"Tristan there's–"

"Shit!" The car screeched to a sudden halt; the tires screamed in protest. We were surrounded. We were in an intersection blocked on all sides by police cars, their lights spinning and dancing across the dark street.

"Get out, get out!" Tristan unclipped my seatbelt and shoved me roughly out the door. I hit the asphalt painfully, rocks tore at my palms and knees, but Tristan's large hands were grabbing me up, hauling me to my feet.

"Tristan Lawrence! Put your hands up *now!*" someone yelled through a loudspeaker, the sound stung my ears. Tristan's face was full of panic as he stared down at me, ignoring the six police cars that encircled us. His molten eyes flashed upward, over my head and his face paled. His large, strong hands grabbed me roughly and shoved me behind him.

"Let her go, let her go!" he shouted, pleading. I gripped fistfuls of his t-shirt, daring a peek behind me. The five other police cars that formed a half circle around us each had a police officer standing beside it, guns drawn and pointed directly at me. Tristan kept one hand clamped firmly on my wrist as he held the other arm up in surrender.

He walked backwards a step, turning me away from the guns but it was impossible, they were all around us. Tears streaked my hot cheeks. My hands were trembling so badly I gripped his shirt harder.

"Get on the ground!" The one with the loudspeaker demanded.

"Okay I will!" He shouted back, his voice was terrified. His hand shook around my wrist. "Just please let her go!"

"Get on the ground!"

"Let her go!" he pleaded. "She has a kid!" The red and blue lights danced across the asphalt, over his fear-stricken face. My heart pounded as I thought of all those guns pointed directly at his open chest, at my back. There was a moment of deliberation before the officer with the loudspeaker nodded to the police officer closest to us.

The officer stepped slowly around the squad car; his face pinched apprehensively as he raised one hand to show Tristan that he was approaching. His other hand still held the gun, but it was now angled carefully towards the ground.

"Tristan!" I shrieked.

Tristan stiffened as the officer stepped closer, I could feel his heart pounding against my hands.

"She'll be okay," the officer nodded, his eyes focused on Tristan as he stepped painstakingly slowly towards us. Tristan hesitated before he pulled my hands off his shirt.

"No! Tristan!" I scrambled to reach for him but he was too strong. He pushed me with shaking hands towards the officer. I fought.

"You'll be okay—you'll be okay," Tristan's voice trembled. I think he was telling himself more than he was reassuring me. Hot tears poured down my face, my stomach twisted painfully, and I thought I would explode. The other officers kept their guns aimed directly at Tristan as he stepped back away from me, his arms up in surrender. He didn't look away from me. The police officer wrapped an arm around my waist and hoisted me away, slamming me down onto the hood of the nearest police car.

"Tristan! Tristan!" My throat burned from screaming. I was a wild beast, thrashing to get free as six officers slowly approached Tristan, not lowering their guns. One stepped behind Tristan and shoved him roughly forward; Tristan didn't fight as he landed with a thud onto the asphalt. He winced at the impact, but his eyes never left mine.

Even as the officer who knocked him down kneeled on top of him, then a second and third. He wasn't even fighting back. Another officer handcuffed him. Red and blue lights streaked across his face, but he never looked away from me. Even as they hauled him to his feet, needing four of them to do so and shoved him roughly towards a police car.

Tristan stopped walking and the officers stumbled around him. "Don't fight them," he called out to me.

I sobbed; my vision swam with tears.

"Keep moving, Lawrence," one of the officers demanded, shoving him. Tristan barely budged.

"Don't fight them," Tristan told me again before willfully taking a step forward. "I love you." He allowed the police officers to finish hauling him to the squad car and shove him inside. The officer pinning me down waited until they had driven away with Tristan, two cars in tow before he released me. He stepped aside and opened the back door of the squad car.

"Get in," he barked.

"A-am I getting arrested?" I stammered.

"What do you think?" he snarled. I swallowed hard but climbed in without protest, he hadn't handcuffed me.

It wasn't like the movies. The police station was quiet and orderly, not bustling with busy police officers like I had expected. They took me to a small room that could have been a storage room at some point, it was so small. A fold out card table was pushed against one far wall with three metal folding chairs.

I sat in the single chair against the wall, my legs curled up to my chest and my head rested against the wall. My head was pounding. After what felt like an eternity, two police officers entered the room. One petite Hispanic woman and one was tall with an ugly mustache.

"I'm Officer Torres and this is Officer Chadwick," the woman said curtly as they took the two empty seats across from me. "Do you know why you're here?"

"I'm being arrested?" I guessed and they both smirked.

"No, you're not being arrested," Officer Torres clarified but it did little to make me feel better. "What do you know about Tristan Kyle Lawrence and his involvement in a robbery at a Valero one month ago?"

"Nothing." It was the truth, but my eyes were hard, unrelenting. They exchanged a look and Officer Chadwick placed something heavy onto the plastic table with a clunk. I blinked. It was Tristan's handgun, smeared with blood in an evidence bag.

"Do you recognize this gun?" Officer Chadwick asked, his voice neutral. I shook my head and wrapped my arms around myself. Officer Torres sighed and pulled out her cellphone. She clicked around before she turned it toward me.

"I'm sorry to have to show you this." It was a grainy, black and white video of a large back truck in a dark alley. A moment later, two masked figures excited the vehicle. No—the smaller one wasn't masked but after a moment he pulled it down.

I didn't recognize him. I could immediately tell by the hulking build of the larger man that it was Tristan. I didn't need to see his face to know. I pressed my lips together. The next clip was in full color, this one was from inside of a liquor store. I didn't look away, didn't show any emotion as there were explosions all around the store as the man behind the counter and Tristan fired their guns at each other.

Tristan stood and fired at the man behind the counter, and he collapsed. Tristan spun around, facing the camera. His mask was off. The video paused. Tristan was frozen in the frame, his face hard with fury but his eyes were alarmed. Officer Torres lowered the phone, and I met her eyes steadily, my lips a tight line.

"Tristan attempted to kill a man named Ronald Quinn. He was a grandfather and husband, married for forty years. His only daughter had just welcomed their first child two months prior to Tristan shooting him in cold blood." The words dripped into my stomach like ice. "The young guy with him also died, his name was Micah Ortega. Just graduated from high school early at the age of sixteen."

I fixed her with a steely glare, my eyes swollen from crying. "What do you want from me?"

"It's clear that you and Lawrence have a relationship," Officer Chadwick began. I absentmindedly twisted the gold band on my ring finger. Officer Torres's eyes flashed down to catch the movement, her face unreadable. "But we were hoping that you could see through his facade. See that he isn't what you believe him to be. Help us get him off the street–him and his crew."

"I don't know anything about that." I shook my head.

"Think about your son, Hunter." Officer Torres leaned forward.

"If I'm not being arrested, I want to go home," I said, glaring.

Officer Torres sat back with a sigh. "We will arrange a ride home for you." They both rose to leave.

"What–what about Tristan?" I asked. They both froze at the door, again exchanging a look before the woman spoke again.

"He's going to prison," she declared. "For a very long time for the murder of Ronald Quinn…and others."

I didn't hear from Tristan for almost two weeks. Each day I was racked with guilt and dread. Guilt for asking Tristan to go on a drive with me, for practically delivering him to the police officers. Dread because I didn't know if I would ever see him again. I had nearly jumped out of my skin when my phone rang, and the caller ID showed the county jail.

"Hello? Tristan?" I gasped.

"This is a collect call from an inmate at San Francisco County Jail," a robotic woman's voice said. *"Do you accept the charges?"*

"Yes!" I shouted. The line clicked a few times then Tristan's voice came over the line, full of static and hollow as if the lines were struggling to connect us.

"Ophelia?" His voice was tight.

"Oh Tristan," I cried. "I'm so sorry."

"No, I'm sorry Ophelia," he sighed. "I've ruined everything. Are you okay? Did they hurt you?"

"No," I shook my head though he couldn't see. "I'm fine but they tried to get me to talk about the crew."

Tristan made a warning sound, and I realized the line was probably recorded. But what I had to say wasn't incriminating. "I don't know anything anyways." Which I realized was probably on purpose. For this exact reason. "How do we get you out of there?"

"You don't." His voice was dark, flat. "This was my third strike baby…it's a wrap for me."

"No," I squeaked. "What happened to 'innocent until proven guilty'? Don't you have a bail?"

"Do you have a hundred grand on you?" His voice was sharp, but he sighed heavily. "They're charging me with voluntary manslaughter, Ophelia. They've been *waiting* to get me back here so I'm sure it'll be a speedy process."

"They said Micah died." There was a long pause on the other end.

"Yeah," he said. His voice sounded far away. "His dad is probably in this jail somewhere too."

I frowned. Something in his words made some deep, instinctual warning ring in me but I couldn't figure out why.

"*You have one minute left,*" the robotic voice cut through and my heart hammered.

"Tristan…" My brain scrambled for something to say, anything. "I'm going to get you out."

"Don't." His voice was hard. "You and Hunter deserve better than this–than weekend visits to prison to see me through a plastic screen."

Panic flared in my chest at the finality of his words. But before I could speak, he hung up.

Ophelia
36

There were a few cars parked inside, the doors of L&L Autobody rolled up high as the sounds of the guys working drifted towards me. I didn't look at any of them as I hurried into the office. The front desk was empty but the door behind it was ajar, the light on. I hugged Hunter tighter and pushed through the door. Charlie was seated at the desk, working on a pile of papers in front of him. He glanced up with a blank expression as I entered that slowly trickled into bored amusement.

"Ophelia," he smirked, his eyes flashed to Hunter in my arms. "What a lovely surprise. What can I do for you?"

"I know you're aware that Tristan was arrested," I began. Charlie raised an eyebrow and leaned back against the seat; the metal groaned. "I want you to help me get him out."

"Get him out?" he scoffed. "I think he's exactly where he needs to be."

"He's your *son*," I snarled.

Charlie just shrugged, a bored expression on his face.

"I looked it up, his bail is one hundred thousand dollars, but I only have to pay–"

"Ten percent," he interjected, clearly well versed in this topic. "So you want me to give you ten grand?" He smirked again and shook his head. "He isn't worth it."

My fist clenched at my side.

"He's only caught up in this life because of you!" I said.

Charlie's head snapped up.

"Is that what he told you?" he said slowly, carefully. "He's *caught up* because of his own actions. Because he is a wild fucking animal that can't control himself. You think Ronald Quinn was his first victim?" He scoffed. "He was one of *many*…and many more to come. I don't know who you think Tristan is, but your perception is screwed."

"I don't know how you could be so heartless." I hugged Hunter tightly.

"He won't be a problem for you much longer anyways," he said dismissively.

"What does that mean?"

Charlie just shrugged again and went back to working.

"Eye for an eye." The words rattled around my head, awakening that warning bell inside of me…something Tristan had said clicked into place suddenly. About Micah's dad.

"It was you…" I whispered. "You gave up Tristan to get him arrested. To put him in the same jail as Micah's dad…for…for revenge?" My vision turned red.

Charlie sighed with annoyance and tossed the paper he held onto the desk.

"It was either him or the crew," he said in a tight voice. "Barry lost his son because of Tristan's hasty actions. I'm not losing *everything* because of *him*." He pointed a finger at me as he spoke.

Any resemblance I thought I had seen between him, and his son had vanished. He was a monster. I couldn't speak. Couldn't breathe. I spun on my heel and ran with Hunter out of the shop. I had to get Tristan out of that jail or at the very least, warn him.

We were at the trailer in just a few minutes. It was locked. I swore under my breath and set Hunter down as I searched through the dirt and rocks beneath the kitchen window for a spare key. Nothing. I looked under the welcome mat but nothing there either. My heart hammered against my ribs.

"Back up baby," I told Hunter as I ushered him away from the front step. I whirled, kicking my leg out like I had seen in the movies. My foot connected with the front door just below the handle, it didn't budge. I took a step back, willing all my strength and kicked again. My shoe left a print where it connected. I kicked again and again, the door frame groaning in protest until it finally popped open.

I stumbled forward, catching myself on the door frame as relief flooded me. I scooped up Hunter and hurried inside, setting him down in the living room as I began my search. I didn't care about the mess I made as I pulled everything out from the cabinets, from under the sink. I knocked on the walls, the bottom of drawers to find where it might be.

I searched the bathroom, spilling all its contents onto the counter, the sink, the floor. Nothing. Every minute it took me searching, the more likely it was that Barry, or his own crew found Tristan… I looked behind the washer and dryer–nothing. I tore the posters off the walls in Tristan's bedroom, the scent of him was strongest here and it made my chest squeeze.

I had to use all my strength to shove his mattress off the box spring, hoping to find what I was looking for, but it was empty. I sank to the floor on my knees and sobbed. I was running out of time. I don't even know what would come next. I could bail Tristan out but then what? They had his face on camera, his gun with his fingerprints and Micah's blood. Would we run? Hide for the rest of our lives?

I slid off my knees onto the floor and leaned back against the ramshackle bed. The entire trailer was in disarray. I didn't know if he would even ever come back here. I couldn't leave it like this. I felt like a failure. As I righted, my eyes fell onto the speakers in the corner of the room by the massive TV. Two large, black boxes stacked on top of each other. My hands acted on their own, shoving the top one over until it crashed onto the floor, wood splintered and fell apart to reveal money. Loose money fluttered in the breeze, landing like leaves around the room. I found it.

"How much longer?" I asked the lady behind the desk. Her hair was slicked back into a painfully tight bun, her face was heavily covered in makeup, and she looked up at me from under her lashes, annoyed.

"Take a seat miss," she repeated. This wasn't my first time asking her. But I was a bundle of nerves, worried about him being so close to those who wanted to hurt him. I had picked my nails down to raw, painful numbs as we waited.

"Look—I get it," I huffed. "You have plenty of inmates back there and paperwork and policies and—whatever. But I paid his bail *hours ago* and my son is getting tired and hungry."

She threw a sneer at Hunter where he played with his toy trucks on the cracked, plastic bench.

"Should have thought of that before whatever actions landed you inside of a jail waiting for your boyfriend." The audacity in which she spoke left me flabbergasted.

"He's my *fiancé*," I corrected. "Bitch," I mumbled quietly to myself and plopped down on the bench next to Hunter. I dropped my head into my hands, my hair fell forward like a dark curtain around me.

There was a loud, long buzzing sound and a door beside the counter where the bitch sat popped open, and Tristan walked out. I leapt to my feet but froze in my spot. He was wearing the same clothes he had been arrested in and holding a plastic bag with his cell phone, wallet, and necklace but more concerning was the way he limped forward.

He winced, bracing his left side and his beautiful, bruised and cut face twisted in pain. What had happened to him in there? His green-blue eyes were flat as he scanned the room before he spotted me. Surprise flickered through his eyes before his jaw flexed.

"What're you doing here?" he demanded.

"Tristan—Tristan, what happened to you?"

"I told you to forget about me," he growled. "You already paid the bail?"

I nodded and he shook his head.

"What happened to you?" I whispered. He was clearly hurt. *Had they already gotten to him?* How much worse would it be after he was officially charged? He shook his head again and walked away from me, out the door. I grabbed up Hunter, stuffing his toys back in my purse and hurried after him. Thankfully Tristan was waiting next to my car, not walking down the street.

I unlocked it and he got in while I buckled Hunter into his seat. Tristan winced as he sat down carefully, clearly trying to support his weight with his arms to not tweak whatever was wrong with his side. He seethed as his body settled into the seat finally and slammed the door closed.

"Where did you get the money?" he demanded once we were long gone from the jail.

"I had asked Charlie—" I started, and he snorted, rolling his eyes. "But he refused. I found the stash you kept in the trailer."

He just nodded, clearly relieved that I hadn't used my own money—which I didn't have anyways.

"Money is replaceable," he murmured and winced as I hit a pothole.

"Sorry," I grumbled. I was elated to have him with me, safe but how much time would we have? How would I keep him out of jail? Tristan stared vacantly out the window as we drove and didn't speak. We finally reached the apartment, but he didn't move to get out. I turned off the engine and silence filled the small car; Hunter was close to falling asleep in his car seat.

"I…I need your help." Tristan said flatly.

"Okay," I said. "Let me get Hunter upstairs and I'll be right back." I scooped Hunter's heavy, sleepy body out of the back and quickly carried him up the stairs and inside. He was completely asleep by the time I carefully laid him in his bed and hurried back to Tristan.

"Tristan!" I shouted in alarm. The passenger door was open, but Tristan wasn't in the car. Instead, he was kneeling on the asphalt, his face twisted in agony as he clutched his side, struggling to stand. I rushed over to him and slung his free arm over my shoulders.

My god he is heavy, even with his help I struggled to help him stand to his feet. Tristan cried out in pain and staggered, nearly collapsing on top of me. I was able to steady us both and shoved him forward towards the stairs.

"Oh fuck," he gritted, breathing heavily as he eyed the staircase that loomed before us.

"One step at a time baby," I urged. Halfway through, he had to stop for a break to catch his breath. His body trembled from the effort, and I bit my lip to keep from crying. The back of his neck glistened with sweat even though it wasn't even sixty degrees outside, the sky thick with roiling clouds.

Finally, we reached the apartment, and he stumbled past the threshold and collapsed onto the couch with a string of swears. He buried his face in the armrest of the couch, the veins in his neck visible under his flesh. I stood there helplessly.

"I need you to ch-check them," he heaved. "Did they tear?" I rushed over and gently pulled his shirt up and gasped. I couldn't even clearly see the wound; it was covered by thick layers of white gauze, but it wrapped around his abdomen to his back at an upward angle. My hands trembled as I carefully peeled the adhesive back and the air caught in his chest. Angry, red skin appeared, puckered, and twisted together by thick, black thread. The wound itself was glistening with dried blood woven through the stitching. This was fresh.

"You…you were stabbed?" The words were just breath. "Today?"

The stitches had held. I quickly reapplied the bandage, worried about exposing such a fresh wound. Tristan pushed up on an arm, his other hand flat against his abdomen like he was about to be sick.

"One of them caught me in my cell as I packed my stuff up." He grunted as he shifted to a better sitting position.

"That's…that's what took you so long to come out?"

He nodded.

"They heard I was getting out on bond and found me." He settled slowly back into the couch and wiped the sweat off his face. "It wasn't Barry…it was some other piece of shit that works for him. Too much of a pussy to do it himself."

Part of me was startled by his casual use of the derogatory word, he never spoke like that around me but I shoved it away.

"Tristan…" I didn't know how to tell him. There was so much going on, so much we were going to have to face. I didn't know how to add this to the pile that I knew would hurt him. But I had to. "Charlie sold you out. I don't know all the details…but he told me he owed Barry for Micah's death. 'An eye for an eye' he had said. Charlie had said it was either you or him."

Tristan's unsurprised, flat eyes met mine.

"I know," he said. "Something like this isn't easily fixed, Ophelia. Micah was just a kid. Of course, Barry is going to want blood for losing him. Charlie gave me up in a heartbeat." Tristan was so nonchalant about the betrayal of his own father.

"We can leave," I grabbed his leg. "We don't have to stay here."

Tristan laughed darkly and wiped a hand over his face.

"And do what? Be on the run for the rest of our lives?" he said. "They've *got me*, Ophelia—for voluntary manslaughter. They have my prints—they even have me on video. I'm fucking done."

I shook my head.

"What about you, huh? You're just going to give up your future for this shit? Lose custody of Hunter because you know they're going to take him away if we run and we get caught. We *will* get caught."

"No." Tears poured down my cheeks. "This can't be how this end."

Tristan's face crumpled. Heavy, deep sobs rocked his body, releasing years of pent-up anger, hatred, sadness and disappointment. I rested my cheek against his thigh, and he laced his fingers through my hair.

"I almost had everything," he choked out, the words barely audible. "I almost had *fucking everything.*"

Tristan

37

Ophelia's optimism was getting to me. Every day she brought up some new plan, some new scheme to get me out of the murder charge. I hated seeing the hope in her eyes die when I would explain–again– why it wouldn't work. I wouldn't have her jeopardizing her own future, Hunter's, for me.

My mistakes were my own. I had always known that my life would end in one of two ways: killed on a run or killed in jail. My path was becoming more and more evident as every day passed. She didn't realize that we were running on stolen time, that my court date was approaching and that would be that.

The letter had come to the shop a few weeks after Ophelia bailed me out. Greg had called me with the information, knowing that if Charlie found it, it wouldn't end well. I genuinely believed that the only reason that I was even alive today was because Charlie didn't know where Ophelia lived. And because the crew hadn't told him. If they came here, found Ophelia and Hunter…I couldn't even think of it.

I traced the long scar on the inside of my left forearm, scarcely hidden under the rose tattoo. Barry wouldn't stop until I was dead. He would burn those who I loved until he got to me. I had already canceled my weekend plans with Millie these last two weeks straight, out of fear for her safety.

Much to Katherine's delight, it gave her another reason to hate me and blame me. But I couldn't tell her the truth. If I found a way out of this shit, I didn't want to give Katherine the ammo she needed to steal Millie away again.

A couple of weeks later, two months after I had been out, a knock came pounding on the apartment door. I hurtled over Ophelia's sleeping body and raced for the door, grabbing the baseball bat that Ophelia kept hidden behind the couch. I flung the door open, ready to bash in someone's head but froze when I saw Greg.

"Dude!" Greg threw up an arm to protect himself when he saw the bat.

"What're you doing here?" I demanded, only half realizing that I was naked.

"Y-you gotta come, man," he rushed. "They burned your trailer, it's on fucking fire."

It could be a trap. A ploy to lure me out. But I'd known Greg for years and I saw nothing but genuine fear in his eyes.

The trailer was gone. I could see the plume of smoke miles before we even reached it. Fire trucks barreled past us on the way there. There was already a crowd of onlookers mixed between the fire trucks, one police car and a single ambulance. I could feel the heat even from inside the car.

I got out slowly, helplessly as I watched all my possessions go up into smoke. All of Millie's things. Luckily, I had moved my cash a couple of days after I got out of jail, it was safely squirreled away in Ophelia's bank account. I staggered to the sidewalk, unable to look away from the fire. I hadn't realized I had walked up on my crew until they were all grabbing at me.

"Aw shit man." Tony shook his head.

"I'm so sorry bro," Louis added. Cherry was there too, a weird expression on her face as she approached me slowly.

"He was the first one here," she said, nodding towards the ambulance. Numbly, I turned to see who she meant. Sitting on the step of the ambulance, covered in soot, and breathing deeply through an oxygen mask was Charlie. My entire body tensed; my vision turned red as I spun around fully. Cherry's hands grabbed my hoodie. "He saw the fire, he's the one who called 911—he searched the trailer for you. He almost died."

"Good." I tore out of her hands and stormed across the narrow street towards my father. Charlie glanced up as he noticed me, his eyes went wide, and he threw his hands up to protect himself as an EMT jumped between us.

"Whoa! Whoa! Calm down sir!" The male EMT shouted.

"It was you motherfucker," I snarled over the EMT's head. "You're fucking dead!"

The commotion caught the attention of the two police officers, and they ran over, jumping in the middle with the EMT.

"Tristan! Tristan calm the fuck down!" A familiar, female voice shouted up at me, a finger jabbing into my chest. I glanced down and recoiled when I recognized Officer Torres with her trusty sidekick. "¡cálmate! Your dad is a hero. He went into your *burning trailer to save you.*"

"Bullshit," I spat. "He probably lit the bitch on fire himself."

Charlie looked weak, exhausted, his face was completely covered in soot, his eyes were bloodshot.

"No bro it's true!" It was Greg. The guys had all ran over and were trying to help the police and the EMT keep me off Charlie. "Charlie and I were out uh—for work stuff and we saw the flames. I was with him the entire time."

Charlie slumped, relieved, against the open door of the ambulance. The mask fogged with his heavy sigh.

"You…you thought I was in there?" I ignored the seven of them, my eyes fixed on Charlie. "You tried to save me?"

He closed his eyes and nodded. Something in my chest tightened, a lump formed in my throat. I swallowed hard and looked away, back to the firefighters who were battling the raging inferno before it could consume the other trailers nearby.

"You two need to talk, it seems." Officer Torres jerked her chin at Office Chadwick, signaling that it was time for them to leave. He narrowed his eyes at me but straightened as he followed his partner back to the police car. Seeing that there wasn't an imminent threat, the EMT went back to checking on Charlie, listening to his lungs with a stethoscope.

"Just some minor smoke inhalation," the EMT nodded to himself. "But we better take you to the hospital to get checked out just in case."

Charlie nodded again, unable to speak. That's when I noticed his hands, burnt flesh peeled away from his red, exposed skin. I winced. I didn't say anything as I watched the second EMT come out from the cab of the ambulance and help the first EMT get Charlie up onto the stretcher and secure him.

"We'll be at Kaiser Permanente hospital–do you know where it is?" The first EMT sighed.

"On Broadway, we know where it is," Cherry nodded.

Her shoulders slumped the moment they were gone, and she threw her arms around my sides. "I'm so glad you're okay."

I absentmindedly brushed my hand against her back, my mind a whirlwind.

It took another hour for them to put out the fire and then another hour on top of that before they would let me pick through the rubble. To *salvage* anything.

"Just get rid of it all," I shook my head at the Fire Chief and he shrugged.

Charlie was released from the hospital later that morning with minor smoke inhalation, second degree burns on his hands and neck and singed nose hair. I debated going to see him once he got home. Fucker had sold me out to Barry. But he had also risked his life to save mine, or so he thought. I was beyond fucking confused. Ophelia had offered to call out of work to stay with me, but I had refused, telling her to go and I would watch Hunter.

I needed a break from her constant worrying, from the apprehensive glances she threw my way and the way she anxiously picked her nails. I loved everything about that woman, but I knew she needed a break from worrying about me.

It was nice to spend some time with Hunter. It was storming outside, the wind and rain sloshed against the windows, so we were stuck in the apartment. After his nap, we made lunch together. He laughed as he slopped a heaping ton of mayonnaise onto his slice of bread, and I couldn't help but laugh as I tried to help him fix it. His handiwork ended up being two slices of bread, way too much mayonnaise and a single slice of turkey lunch meat but he was so proud. I scooped a handful of crackers onto his little plate and plopped him down on the floor between the couch and the coffee table with me.

"Don't tell mom I let you eat in the living room," I winked at him.

"Okay, okay," he nodded excitedly and grabbed his sandwich. After lunch, we cleaned up and played a game of tag which was surprisingly difficult. He was tiny but he was fast. Hunter had me leaping onto the couch, running along the back with my head ducked to not slam into the ceiling and lunging over his head for a clearing.

After about twenty minutes, I was exhausted. I rolled across the carpet and snatched him up in my arms, holding him tightly to my chest. He laughed and squirmed until I let him go. I sprawled out on the floor with my arms out wide as I struggled to catch my breath.

"We're going to have to pick up all those couch pillows before mom gets home," I laughed.

"Okay, love you," he chirped. I froze. He was only three and didn't know what it meant but every fiber in my being had loved him as my own since I first met him. Hunter and Ophelia were my family. I had every intention of being Hunter's father, especially now with Jimmy completely out of the picture. I just didn't know how that would work now with my court date fast approaching.

My throat was tight as I scooped Hunter up in my arms and buried my face in his soft, blonde hair. "I love you too bud."

I needed to see Charlie. I needed to understand.

I called Tamara and she, begrudgingly, agreed to watch Hunter. Something in our dynamic had changed since I got out of jail. I could see the distaste in her hazel eyes, the way she pressed her lips into a thin line when she saw me that first time. I hated knowing what she was seeing: another Jimmy. Another disappointment that had latched onto her daughter. I didn't blame her.

The storm hit with its full fury, painting the sky black as it poured down onto the world. It was nearing twilight, but the storms threw the earth into a premature night as I drove into Oakland. The headlights were weak against the onslaught, the wipers struggled to keep up. I knew these streets and highways like the back of my hand but even I got nervous once or twice when I hit a deep pocket of water and the Cutlass swerved.

The lights were on in Charlie's house, the gold and black Chevelle parked in the overgrown driveway. Fresh tire marks marred the front lawn, the guys must have been here checking on him earlier. The rain was only a light drizzle as I got out of the Cutlass and jogged over to the front porch. I grabbed the door handle to let myself in but thought better of it and knocked instead.

After a minute, the door opened, and Charlie's eyebrows shot up his forehead. He had a plastic tube in his nose for oxygen, a portable tank in a little cart with wheels was in his hand. We stared at each other silently for a long pause before he turned and walked back into the house, leaving the door open for me. I entered after him and followed him into the kitchen.

There were beer bottles on every flat surface, cigarette butts floating in some of them. A pizza box sat on the littered table in front of him.

"You hungry?" He nodded to the box as he slowly eased himself into one of the wooden chairs. I stood in the entryway but leaned against the wall and shook my head.

"Nah, I'm good." My voice was flat. I studied him. He looked like his trip into a blazing trailer had aged him. His shoulders were slumped forward, his hair uncombed and his hands were wrapped in bandages. With a shaky, injured hand, he pressed the tubing against his nostrils and took two deep breaths, the second caught in his chest and he coughed harshly. It took a long moment for him to catch his breath, heaving for air.

"Why did you do it?"

"Do what?" His voice was hoarse, still struggling for air but he was calmer now.

"I get why you gave me up to Barry," I said. He looked at me with surprise. "You've always been a selfish bastard. But why did you try to save me?"

Charlie looked down at the table, toying with a beer bottle cap between his fingers.

"I made a mistake," he said finally. "Not just with Barry…but a long time ago. I made a lot of mistakes with you a-and–I'm sorry, son."

We both looked away, uncomfortable.

"I'm not getting back with the crew," I said.

"I don't want you to," he chuckled dryly. "But we could use you around the shop, all the same."

I nodded.

"That would be alright," I said. "Until my court date." Charlie winced.

"When is that?"

"Couple months," I shrugged again.

"Well, you're welcome at the shop as long as you want." He coughed and ducked his eyes. "I have something for you." He stood up shakily, tugging the oxygen tank after him as he crossed the kitchen to the counter. He rummaged through the papers and trash there until he found what he was looking for. Something flashed as he tossed whatever it was towards me.

I caught the keys in the air and raised an eyebrow at him.

"What's this?" I had seen these keys my entire life. I knew what they belonged to. But I didn't understand the gesture.

"The Chevelle, you've wanted it since you were a kid–it's yours," he grinned. "I'm not good at this shit but I don't know how else to tell you that…I'm sorry."

"You don't have to give me the Chevelle." I shook my head and handed the keys back to him, but he didn't budge.

"I know I don't," he chuckled. "But I want you to have it, son."

My vision blurred as the knot constricted in my throat.

"I–uh, thanks," I stammered. "But I have the Cutty here…"

He made a gesture to hand the keys to him.

"I'll drive the Cutlass back to your place, we drop the Chevelle at your place and bring me home," he said nonchalantly. "It'll be a lot of driving but if we hurry up and go, we can hurry up and come back." I was too overwhelmed. I was too excited to hear the edge in his voice, the persistence in which he urged me.

"O-okay." We switched keys, my mind numb with surprise. I couldn't absorb what had been exchanged in the short time I was here. Charlie tugged a jacket on, fixing his oxygen tubing as we stepped out of my childhood home. The storm had stopped for now, leaving the earth sopping wet and dark in the meantime.

"Fuck," I shivered and pushed my hands into my hoodie pocket.

"Let's hurry up, it's cold as shit," Charlie grumbled. My heart picked up its pace as I jogged across the damp lawn and mud to the Chevelle. The heavy door swung open, welcoming me inside. I jumped in excitedly, the smell of leather and cigarettes a familiar greeting as I gunned the engine to life. I chuckled as the entire car shook with power around me, it vibrated up the steering wheel and down my arms. I looked in the rearview as Charlie started up the Cutlass, flashing the lights to let me know he was ready to go.

I didn't even bother with the radio as we drove down the dark, quiet roads. I just wanted to listen to the sound of the 502-engine roaring with life and power. The car felt like home. I had played with Donny in the back seat and now maybe Millie and Hunter could play together one day. We made our way slowly so I could relish the feel of the Chevelle, the Cutlass headlights were steady in my rearview mirror.

I turned on Snell Ave, a particularly long and desolate road that was a backway to Ophelia's apartment. There weren't any streetlamps here, the only light came from my headlights as they bounced off the thick row of redwoods on the right side of the highway and reflected off the wet asphalt. There was a small beep. I glanced down at the dashboard as it lit up, every warning light came on at once.

"The fuck?" I frowned. The engine began to sputter, the Chevelle lurched, struggling to move forward as I pressed on the gas. I looked up in the rearview mirror, but the Cutlass headlights were gone. The Chevelle stalled with a loud clunk. I killed the engine and tried to start it back up, but the Chevelle just sputtered. "Motherfucker!" I hissed.

I got out and made my way through the dark, using only my phone as a flashlight now that the entire car was dead. I popped the hood and peered through the mist but couldn't see shit. I reached for the oil cap but recoiled as my hand burned.

"Shit!" I pulled my hoodie off over my head, leaving my torso bare to the drizzling rain to protect my hand as I tried again. Headlights flared too brightly in this dark space, and I squinted. *Charlie must have got hung up at a redlight,* I realized. But the car sounded wrong. The headlights were too bright. It wasn't the Cutlass I realized as I heard the distinct sound of the approaching car speed up.

The car banked to the left suddenly, slamming into the back of the Chevelle. The impact sent me flying, I landed on the asphalt on my bare skin as pain lashed through me. My head connected with the ground with a sickening crack and my vision swam. My entire body was on fire, but I couldn't catch my breath. Groaning, I rolled onto my stomach as the fire in my skin flared. I grunted, my stomach twisted, and I thought I was going to puke. Warmth trickled down my neck, too warm for the rain that had picked up in strength as it splattered around me. I realized, numbly, that my head was bleeding profusely from the impact.

Someone got out of the second car, heavy foot falls as they approached me.

I weakly pushed up onto my knees, but a boot slammed into my back and shoved me back down.

"P-please," I gasped as the agony tore through me. My mouth tasted of blood. It trickled out of my ears and down the sides of my neck. Black spots filled my vision, stars burst in the darkness. The toe of the boot connected with my ribs, kicking me over and onto my back. I landed with a huff as the remainder of the wind was knocked out of me. Rain pelted my face, my naked torso as I struggled to see through it, see through the double vision that swam dizzyingly in my eyes.

Barry. He must have either served his time or made bail too.

He looked down at me with a blank expression. There wasn't malice or anger. Only justification. Blood bubbled up in my mouth, choking me and I turned my head to cough it out, weakly. Once I could breathe, I looked up at Barry, my eyes full of pleading. Begging.

"Please…please…" It was all I had the strength to say. "I'm sorry son," Barry's voice was flat as he leveled the gun with my head.

Ophelia
38

I was exhausted and sweaty after work. It had been an extra-long and hard day, so many of the residents needed help with showers and diaper changes today. I was excited to get home, shower, eat something quick and curl up in bed with Tristan. I had tried calling him earlier, but he didn't answer. *Probably just busy with Hunter*, I figured. It was after 10PM so I wasn't surprised when I pulled into the parking lot and all the lights in the apartment were off.

I tugged my coat tighter around me as I hurried across the lot but stopped before I reached the stairs, at the bank of mailboxes just before the stairs. My hands were already numb from the cold, so I fumbled with the key before I was able to pop open the mailbox. The application period for the nursing program had closed two weeks ago which meant I should, hopefully, be hearing from someone very soon. Excitement jumped through my veins as I saw the mail stuffed into the little metal box. I stuffed it into my jacket to protect it from the rain and ran up the stairs.

The boys were asleep, I figured so I quietly set my stuff down on the table. *Just wait*, I told myself. The eagerness and excitement to tear through the mail was too great but I wouldn't get this moment back. I took my time tiptoeing around the kitchen, spooning leftover lasagna onto a plate and heating it in the microwave.

I filled a cup of diet soda and sat down at the table. I avoided even looking at the pile as I shoveled food into my mouth, so hot that it burned my tongue. With the lasagna eaten, I chugged the diet soda. But still, I did not open the mail. I snickered to myself as I washed my plate and set them in the drying rack.

"Okay…" I told myself, working to calm my racing heart. "Now." I leapt for the mail, sorting it quickly without fully reading the return addresses. Mostly junk. The last envelope was thinner than the rest. I flipped it over and stifled my shriek as I saw the return address as one of the schools that I had applied to. *Okay, okay okay*, I took three deep, steadying breaths. Reminding myself that this could go either way. With one final, deep breath I tore the letter open.

I couldn't help the scream that bubbled out of me.

On behalf of Meritt City College, we would like to congratulate Ophelia Black for her conditional acceptance into the Associate of Nursing (ASN) program.

I screamed again, jumping up and down as I read the acceptance letter over and over again, not fighting back the tears that flowed freely. A small part of my mind that wasn't distracted, registered that my phone was ringing. Vibrating on the counter by the microwave. I rushed over to it but frowned when I saw that it hadn't been ringing. However, there was a text from my mom.

Tamara: Are you picking up Hunter tonight? I don't mind him sleeping over but Tristan had said that he would be picking him up in a few hours. That was quite a while ago. Anyways, just making sure you're okay.

– Love mom

I frowned down at my phone. *Why was Hunter at my mom's?* Where was Tristan? I suddenly realized that the house was too still. Too quiet. Tristan hadn't woken up from my cheers. The buzzing continued.

Horror dripped into my stomach like ice as my eyes shifted from my quiet cell phone to where the buzzing was coming from. The drawer rattled softly as the vibrating continued. The drawer where I had tossed the black phone Tristan had given me and never thought of it again.

It continued ringing.

10 Years Later

Ophelia

I'm exhausted. My entire body feels like it's seeping into the car seat into a puddle as I struggled to keep my eyes open and focused on the road. It took longer than usual to give report at shift change to the oncoming nurse because a patient had coded just before the end of my shift. The *code blue* alarm still echoed in my head and pulsated in time with the headache blooming in my eyes.

The feeling of ribs cracking under my palms as I desperately tried to pump a patient's dead heart wasn't something I would easily forget. The faces of the patients became a blur over the years, some we could bring back but others we could not. Not many affected me.

Until it was Jimmy.

I had been a Registered Nurse for three years at the time when I answered a code. A 35-year-old male had suffered cardiac arrest after his endocarditis resulted in a massive left central artery stroke. By then I hadn't seen Jimmy in years, and I hardly recognized him then; sickly yellow and filthy. I was in my first round of CPR compressions when I realized that I recognized the faded tattoo of a horse on his chest.

By the time the code was called, Jimmy was dead. He had been homeless for some time and have developed a heroin addiction that landed him in the hospital with a fungal infection of the blood and a bacterial infection of the heart that led to his stroke. I didn't tell Hunter when I got home; he hardly remembered Jimmy and never asked about him. That was five years ago, and I never talked about it.

I rubbed my tired, blood shot eyes and glanced at the time on my electric dashboard. Hunter would be done with lacrosse practice and headed home soon. I punched the Bluetooth button on my steering wheel and called our favorite pizza spot as I pulled my car into the garage. The house was quiet, and I tip-toed on sock covered feet across the large expanse of marble floor, my dirty work shoes left in the garage.

"Hi bud," I greeted with my arms stretched out wide. Hunter dropped his heavy lacrosse bag onto the floor of the entry way, and I winced the way his cleats marked the marble.

"Heya mom," Hunter smirked in that half-smile that I loved. It made his dimples pop out against his tan skin. His hair had lightened over the summer and the contrast with his dark eyes and tan skin was remarkable. He dramatically dragged himself over to me before enthusiastically throwing his arms around my shoulders. At thirteen he was already my height; he was going to be a giant. I kissed his sweaty hair and winced again from the smell.

"How was practice?" I made a show of waving my hand in front of my face and he flicked his sweaty practice jersey at me.

"Good, we're going to crush Greenwood next week."

"Mooooooommmmm!" A small, high-pitched voice whined from behind Hunter. Rose stormed up the front steps and into the entry way, her dark eyebrows knitted tightly together over chocolate-brown eyes. "Hunter said I was being a butt-face!"

"No, I didn't!" Hunter laughed but quickly made work of making his face serious as he glared down at his little sister.

"Yes, you did!" Rose stomped her foot and put her fists to her hips, making her beaded bracelets crinkle against each other.

"All right that's enough you two, your mom just got home from work she doesn't want to hear you two fighting." Hayden stepped in behind them, balancing two boxes of pizza in one hand and closed the door with the other.

"Hmph!" Rose stomped her foot again before she took off running into the house as Hunter chased her, his laugh trailing down the hall behind them.

"Hi baby," Hayden smiled my favorite smile, the one that made the corners of his blue eyes crinkle, and I felt my heart skip. Hayden and I had been married for six years and I never got over the way his smile made me feel. He leaned down and I kissed him eagerly.

"A butt-face?" I cocked an eyebrow up at him.

"He did," Hayden shrugged. "And she was."

I laughed and took the pizzas from him so he could change out of his suit.

After dinner, Hayden and I stretched out on the couch while the kids played in their bedrooms upstairs. Some movie was playing on the flatscreen over the fireplace, but I was too sleepy to pay much attention. Hayden absentmindedly rubbed my feet in his lap, and I couldn't help but admire how handsome he was.

His brown hair was flecked with grey around his temples, a lovely testament to our time together stretching towards forever. Icy blue eyes and the darkest eyelashes. Tall and strong, he was my best friend and an amazing father.

Hayden lifted his wine glass to take a sip as Rose jumped up from behind the couch with a shriek that stung my ears.

"Boo!" She beamed as she startled her father causing him to flinch and spill his red wine on his white t-shirt. I bolted up right, my hands out to do something but they hung uselessly in the air as I stared at the dark red seeping into my husband's shirt. "I'm sorry!" Rose's eyes flew wide as Hayden jumped to his feet.

"Oh shoot," Hayden chuckled. "I look like I've been shot." Hayden sighed down at the mess, relieved the couch hadn't been a victim. "Come on baby girl, you're going to learn how to start a load of laundry." He scooped her up and they walked off together to the back of the large house.

I was still perched on my knees, my hands reaching out aimlessly as my stomach churned. I stumbled to my feet numbly and hurried out the glass doors that made up the back wall of the house. The cool air hit my burning skin and I sucked in deep gulps of air, willing my heart to settle.

"You're okay, you're okay, you're okay…" I told myself between breaths. When the pounding in my ears subsided, I opened my eyes slowly and looked out across the water. We lived pushed up against a large lake, our private dock was an extension of our backyard. The sound of a gun firing, muffled by a couch pillow blasted from behind me and I spun with a gasp.

Hayden's eyes met mine, at first confused then tinged with alarm as he closed the glass door behind him.

"Oh Ophelia," his brows knitted together over his sad eyes. "I'm sorry, I shouldn't have said that I was just making a joke."

"I know," I tried my best to smile but his expression told me that he wasn't buying it. He walked over onto the dock and wrapped his arms around me. I buried my face into his strong chest and breathed in the familiar scent of him. He smoothed my hair down my back and rocked us gently until my heart was beating normally. I turned my face to look out over the water. I wasn't typically caught off guard like this, with random flashes of…Tristan.

His name was easier to think to myself now than it had been for the first few years after his death. No longer did his name or thoughts of him send a burning pain through my chest. I wrapped my arms around Hayden's waist and hugged him tightly. My time with Tristan had been a whirlwind of pain, love,
and betrayal—something I never had to worry about with Hayden. For a few years after Tristan's death, it was just Hunter and I. Tristan's crew had stuck to their word of paying me Tristan's portions of their jobs and without it I wouldn't ever have completed nursing school.

Even after their crew disbanded after they found out that Charlie had sold out Tristan. It lasted a few years until I graduated and then I never heard from the boys again. I would forever be grateful for them and even Cherry for what they did for Hunter and me. That time of my life was long over except for when small cracks would appear, taking me off guard and letting memories slip through.

I couldn't be more thankful.

Though I had loved Tristan from the deepest parts of myself at the time, I knew now that our relationship never should have existed. Tristan was toxic and hurtful; I often mistook those traits for romance and passion, naively. I ached for how hurt he had been all his life but part of me took comfort in knowing that he didn't have to hurt anymore.

Hayden slid his hands up to either side of my head so that I was looking up at him. His blue eyes were full of patience, love and acceptance and my heart squeezed.

"I love you," I whispered. Hayden touched his lips against mine gently at first then more hungrily.

The End.

Acknowledgements

I cannot even begin to express my upmost gratitude for those who helped make All My Life a reality. First & foremost, I want to thank my husband for pushing me to finally finish my manuscript, to get my trauma out & onto paper. This has been such a cathartic experience that I hope will resonate with other young, single mothers torn between their hearts & their minds. I also would not have gotten here if it wasn't for my journey exploring traditional publishing that brought me to Lauren Kay Writes & her treasure trove of resources.

My editor Suzy Pope was always accessible even for being on the other side of the world. She fell in love with my characters & story but cut down all my over-writing that my ADHD brain loves to do. My beta readers, my friends & family who sometimes had to read looking between their fingers but encouraged me every step of the way.

My son. For giving me a purpose & a reason to do better.

Lastly, for the failed relationships, the holes-punched-in-walls, the sleepless nights & lost tears. Though ugly & hurtful as they were, they shaped me into the woman I am today. All My Life would not be here without any of you.

About The Author

As a first-generation college student and (past) single mother who has overcome similar trauma to Ophelia, exploring her story has helped Brianna better understand her own. She is a romance novelist living in Folsom, California, where you can find her by day as a nurse, and by night with her nose in a book.

www.ingramcontent.com/pod-product-compliance
Lightning Source LLC
Chambersburg PA
CBHW031846310726
48972CB00005B/1426